For Dexter

Knaves on Waves

By Jim Parfitt

This is a work of fiction. Names, characters, places, and incidents either are the product of the author's imagination or are used fictitiously. Any resemblance to actual persons, living or dead, events, or locales is entirely coincidental.

Copyright © 2021 by Jim Parfitt

All rights reserved. No part of this book may be reproduced or used in any manner without written permission of the copyright owner except for the use of quotations in a book review. For more information, address: jim.w.parfitt@gmail.com

First paperback edition October 2021
ISBN: 9798481097954
Cover design by Kenneth Kolloen

Acknowledgements

All stories reflect the soul that composed them. Their thoughts, emotions, and experiences. Mine is in no exception. My family, friends, and even brief acquaintances have shaped the man I am, and thus the tales I tell. For this, I thank them. There are three, however, who deserve to be mentioned above all others.

My Mother, who lit the fire.

Sasha, who kept it stoked.

Aga, who brought it back to life.

This book wouldn't exist without you. Thank you, from the very depths of my heart.

Chapter One

The sea was still, a sheet of glass fixed to the contours of the world. The vessels upon it were a different affair, the salt-stained timbers buckling under the frenzied movements of captain and crew. The sole exception was Trigger, who stood at the prow with quiet reserve, studying the distant crowd. The White Harbor was lost beneath the thronging masses, their cheers eclipsing even the screeching gulls. The hands and voices of countless races called out to him, yet Trigger paid them no heed, searching the private balconies for the one group of faces which mattered.

He found them without too much trouble, their family sigil resting only three tiers below the Empresses' own. Clearly, his absence had served them well.

Miraculously, his sister turned to face him at precisely that moment, their blue eyes locking across the crowded sea. Her features were expressionless as she considered him, the only change occurring in her thin and pale lips, which parted the slightest degree. What she said he would never know, yet it gained the attention of his parents, who turned their gaze to him with obvious reluctance.

They stood like this for several moments, staring at each other without word or movement. It was Trigger who broke the spell, raising his scarred hand in a tentative wave.

His family considered the action, the gentle breeze tugging at their pristine hair. Each of them had dressed for the occasion.

Then, one-by-one, they showed their backs, returning their attention to the legions of false-friends and sycophants baying at their heels. His sister was the last to turn, with what Trigger fancied to be a trace of hesitation.

He knew he was probably wrong.

A regal horn cut off his sigh, drawing his focus to the highest balcony, its ivory banister stretching three-times the length of any other. A ceremony of the highest pomp was beginning to take place on its polished floors, signaling that the Empress would soon arrive.

It was time he got to work.

"Alright men, it's minutes till the horn blows!" He roared, spinning around to face his crew. "How fares my wonderful ship?"

He knew the answer before he turned, his men having proven themselves reliable time and time again. Yes, many of them came from the empires more... uncivilized regions, but that was to be expected, considering their current form of employment. One didn't become a pirate if they were swimming in prospects.

Gods, most of his crew couldn't swim at all.

"Quick, clean and ready to sail!" His men boomed back, giving salutes that would put the navy to shame. All save their newest recruit, who continued mopping the deck with his usual amount of disinterest. He wasn't the brightest boy, or the most enthusiastic, yet that was of no real concern. Trigger knew there was a real sailor hiding beneath that scrawny physique. He just needed to bring him out.

Besides, even if he was wrong, it didn't really matter. You don't need a brain to swab a deck.

Another horn echoed across the motionless sea, silencing the ecstatic crowd. The Empress's balcony was now completely still, not a single soul present on its gleaming surface.

The people held their breath, as did Trigger's crew. He alone stood in contempt, all-too aware of the psychology behind these theatrics. All the Empress needed to do was blow a simple horn. He wished she'd just get on with it.

A low drone began forming on the periphery of his senses, a gentle pulse that grew into a cacophonous rumble, turning the calm waters into a seething abyss. The crowd trembled on the shore, and he was somewhat amused to see his family clutching their banister for support, desperate to remain upright, lest they lose even more of their precious social standing.

The Empress's balcony was all that remained untouched, a single point of stability in the quaking world. A ghostly white mist was forming within, billowing across the floor and out into the sky beyond. A few stray tendrils trickled downwards, where they were greedily inhaled by the nobles below, their privileged lungs desperate to suckle at any trace of their ruler's discarded glory.

Then, just as suddenly, the tremors ceased, sending the white mist spiraling back upon itself, thickening and thickening until it was solid as a wall. The horn sounded once again, and with one final display the mist blasted upwards, streaming into the heavens as an enormous pillar. With each passing moment the column faded, stretching thinner and thinner as it climbed beyond sight. Its recession revealed a form within, their flowing gown and porcelain mask marking them as the woman all had come to see.

The Empress strode forward, placing her hands on the banister with confidence and poise. Every eye present followed the movement, captivated by her power and beauty.

Trigger had to admit, it was a damn good entrance.

****

Barnaby clutched the mop with trembling hands, unable to believe his eyes. The Empress was *right there*, no more than a mile beyond his reach. He'd dreamt of this moment a thousand times, whether it be awake or asleep, and now that he was finally here, actually living the fantasy, he couldn't accept it as fact.

Glancing around, Barnaby gave himself a discreet and forceful pinch.

Nothing changed. The Empress was still on display, and he was still on this fucking ship. His dream was actually coming true.

Now, if the Empress would just lift her dress and bend right over, he might be able to fulfil the rest of it.

"My good people."

Barnaby grinned as the enhanced voice danced across his ears. The Empress sounded smoother than honey, a bright fire in a dark and lonely night. She had no need to raise her voice, her power alone carrying it to every soul in sight.

"Welcome." She continued, turning her head so that all could catch a glimpse of her porcelain mask. The cut of the eyes was a miraculous design, giving the illusion that no matter where you were, her majestic gaze was directly upon you. Barnaby knew this, yet still, he couldn't help but swoon.

His attention wavered, however, as the Empress began the speech that he and every other citizen of the empire had heard a dozen times before. A heartfelt tribute to her Imperial Majesty's ancestors, and a prayer of thanks to the benevolent Gods, who had allowed them so many years of unfettered peace. It was all bullshit, of course, as anyone from the outer fringes could plainly see, yet it still appeased the ignorant masses, feeding their delusions of safety and grandeur.

Barnaby let his eyes roam as the platitudes descended, studying the decks and banners floating beside their own. While none of the vessels and pirates present were quite as intriguing as the Empress herself, Barnaby had heard their names enough to know that more than a few were living legends.

The twin Captains, Jack and Henry Falcon, were the closest he could see, their sleek vessel sitting lower than any other. This afforded him an unfettered view of their chaotic deck, the crewmen scurrying to the directions of their famous Captains. Only Henry was present, however, a fact which struck Barnaby as extremely peculiar, considering that all tales suggested that the brothers were inseparable. Henry himself seemed distracted, his desperate eyes studying the shore.

Leaning forward to observe the unfolding drama, Barnaby was somewhat disappointed when a passing vessel obstructed his view, its mighty hull eclipsing their own. His sorrow was short-lived, however, as a single glance at its fluttering flag revealed the vessel's owner, sending a shiver of delight down his aching spine.

Captain Hargrave Longsteel, the lightning terror of the southern seas. Both the man and his ship were the subject of hushed whispers, their countless victories ensuring them a place in every naval man's nightmares. Rumor held that he had earned his last name through being the finest swordsman alive, a claim which added further interest to the vessel currently avoiding their starboard side.

Captain Jacques Beaufort was a gentlemen and scholar, by all accounts. Self-raised on the wild streets of Melbrax, he paid his way through cage-fights and petty thefts, using the money to improve his swordsmanship and education. The result was a mass-murderer more cultured than most noblemen, who was widely considered to be peerless with a blade. He and Captain Longsteel had never met, yet fate had finally seen fit to draw them together for this monumental event, and Barnaby couldn't wait to see who would come out on top. He wasn't the only one. Half the empire had been placing bets, the mere promise of that battle garnering almost as much attention as the race itself.

"Big boats." Declared a voice at his side, the woody tone filled with wonder. Barnaby regarded the speaker with mild trepidation, Magwa's dark-skin and tribal scarring lending his appearance more than a slight degree of pants-shitting ferocity. Still, the Kalyute warrior was the only person aboard who considered him worth speaking to, making him the closest thing Barnaby had to a friend.

"Ships, not boats." He corrected. "When they're that big, they're ships."

"It float, it boat." Magwa replied, giving him a friendly grin. Three of his front teeth had been filed into points.

"Don't let the Captain hear you say that." Barnaby warned. He meant it, too. Trigger was a kind man, yet strict as a priest on protocol.

"Trigger not care how Magwa say boat, so long as Magwa stay strong." Magwa shrugged, running a hand along his hideous arm. The scars were beyond counting, the mottled flesh rising and falling as though it were a mountain range. Magwa had let him touch them once, the puckered lumps proving far harder than he had anticipated. The shock in texture had made him retch, a fact which Magwa found most amusing.

"Pretty woman talk for very long time." The Kalyute frowned, gazing at the Empress with obvious frustration. "When we set sail?"

"When her Imperial Majesty is good and ready." Barnaby replied, frowning at the disrespect. He may come from the outer fringes, yet that was still close enough to hear the songs of the Oracle Birds. Magwa had no such fortune, his own home bordering the fearsome jungles which housed the empire's most tenacious foes. In all honesty, Barnaby wasn't completely sure that Magwa wasn't one of them. It was a thought that many of the crew had voiced, at least at first. Captain Trigger had shut them down without a moment's hesitation, threatening to hang any man who questioned Magwa's integrity. The Kalyute had been given a wary berth ever since.

That said, Magwa had a point. The Empress had been speaking a very long time. Fortunately, she finally seemed to be winding down.

"For two-hundred and fifty years, the Tides of Redemption have given us hope." She declared, throwing an arm wide and sending a river of silk spilling over the banister. "Hope that a soul can rise above its misdeeds, that one who has faltered can regain their footing, and find the righteous path."

Barnaby snorted. Sure, there wasn't a pirate alive who wouldn't brave the Tides of Redemption, yet most of them only did it for the promise of future debauchery.

"The challenges will be great, and the foes they face fearsome." The Empress continued, her voice as resplendent as her stunning frame. "For they battle not only the elements and beasts, but their own base and hideous nature. Each soul here is tainted by vice, a selfish disease that consumes not only themselves, but every being they have ever touched. You see before you a fleet of the damned, seeking a prize that only one vessel may claim. History has taught us how they will respond, and thus there remains but one question we must ask."

The Empress paused for dramatic effect, and to his surprise Barnaby found that even he was leaning forward, despite having heard it a thousand times before.

"Who will win?"

The crowd screamed, stamping their feet and clapping their hands. Her Imperial Majesty allowed the display to continue for almost a minute, before silencing it with a gesture. Her arcing hand summoned forth a muscle-bound champion, his biceps bulging beneath the weight of a decorated horn.

The Wind of Summons. Barnaby was seeing it with his own two eyes.

They were beginning to fill with tears.

"To those about to sail, we offer our prayers." The Empress declared, placing her palm against the gilded mouthpiece. "For your success, and your redemption. May you right the wrongs that define your past, or find solace in a death that clears the slate."

As she spoke the final words, her gaze shifted once more, her mask failing to conceal the tiny movement. The Empresses' eyes were on Barnaby's vessel, fixed on the man at its bobbing prow.

Trigger met her focus without a trace of fear, his faded naval jacket billowing in the growing wind. Whatever reaction the Empress expected, she clearly didn't receive it.

"Very well." She announced, beautiful voice filled with disgust. Her delicate hand lifted the porcelain mask, just enough to expose her luscious lips. These the Empress puckered, placing them against the horn. Then, with a deep breath, her Imperial Majesty began to blow.

Chapter Two

A thousand thuds filled the air as every sail caught the wind, launching their vessels forward with a familiar groan. The *Blackbird* wasn't the swiftest, nor the largest or most maneuverable, yet its aging timbers possessed a strength and character that Trigger couldn't help but respect. Their prow cleaved through the growing waves with dogged determination, clawing through the press of hulls forming at the harbor's edge. The first leg of the race was always one of the most exciting, a result of cramming so many vessels into the White Harbor's narrow confines. Even now the splinters were flying, dozens of ships striking each other as they sought to be the first on the open seas.

"Starboard, swing starboard!" Trigger roared, as an armored monstrosity reared up before them, its heavy prow coated in jagged steel. He didn't recognize the vessel, or its owner, yet he didn't need familiarity to know that even a light collision would see their own ship totally destroyed.

His crew responded with expert precision, guiding the *Blackbird* with leathered hands. They avoided the behemoth by inches, its crew leering down from its lofty heights. More than a few of the bastards offered coarse and savage challenges, yet Trigger ignored them, as did his men. He had given them orders to avoid any confrontation, and was proud to see that they had followed his instructions. Judging by the growing sounds of swords and gunfire, many Captains had not been so fortunate.

"Captain, someone's gaining on our rear!"

Trigger clicked his tongue in annoyance, peering over his shoulder at the vessel surging towards their own. Again, its colors were unfamiliar, yet the speed and ferocity of its approach made this a secondary concern.

"Swing to port!" He cried, scanning the sea for unoccupied space. The world had become a hurricane of timber, every inch occupied by a bellowing hull.

Again, his men responded with fantastic speed, turning the *Blackbird* as deftly as most would handle a mare. The action guided them into a thin strip of unclaimed blue, cutting off the passage of three other Captains, who hurled abuse from their saturated prows.

"Fuck off, ya cunts!" Sneered Three-fingered Frank, waving his titular hand for emphasis.

"That's half-rations for a week, Frank!" Trigger declared, earning a laugh of approval from his crew. At first, they had resented his attempts at introducing civility, yet after a while they had taken to it with a surprising affection, enjoying the air of sophistication he had cultivated onboard.

"Aye, Captain, fair enough." Frank conceded, lowering his hand.

The vessel they had avoided soared past, colliding with four other ships as it made its journey towards open sea. Trigger could barely see its careless Captain, yet the man's visage alone was cause for alarm, his pale features twisted into a cheeky grin, despite the horrendous damage he was inflicting to his own vessel.

Then the madman was gone, lost behind a forest of heaving hulls.

"Sunniday, what's happening?" Trigger called, gazing up at the crows-nest. The ships around them seemed to be freezing in place, halting their progress towards the sea.

"It's Carnage, Captain. He's making himself known, and he's putting on one hell of a show."

"More specifics, if you'd please."

Sunniday cleared his throat, his brow creasing in beleaguered thought.

"Maybe come up here, Captain. It's a bit beyond my scope."

"Right then." Trigger sighed, making for the mast. He paused only to address his First Mate, who was gripping the wheel with manicured hands.

"Keep an eye out for openings." He declared, giving her a nod. "The second one appears, take it. It doesn't matter who we go through."

"Aye, Captain." Sheridan nodded, blonde wig shifting on her hairless scalp. They should really find a way to fix it in place.

Without further delay he ascended, reaching the nest in a matter of moments. Their vessel travelled slightly in the tiny interval, yet nowhere near the distance it should, the ships around them locked in a fearful huddle.

Gazing down, Trigger could see why.

Captain Carnage owned the harbor, every vessel giving him the widest of berths. The driving cause was a healthy dose of fear, followed by practicality. All it took was a single disease to cripple any crew, and where Carnage sailed, plague itself was sure to follow.

Carnage wasn't human, nor were his crew. They were comprised entirely of Thrallkin, their terrifying features and blood-red skin marking them as both the empire's greatest weapons, and its greatest threat. Natural Thrallkin were smaller, their faces less pointed, their skin unstained by countless generations of bloodshed and war. Carnage and his crew were the empire's home-grown variety, however, a breed made solely to fight its battles, and slay its enemies. Most were kept under permanent lock-and-key, released only when the war demanded swift and brutal action. How Carnage and his men escaped was a source of much speculation, yet there was one thing that every one did know. If you see the Red Thrallkin coming, don't bother to run. Just slit your own throat, and see the matter ended.

"A path, for me? You shouldn't have!" Carnage boomed, shouldering his war-hammer as though it were weightless. Most men could barely move it.

Looking now, Trigger could see that the beast was right. The ships had indeed parted, creating a clear space between Carnage and the ocean. At first, such cowardice annoyed him, yet Trigger was eventually forced to concede that it was probably the wisest choice, especially considering Carnage's choice of decoration.

The Thrallkin's ship was covered in corpses, their rotting flesh strapped to the hull by an endless network of ropes and chains. A horde of flies and maggots writhed beneath the sodden meat, while blood-thirsty rats scurried across the deck, their bulging bellies filled to burst with the taste of humanity and death.

Such grizzly horror held two purposes. One was intimidation, at which it succeeded admirably. The second was far more important, however, and was one of the reasons why Carnage had won the Tides every year for the past decade. The beast's vessel was a plague ship, the rotting meat and vermin carrying every disease known to man. Carnage and his crew were entirely immune, their hardy nature leaving them resistant to most mortal frailties. Other ships were not so fortunate, a single piece of flesh carrying enough disease to kill an entire village, let alone a single ship.

"Falcon. Where is Captain Falcon?" Carnage sneered, adjusting the tricorn hat perched precariously in his hair. It was a trophy from his first kill, and thus several sizes too small. All that held it in place was Carnage's thick and ropey locks, their knotted lengths studded with countless skulls, bullets, and sticks.

"Who asks?"

Trigger nodded with approval at Falcon's reply, watching as the Captain made himself known. His sleek vessel had navigated the masses with ease, putting him perilously close to Carnage's own. It was a valiant display of defiance; one which Trigger couldn't help but respect.

"You're looking well, Captain." Carnage sneered, leaning against his vessels edge. "Even your ship looks in good order. Quite a feat, considering you're down a man."

A potent silence swelled as Carnage finished his taunt, every Captain present having noticed Jack's absence. The twins never sailed alone.

"The fuck are you talking about?" Falcon snarled, unable to keep the dread from rising in his tone.

"Oh, there's no need to worry." Carnage laughed, motioning to his crew. "We found him drinking at the docks earlier this morning. Shared a joke or two, got along like old friends. Shit, he kept on begging to join our crew!"

Carnage's men were hauling something up from the bowels of their festering ship. Their huge bodies hid it from Trigger's view, yet he already knew what they were planning to reveal.

"What have you done to my brother!?" Falcon roared, drawing his sword in fury.

"I told him no, at first." Carnage shrugged, completely undaunted by Falcon's rage. "But then I started thinking. It has been a while since we had a good figurehead."

Carnage stepped aside, revealing the package his crew had extracted.

"Gods' above." Sunniday whispered, taking a nervous step back. Trigger could hardly blame him.

Jack Falcon was a hard man, in every sense of the word. Tough, honest, and completely foreign to the concept of fear. All of that was gone, his broken body leaking as he was dragged towards Carnage's beckoning arms, the Thrallkin Captain embracing him as though they were the oldest of friends.

"Say hi, Jack." Carnage grinned, making his plaything wave. They'd slit the tendons in Jack's arms, leaving him malleable as a child's doll.

"Jack!" Henry screamed, tears forming in his proud eyes. His brother couldn't respond, his senses robbed by the tortures he'd endured.

"Ah, he's fine!" Carnage waved, lifting Jack above his head and drawing attention to the many hooks embedded in his bruised and bloodied back. Each one was connected to a length of rusted chain, the links vanishing beneath dozens of Thrallkin feet.

"He's just going to be with us for the duration of the race. You can have him back when we're done."

With that, Carnage hurled his prisoner overboard, the hooks snagging his flesh and sending him slamming roughly against the ship's hull. The pain awakened Jack, who screamed as the metal tore at his frame, piercing deeper as gravity had its way.

"Jack!" Falcon cried, openly weeping with rage. There was nothing he could do. To challenge Carnage in such restricted confines would spell certain death, the countless corpses ensuring that even if he got close enough to free his brother, they would both die of disease only a few days later. Sure, the same diseases would ensure Jack's death before the race's end, yet it would be an agonizing demise, a torture.

Trigger frowned, more and more annoyed by the sound of Carnage's laughter.

BOOM!

The shot rang out across the harbor, Jack slumping forward as the bullet pierced his skull. His limp corpse ceased its convulsions, swaying gently in the wind.

Carnage ceased his laughter, dark eyes widening with outrage.

"Who did that!?" He snarled, slamming his hammer against his ship. "Who ruined my fun!?"

All eyes turned to Trigger, who returned his smoking pistol to its holster.

"That would be me." He declared, taking a step forward.

"Oh shit, Captain." Sunniday whispered. "What did you do?"

"That's half-rations for a week." Trigger replied, keeping his eyes on Carnage.

****

What the fuck had the Captain done?

Barnaby held his cheeks, looking from Trigger to Carnage, his head swiveling back-and-forth as he considered the madman who had doomed them. Everyone present was doing the same, holding their breath in anticipation of Carnage's response.

The Thrallkin rose to his full height, puffing out his muscular chest and regarding Trigger with narrowed eyes.

Barnaby felt his bladder going, preparing to void itself at the first sign of the coming slaughter.

"That was a difficult shot." Carnage declared, red face splitting into a wide grin.

A moment of silence as Trigger weighed his reply.

"I've a very good aim."

They all looked back to Carnage, each person still holding their breath.

"Heh." Carnage chuckled, scratching his scalp with his hammer. "You've got balls. I like that."

It wasn't witty, and it didn't make much sense. From a mouth like that, however, it was terrifying.

"Might I suggest you cut his body loose?" Trigger asked, using a handkerchief to wipe the gunpowder from his hand. "The game is over, it does you no good."

Carnage snorted, though his smile didn't waver as he considered the request.

"Let it go." He shrugged, motioning to his crew. There was a flurry of movement, and a metallic clink as the chains were struck. Jack's body fell, striking the water without grace or ceremony. It didn't take long for the chains to drag it down, confining the corpse to a watery grave.

As burials go, it wasn't exactly proper. Still, it was better than what Carnage had planned.

"Thank you." Trigger declared, nodding at the display.

"Oh, don't thank me." Carnage laughed, adjusting his tricorn hat. "I agreed because he'd run out of uses. I've got my eyes on a new trinket now."

The Thrallkin's gaze roamed across Trigger's body, peeling back the layers as though he were ripened fruit. Barnaby was certain that he actually licked his lips.

"I'll see you on the waters, Captain."

Barnaby had never been happy inside his own skin. Still, at this particular moment, he was fucking glad to not be Captain Trigger.

"I look forward to it." Trigger replied, without the faintest trace of fear.

Carnage snorted, though from amusement or anger, it was impossible to tell.

"Alright lads, we've held things up enough!" The Thrallkin suddenly announced, turning to his crew. "Let's get the race going and give these fine citizens everything they want!"

A roar of approval rose from Carnage's crew, their massive limbs setting to work on the rigging. With a dreadful groan the *Bloodbath* obeyed, stalking across the sea with predatory grace.

Even from here, Barnaby could smell its taint on the wind.

Not a single ship moved as Carnage left the harbor, the Thrallkin gazing back at them with imperious disdain. Only when the *Bloodbath* was safely ahead did the first few vessels resume their motion, the *Blackbird* shifting as First Mate Sheridan began pushing for advantage.

"Large woman knows how to steer a boat." Magwa grinned, as the First Mate guided them to the front of the pack.

"Large woman will rip your head off, if she hears you call her that again." Barnaby replied, craning his neck. Countless other vessels were beginning to obstruct his view, yet he was still able to make out Falcon's weeping form, the Captain slumping forward as he considered his brother's unmarked grave.

Swallowing nervously, Barnaby looked to Trigger, his scarred face unreadable beneath the brilliant sun. He appeared terribly calm, for a man who'd doomed them all.

"Bastard." Barnaby whispered, slamming the mop against the deck.

"That's half-rations." Announced First Mate Sheridan, glancing at him from the *Blackbird's* wheel.

Sighing, Barnaby retrieved his fallen tool, its ancient handle filling his palm with splinters.

He was beginning to feel that he'd made a mistake.

Chapter Three

Trigger set aside his quill, leaning back into his chair with a moan of appreciation. There hadn't been too much damage to record, Carnage's display putting the other competitors in a rare mood of compassion and civility. Gods, the remainder of the ships were practically polite as they made their exit from the harbor, hitting open water with a pace that almost implied hesitation. Trigger could understand their reluctance. No one wanted to be caught downwind of the Thrallkin vessel.

"You alright, Captain?" Sheridan asked, turning to face him. His First Mate had been gazing out the port-side window, watching as the last of their competition faded from sight. The sun was setting, and their formerly tight ranks were beginning to disperse, each Captain deciding which path would see them finish the race with the greatest amount of haste.

"I'm fine." He replied, running a hand across his face.

"No, you're not." Sheridan laughed, removing her wig and placing it on his desk. Even in the fading sunlight, her bald scalp appeared to glow. "Is it Carnage? I'd be nervous too, if I'd pissed that beast off."

"I'm not worried about Carnage." Trigger frowned. "You know me better than that."

"I do." Sheridan replied, taking a seat on his desk. "Which is why I'll rephrase. Forget your family and focus on what matters. The men need their Captain strong, especially since we aren't even a day into the race, and you've already managed to slight the reigning champ."

"Making enemies is good." Trigger shrugged. "It shows you live by your convictions."

"And guarantees you die by them." Sheridan replied. "A fact which understandably concerns your crew."

She had a point. Then again, Sheridan usually did. It was why he'd made her First Mate.

"I'll talk to them in the morning." He assured. "Give a rousing speech and inform them of our route. Will that suffice?"

"If the route is satisfactory. How many are there to choose from?"

"Five, though each of them comes with their own set of issues."

"Of course. I assume we'll be taking the safest?"

"There's no need for sarcasm." Trigger warned, sweeping back his hair.

"That statement will never be correct." Sheridan replied, unfastening her dress.

"Must you do that here?" Trigger asked, as she slipped the material from her broad and tattooed shoulders.

"Yes. The men have drilled a hole into my private quarters, and while I have no issues with blinding the next one who chances a peek, I thought you might object."

"Not if it's only the one." Trigger declared, as Sheridan's dress slumped to the floor. "They can be a warning to the rest."

"Am I taking both eyes?"

"Just one, please. We don't want to ruin the man."

"Fair enough."

Sheridan returned to the window, spreading her arms as the sunlight touched her skin. Despite himself, Trigger found his gaze roaming the spirals inked into her flesh, each tattoo flowing into a complex labyrinth of artistic design.

"Most men would be looking somewhere else." Sheridan grinned, glancing at him over her shoulder. She'd been watching his reflection in the window.

"I'm not most men." Trigger replied.

"Isn't that the truth." Sheridan remarked, turning around to fiddle with the bandages strapped across her breasts. It wasn't that she was attempting to hide them. They were just so bloody big that something was needed to keep them in check.

"Uncomfortable?" Trigger asked, placing his feet on his desk. The tension of the day was beginning to ease.

"You know it. Still, it's better than the alternative."

She wasn't wrong. Most of Sheridan's people had their breasts removed to increase mobility. Sheridan had declined, to his crew's eternal joy.

"I noticed this was new." Trigger began, indicating her discarded dress. "Did you make it for today?"

"I did." Sheridan nodded, sounding immensely pleased. "I wanted to look good for our big day."

"You were stunning." Trigger grinned, receiving one in reply. He wasn't just being kind. At her height and breadth, Sheridan captured the attention of any who saw her, regardless of her outfit. That she only dressed in the finest garments was of secondary concern, her immaculate taste further enhancing her natural allure.

At least, that's how Trigger felt. Sheridan's own people were another matter entirely.

"I still can't believe we made it." She declared, studying his quarters in wonder.

Trigger could. He'd always known the value of hard work, and the pair of them had worked hard indeed.

"We haven't made it yet." He replied, opening his desk and retrieving a bottle of wine. "Not until we cross that line."

"True enough." Sheridan nodded, accepting the glass he offered. "And I guess that's easier sai-"

"Captain!"

Trigger sighed, placing his glass aside.

"I think you're needed on deck." Sheridan teased, downing her own. "Don't worry, I promise I'll save you a glass."

"I'd prefer if you saved me the wine." Trigger replied, knowing Sheridan's humor.

"That, I cannot help you with."

****

Barnaby watched with the others as it wavered on the horizon, fading in-and-out beneath the growing moon.

"Barnaby see before?" Magwa asked, nudging his shoulder.

"No." Barnaby replied. "I don't think anyone has."

"Captain!" Sunniday repeated, his voice almost hoarse.

"Yes?" Trigger replied, emerging from below with a hint of irritation.

"Another ship, sir!"

"I hardly find that surprising. We are in a race, after all."

"No, Captain, she wasn't in the harbor. I've never seen her like!"

"Who has the telescope?" Trigger asked, studying the crew. It was Bearded Gary who stepped forward, offering the scope with a sheepish bow.

"Why did you have this?" Trigger frowned.

"I wanted to check something, Captain."

"Check what?"

"A lump."

"A lump?"

"Yes, Captain. I... I wanted to know if it was a wart."

"We do have a doctor, you know."

"Aye, Captain. It was just a bit...personal."

Trigger looked at the telescope, and then back to Bearded Gary.

"That's half-rations, Gary. Next time, see the doctor."

"Aye, Captain."

With a small amount of hesitation, Trigger raised the telescope, squinting through the lens with quiet intensity. What exactly he was seeing, Barnaby couldn't be sure, yet if it was an up-close view of what they could already discern, well, he didn't envy the Captain.

The ship was decaying, whole sections of its hull rotted away, exposing the skeletal decks below. Not a soul stirred in their barren depths, be it human or otherwise. Even the vermin had fled. The sails were scraps, soiled tatters flailing in the wind. This made the vessels motion all the more uncanny, as while it seemed to lack any direction, its prow waving back-and-forth like the snout of some great predator, it still maintained a frightening speed, surging across the sea at a pace that no regular vessel could match.

"Empty boat is bad omen, Captain." Magwa declared, caressing the dagger at his hip.

"It's not empty." Trigger replied, lowering the scope.

Barnaby squinted, studying the abandoned decks. With every moment, they were steadily drawing closer.

"Looks empty to me." He murmured, forgetting himself.

Trigger glanced at him, and for a second Barnaby wondered whether it was possible to survive off quarter-rations.

"Look closer, then." Trigger eventually declared, offering him the scope.

Barnaby accepted it with a sigh of relief. He was skinny enough already.

With bated breath he peered through the glass, running his gaze across the spectral sight. The vessel's decay was truly astonishing, the timbers blackened and scarred by some unknown corruption. Several beams were warped by festering growths, their grey and bulbous heads slick with ooze. It was disgusting, yet still, it didn't confirm the Captain's claim.

"Where are they?" He asked, swiveling the scope from side-to-side.

"The wheel." Trigger declared. "Look closely."

Barnaby did as he was told, focusing his attention on the fractured circle. Many of the handles had been torn away, leaving only jagged spikes in their place. At first, that was all he could see, the wheel appearing as abandoned as the vessel it steered.

Then he saw it turning, the dusty wood commanded by thin and spidery hands.

The vessel's helmsman was not a large man. He may not have been a man at all. Most of him was obscured behind the wheel's mounting, while the rest was swaddled in a dark and heavy robe, blending seamlessly into the blackened deck.

At first, Barnaby believed the man to be suffering from tremors, his robed frame shaking against the wheel. Then he realized that the shudders were his own, his arm struggling to keep the scope level as waves of terror swelled in his chest. An ocean of spit soaked his lips as he fought to keep control, to understand what it was that filled him with such dread. The man at that wheel scared him more than Carnage, that tiny frame holding an air of menace beyond any amount of muscle.

As if in answer to his thoughts, the shadowed hood twisted, swiveling with measured pace. When eventually it paused, the man's thin face stood revealed, as did his dark and horrifying eyes.

Eyes that were fixed directly on him.

With a yelp of fear, Barnaby lowered the scope, offering it to the Captain with trembling hands.

"What did you see?" Trigger asked, frowning.

"He saw me." Barnaby mumbled, stepping back and staring at the corrupted vessel. It was still far away, too far for anyone to have seen him unaided.

"Think Barnaby's a bit spooked." Grinned Three-fingered Frank, though his own voice held a waiver of fear.

"Then Barnaby has a head on his shoulders." Trigger replied, retracting the scope with a decisive snap. "Any vessel that sails without wind or crew is one best left alone."

"What's your orders then, Captain?" Frank asked, clearly chastened by Trigger's remark.

"She doesn't seem to be aiming for us." Trigger declared, after a moment's consideration. "Or anyone, come to think of it. Even if she was, we can't outrun her. It's best we stick to our course, and wait to see how she responds. When we know which passage she intends to take, we'll simply pick another one."

Everyone nodded. It wasn't a particularly brave plan, yet it was sensible, and in the end, that's what a good Captain was there for.

"Alright men, return to your duties." Trigger declared, tucking the scope into the depths of his coat.

Probably to keep it away from Gary.

The others dispersed, returning to their tasks with swift diligence. For his part, Barnaby resumed mopping, though it was with far less enthusiasm. He was getting bloody sick of the mop.

"Oy, Barnaby!"

He closed his eyes as he heard his name. He had two primary duties he was expected to perform, and while he despised mopping, it was still the lesser of two evils.

"Yes?"

"Your boss has left you a present in the kitchen. I'd get on it quick, before the cook decides to feed it to you."

"Thanks, Johnny."

"Don't mention it. By the way, when you're done, re-mop this deck. It stinks."

Barnaby wasn't surprised. He'd been pissing in the mop bucket for weeks now. He saw it as fair. They kept complaining every time he mopped. He may as well give them a reason to.

Sighing, he made his way into the *Blackbird's* bowels, taking care not to disturb those slumbering in their hammocks. At first, he had struggled to navigate the ship, its swaying decks throwing him into doorways and walls. More than once he had toppled into the embrace of a sleeping crewman, the rough collisions earning him several black eyes.

He wasn't really surprised. Pirates were seldom known for their pleasant dispositions.

The cook was indeed livid when he stepped into the kitchen, his purple face made darker by a copious helping of wine and rage.

"Where the fuck have you been?" Rumbling Rogers demanded, hurling a skillet at Barnaby's head. He avoided it, the copper pan striking the wall with enough force to kill, or at least seriously maim.

"Mopping."

"Mopping!? Mopping he says! Like it's the most important thing in the fucking world!"

Barnaby didn't agree with this assessment of his tone. Still, he knew better than to argue.

"I'm sorry, sir."

"Oh, you better believe you're sorry!" Rogers bellowed, picking up a steaming pan of what may have been soup. Then again, it could simply have been dirty water. With Rogers, it was hard to tell.

"I don't spend my days slaving in a kitchen, just so you can slack off and bugger it up! What if he'd gone in the soup, Barnaby? What then?"

Truth be told, it would probably improve the meal. Barnaby had the sense not say to this, however.

"Where is it?" He asked, trying to appear contrite.

"Over there." The cook snarled, jerking a thumb towards the stove. "The culprit's sitting beside it."

"Of course he is." Barnaby sighed, heading towards the stove. He smelt his target long before he saw it, the fishy odor bringing tears to his eyes.

A pile of droppings sat on the floor, so fresh as to almost be steaming. Beside it sat the ship's cat, his pretty face fixed on Barnaby's own. It was as though he'd been waiting for him.

"Why can't you ever go on the top deck?" Barnaby asked, stooping and shaking his head. The cat replied by rubbing against his arm, purring with contentment.

The ship's cat had a name, though it was known solely by the Captain. The feline and he were apparently old friends, having served on every vessel together since the start of Trigger's career. This was more than could be said of any other crewman, and it was a well-known fact that the Captain regarded this cat as far more than a simple pet. It was his best friend and companion, and woe betide any member of the crew who dared to mistreat it. Fortunately, this was no real concern, as the rest of the crew had adopted him as their own, the creature's prowess as a hunter ensuring that the only vermin seen on the *Blackbird* were already long dead, the cat often laying his kills at the Captain's very feet.

The downside to this wonderful relationship was that it gave the cat a status outranking Barnaby's own. Whenever he wasn't mopping, Barnaby's other duties revolved around making the feline as comfortable as possible, whether it be feeding him, or clearing away his waste.

He needed to do both an awful lot.

"This is disgusting." He groaned, breathing through his mouth. He had neglected to bring a bucket, and was forced to remove the droppings by hand, the brown lumps warm against his palm.

The cat brushed against his legs, its muscular frame almost causing him to trip. Barnaby couldn't be sure that this wasn't its intent.

"Oh Gods, Barnaby, that's disgusting." Rogers gagged, pinching his nose. "Take it outside!"

What the fuck did he think Barnaby was going to do?

He raced up the stairs with the cat in tow, its little paws tapping against the wood. The night was cool as he emerged above deck, the setting sun replaced by stars and moon.

The spectral ship still hung in the distance, yet closer than before. By midnight, it could very well be upon them.

Keeping his eyes on the ship, Barnaby moved to the banister, hurling away the droppings with a hiss of distaste.

The cat brushed gently against his knees, gazing up at him with friendly eyes.

Barnaby looked down at it, glancing at the brown chunks smeared across his hand.

"I'd pat you, but I don't think you'd enjoy it." He declared, giving the cat an apologetic grin. The creature seemed to understand, leaping onto the banister with effortless grace. A second later it was nuzzling his arm, giving an endless series of joyful purrs.

Well, at least someone here liked him.

Chapter Four

Trigger stood on deck, watching as the spectral vessel began to turn, making for the Western Crunch.

"Well, that is unfortunate." He remarked, running a hand through his hair.

"Aye, Captain."

Crossing his arms, Trigger pondered their options. The whole crew was on deck, each of them gazing at him with curiosity and fear. The Western Crunch was not the easiest route, yet it represented a comfortable middle-ground between speed and danger. It had been Trigger's first choice of passage, yet now that it was denied him, he was going to have to improvise.

"We could always play it safe." Sheridan shrugged, giving him an easy grin. She knew that was never an option.

"We aren't taking the Coward's Path." He assured her. "Or the Blind Man's Way."

"Then you'd better tell the men to say their prayers. They'll be wanting the God's on their side."

Trigger bowed his head. She was right. The required speed left them only two options, both of which were usually fatal. He just had to decide how much danger he was willing to risk.

"Do we know which direction Carnage took?" Sheridan asked, delicately fanning her face. It wasn't particularly hot, yet his First Mate enjoyed the novelty of the habit.

"He always risks the Snares." Trigger replied. "He knows he can take the tribes, and if he loses his ship to the falls, well, he and his men can steal another."

"Well, considering how eager he is to hang you from his mast, might I suggest we choose another direction?"

"There's only one left." Trigger sighed.

"I know."

"And you think I should take it?"

"I do, though, I'm not the one who has to tell the crew."

"No." Trigger whistled. "I suppose you're not."

He returned his focus to his men, who had observed their conversation in respectful silence.

"Alright men, it's time we start in earnest." He declared, his words met by rousing cheers. "Firstly, an extra ration of ale for every one of you. You just showed tremendous patience, and I am very proud."

The next wave of cheers eclipsed the first, and actually brought a smile to Trigger's face. It didn't last long.

"Secondly, I have decided on our route. I have listened to your complaints, and acknowledge them as valid. We will not be following that vessel into the Western Crunch."

A roar of approval from his crew. He'd built them up high. Hopefully high enough to handle his decision.

"Instead, we will be travelling through the Howlers. From start-to-finish they are the shortest path, and should we succeed in navigating them, our victory is all but assured."

Silence. Terrible, awkward silence.

"Good one, Captain." Laughed Three-Fingered Frank.

"It isn't a joke, Frank."

"Oh."

Another hush, this one filled with uncertain glances, and the low drone of uneasy murmurs.

"I realize that you have concerns." Trigger announced, raising a hand. "This will not be an easy journey. If you have any misgivings, now is the time to voice them."

He was almost bowled over by the chorus of voices, his men taking him at his word.

That was something, at least.

"The Howlers, Captain?"

"No one's ever sailed the Howlers!"

"Yes, they have! Captain Randigold took them thirty years back, and she won the bloody Tides!"

"Bollocks, Steve. Everyone knows that's a myth!"

"My uncle was part of her crew!"

"You never knew your father, let alone your uncle!"

A round of laughter sounded, an opening that Trigger swiftly seized.

"Please men, one at a time. Raise your hands and speak when I address you."

Almost every arm present shot into the air. Only Magwa, Sheridan and Barnaby appeared to be content.

"Alright. Frank, you may go first."

"Thank you." Frank declared, licking his titular hand and flattening his hair. Frank fancied himself the crew's official spokesman, a belief that no one had ever bothered to address.

"You see, Captain, the Howlers aren't exactly the easiest route. I mean, sure, they're the shortest in terms of distance, but surviving them is another matter entirely. Most crews don't make it past the Howlers themselves, let alone the dangers beyond. There's a reason no one takes them. They're just not worth the risk."

The crew murmured their agreement, most hands descending as Frank made their point for them.

Rubbing his thumb against his finger, Trigger considered his response. Were he still with the navy, he could simply threaten his men into obedience. A pirate crew was a democracy, however, forcing him into a more diplomatic approach.

Fortunately, he was a noble's son, and knew what it took to sway a crowd.

"Aye, valid concerns." He nodded, making sure that his posture remained calm and relaxed. "Most crews have failed when they've challenged the Howlers. Most turn and run with their tails between their legs, while a small few succeed in scraping through, only to perish a few days later. It is a dangerous path, one that should never be taken lightly."

He could see men nodding, focusing on him as he started pacing back-and-forth.

"Which is why I would never make this proposal to other men. To *lesser* men."

He ceased his pacing, placing both hands on the banister and leaning forward.

"Instead, I make it to you. The finest gathering of pirates and scoundrels the world has ever seen."

Cheers of agreement rang out from the crew. Trigger failed to contain his grin.

"Every man here is worth a hundred on the shore. You are the villains who haunt their nightmares and grace their women's dreams. You do not fear the sea, or its terrors, for you *are* the crushing waves, you *are* the bloody terrors. We are the last free men, the last great men, a fact which we shall mark in history, the moment we cross that finish line, and return in glory to the bright White Harbor."

Most of the crew were nodding now, looking to each other with beaming faces.

"That is what I promise you." Trigger declared, throwing open his arms. "Glory, riches, women and freedom. All I ask in return is that you be *who you already are.* Men of action, men of courage. So, tell me, my brave crew. Are you willing to defy one last antiquated folly? Are you willing to stretch the boundaries of what men believe is possible? Will you sail through the Howlers, to the promise of a life grander than anything you have ever imagined!?"

"Aye, Captain!"

Trigger bowed his head as the cheers continued, the men working themselves into a frenzy of adulation.

"Bit over-the-top, wasn't it?" Sheridan whispered, giving him an amused smirk.

"I had to be sure." He shrugged, running a hand through his hair. "After all, I am asking them to risk their lives. Which reminds me…"

He returned his gaze to the crew, holding up a palm for silence.

"You know what?" He began, lowering his hand.

"Make that two extra rations of ale."

He didn't stay to watch what followed. The cheers were loud enough.

****

Barnaby held his head, as did the rest of the crew. The ale had seemed a good idea at the time, as it always does, yet in the cold light of morning they were all feeling remorse, not to mention the worst fucking headaches. Considering their destination, this was not ideal.

"Here."

Barnaby looked at the hand before him, its dark palm filled with wax.

"Thanks." He said, taking the wax between his fingers. Magwa nodded in acknowledgment, sitting beside him with a mild groan.

"Magwa didn't think Barnaby would take enough." Magwa declared, giving him one of those pointy grins.

Barnaby hadn't taken any, truth be told. He'd been too hungover to find the man distributing it.

"Can Barnaby believe the Captain?" Magwa asked, gazing at Trigger with unabashed awe. "Brave man."

"That's one word for it." Barnaby grumbled. Frankly, he was still a little pissed that Trigger had swayed the crew so easily. Now, not only had he convinced them to sail into certain death, he'd also found a way to make them admire him for it.

"Man who knows what he wants is no fool, nor is a Captain who guards his crew."

Barnaby scowled at Magwa, the Kalyute's constant good cheer grating on his rattled nerves.

"Most men who hear the Howler's go insane, you realize? He's not being brave. He's putting us all in danger, even more than he's already put us in."

"Why? Captain's the one who'll hear them."

"And you can't see the peril in having a lunatic Captain?"

"Most leaders already lunatics. Trigger get too bad, we kill him and find new one."

Barnaby decided not to contest this point. Truth be told, it had some merit.

"Alright lads, start waxing up!" Yelled Sunniday, leading by example. "I can see the rocks, and it won't be long until we hear them, too!"

Barnaby watched as the crew filled their ears, each man making sure he was perfectly positioned to continue his duties. There would be no real communication for the next few miles, and a single misplaced crewman could lead them into disaster. It was during times like these that Barnaby relished his unimportance, his lack of skills ensuring him a peaceful hour of lazy mopping.

"It would be a journey, to hear the Howler's song." Magwa mused, considering the wax in his hands.

"Not a pleasant one." Barnaby warned. Even in the outer fringes, the dangers of the Howler's were known far and wide. "More than a few sailors have tried their luck, and nearly all of them end up guiding their ship prow-first into the rocks. Apparently, death is the preferable option."

"Why?" Magwa asked, gazing at him with fierce curiosity.

"No idea. The people who do survive are tellingly few, and never in the mood to speak about what they heard. The majority end up completely insane."

"Hmm." Magwa frowned, weighing the wax. A moment later, he was stuffing it in his ears, sealing them shut with the utmost care.

"I'm surprised you did your duties so quickly!" He yelled, making Barnaby jump. "I would have thought he'd be harder to catch!"

"What?" Barnaby asked, extremely confused.

"What?" Magwa repeated, pointing at the wax in his ears.

"Who are you talking about!?" Barnaby yelled. "Who would be hard to catch!?"

Magwa simply shrugged, shaking his head in amused surrender.

Taking a deep breath, Barnaby resisted the urge to strangle the savage. Gods only know what he was talking ab-

The cat.

The bloody cat.

He hadn't blocked its ears!

"What's wrong!?" Magwa called, as Barnaby sprinted below deck. He didn't stop to answer.

"Shit, shit!" Barnaby panicked, racing up and down the halls. "Where are you!?"

"A mile till the Howlers, boys!" Sunniday boomed from above. "If you haven't clogged your ears, I'd hurry up!"

Barnaby paused, considering his options. He could clog his ears and forget the cat, yet to do so would be leaving the poor creature exposed, a failure that may well see him hanged. Peg-Leg Greg had once moved it roughly with his foot, only to suffer the direst of retributions. Prior to that, they'd simply called him Greg.

No, abandoning the cat was not an option.

A flash of white, in the corner of his vision.

Barnaby turned towards it, and was rewarded by the sight of a snowy paw, vanishing around a nearby corner. Willing himself not to run, Barnaby began a stealthy pursuit, keeping low as he traversed the hallway, rounding the corner with bated breath.

The cat had entered the food stores, its black-and-grey tail vanishing behind a groaning stack of shelves. The sheer volume of food guaranteed that it was cornered, a fact which gave him some comfort. If he could do this quickly, there should be no danger.

He snuck his way towards the shelves, peering around them for some sign of his quarry. He found it perched in a shadowed corner, its fluffy paws resting on the corpse of a rat.

"Aw, good boy." Barnaby soothed, stepping calmly towards it. "Clever cat, beautiful cat. You're a great little hunter, aren't you?"

The cat regarded him as he spoke, rolling onto its back and stretching its paws.

"Good boy, good cat." He continued, kneeling and reaching towards it. It clawed playfully at his sleeve, its closed eyes slowly opening.

"That's it." He smiled, attempting to drag it closer. He wasn't certain, yet he was beginning to feel as though he could hear something in the distance, a strange and fierce buzzing that left a sour taste on his tongue.

The cat rolled from his grasp, leaping to its feet with preternatural grace.

"It's ok." Barnaby assured, struggling to keep his voice level. He was sweating now, though whether it was from the noise or fear, he wasn't completely sure. "All I want is a cuddle."

The cat stared right at him as it picked up the rat, clamping its corpse between its jaws. He could see the mischief in its golden eyes.

"No." Barnaby scolded, his hands balling into fists. The buzzing was growing louder, an insistent clawing at the base of his skull. It made his scalp itchy, while the backs of his eyes were burning. By contrast, the cat seemed entirely unaffected.

"Put it down." Barnaby ordered, shuffling towards the cat. It backed away, swaying from side-to-side.

"Look, just come here, ok?" Barnaby begged, reaching. With uncanny speed its paw lashed out, swiping his hand away.

Fuck it. He'd tried being gentle.

Barnaby leapt, slamming face-first into the wall as the cat danced around him. He heard the tip-tap of its paws as it sprinted past the shelves, and for a moment he feared he'd lost it, until a simple glance revealed that it had come to a halt, studying him with expectant delight.

"Is this a fucking game to you?" Barnaby asked, cradling his bleeding nose.

The cat purred and turned in a circle, still holding its limp prize.

"Right." Barnaby declared, rising to his feet. The noise was almost unbearable, as though it were vibrating through his very bones, grinding his brain to paste.

"Come here!" He yelled, sprinting at the cat. It took off with blinding speed, yet made the mistake of pausing at the door, checking to see if he would follow. Barnaby took advantage, diving forward and slamming the door with a victorious cry.

"Nowhere to run." Barnaby mocked, his dive having spread him across the floor.

Was that blood trickling from his ears?

The cat dropped the rat, nudging it towards his face. Too panicked to consider the diseases, Barnaby picked it up, placing it in his pocket. He hoped the display would soothe his prey, and lead it into his waiting arms.

The cat turned its back on him, flashing its arse-hole as it scurried beneath a shelf.

"I thought we were friends." Barnaby whined, dragging himself after it. Closing the door had dampened the sound, yet it was still growing, the buzzing morphing into something else entirely. Whispers and shrieks. The voices of his family, and people he knew were now long-dead. They dripped into his mind like rain, building in intensity with every second. He couldn't understand them, not yet, though their whispers filled him with dread.

Barnaby coughed as a desert of dust brushed his lips, drying out his mouth in moments. He cursed the cleaner's lazy nature, before remembering that the storage floors were his responsibility.

The cat had positioned itself against the far wall, its shivering body finally reacting to the Howler's terrible cries. The feline was on its side, its uneven breaths causing its stomach to rise and fall in rapid intervals. He didn't have much time.

Barnaby increased his pace, the voices growing stronger in his aching mind. They were conjuring images now, his life flashing before his eyes, though each of the scenes were subtly altered, twisted into demented mockeries of what had really occurred. At least, he thought they were. Between the constant pain and bombardment of his senses, he could no longer be sure.

He seized the cat and dragged it close, carving a groove in the powdery dust. This time, the creature offered no resistance, meowing weakly in his folded arm.

"It's alright." He soothed, coughing again. His vision was fading now, the world wavering before his watering eyes.

Extracting the wax from his pocket, he clamped it against the cat's ears, trying to mold it into the unfamiliar shape. The change was instant and encouraging, the feline ceasing its shivering as its breathing returned to normal.

That was when the Howlers really began to sing.

Barnaby convulsed as the sound tore into his mind, existence slipping away as he fell into a prison of his own corrupted memories. He was vaguely aware of the cat, its fragile skull still clutched between his fingers. He had failed to plug its ears, only his quivering palms keeping the wax in place. If he shifted even slightly, the sound would slip through, and at this intensity, he doubted the creature would survive a single second of exposure.

Curling around his furry ward, Barnaby clenched his teeth, the pain and madness growing with every moment. He had two options. Sacrifice the cat, and save himself, at least until the Captain killed him, or brave the Howlers cry, a feat failed by thousands of better men.

One guaranteed death, while the other merely made it probable.

Barnaby had always been keen on self-preservation.

Chapter Five

Trigger walked across the misty docks, his palms wet with excitement. Thick-set sailors were bustling all around him, cursing beneath the weight of cargo, or leering at the giggling whores. He'd never been this close to the ocean before, never smelt or seen such base humanity. It was intoxicating, the stench of sweat, tar and semen mingling with the salt-stained air. A hint of ale guided him to what he assumed was a tavern, the faded sign too worn to read. The revelry within was all too clear, however, and Trigger would be damned if he'd miss this opportunity. With bated breath, he seized the greasy handle, twisting it downwards and throwing open the door.

It led him into a derelict alley, its cobbled streets abandoned, save for the hatted stranger reclining against a discarded barrel. His head shifted, giving Trigger a flash of two jade-green eyes, and the most stunning grin he'd ever seen.

Barely able to contain his excitement, Trigger advanced towards him, casting aside his heavy coat. This is why he'd left his family. This is what he'd come here for. This, this is what he'd always wanted...

No, it wasn't.

Trigger slumped against the banister, trembling hands failing to support his weight. His knees buckled, sending his head slamming into the dense wood. The darkness reared once more, closing around his vision as Sheridan touched his arm.

His sister was laughing, pointing at something in the tightly-packed crowd. Trigger followed her gaze, and started laughing as well, just as the Empress embraced his sides. Her body felt tight against his own, firm, despite the depths of her billowing dress. With nervous hands he caressed her mask, clutching its edges and sliding it up.

His sister was still laughing, her thin finger pointing at the growing crowd.

Trigger shook his head as Sheridan helped him to his feet. She yelled something in his ears, yet the Howlers owned the world, his eyes spewing blood down his cheeks.

He was falling, clutching the Empress to his waist. His grip was tight, so tight it hurt, yet the Empress didn't mind, her delicate hands wrapping around his neck and pulling him towards her gaping mouth.

The mouth became a cannon, smoke and powder filling the air as she loosed another volley, Trigger standing at her side and screaming for all he was worth. A ship burned in the distance, the men upon it diving for cover as he ordered their demise. One of their corpses caught his gaze, their regal face crushed by a glancing blow. A single eye was dangling free of the socket, its burst vessels drawing him in...

His sister was still laughing, and the crowd was beginning to join her...

"The crew...can't see...me...like this." Trigger spat, clutching the collar of Sheridan's dress. He didn't know if she could hear him, yet all the same she held him close, dragging his limp form towards the cabin.

The cannons were gone. There was only the Empress. Trigger rolled from her in shame, her hand touching at his fleeing shoulder. A grin touched his face as the grip became strong, forcing him to stop, keeping him rooted in place.

The door burst open, a beam of candlelight cutting across his bedroom floor.

The crowd was laughing now, their eyes and fingers turned to him. The Empress glared at him from above their heads, her porcelain face twisted by hate. His sister was beside him, little more than a foot away. She wasn't laughing now. Her bright blue eyes were stained with tears.

He was on his side, his shoulder pressed against a wooden floor. He'd thrown up, staining the surrounding timbers. The air was still filled by a terrible buzzing, the hideous sound assaulting his very core. His stomach churned as the vibrations tumbled through it, folding him in half and sending another wave of nausea crawling up his throat. This time, however, he was able to suppress it, the sound gradually abating as they sailed onwards, the floor swaying softly beneath his cheek. Eventually, it ceased entirely, replaced by lapping waves, and the gentle creaking of a wind-touched mast.

Slowly, he unfurled, rolling onto his back and caressing his aching stomach.

A woman stood high above him, her fearsome features creased with concern. A blonde wig sat unevenly on her scalp, while a vivid pink dress was draped about her shoulders. She looked utterly absurd, and yet entirely familiar.

"You okay, Captain?" She asked, kneeling beside him.

"I know you." He replied, cracking his aching jaw. He had no idea how long he'd been keeping it clenched.

She tilted her head as she studied him, knocking her wig askew and revealing a wax-clogged ear. It stirred something in his fractured mind, the words trickling from his lips without thought or consideration.

"You don't need those, not anymore. The noise has stopped."

He touched his own ears for emphasis, watching as the burly maiden tentatively removed her earplugs, wincing expectantly as she pulled them free. For a moment, her hands lingered, prepared to stuff them back at the first sign of trouble, yet after a few seconds of silence she relented, tucking away the wax into an unseen pocket.

"How do you feel?" She asked, putting a hand to his forehead. Such an obvious display of familiarity reinforced his belief that he should know who this is, yet the memories still eluded him, dancing like smoke at the edge of his fingers.

"Parched, exhausted and confused." He replied, deciding that honesty would serve him best. "And not entirely sure who you are."

She retracted her hand, hazel eyes narrowing as though she were insulted. She probably was.

"I'm your First Mate." She declared, rising and moving towards a nearby desk. His desk, he vaguely recalled.

"My First Mate." He echoed. The statement rang a bell.

"Aye, First Mate Sheridan." She continued, pouring water into a bowl and cup. "We found each other at the Golden Stag, probably the least salubrious tavern in the whole fucking empire."

"That's half-rations." Trigger announced, surprising himself. At first Sheridan smiled, though his confusion must have been clear, as the expression faded from her lips.

"You're not a fan of swearing." She informed him. "And your policies reflect that. The first words I ever heard you say were 'a man's language reflects his soul'."

Another bell rang in the back of Trigger's mind.

"Rather pretentious, yet it sounds familiar." Trigger conceded, accepting the cup and downing a swig.

"To be fair, you were blind drunk, and attempting to defend my honor."

"You don't look as though you'd need defending."

"I don't, though, considering it was seven-on-one, I appreciated the effort."

The words opened the floodgates of his memory, the scene spilling free with the force of a hammer. Half-melted candles flickering in cobweb-coated holders, the blood-and-piss-stained walls quaking as Sheridan hurled a scoundrel against them, cracking the wood with his empty skull. His friends had leapt to defend him, their mead-pickled tongues screaming tasteless insults. He had struck one with the base of his mug, his own drunken mind taking a stab at poetry and wisdom.

"You dropped them all in under a minute." He beamed. "Though, you looked an absolute mess afterwards."

Sheridan grinned, extracting a handkerchief and dipping it in the bowl.

"I looked a mess beforehand, as well. Wigs and dresses are expensive, and you don't make much on a barmaid's wage."

"Do you still have that dress?" Trigger asked, as she began cleaning the blood and vomit that had caked on his face.

"I do. I pull it out from time-to-time, just to relive that night. It still has the stains."

"It was a good one." Trigger replied, as she curved the cloth around his cheek. "Though, I have to admit, your current outfit is far more complimentary."

"Piracy pays." Sheridan shrugged, tossing the handkerchief into the bowl. "It's the most redeeming feature."

"Can't argue there." Trigger groaned, as Sheridan helped him to his feet. "How much did the men see?"

"They saw you bleeding from the eyes and ears, and they watched you stumble. I got you inside before the vomiting, however. So that's okay."

Trigger nodded, pondering the day's events. He was steady on his feet, yet his eyes were sensitive to light, while his thoughts and memories were cluttered, resistant to any effort to right them. It was as though his head were deep underwater, the pressure crushing his skull. Still, he didn't need a clear mind to stride across the deck, or to congratulate his crew.

"I'll let them see me." He announced, adjusting his coat.

"Good plan." Sheridan nodded. "You're clean, and from a distance look perfectly fine. If the men can boast that you passed through the Howlers and came out strutting, well, that will do wonders for morale, and your reputation."

"Thank you." Trigger replied, giving her a grateful smile. As First Mates go, he couldn't have made a better choice.

"Should I go first?" Sheridan asked, moving to the door.

"No." Trigger declared. That would make it look as though he were being escorted. He needed to appear strong, in control.

Sheridan nodded and stepped aside, giving a mock-bow towards the doorway. Shaking his head at her sarcasm, Trigger thrust it open, trying not to wince as the sunlight seared his gaze. For a moment he was blinded, yet the whiteness was quick to fade, revealing his crew on the *Blackbird's* deck. Every face was turned to him, mouths wide with blatant awe.

Despite the throbbing in his skull, Trigger felt a trickle of pride. Yes, it had brought him to his knees, yet he had listened to the Howler's, and now stood proud despite them. It was a tale these men would tell their children, a legend that would be whispered in the harbors of the world.

Perhaps they would reach his family, if the fates were feeling kind. Perhaps they would actually care.

"You can clear your ears!" He declared, tapping at his own. The brighter crewmen understood, removing the wax and indicating that their less-astute comrades should probably do the same.

Trigger waited until all ears were empty to begin his speech. It wouldn't be as passionate or articulate as many he had given before, yet he sensed that his men would understand. Gods, they'd probably approve.

"My crew." He began, leaning against the banister. His legs were feeling the strain. "We made it!"

The crew erupted into roars of approval, thumping their chests and slapping each other's hands. Trigger allowed them the display, using the time to recover.

"Each of you have shown courage, conviction and determination." He declared, once the noise had abated. "I could not be prouder, or more grateful for your service. You have done well, and I applaud you."

"Aye, don't clap for us, Captain!" Frank bellowed, earning a round of cheers. "You just sauntered through the bloody Howlers! We should be yelling for you!"

The crew clearly agreed, letting loose a mighty roar that tripled Trigger's headache. Still, it felt fantastic. It had been so long since people cheered his name, rather than hissed it in disgust.

"Thank you, thank you." Trigger waved, bowing his head. "We have all performed an admirable task. We are not quite done, however, and must pull clear of these final rocks. Return to your duties for now, and when we are done, we shall celebrate in the proper manner."

"Aye, Captain!"

The men obeyed with boundless enthusiasm, many of them sneaking admiring glances as Trigger moved among them. His destination was the stern, and as he stood upon it, he retrieved his scope, squinting through the treated glass.

The Howlers sat in motionless contempt, not a single creature present on those cold and empty stones. They were bastions of isolation, solitary sentinels amongst the rolling waves. There was no trace of the creatures who had almost shattered his mind. They lived unseen by man or beast.

Isn't that the way of all great terrors?

"Captain."

The deep voice of Magwa beckoned, and with an expectant snap Trigger closed the scope, turning to the Kalyute with a mild grin.

"Magwa. How did you find the passage?"

"Quiet."

Trigger nodded at this response. The Kalyute were a direct people.

"How may I help you?"

"Crewman missing. The small one, Barnaby."

Trigger suppressed a sigh, running a hand through his tousled hair. It had been too much to expect a perfect escape.

"Where was he last seen?"

"Sprinting below deck. Magwa gave him wax, believing Barnaby foolish enough not to get his own after seeing to cat. Apparently, Magwa gave too much credit. Barnaby had forgotten cat, and himself."

"Gods." Trigger whispered, closing his eyes. He allowed himself to feel the frustration, using it to suppress the growing fear and concern. Barnaby could be replaced, yet if anything had happened to his cat…

No. Only sorrow lay in that direction, and hope was still in reach.

"Did you see what direction he went?" Trigger asked, as Magwa followed him below deck.

"No. Barnaby run without warning."

"Can you track him?"

"Yes. Barnaby awful at mopping."

Magwa indicated a pair of tracks in the dusty floor, four tiny paws pursued by clumsy feet. The trail led them to the storeroom, the burdened shelves releasing a noxious odor.

"Vomit." Magwa declared, sinking into a crouch.

Trigger nodded in agreement. If Barnaby had failed to use the wax, then a puddle of vomit made total sense.

His concern grew.

"Where are they, then?" He asked, wandering the cramped aisles. Grooves of pursuit had been carved in the dust, yet of the pair who made them, there was no sign.

"Here." Magwa replied. Backing out of the shelves, Trigger watched in amazement as the Kalyute scurried around on all fours, peering under the supplies as though he were some enormous crab.

"What can you see?" Trigger asked, dropping to his knees.
"Barnaby. Curled up, covered in blood. Magwa think it his."
"The cat?"
"Behind him, maybe."

Moving forward, Trigger attempted to insinuate himself beneath the shelves. His shoulders proved too broad, however, catching on the wood and blocking his passage.

"Here." Magwa declared, pushing him aside. The Kalyute's lithe frame was smaller than his own, allowing him to slither under without concern. His compact muscles were efficient, however, and in a matter of moments he was dragging Barnaby free, the cat less than a second behind.

"Hey, boy." Trigger beamed, as it raced over to nuzzle his palm. He swept it up with gentle arms, rubbing his forehead against its own.

"Is Barnaby alive?" He asked, rising to his feet. Magwa rested a hand against the boy's lips, nodding as breath touched his dusty fingers.

"Find a man to help you, and place him in my quarters." Trigger ordered, giving his cat a loving squeeze. "I'll fetch the doctor."

"You want to leave, then leave! You think we care?"
"Mum, please…"
"I'm not your mother. Sons love their mothers. All you are is a selfish little prick, who cares more about some fucking ship than he does his own family!"

Barnaby hung his head in shame, yet didn't stop edging towards the door. Bethany sat to his right, watching with indifference.

His mother caught him looking, and began the tirade anew.

"And what about your wife? Have you given a single thought to how she feels?"

She didn't care. He knew that. Shit, she was probably glad he was leaving. She'd never wanted the marriage, neither of them had. He wanted a life beyond the village, and she wanted a husband who wasn't a hideous failure.

"This is best, mum." He replied, opening the door.

A flood of flesh struck him from the other side, smashing him against the floor and dragging him back towards his mother.

"No!" He yelled, lashing out at the mouths screaming around him. "I don't want this. I don't this!"

"Well, I don't want you either, you ungrateful little shit."

Barnaby's eyes snapped open, landing on the bulging shoulders of the most enormous -and fashionable- woman he'd ever seen. Still, something about her features fanned the sparks of recognition.

"Do I know yo-"

"Oh, not this again." The woman replied, rolling her eyes. With one meaty hand she slapped his cheek, snapping his head sideways.

"Remember me now?"

"Gods above, woman!" An angry voice declared, shoving her away. It took Barnaby a moment to regain his senses, yet when he did the picture had changed, the face above him resembling a kindly grandfather.

"Hey." Barnaby rasped, his throat unbelievably sore.

"I'm sorry about Sheridan." Said a familiar voice to his left. "Her people have a very…rough, concept of medicine."

"Aye, Captain." Barnaby croaked. "No harm done."

"See?" Sheridan exclaimed. "I fixed him!"

"You almost snapped his neck." The ships doctor frowned, stroking his voluminous beard. "Though, it does appear that the blow was successful in restoring him…"

"Will one of you please get him some water?" Trigger remarked, his tone commandingly stern.

"Aye, Captain." The doctor replied, handing Barnaby a cup. He downed the water in one mighty gulp, the pain in his stomach suggesting that this was quite the mistake.

"Sorry, I should have warned you to go slow." The doctor winced, watching as Barnaby seized his sides. The movement disturbed the ships cat, who was curled up on his waist.

"We found him with you." Trigger explained. "And he hasn't left your side."

Barnaby was oddly touched.

"Has he been making sure that I'm okay?" He asked. Nothing had ever cared so much for his well-being.

The trio around him shared several awkward glances.

"Not…exactly." Sheridan conceded, rubbing the back of her head. Her eyes had fallen on Barnaby's right hand, which, while cleaned and treated, bore the unmistakable marks of tiny teeth.

"He wanted to eat me!" Barnaby exclaimed, gazing at the cat in horror. The creature rolled onto its back, lifting its legs, and purring softly.

"I'd take it as a compliment." Trigger shrugged. "Cats are picky."

Barnaby tried to bury his resentment. After all, judging by the depth of the wounds, the cat *had* stopped as soon as it realized he was alive.

"Captain! There's something you should see!"

Trigger sighed as he rose from his chair, Sunniday's voice filled with urgency.

"Can I trust you to keep an eye on him?" He asked, looking to Sheridan.

"I won't slap him again, if that's what you're asking."

Barnaby felt a wave of relief. His cheek was fucking sore.

"Captain!"

"I'm coming, I'm coming." Trigger muttered, adjusting his coat, and stepping out the door.

"I'd best go as well." The doctor declared, clearing away his equipment. "When Sunniday's voice hits that particular pitch, my services are usually required."

"Thank you, doctor." Barnaby nodded, the motion making his forehead ache.

"Eh, don't thank me. I didn't actually do much. Just gave you some water and looked at your eyes. That's all medicine is, really."

Barnaby couldn't tell if the doctor was joking. He wasn't sure if he wanted to know.

The doctor waved as he slipped through the door, shutting it gently behind him. Sheridan and Barnaby shared awkward glances in the ensuing silence, the discomfort between them palpable.

"So." Sheridan began, producing a file from the depths of her dress. "Tell me about it."

"About what?"

"Your hometown, your life before the ship."

"Oh! Well, it's…not actually someth- "

"I was kidding, Barnaby. I don't give a fuck. I want to hear about the Howlers. What did they do to you? What did you see?"

Barnaby bit back a scathing reply. He seemed to do that a lot.

"They're a bit connected, actually. I saw my life, though it was…fractured. Distorted."

"Distorted?"

"Aye. Things were happening out of sequence, and in ways that weren't quite right…well, at least, I think they weren't right. The false memories have mingled with the real ones, and it's hard to tell which came first."

"Sounds unpleasant." Sheridan replied. "Though, not as awful as I'd expected."

"You don't see a problem with losing your past?"

"Gods, no." Sheridan replied, running the file across a manicured nail. "I think it sounds wonderful."

Barnaby studied her extravagant frame, her wig, nails and dress in complete defiance of the body beneath.

"You do look like someone who's trying to escape themselves." He ventured, fearing that he may be pushing the conversation a hair too far.

"On the contrary, I'm exactly who I want to be." Sheridan replied, tucking away the file. "It was my past that stood in my way. If the Howlers can erase that, well, I'm more than a little tempted."

"They're altered, not destroyed." He declared. "And I don't think it's for the better."

"Mine can't get any worse." Sheridan shrugged. "I'd be interested to see them try."

Barnaby bowed his head in consideration, relenting as the pain intensified.

"It sounds like quite the story." He conceded. "I'll tell you mine, if you tell me yours."

He hoped that she'd accept. He was genuinely interested, and Gods know, he needed the friends.

Sheridan considered him, sizing him up.

"Yeah, okay." She grinned, leaning into her chair. She must have decided he wasn't a threat. Barnaby could have told her that.

"Sheridan!"

Trigger's voice was commanding, bringing Sheridan to her feet on the first syllable.

"We'll have to do this later, I'm afraid." She declared, giving him a friendly wave. "Rest up, and try to look alive. I think the cat's still hungry."

Barnaby grinned, giving the creature a comforting pat. It purred softly as he touched its fur.

"I think we're good." He nodded, as Sheridan opened the door.

"I can see that." She replied, taking a moment to position her wig. "You should be proud. He's an excellent judge of character."

She exited the cabin, leaving Barnaby in the soothing quiet. Feeling oddly content, he let his head sink into the downy pillow, feathers cradling him like a lover's lap.

"I think I made a friend." He whispered, giving the cat a tender stroke.

Chapter Six

"What is it?" Trigger bellowed, glancing up at Sunniday. The crewman was almost hanging outside the crow's nest, one hand raised to ward off the sun.

"Wreckage ahead, Captain! More than I can count!"

Trigger moved towards the portside, stretching out his scope and raising it to his eye. For the first time he took note of the landscape around them, the shores pinched so close as to almost form a river. The land beyond was arid, steely clumps of grass erupting from parched and sunbaked dirt. The few trees in sight were thin and skeletal, their scant leaves a mottled mix of browns and greys.

"Nice place." He murmured, swiveling his gaze towards their prow.

"Ah." He declared, lowering the scope. It wasn't exactly needed.

The wrecks occupied the shoreline, their rotting hulls beached like whales. Some had been repurposed, countless birds crouching in their shade as they studied the seas for prey. Most had been reclaimed, nature decaying them until they were little more than paper structures, their ancient frames waiting for a gust of wind strong enough to finally knock them down. Their makes and models differed an astounding degree, yet one feature remained static about every moss-strewn vessel.

The bones.

Skeletons adorned them as though they were jewelry, the bleached surfaces made blinding by the brilliant sun. The scale of death was beyond calculation, leaving Trigger utterly speechless.

"Aye, it's a nasty sight, isn't it Captain?"

Frank, however, was apparently unaffected.

"That it is, Mr. Frank."

"You reckon' it was the Howlers?"

"That I do, Mr. Frank. I believe these were the crews who attempted them before us, without the benefit of wax."

Frank whistled through his front teeth, gazing at the wreckages with predatory wonder.

"You reckon' there's treasure onboard?"

"If there is, we aren't stopping to pick it up."

Frank sighed, wiping his sweaty forehead with a filthy hand.

"Aye, Captain."

"Captain!"

Trigger glanced upwards, repressing a sigh of his own. He liked Sunniday, yet he was getting rather sick of hearing his voice.

"Yes?"

"There's another wreck ahead!"

"I find that unsurprising."

"No, Captain, this one's different! I think it's fresh!"

"Fresh?" Trigger mused, heading for the prow. Frank followed, his grimy face a mask of confusion.

"You think someone else tried to sail the Howlers?" He asked, scratching at his chin.

"Anything is possible." Trigger replied, peering over the banister at the churning waters ahead.

"Oh, fuck me." Frank declared, gazing at the grizzly sight.

"That's quarter-rations, Mr. Frank."

"Aye, Captain."

Trigger returned his eyes to the vessel before them, its mighty hull crushed against the barren shore. Broken beams and bleeding bodies churned in the waters around it, punctured skulls bobbing in-and-out of view. Those still on the vessel had fared little better, their corpses draped across the woodwork in various displays of man's fragility. Some had obviously been butchered, stab wounds and slashes appearing ludicrously large beside their bullet-born companions. Others were more abstract, some having clawed out their own eyes, ears and throats in an attempt to escape whatever madness the Howlers wrought. One poor soul lay crushed beneath the dislodged wheel, its spokes driven through the side of his skull. It was impossible to tell whether it was self-inflicted.

"Excuse me, good sirs! Over here if you please!"

Trigger almost jumped as the voice addressed them, the heavy accent sounding ridiculous in such dire surroundings. It took him a few seconds to identify the source, the speaker standing camouflaged amongst his murdered companions.

"Who asks?" Trigger demanded, slyly indicating that they should maintain their current course. There was every chance that this was a trap.

The addresser rose to his full height, wiping away the bloody water clinging to his chest and arms. He was stripped to the waist, revealing a husky frame that was tailor-made for ending other's lives.

"My name is Captain Jacques Beaufort." The man declared, giving a modest bow. All around him, Trigger's crew began to murmur, glancing at one another with astonishment. Trigger ignored them, refusing to let the man's reputation cloud his judgement.

"What happened to your crew?" He asked, studying the scene for signs of foul play. It was impossible to discern amongst such brutal slaughter.

"Zey wished to hear ze Howlers." Beaufort replied, shaking his head. "Ze strain proved too great, and in a bout of madness zey fell upon each ozer. What followed was…unpleasant."

Trigger frowned at the Captain's accent. It was a somewhat effective imitation of an Urlranesian noble, yet in many cases it missed the mark, lacking the true air of pretention that all Urlranese possessed.

"How did you survive?" Trigger asked, quite sure he already knew.

"Zeir insanity lacked direction." Beaufort began. "Zey attacked each other, and zemselves, as zough zey were feral beasts. Some did come for me. Fortunately, I am razer…efficient, with a blade. According to some, at least."

The comment caused another rumbling from the crew, this one filled with excitement. Again, Trigger paid them no heed. A Captain who kills his crew is not one to be celebrated.

"Why didn't you block their ears?" Trigger asked, scowling. "It would have preserved their sanity, and their lives."

"Zey wanted to hear ze song." Beaufort shrugged. "And I am merely zeir Captain, not zeir fazer. It is a tragedy, yes, but what are you going to do?"

Trigger folded his arms, his opinion of Beaufort rapidly declining. His men, on the other hand, appeared enraptured.

"Did you hear the song?"

"I did." Beaufort replied. "Awful, zough I don't quite see what ze fuss is about. Zough to be fair, I am partially deaf, so my opinion may be skewed."

Beaufort tapped the right side of his hairless scalp, drawing Trigger's attention to a prominent ding.

"An old wound." The Captain continued. "I killed ze man who gave it to me, yet I am beginning to zink zat he did me a favour. When next I am in town, I shall place flowers on his grave."

"How generous." Trigger replied, hand slipping towards his pistol. Their ship had drawn parallel with the wreck of Beaufort's own, and he was still uncertain whether this was some kind of deceit. "I wish you luck in your journey home."

Beaufort's face crinkled in surprise, as did the majority of Trigger's crew.

"You're just going to leave him here, Captain?" Frank asked, seizing his sleeve. With one look, Trigger made him let go, and sent him scurrying back three paces.

"That's Captain Jacques Beaufort." Frank continued, judging himself safe. "He's a living legend. Every man on this ship knows his name, and more than half of us have money riding on his duel with Longsteel. Some of us stand to make a fortune!"

"No one knows if that duel is even going to occur." Trigger replied, waving him away.

"Well, if you leave him here, I'd say the odds of it happening drop pretty bloody far." Frank declared. "I mean, what do you think his chances of getting home are? This place is a deathtrap."

Based on what he'd seen so far, Trigger doubted that Beaufort could find his own arse. Still, it would be irresponsible of him to risk his crew for the sake of one man's life, regardless of how badly they wanted it. Then again, he had always tried to run his vessel as a democracy, and in this matter, it seemed that there was clear contention.

"Sheridan!" he called, his cry causing Frank to jump.

"Does that mean you're considering it?" Frank ventured, chancing a grin.

"I'd stop talking, Frank. You're on quarter rations as it is, and I'm still deciding whether 'bloody' counts as swearing."

"Aye, Captain."

It didn't take long for Sheridan to appear, her angular features resting half a head higher than the rest of the crew. She made an odd sight, a warrior woman dressed in regal attire, yet this also made her an imposing one, a fact for which Trigger was extremely grateful. Her presence alone served as a visual threat; one he was all too happy to make. Beaufort had been entirely silent during his and Frank's exchange, and Trigger sensed that it was because he knew exactly what the crewman was requesting, and had been expecting his reputation to gain him passage from the start. It was a hideous display of arrogance, one that Trigger was all too happy to contest.

"Oh, wow." Sheridan declared, gazing at their surroundings. "This is bleak."

"Indeed." Trigger replied. "That's not why I called you, however."

He directed her towards Beaufort, who was considering them with a friendly grin.

"Is that Captain Beaufort?" Sheridan asked, sounding mildly impressed. Trigger barely repressed a sigh.

"It is. Frank believes that we should pick him up."

"Frank would. He's got a fortune riding on the Longsteel duel. Most of the crew do."

Trigger frowned. He had managed to ween the men away from swearing. Perhaps gambling should be his next opponent.

"What do you think?"

"He's an extra-mouth to feed." Sheridan shrugged. "Though, it's a pretty famous mouth. One that might deter anyone looking for a fight, which, considering your display at the harbor, may very well be coming. Plus, we can raid his ship for supplies, something that will be easier if he's compliant."

Trigger ran a hand through his windswept hair. Unfortunately, she made several excellent points.

"So, you're saying we should pick him up."

"No, I'm telling you why it's a good idea. What you do with that knowledge is in your hands."

Trigger considered her, uttering a silent thanks to the moments that had brought her to his life.

"Captain Beaufort!" He declared, returning his gaze to the grinning survivor.

"Yes?"

The word was so smug that he immediately regretted his choice. Still, it was never wise to appear indecisive.

"Would you care for a ride home?"

"Aye, zank you, I zink I would!" Beaufort beamed, already moving towards their ship.

"We'll just need to grab some of your supplies." Trigger began. "Food, water and any of your belongings that you might- "

"I have zem already!" Beaufort waved, seizing a rope that Trigger had missed. Following its length, he saw that it connected numerous barrels and chests, cunningly concealed within the vessels cracked hull.

"Of course you do." Trigger murmured, watching the Captain approach. His regrets were growing.

It didn't take them long to haul up Beaufort's booty, or the man himself. The crew formed a bustling crowd as he sprung onto the deck, eager to see if the man equaled the legend. Trigger had to admit, in a physical sense, he rather did.

Almost as tall as Sheridan, and at least as broad, Beaufort's body rippled with menace, every inch of him covered in scarred and mottled flesh. He looked as though he'd been pounded out on a blacksmith's anvil, though not by a skilled one. The blacksmith who made Beaufort would have to be blind, with hooks for hands and dog shit for brains. The man's nose was a hideous tapestry of breaks and fractures, his lips missing several scraps of flesh, revealing cracked and yellow teeth beyond.

"Quite ze ship you have here." Beaufort declared, gazing around in admiration. "What is her name?"

"The *Blackbird*." Trigger replied, stepping forward and extending his hand. "Welcome aboard."

"Ah, a beautiful name for a beautiful ship." Beaufort replied. "What do I call her Captain?"

Trigger suppressed a wince. He hated this part.

"Trigger. Captain Trigger." He announced, as Beaufort seized his hand.

"Trigger…" Beaufort murmured, frowning with recognition. "Ze naval officer? Captain Trigger-happy?"

"Just Trigger. But yes, that is me."

He could see the amusement in Beaufort's eyes. As far as this man was concerned, he'd practically struck gold.

"It is an honor." Beaufort replied, bowing from the hips. "It is an amazing feat, to have risen so far above such disgrace."

"Thank you." Trigger nodded, increasing the firmness of his grip. Beaufort responded in kind, almost breaking his palm.

"I am ze one who owes zanks." Beaufort shrugged, releasing his monstrous grip. Trigger resisted the urge to cradle his hand. "I would surely have perished in zis terrible place. In return, I promise you whatever aid I may give. You have my back, my brain and my blade."

As far as Trigger was concerned, only two of those were useful. Still, he'd take what he could get.

"Excellent." He replied. "In that case, welcome to the crew, Mr. Beaufort."

He caught a glimpse of anger at the lack of 'Captain' in his address. Beaufort hid it well, however, swiftly producing another easy grin.

"I am proud to be a member." He declared, gesturing at the crewmen. "Now tell me, how may I be of use?"

"I'll leave that to Mr. Frank." Trigger began, gesturing at his crew's unofficial spokesman. "I'm sure he'll be happy to show you around."

Frank was at his side before he'd even finished speaking, gazing at Beaufort with shameless adoration.

"Hello zere." Beaufort greeted, giving Frank a friendly nod.

"Hi." Frank replied, blushing like a schoolgirl. "Would you like to come with me, sir?"

"You are my superior." Beaufort, shrugged, patting Frank's shoulder. "You tell me."

Trigger was genuinely concerned that Frank was about to melt.

"Okay." Frank breathed, eyes dangerously wide. He turned towards the lower decks, the rest of the crew following as he led Beaufort to his new quarters.

"Ah, men?" Trigger snapped, regaining their attention. "I think Frank can manage alone."

The crew shared looks of bitter disappointment. Trigger didn't budge.

"Aye, Captain."

****

Barnaby held the banister as he staggered across the deck, regretting the third cup of ale resting in his hand. He'd hoped that the drink would help his recovery, yet was quickly discovering that alcohol was not, in fact, a solution to any problems. Indeed, it usually seemed to be the cause.

"Drink it down, drink it down, smash that ale till you drown!"

He winced as the song crashed against his ears. Drowning didn't sound a half-bad proposition.

"Tilt it back, tilt it back, smash that ale till you see black!"

He looked towards the source of the commotion, a circle of crewmen surrounding a thoroughly tapped keg. Two men stood beside it, both shirtless and dripping with sweat. For Beer-bellied Bradley, this was a common look, his hairy stomach constantly bulging from the strain of drinking. The newcomer's chiseled physique could not be further opposite, yet Beaufort was more than holding his own, matching Bradley ale-for-ale, with far less of a sway in his steps.

"Jacques Beaufort." He heard Gary whisper, the crewman shaking his head.

"I know." Frank replied, watching the contest with excitement. "What a man!"

Barnaby chuckled at their blind adulation. From what he could gather, Beaufort had sailed his men through the Howlers without a hint of protection, slaughtering them all a few hours later. He might be an amazing man, yet he was a fucking terrible Captain.

"The Captain didn't seem too excited to have him on board, did he?" Gary ventured, lowering his voice. Somehow, Barnaby had completely escaped their notice. He'd always been told he was unremarkable. Yet wasn't that, in and of itself, a form of remark? He was tempted to pursue this line of thought, yet decided against it. This conversation was important. Drunken ponderings could come later.

"Aye, which shouldn't be surprising." Frank shrugged. "I'm amazed he managed to put a crew together in the first place, and I'm sure he thinks so as well. He'd always be on the lookout for dissent, and with one of the greatest Captains to ever live currently on offer…well, he must be shitting bricks."

"Language." Gary warned.

"Aye, that's something I bet Beaufort allows." Frank grumbled. "Sometimes a man just needs a good swear."

"You know what else Beaufort allows?" Barnaby declared, feeling an inexplicable surge of frustration. "For his men to sail through the Howlers, completely unprotected. A Captain's place is to be effective, not popular. The man can swing a sword, hoo-bloody-rah. That doesn't mean he can lead a ship."

He ceased his rant, taking a deep and bracing breath. Frank and Gary stared at him in astonishment, while Barnaby's gaze slipped towards his cup.

Seriously, how much had he drunk?

"Piss off, Barnaby." Frank sneered, taking a step towards him. "Who do you think you are, talking to us like that? Gods, Beaufort's been with the crew less than a day, and he's already more useful than you."

He shoved Barnaby with his deformed hand, a blow which proved too savage for his already-struggling legs. Barnaby toppled over, striking the deck with a feeble cry.

"Such a runt." Frank chuckled, shaking his head. "Is one push really all it- "

Barnaby didn't see the strike coming, and neither did Frank. One second he was standing, and the next, he was flat on his face, the arm that struck him covered in a sleeve of moon-white silk.

"Help him up, Gary."

Gary did as he was told, hauling Frank to his feet. The crewman was still severely dazed.

"Now, go join the rest of the crew." Sheridan instructed. "Get drunk and forget this ever happened."

"Aye, Mam."

Groaning with effort, Gary pulled Frank into the rowdy circle, the ranks closing around them like an oysters shell.

Barnaby prepared to thank his savior, yet before he could speak her hand was on his collar, yanking him upright with ease.

"Are all your people that strong?" He asked, as his boots touched down on the comforting deck.

"Stronger." Sheridan replied, studying her gloves for any sign of damage. "Most of them spend all day training. Waste of time, if you ask me."

Reports on Sheridan's people were far and few between, especially on the outer fringes. All Barnaby knew was that they lived for war, and that the women of their tribes did all the fighting. This was understandable, as they tended to be twice the size of your average male.

"Thanks for that, by the way." Barnaby declared, nodding towards the cheerful singing, in which Frank and Gary were now thoroughly involved.

"Not a worry." Sheridan grinned. "Frank's always in need of a good slap, and my gloves held up just fine."

She raised them for Barnaby's inspection, their milky fabric unscathed.

"They're beautiful." He replied, studying them closely. The compliment was completely sincere. "Where did you buy them?"

"I made them, thank you very much." Sheridan laughed. "Though, I suppose that implies an element of professionalism in my work, which is never a bad thing."

"Do you make all your garments?" Barnaby asked, genuinely surprised.

"The vast majority." Sheridan replied. "Being a pirate gives you an awful lot of access to raw materials. Every time we take a vessel, I claim most of the fabrics. It serves me better than gold."

"You'd rather clothes than money?"

"People use money to buy what interests them, or the few real essentials. I already have everything I need, and am interested in fashion. Gold is just a middle-man that I no longer require."

"Huh." Barnaby remarked, cocking his head. "Fair enough."

"I think so." Sheridan shrugged, leaning against the starboard banister. "Is that why you're here, then? To grab yourself some easy gold?"

"If I wanted easy, I wouldn't be on this damn ship." Barnaby laughed, leaning awkwardly beside her. "Making a living was simpler back home. You ploughed your land, your wife, and then you went to bed. Rise the next morning and repeat until you die. If you had a few children along the way, well, all the better."

"You look a bit young for kids and a wife." Sheridan replied, studying him.

"And yet, I have both." Barnaby sighed, rubbing the back of his neck.

"Bullshit!" Sheridan exclaimed, forgetting herself. They both stood to attention for several moments, yet calmed as Trigger failed to appear.

"You're kidding, right?" Sheridan reiterated, narrowing her eyes.

"Nope."

"You don't look a day above fifteen."

"I'm not."

"Then, how?"

Barnaby took a breath, fidgeting with the rope he used as a makeshift belt.

"The village where I come from…well, it's not actually a village. It's a group of farms, just close enough for the owners to share a small amount of interaction. A Hanger lives in the area, and spends a week living with every family. We feed and shelter them, and in return they let us watch their mirror. That's our only glimpse of the world at large, of a life beyond the farm."

"Sounds restricting." Sheridan frowned.

"It is." Barnaby replied. "The land is empty. Nothing around but fields, forests, and animals. You're never raided, never threatened. No one can be bothered to make the journey."

Sheridan snorted in amusement, or maybe pity.

"Anyway, once you hit a certain age, you're given a plot of land, and whichever fine maiden your parents picked out for you. In my case, it was Bethany, one of the most stunning girls you'll ever see. Every man wanted her, but my parents, well, what they lacked in ambition or personality, they more than made up for in farming prowess. No one could match their dowry."

"So, a beautiful girl, who could have had anyone she wanted, is forced to marry you?" Sheridan mused, raising a brow.

"Yeah." Barnaby shrugged. "It went as well as you're guessing. We both did our part, in the beginning. Had the wedding, endured the wedding night. Out comes the baby, and surprise, we're still miserable, only now there's a kid screaming, as well. One day, I'm coming back from the field, and I see a strange horse tied up to our fence. I walk up to the door, press my ear against it, and…well, I've been around enough to know what I was hearing."

"Damn." Sheridan replied, appearing genuinely upset. "Did you know who it was?"

"I did. Probably the man Beth would have picked, if she'd been given a choice."

Sheridan nodded, considering him with what Barnaby supposed was empathy. He'd never received it before and couldn't really be sure.

"So, what did you do?" She asked, folding her arms.

"I gave her a choice." Barnaby replied. "Went to the barn, saddled up, and rode off without a backward glance. I lingered in the closest taverns, waiting to see if she'd organize a search party. She never did."

"That had to sting." Sheridan declared.

"Not really. She didn't love me, and I didn't love her. I miss my son, occasionally, but I imagine they'll just lie about his father, or maybe tell him that I'm dead."

Sheridan considered him, her expression shifting. This time, it was bordering on…respect?

"You're a weird one, Barnaby." She eventually announced, shaking her head.

"Thanks?"

"It was a compliment. Not many people could take that situation with such an…accepting perspective. It shows a lack of ego, which can carry you just as far as an overabundance."

"Aye, I'm living the life." Barnaby chuckled, pretending to mop the deck.

"You're sailing on the *Blackbird,* during the bloody Tides of Redemption." Sheridan snorted. "You've heard the Howlers, and lived to tell the tale. You play your cards right, and before you know it, you'll end up a tavern song."

"I can hear it now." He laughed. *"The Ballad of Bungling Barnaby."*

"Has a nice ring to it, actually."

"And what would yours be?" He asked, enjoying the game.

Sheridan paused a moment, creasing her brow in consideration.

"The Saga of Salty Sheridan."

"Salty Sheridan?" Barnaby chuckled, raising an eyebrow.

"I'm a woman." Sheridan shrugged. "They always call us salty."

Barnaby pondered the shanties he'd heard. She had a point.

"And what would your saga consist of?" Barnaby asked. "You promised to tell me, after all."

"I did, didn't I?" Sheridan replied, extracting her fan and fluttering at her cleavage. If she meant it as a distraction, it was bloody effective. Still, Barnaby didn't push her, listening instead to the gentle slap of waves breaking against their hull. They were growing in intensity, their delicate pattern disturbed from its usual rhythm.

Barnaby peered over the banister, studying the black below. All he could see was darkness, flecked by the crests of white-topped waves.

"It would start in a city." Sheridan began, her low voice instantly regaining his attention. "Though, no one here would consider it such. It's a city of stone and jungle, where the works of mortal hands flow through nature without interruption. We built around our world, not through it."

"Sounds beautiful." Barnaby replied, for lack of a better response. He could scarcely imagine such a place, yet still thought it best to be polite.

"It's the same as anywhere." Sheridan shrugged. "With its own charms and flaws. It's a savage place, and only the savage make it their home."

Barnaby nodded again. He sensed that Magwa would love this tale.

"At first, I fit in." Sheridan continued. "Trained with the others, dressed like the others. I was the very definition of what a woman should be. Fast, strong and wild."

She flared her eyes mockingly at the last word, shutting her fan with a decisive snap.

"Then, one day, a royal emissary steps out of the wilds, his whole company sick with fever. They'd failed to prepare for the journey, and had suffered the consequences. We took them in and did our best to heal them. Most died, yet one of the survivors was the emissary's wife, who'd somehow brought her entire wardrobe along for the trek."

"I'm guessing that was quite a feat." Barnaby declared, as a particularly fierce wave crashed against their hull.

"Oh, it was." Sheridan grinned. "I still understand why she did it, though. She had the most magnificent outfits you've ever seen, and could style herself in a matter of moments, with impeccable results. She was everything a noblewoman was meant to be."

"Sounds…impressive?" Barnaby ventured, lacking Sheridan's enthusiasm, yet attempting to understand it.

"My people fucking despised her." Sheridan replied, shaking her head. "She couldn't fight, couldn't hunt. Gods, she relied on men for everything, her sole occupation being her garments and appearance, which the rest of my people considered entirely unimportant."

"You disagreed?" Barnaby asked, beginning to see the picture.

"I did. Yes, her needless dependence was a failing, yet I saw nothing intrinsically wrong with the way she cared for her clothing and visage. I much preferred them to the stinking skins and furs that my people chose to wear, and I would give my left arm to have hair half as glorious as hers. I told her as much, and she was more than happy to share. They'd even lugged along an enormous mirror, so I could inspect her handiwork when she was done."

"And what did you think?"

"I loved it." Sheridan shrugged. "For the next few weeks, I spent every day in her quarters, trying on outfits with the door firmly locked. Most thought we'd become lovers, so they didn't really care. It was only when a friend spied me through the window that they told me I had to stop. Said I was embarrassing them, that I wasn't behaving as a woman should."

Barnaby blinked, slowly. It was a vast and confusing world.

"So, what did you do?"

"I told them to go fuck themselves and started living my life the way I wanted to. No one has the right to tell me who I should be."

Barnaby nodded.

"Shit, I'll drink to that."

He went to raise his cup, then realized he'd dropped it in his earlier fall.

"It's fine." Sheridan grinned, sipping from hers and then offering it to him. "I'm happy to share."

"Cheers." Barnaby beamed, downing a modest swig.

"Good thing Trigger's asleep." Sheridan mused, as another powerful swell smashed against their ship. "The way we've been swearing, we'd both be on quarter rations."

"Aye, that's true." Barnaby remarked, seizing the banister to keep himself standing. "What's his story, anyway? I know that he used to be in the navy, yet beyond that, nothing."

"Bit of a swell building, isn't there?" Sheridan observed, watching as the mast swayed back-and-forth. Eventually, she returned her gaze to Barnaby, considering him with suspicious eyes.

"You've really never heard of Captain Trigger?"

"Not until he picked me up."

"Captain Trigger-happy, who emptied his load in the Thrangish harbor?"

"What?" Barnaby asked, frowning.

"Gods, you did live far out." Sheridan chuckled, before grabbing the banister as a fierce spray dashed against their hull.

"Where are these tides coming from?" She asked, concerned. "There's no bloody wind!"

Barnaby held up a hand, feeling a tender kiss as a faint breeze blew.

This was rather strange.

"Sunniday!" Sheridan roared, causing Barnaby to jump. Gone was the softness she had so recently expressed, replaced by a resolve that put iron to shame.

"Yes, mam?" The lookout replied, stumbling from the circle of now-silent drunks. They too had noticed the foul turn, years of sailing instinct serving to sober them up, at least to a partial degree.

"Get into the nest and tell me what you see."

"Aye, mam."

Even hindered by alcohol, Sunniday's ascent was something to behold, his lean shoulders rippling as he scaled the ropes.

Still, Barnaby couldn't help but feel as though it were a wasted effort. Even from here, he could see there wasn't a cloud in the sky. The stars were glistening from prow-to-stern, the moon perched nimbly above their rudder, a silver crescent in the heavens above.

One that was rapidly being consumed.

Barnaby stumbled backwards as the darkness grew, engulfing the moon and a portion of the stars. At first, he thought they were dying, their light extinguished by some celestial disease, yet as the darkness shifted he realized that they had simply been obstructed, blocked by a frame of colossal size. The water running from its shoulders was sufficient to drown a man, trickling to the sea like waterfalls.

"By the Gods." He heard someone whisper, speaking the words that all were thinking.

Emerald eyes snapped open, twin orbs shining in the velvet black. The darkness rose once more, throwing back its monstrous head and releasing a roar that curdled his blood.

"Everybody, hold on!" Sheridan screamed, seizing Barnaby and slamming him against the banister.

The head came crashing down, revealing a flash of two curved tusks, set within the monster's chin. With a thunderous boom they struck the stern, punching through the deck as though it were made from cheese. It had broken straight through to the Captain's cabin.

"Trigger!" Sheridan howled, releasing her grip as she prepared to charge. She was sent sprawling a moment later, as two more crashes escaped the hull, the titan's arms seizing them in a monstrous embrace. The whole ship shuddered as the creature braced, hoisting their prow right out of the sea. Sheridan flailed for purchase as she began to slide, and with a massive stretch Barnaby grasped her forearm, the woman's bulk almost tearing his shoulder from the socket. Still, he held her, the two of them watching in horror as their vessel rose, threatening to spill them into those vast, gaping jaws.

"Trigger." Sheridan whispered, watching as the Captain's cabin continued to collapse.

"What's happened to Trigger?"

Chapter Seven

He awoke to a shower of splinters, the walls of his cabin groaning as the ceiling buckled inwards.

"What?" He pondered vaguely.

Were those tusks breaking through his roof?

A sudden motion made the question redundant, his bed skidding across the floor as the ship began to move, rising beneath him like a savage tide. His bedframe struck the wall with stunning force, bouncing him against the timbers and bloodying his nose. The movement put him near the window, the screams of his crew setting his senses ablaze. He was their Captain, and he was needed.

Trigger rolled across the mattress, snatching his coat from the nearby post. The ship tilted yet again, and in a moment of clarity Trigger leapt from his bed, barely avoiding his tumbling desk, which cracked against the wall with lethal force. He landed badly on the floor, which appeared set on becoming completely vertical. Throwing his coat around his shoulders, he began climbing for the door, pausing only to dodge a falling chair, from which he seized his sword and pistol.

All he'd wanted was a good night's sleep.

With a snarl of effort, he lunged for the handle, grabbing hold and wrenching the door open. It's wild swing almost sent him tumbling backwards, yet he caught the edge, pulling clear of his cabin as the ceiling buckled in.

"Captain! You're alive!"

Bracing himself against the nearest wall, Trigger found himself in good company, most of his crew pressed against it as well. They stank of fear, sweat and ale, yet danger appeared to have granted them sobriety, the majority having managed to anchor themselves in place.

"What is going on, exactly?" Trigger asked, as a deafening bellow sounded overhead.

"Giant sea-monster." Beaufort declared, appearing at his left. "Quite large, and very stro- "

Beaufort never finished, as the beast in question renewed its assault, shaking their vessel with ferocious intent. The hull screamed beneath the pressure, several beams cracking as the *Blackbird's* own weight was used against it.

"We need it to release the ship!" Trigger roared, pulling his pistol from its holster. "What are its anchor points?"

"Both sides of the hull!" Came a familiar voice. Trigger relaxed, glad to see that Sheridan had remained unharmed. "And the stern! It's tusks are acting as hooks!"

"Right then." Trigger mused, cocking his pistol. "Frank, take three good men and clear our starboard, I don't care how you manage it. Beaufort, same orders, only for our portside. Understand?"

"Aye, Captain." Replied Frank, selecting the men with a wave of his hand. "You three, with me."

"You are placing much trust in me." Beaufort declared, studying him intently.

"You're meant to be a capable swordsman." Trigger replied, seizing the edge of the groaning stern. "Go prove it!"

He didn't wait to see if Beaufort obeyed, pulling himself across the banister, and coming face-to-face with the enormous beast.

As faces went, he'd seen few worse.

The behemoth's jaw stank of rotting fish, decayed seaweed hanging in slick, uneven clumps. Its immense eyes were fixed upon him, jade torches set within a misshapen skull.

The creature was offering a steady growl, exposing countless rows of spiraling teeth. Bones and debris were perched between them, relics of earlier feasts.

Trigger didn't waste time with a snappy line. He just wanted it off his ship.

He fired directly into its shining eye, a spray of fluid coating him as the bullet broke the membrane. The titan bellowed as its lid slammed shut, strength failing as it reeled in pain. Unfortunately, its mighty tusks were hooked too deeply, and as their ship fell so too did the beast, nearly tearing the stern free as they slammed against the sea. Dozens of splinters peppered

Trigger as the timbers cracked around him, slicing his chest and palms as he desperately shielded his face.

"Captain! Captain, are you alright!?"

He opened his mouth to reply, yet it was lost beneath the creature's fury, a blast of moist and stinking breath breaking against his cheeks. Trigger turned back to the monster, and saw that both eyes were open, the one he had damaged glaring at him through a thick and squinting lid.

He was all out of bullets.

"Alright then." He muttered, drawing his sword. "Old-fashioned it is."

Trigger lunged, slashing across the creature's snout. The blade bounced harmlessly away, failing to leave so much as a scratch.

Trigger stepped back, watching as the beast's eyes swelled with murderous rage.

He was very tempted to swear.

The creature's head drove forward, timbers shrieking as it's tusks tore against them. It was their resistance alone that saved his life, the rugged shards causing the assault to pull up short, so that the behemoth's lips barely grazed Trigger as he threw himself sideways, desperate to avoid those gnashing jaws. The force of the collision was still titanic, blasting him across the deck. His coat billowed outwards as he flew across the sky, his ascent abruptly halted by a vast and sturdy sail. A dull thud sounded as he sank into its depths, before being expelled as though he were well-chewed tobacco. His meeting with the deck was far less comfortable, his shoulder popping from the socket as he slammed against the beams.

"Captain!"

He wasn't given a moment to recover, Magwa dragging him to his feet, and regarding him with an excited grin.

"Thank you." Trigger nodded, snatching up his fallen sword.

"Magwa's pleasure. The Great Green Eyes lives in many of my people's legends. It is a terrible omen."

"You don't say." Trigger murmured, caressing his shoulder as he studied the beast. It appeared to be resting, allowing the

Blackbird to take its weight while it recovered from the wound he'd inflicted. Even so, his men appeared incapable of breaking its grip, its massive arms proving just as durable as its awesome snout.

"Magwa, do any of your legends say how we kill it?"

The Kalyute considered a moment, before shaking his shaggy head.

"No, Captain. Story always end the same. Hero meets beast, beast kills hero. Magwa is honored to have seen such a creature."

Trigger stared at Magwa, willing himself to remain calm.

"Magwa?"

"Yes, Captain?"

"That's half-rations."

"Fair enough."

Their next exchange was lost as the beast released a bellow, rolling its shoulders forward and locking them in place. The motion revealed two slits in its carapace, each one containing a glistening spike.

Trigger sighed, taking a moment to button his coat. If they were going to sink, he may as well make a proper corpse.

The spikes burst forth in a spray of stringy fluid, revealing themselves as the talons of two long and spidery legs, their bulbous joints creaking as they rose into the sky. All motion ceased as his men watched the horrific display, the limbs blocking out the heavens as they swayed slowly back-and-forth, pointed tips reflecting the silvery moon. The sight was hypnotic, and almost caused Trigger to overlook their target, which became all-too clear as the legs speared forwards, driving towards their fragile sails.

"No!" Trigger roared, sprinting across the deck and seizing a crewman's pistol. With a wild spin, he took aim and fired, placing the bullet in a bulging joint. The creature howled as its blood coated the deck, the leg retracting slightly in a convulsion of pain. He couldn't stop the second, however, the spike tearing through their sails as though it were aging parchment, creating a gash that would take hours to fix. A few more of those, and it wouldn't matter if they forced the beast to fall back. They'd be still in the water, and completely at its mercy.

"Magwa, how many men are still below deck?" Trigger asked, motioning for his crew to fire at the legs.

"Fifteen or so. The beast's arms are compressing the cannon-ports, and knocked several loose. Many wounds."

Trigger motioned for Frank's pistol, plucking it from the air and placing another bullet in the monster's throbbing joints. The creature howled again, its limbs leaking a steady flow. Still, it remained defiant, one of its legs slashing across their sails with unstoppable ferocity. This gash was twice the size, the fabric flailing like tattered skin.

This creature was butchering his ship. If he didn't act now, his whole damn crew was lost.

"You say it's blocking the cannon ports?" He asked, turning once more to Magwa.

"Aye, Captain."

"Well, then." Trigger nodded, beckoning for another pistol. "Perhaps we should unblock them."

****

Barnaby was shitting himself.

Prior to today, the largest creature he'd ever seen was his father's prize bull, a portly beast whose desire for food was matched only by his insatiable lust. This monster seemed just as intent on feeding, and Barnaby was desperately hoping that it failed to share the bull's other great appetite.

"Keep at it!" Gary roared, refilling his pistol and firing. For his part, Barnaby continued attacking the arm that was fixed to their starboard side, his lack of weaponry forcing him to make use of his most frequently wielded implement. Unfortunately, his mop had failed to produce any damage, the only trace of his efforts being a particularly spotless patch on the creature's filthy hide.

"Gary!"

Trigger's voice called them all to attention, though none ceased their efforts in repelling the monster's stabbing limbs, even Barnaby's limited experience informing him that if the creature destroyed their sails, they were well and truly fucked.

"Gary, take half the men below deck, and return the cannons to their proper positions!"

"Aye, Captain." Gary replied, his voice strained and somewhat confused.

"Once they're in place, I want you to fire. All of them, at the same time."

"Aye, Captain?"

The crew shared several concerned glances, yet made to follow Gary, their trust in Trigger's judgement running amazingly deep. Beaufort, on the other hand, was another matter entirely.

"You will blow out half ze ship!" He protested, lowering the fishing pole he had been using to hack at the creature's arm.

"Better half a ship than none." Trigger replied. "Go now, Gary!"

The crewman nodded, motioning for others to follow. Those remaining on deck continued firing, failing to halt the titan's flailing limbs.

"Beaufort, Sheridan, Magwa!" Trigger cried, holstering a pistol and striding across the deck. "With me!"

The others followed, Sheridan stooping down to claim a fallen sword. Beaufort unsheathed his own dagger and blade, while Magwa hefted his obsidian hatchet, the black stone glinting with primal menace.

"What's the plan?" Sheridan yelled, as the group drew closer to the crumbling stern. The beast was resting its full weight upon it, clearly unaccustomed to supporting itself above water for such an extended period.

"See those legs?" Trigger asked, pointing with his cutlass.

"What about them?"

"Hack them to pieces."

"Aye, Captain."

The group charged, splitting in two as they chose their sides. Magwa and Trigger made for the right, while Sheridan and Beaufort swung to the left. The monster snarled as they made their approach, gnashing its teeth and twisting its head, attempting to extricate itself from the beams about its tusks. Its efforts failed, yet created enough room for it to lunge forward, its murderous jaws snapping towards Beaufort's crouching frame. Despite his size, the swordsman proved incredibly nimble, dancing away from certain death. His reply was just as swift, his blades striking out against the creature's teeth and gums, cracking one and opening the other. A smile lit Beaufort's face as blood sprayed across his forearm, the wound providing Sheridan the opportunity she needed to leap onto the monster's carapace, her stunning gown dripping with wretched gore. She paid it no heed, lunging towards the creature's leg. Her first three blows went completely unchallenged, the beast howling in agony as she cut it almost to the bone. Her fourth was interrupted, however, as the creature's leg slid into its shell, the curved talon arcing towards her back.

"Sheridan!" Barnaby screamed. She must have heard him, as with lightning speed she fell to one knee, rolling away to land nimbly on her feet. The creature's talon struck its own carapace, smashing loose a spray of grit that knocked Sheridan's wig from her scalp.

"You bastard!" Sheridan roared, as the golden curls dropped to the foaming sea. With a cry of anger, she struck again, cracking the talons surface. It must have been excruciating, as it gave the beast the strength it needed to wrench its jaw free from the stern, throwing its head back with a deafening howl. The motion almost hurled Sheridan into the freezing depths, yet at the last moment she caught hold of the oozing talon, the viscous fluid staining her glove a staggering shade of blue.

"Sheridan!" Trigger roared, as his First Mate struggled to maintain her grasp. The beast was flailing back and forth, its monstrous grip causing the *Blackbird* to veer wildly in the water, sending Barnaby and the rest crumbling to their knees. Despite this, Trigger stood tall, keeping himself steady as he took careful aim.

He fired, though this time the creature was ready, eyelid snapping shut and stopping the bullet cold. With a raging bellow, it extended its leg, launching Sheridan across the deck as though she were a bundle of sticks. Barnaby winced as the

First Mate slammed against the timbers, an uncertain crack suggesting that she may have broken her neck.

Barnaby looked back to the beast, watching as it considered the morsels before it. The great green eyes swept between the trio, finally settling on Beaufort, the man who had most recently harmed it.

The swordsman raised his blades, knees bending in preparation.

The creature struck, though this time it was unimpeded by the sturdy timbers, its jaws lashing forward with astounding speed. Beaufort attempted to dodge, his powerful legs hurling him backwards as those enormous teeth snapped shut, spraying spit and splinters. Barnaby watched as Beaufort fell from the stern, striking the deck with a heavy thud. At first, he was amazed that he had avoided such a furious attack, yet as Beaufort groaned, Barnaby realized his mistake. The gnashing fangs had caught their target, severing Beaufort's leg just below the knee. His trousers hid most of the wound, the flapping fabric saturated by a growing pool of blood.

Barnaby considered the crew around him, and saw the disappointment in their faces. The majority had their future riding on this man's skill, which had just been swallowed by a raging beast.

Still, Beaufort was part of their crew, and if he didn't get help soon, he would swiftly bleed to death. The only problem was that no one else seemed prepared to give it, and if Barnaby moved to do so, he'd be getting awfully close to the battles center.

"Fuck." He whispered, hoping the Captain was too occupied to hear. Judging by the furious roar currently shaking the deck, he probably was.

The creature had sunk low, eyes level with the stern as it pondered its remaining targets. Neither Trigger nor Magwa gave an inch as it snarled, snapping in their direction. Whatever the creature was, it clearly knew how to hold a grudge, as with a deliberate slowness it settled on Trigger, injured eye flashing with the promise of vengeance. The Captain stared right back, hoisting his cutlass in defiant challenge.

"Come on, then!" He roared, stepping towards the beast. "Fire!"

The cry wasn't loud, nor was the sound that followed. A muffled squelch, followed by a quaking that engulfed the whole ship. Barnaby tumbled over as the timbers shifted beneath him, splitting his chin and wincing as a tooth burst through his upper lip. The pain was blinding, yet he quickly forgot it as smoking flesh fell against his back, the chunks too large to ever be human.

The creature writhed in the water, the stumps of its arms waggling as wads of molten flesh rained down around them. As Barnaby watched it flail, he saw that much of the skeleton remained, its once-mighty forearms now comically thin beside its bleeding biceps.

The blood roused his memory, and sent him sprinting across the deck, sliding to a halt beside Beaufort.

"Serves ze bastard right." Beaufort remarked, observing the creatures pain. His voice was rather weak.

"Keep still." Barnaby informed him, removing his shirt and tearing off strips.

"Shouldn't be hard." Beaufort replied, gesturing at his missing leg.

Barnaby bound the wound, trying not to be unnerved by the Captain's good cheer. If that were him, he'd have passed out and shit himself.

"Your Captain is a brave man." Beaufort declared, leaning on his elbows. "He blows up his ship, and allows you to be his doctor. Honestly, look at zose bandages."

"I'm not the doctor." Barnaby replied. "I mop the deck."

Beaufort regarded him for several awkward moments.

"And did you wash your hands before you touched my wound?"

"Did it look like I had time?" Barnaby snapped back.

"Fair enough." Beaufort shrugged, shaking his head. "You know, you really a- "

The deck shuddered, throwing them onto their backs. A murderous snarl filled the air, and with a jolt of horror Barnaby saw the creature's face, rising into the heavens as it prepared another blow.

"I'd hold on." Beaufort declared, securing them against the timbers.

The beast struck, an enormous fissure forming as the deck threatened to snap in two. They had forced it into its death throws, and in its final moments the creature was ensuring that they'd join its corpse at the bottom of the sea.

Spiteful prick.

The beast pulled its maw from the shattered timbers, shaking them from its flesh. In that moment of weakness, Magwa seized his opening, springing onto its face with a primal cry. Barnaby couldn't understand the language, yet as Magwa raced across the beast's maw, hacking and slashing with reckless abandon, Barnaby had no doubts that it roughly translated into a hearty 'fuck you'.

He wondered if Trigger would give half-rations for that?

The musings ceased as Magwa reached the beast's eye, using his knife to pin the eyelid in place. His obsidian axe shone as he pumped it back-and-forth, each blow driving the creature deeper-and-deeper into the chilling seas, as though Magwa were striking with the force of ten men. Barnaby stood so that he could keep watching, observing in awe as the Kalyute forced the creature's jaw below the shattered stern. His darks skin was lost beneath the flowing green, the creature's eye completely obliterated beneath Magwa's still-swinging axe. It was the stuff of legend, and it was the reason he didn't see the creature's leg until it was far too late.

The talon struck Magwa across his side, red blood joining the green as he was flung sideways, tumbling into the merciless sea.

"Magwa!" Barnaby cried, though his voice was joined by another, that of Captain Trigger, who had extricated himself from the stern's wreckage, just in time to see the crewman fall. He was covered in a hundred small wounds, and a layer of sawdust that rendered him white. Before him, the creature swayed, its one good eye still fixed on their ship, the green orb filled with animal hate.

Trigger turned and studied the ship, his gaze resting on Barnaby, if only for a second. It was long enough to read his expression, and see the resolve that had settled within.

Turning back to the beast, Trigger raised his cutlass, levelling it at the creature's maw. Then, without a trace of hesitation, he leapt towards its gaping jaws, and straight down its stinking throat.

Barnaby watched in shock, the creature rearing backwards as it greedily swallowed.

"What the fuck?" He whispered, falling to his knees.

"Brave, brave man." Beaufort whispered, shaking his head.

The beast's reaction was violent, and almost immediate. The snarling face turned inward, studying its stomach as it folded in half, uttering a keen of pain. Then, with a savage howl, it threw its head backwards, green blood spraying from its filthy lips. Its writhing's churned the sea into a snow-white foam, the beast throwing itself from side-to-side in a desperate attempt to destroy the meal that was tearing it apart. It failed, and with a final bellow it collapsed to its side, launching an avalanche of water across the broken deck. For an instant, Barnaby was blinded, and when his sight returned the creature was gone, not a trace of it left in the stilling sea.

"He's gone." Barnaby declared, feeling numb.

"The fuck he is!"

He barely felt the wind as Sheridan streaked past, springing from the deck without a backward glance. A dagger was clasped in her gloved hand, its steely surface glinting as she struck the sea below.

Barnaby edged towards the shattered banister, peering into the void. The water was completely still, not a single wave cracking its glassy sheen. Behind him, the remaining crew were emerging from the decks below, their worried murmurs rising as they beheld Beaufort's wound, and found no trace of their noble Captain.

"What happened?" Frank demanded. "Where's the Captain?"

Barnaby didn't reply. He kept his gaze on the freezing water, hoping it would be answer enough.

It was.

"Oh." Frank whispered, coming to stand beside him.

As far as Barnaby was concerned, that single syllable summed it up. He could barely fathom such a devastating loss.

"How long have they been down there?" Frank asked, regarding the water with somber resolve.

"Not long." Barnaby replied, trying to find some semblance of hope.

Frank put a hand on Barnaby's shoulder. The grip was firm, yet oddly comforting.

"I think it's time to step away." Frank began, attempting to steer him from the edge. "The waters here are cold and perilous, and there's work to be done if we want to survive."

"A few more minutes." Barnaby replied, shrugging aside his hand.

Frank studied him, a sad grin etched across his lips.

"Sure, kid. Take as long as you need."

Frank returned to the others, voice rising as he barked order after order, setting the crew's attention towards repairing their ship.

Barnaby watched the water, searching for a sign of life. In a spectacular display of splashing and gasping, his efforts were abruptly rewarded.

"Frank, Frank!" He cried, gesturing at Sheridan, and the unconscious forms of Trigger and Magwa, who she had clamped between her mighty arms.

"Fuck me." Frank murmured. He recovered quickly, calling for a rope and four able-bodied men. It didn't take them long to reach the struggling trio, two pairs forming to support Trigger and Magwa, while Sheridan proved able to care for herself, once relieved of their heavy forms.

"Are they alright?" Barnaby asked, as Frank lay Trigger across the deck. The Captain's eyes were closed, his hands and face oddly red, as though he'd been burned by heated oil. By contrast, Magwa was almost blue, his dark body shivering on the uneven timbers.

"Where's the damn doctor?" Frank roared, looking around the ship.

"I'm right here." The doctor declared, rising from Beaufort's side. He had reapplied some bandages to the former Captain's wounds, and studying them now, Barnaby could see that his earlier work had indeed been a haphazard affair.

"They're both breathing." The doctor announced, after a moment's analysis. "Though Magwa needs to be warmed."

"Light a fire!" Frank ordered, pointing to two men.

"Gods, no!" The doctor gasped. "We need to do it slowly. The two of you, take him to your quarters, and place him in a hammock. After that, undress, and lie down on either side of him, taking care to keep your skin pressed firmly to his."

The crewmen regarded the doctor as though he were taking the piss. Somewhere in the crowd, someone sniggered.

"Do it!" Frank roared, sending the pair into a panicked frenzy. In a matter of seconds, they held Magwa between them, carrying him below deck with only a trace of hesitation.

"What about Trigger?" Sheridan asked, coming to rest at Barnaby's side. She was sopping wet and heavily bruised, yet if she were in any discomfort, she wasn't showing it.

"Partially suffocated, and moderately burned. Where was he when you found him?"

"The creature's stomach." Sheridan replied.

"Acid, then." The doctor mused. "Nothing I can do for that, really, bar some pastes and oils. We need to bathe his wounds, and after that, it's a matter of seeing if he wakes."

"Is that likely?" Sheridan asked, scooping Trigger up into her powerful arms.

"Depends on the degree of suffocation. He may have simply passed out, or he might be completely brain-dead. There's no way of knowing until he awakes."

It was to her credit that Sheridan held her composure. Barnaby certainly couldn't

"Do you need a hand?" He asked, trying to take a portion of the Captain's weight.

Sheridan regarded him with watering eyes, her features shifting into a tiny smile.

"Yes, Barnaby. Thank you."

Chapter Eight

Hot, moist wind. So fierce as to be burning. Tight, slick walls, pushing and squeezing. Mild disgust, dampened by adrenaline. A growing darkness, a sense of an inevitable end.

A woman, bursting in.

Trigger's eyes fluttered open, wincing at the sun pouring into his cabin. Well, what remained of it.

"What happened?" He asked, trying to rise. He failed on both counts, his raw throat barely managing a rasp, while his exhausted body assailed him for simply attempting movement.

"Captain?" He heard Sheridan ask, the First Mate having noticed his croak. She was sitting at the end of his bed, patting the cat wrapped snugly about his feet. He looked to her with sluggish eyes, managing a feeble grin. He was so damn happy to see her alive.

"How are you?" Sheridan asked, speaking slowly and clearly, as though he were a child. "Can you understand me?"

Trigger would have frowned, yet the effort was too great. Instead, he flicked his eyes towards his desk, and the jug of water it usually contained. Unfortunately, his desk was no longer there, reduced to kindling by the creature's assault. Indeed, most of his cabin was no longer there, the ceiling almost destroyed by their recent battle.

Fortunately, Sheridan knew him well enough.

"Here." She said, offering him a cup. "Go slow."

Trigger failed to nod, using the entirety of his strength to support the cup. With a shaking hand he put it to his lips, downing the water with measured sips.

"Thank you." He gasped, putting aside the empty cup. "Where are we?"

"About two weeks from the first fixture."

"I've been out that long?"

"You're lucky you weren't out longer. Your burns became infected, and we barely managed to get a handle on your fever. The doctor says he doesn't do much, but I swear, the man's a miracle worker."

"That's why I recruited him." Trigger shrugged, the motion hurting his shoulders. They were swaddled in bandages, the woolen fabric soiled by his blood and lymph. The pain reminded him of the battle, and his companion's own terrible wounds.

"What about Magwa?" He asked, panicking slightly. "Did you find him? Did Beaufort survive?"

"Magwa is fine." Sheridan replied, placing a hand on his chest. "Beaufort as well, though his balance is shot. The men who had bets are quite distraught."

"Unsurprising." Trigger chuckled, placing his hand on hers. "I'm glad you're okay."

"My garments aren't." Sheridan sighed, her voice brimming with woe. "I lost my best wig, and my new gloves are little better than rags. Still, I'm managing."

Indeed, she was. His First Mate had donned her back-up wig, a shoulder-length, brunette affair, which really highlighted her gorgeous eyes. As for her dress, it was a dazzling shade of ocean blue, which clung to her frame in a most complimentary fashion. She had completed the ensemble' with a cream parasol, which she was using to shield them from the glaring sun.

"You look radiant." He grinned, removing her hand and rising. She made no attempt to stop him, and after a few moments of light-headedness his feet were on the floor, skidding across shards of shattered timber.

"My cabin's seen better days." He remarked, standing. He wobbled uncertainly, yet Sheridan caught his shoulder, keeping his balance in check.

"The beast did some damage." Sheridan conceded, tapping his only remaining wall. The motion dislodged two wounded beams.

"I would wager it did." Trigger replied, wincing as he took a cautious step. "What I need to assess is exactly how much."

He staggered out onto the main deck, and the answer became disturbingly clear.

The deck was cracked and warped, as though the *Blackbird* were a sponge in the middle of being squeezed. The sails were a patchwork of hastily sewn fabrics, catching the wind effectively, yet threatening to tear at any given moment. Random bits of timber were strewn about his vessel, valiant attempts to seal the dangerous breaks. His crew worked around these hazards with diligence and care, yet he could already see that a few had suffered, small bandages and cuts marking those who had failed to maintain their vigilance.

"Gods." He breathed, running a hand through his hair.

"Aye, she's taken some hits." Sheridan consoled, placing a hand on his shoulder.

"Where's the rest of the timber?" He asked, studying the ship. "There should be more than this."

"Below deck." Sheridan replied. "We needed most of it for the real wounds."

"Of course." Trigger sighed, remembering his gambit. "Would you help me down, please?"

"My pleasure."

Sheridan took his arm, supporting him across the deck. One-by-one his crew stopped to watch, their jaws dropping as he shuffled past.

"Captain-on-deck!" Sheridan yelled, once it became clear that they would never pass unnoticed.

All motion ceased, every man pausing to give a salute.

Trigger saluted back, their loyalty lending strength to his wounded limbs.

"Relax, men. You've done well in caring for our ship, and I can honestly say that I've never been so proud. No Captain's ever had a finer crew."

His men cheered, yet kept their focus on him. When a voice spoke out, Trigger was pleased to hear that it was Frank. Say what you want about him, the three-fingered scoundrel could certainly run a ship.

"If you don't mind me saying, Captain, we're the ones who are proud. Not many crews have a Captain who'll tear a sea-beast from inside-out. You died for us. That's something we won't forget."

The crew gave another cheer, though this was more subdued. Pirates were not accustomed to showing humble admiration.

"I'd do it again, if I had to." Trigger replied. "Though, hopefully not too soon."

His men chuckled, nodding at his good cheer.

"Which reminds me. Sheridan, how's the ale situation?"

"Well-stocked, Captain."

"Let's change that, shall we? Double-rations for the next two nights. We can restock at the fixture."

The men let out a roar of approval, allowing Trigger and Sheridan to continue below deck. The night crew slumbered all around them, their hammocks swaying with the motions of the sea. One of them was Magwa, who appeared completely unaffected by his ordeal, minus the gash on his side.

"He almost killed that creature with a stone-axe." Trigger remarked, shaking his head in amazement.

"That's nothing." Sheridan grinned. "He was still holding that axe when I found him."

Trigger looked at Magwa's belt, astonished to see that her words were true. The obsidian weapon sat firmly against his thigh, not so much as chipped from the furious battle.

"Unbelievable." Trigger smiled, shaking his head.

"A breathing corpse, and yet he stands amazed."

Trigger turned towards the speaker, who revealed themselves with a wooden dunk. Beaufort's new leg was not fashioned for stealth, the timber stump thumping with every step.

"You're walking well." Triger declared. "Considering your wound."

"Yes, I am. Zough, I have always healed quickly. It has been a necessity in my life." He stopped a moment to tap his prosthesis, nodding in approval. "Your doctor, he does good work."

"That he does. You earned it, however. You fought with courage, to defend a ship that isn't yours."

"You took me in." Beaufort shrugged. "I owed you a favor. Besides, if your ship dies, I die. I am a man of common sense."

"Fair enough." Trigger laughed, appreciating the honesty. "Would you care to join us? We're going to inspect the lower decks."

"Alas, I am restricted for a few more days." Beaufort shrugged. "Stairs are difficult, and the chafing is most uncomfortable."

"I bet." Sheridan remarked, studying his wooden leg. "How has it affected your balance?"

"Well, it certainly hasn't helped." Beaufort grinned. "Still, it could be worse. Ze beast could have taken my head, or somezing even more important."

"What could be worse than your head?" Sheridan asked, chuckling.

"An arm." Beaufort replied, completely serious.

"You can live without an arm." Sheridan frowned.

"Not in any way I'd wish." Beaufort declared. His tone was pleasant, yet suggested that their discussion had reached its end.

"Well, we'll let you return to your rest." Trigger nodded, nudging Sheridan down the hall. "Once again, thank you. We appreciate your sacrifice, and will care for you as best we can."

"I have no doubts, Captain. Zank you."

Beaufort retreated into the crew's quarters, his gait awkward and uncomfortable. Still, the man never stumbled, or offered a grunt of complaint.

"Tough bastard." Sheridan remarked, as they made their way towards the stairs.

"Unsurprising, considering his history." Trigger replied. "Though, I have to admit, I doubt I'd be as calm, were I in his position."

"Don't sell yourself short." Sheridan laughed. "The creature only ate his leg. That's four limbs less than you."

"True, yet I managed to avoid the teeth." Trigger shrugged. "So, really, I…oh, oh Gods."

They stepped out onto the gun deck, giving Trigger a view of his vessel's fractured hull. The *Blackbird* had been blown wide open, rivers of sunlight spilling in through the obliterated ports.

"Yeah." Sheridan winced, surveying the grizzly scene. "We tried our hardest to repair what we could, but…well, we're pirates, not carpenters."

"Gary *was* a carpenter, before he signed on."

"Not a good one." Sheridan replied. "That's why he signed up."

Trigger sighed, yet made no further complaint. As always, she had a valid point.

The crew had made use of his shattered cabin, sealing the larger gaps with oddly shaped fragments, regardless of their former purpose. He could see his desktop stretched across a starboard break, while the scraps of his favorite painting were smeared across a newly built wall. It was a hideous affair, one that left the *Blackbird's* hull skeletal and exposed, vulnerable to whatever the ocean saw fit to inflict.

"Two weeks to the fixture, you say?" He asked, turning to Sheridan.

"Aye, give or take."

"Is there any timber left?"

"No. There are trees on the shore, yet felling them would take time."

"And I imagine we've lost quite a bit already." Trigger sighed, running a hand through his crunchy hair. He really needed a proper wash.

"So, what's the plan, Captain?" Sheridan asked, after several moments of quiet contemplation.

Trigger rubbed his finger against his thumb, weighing up their scarce options.

"We carry on." He announced, nodding with resolve. "And pray that the remainder of our journey proves far less harsh."

"That seems risky."

"Well, the crew have always enjoyed a good gamble." Trigger replied, folding his arms. "Maybe it's time I joined in."

****

"No way."

"Are you calling me a liar, good sir?"

"No, no! It's just that Barnaby's never been the most…effective crewman."

"Well, he was effective enough zat evening!" Jacques declared, giving Barnaby a hearty slap. "I have never seen such courage and speed!"

The circle around them regarded Barnaby with a mixture of suspicion and awe. It was far better than their usual disdain.

"I mean, look at him!" Jacques continued, jerking his thumb at Barnaby's slightly swollen lip. "Ze Captain burns, Magwa drowns and I lose my favorite leg. All Barnaby gains is a handsome scar. I owe zis boy my life."

He gave Barnaby another affectionate slap, his great palm striking like a torturer's whip. Still, Barnaby took it, knowing that the swordsman meant well. Ever since the attack, he had taken Barnaby under his wing, doing everything he could to change the crew's perception of him as both a pirate and a man.

Success had been mixed.

"Anyway, zat is a long enough break." Jacques announced, rising and unsheathing his swords. "Who is my next opponent?"

The crewmen looked to one another with shameless apprehension. At first, most had leapt at the opportunity to train with Jacques Beaufort. Sadly, they had quickly discovered that his reputation was more than deserved, and that 'going easy' was not a term with which he had any familiarity.

"Perhaps Barnaby could spar with you?" Gary ventured. "Show off some of those sea-beast skills."

Barnaby fought the urge to piss himself, he really did. He would have failed, however, if not for Jacques quick-thinking.

"Would you wish to strike your savior?" He asked, scowling at Gary. When Jacques Beaufort scowled, the whole world seemed to darken. "Would you stride up to your noble Captain, and slap him in ze face, after all he has done for you? I could no more harm Barnaby zan you could hurt your own mozer."

A crewman giggled at the way Jacques pronounced 'mother'. Whoever they were, they were a brave man indeed.

"Well, okay then." Gary sheepishly replied, trying to back away. The crew had sensed what was about to occur, however, and descended like a pack of rabid hyenas. All avenues of escape were instantly cut-off, forcing Gary into the perilous circle.

"Zank you for volunteering." Jacques grinned, his wooden leg thumping as he paced back-and-forth. He'd had the appendage for less than a month, yet had managed to remain astonishingly spry.

Gary glared at the crewmen who had doomed him, receiving only mischievous grins.

Say what you want about pirates. When they fix themselves to a common goal, nothing in the world can stop them. Especially not Bearded Gary.

Barnaby didn't move as the fight began. He didn't really get the chance. One moment Gary was standing, his cutlass at the ready. The next, his blade was flying through the air, the poor bastard sprawling across the deck as a nasty bruise formed in the center of his head.

Jacques sighed in disappointment, sheathing his swords and lifting Gary to his feet.

"None of you are very good at zis, are you?"

"We're pirates." Bradley declared, taking Gary's weight as he slumped against him. "We show up, and they usually just give us what we want. You'd be surprised how rarely we actually fight."

"And your Captain? Trigger?"

"Well, he's a navy man, and a noble. Somewhere along the way, someone taught him to swing a sword. Even then, he's not our best. You'd want Sheridan, or maybe Magwa, though he only uses that bloody axe."

"Zat could be fun." Jacques mused, retaking his seat beside Barnaby. He sat in thought for a few quiet seconds, then raised his head, exposing them all to a yellowish grin.

"I'd say zat is enough for today. My leg is beginning to ache, and I'm sure zere are duties to which you must attend."

The men nodded, waving their goodbyes as they spread across the deck. After a few rounds of training, they were never quite so eager to spend time with Jacques.

"Do you not have duties?" Jacques asked, fixing Barnaby with a curious stare.

"The cat's napping." Barnaby shrugged, pointing to the remains of the Captain's cabin. "And I've already mopped the deck. It's easy now, considering there's about half as much as there used to be."

Jacques chuckled, giving his shoulder an affectionate punch. Barnaby's arm went completely limp.

"Thanks for doing all this." Barnaby began, rubbing life into the tingling limb.

"Doing what?"

"Speaking against the crew, standing up for me. I'm grateful."

"I would have bled out if not for you. Singing your praises is no great burden."

"Still, you didn't have to do it. It must be a pain, especially considering what you're already going through. I'd be a sobbing mess in your place. You're already on your feet- "

Jacques looked at him with a quizzical brow.

"-You're already out of bed." Barnaby corrected. "Training and laughing, as though nothing ever happened. Gods, a few of them are actually calming down about the bet. They're thinking you'll still win, regardless of your injury."

"Zey are kind." Jacques smiled, inspecting his wooden leg. "What do you zink?"

"I wouldn't bet against you." Barnaby replied. "The way you move, your ferocity. I wish I could be one-third the fighter."

Jacques chuckled, though the laughter was strangely empty. The smile on his face began to fade, his lips twisting towards the deck.

"What do you know of my story, Barnaby?"

Barnaby considered the question, thrown off by the swordsman's change. Eventually, he decided to settle with honesty.

"The basics, really. That you were raised on the streets, fighting your way through lif- "

"Wrong."

Barnaby halted, afraid that he had offended the former Captain. Jacques was smiling again, however, though it was the grin of a man who is supremely tired.

"I wasn't raised on the streets." Jacques began, shaking his head. "Everyone gets zat wrong. I was raised in a basement. My mother sold me as a child, to a man wiz very…specific tastes. He kept me down zere until I was too old to fulfill zem."

Barnaby said nothing. He wasn't certain that there was anything he *could* say.

"He fed me well enough, kept me in good condition. As he said 'no one wants just skin and bones'. Zis kept me strong, so zat when I was old enough, he could put me in ze fighting pits. I can still remember ze first day I saw zem. Ze sun was scorching, ze crowd was deafening, and ze pit stank of blood and shit. It was ze first day I'd been outside since my fourth birzday. It was ze best day of my life."

"Gods." Barnaby whispered, unable to stop himself.

"I doubt zey were present." Jacques shrugged. "Do you know what he said to me, before my first bout?"

"No." Barnaby replied, feeling oddly helpless. How do you comfort such horrendous deeds?

"He told me zat I must win, no matter what. Zat if I lost, I was going back into ze basement, and zat I would be visited by men who *didn't* mind my age. Zat thought, zat knowledge… it terrified me. How do you think ze fight went?"

"You won?" Barnaby ventured, desperately hoping that he was right.

"I did. I killed the ozer boy in under a minute. Smashed his skull against a rock. My terror gave me strength and power. My hate made me unstoppable. Zat was the day I learned life's one great secret, one I am happy to share with you."

"What is it?" Barnaby asked, so focused on Jacques that he was nearly bent double.

"Zat motivation can come in any form. Zat the key to taking what you want, is to accept zat bad zings happen, and zat zere is only one zing you can do in reply. You take zem, and you use zem to make you stronger. I am furious zat I lost my leg. It is a travesty, anozer item on a list of countless injustices. Zat rage is why I am out here training. It is why I laugh louder zan any ozer man. I cannot bear the zought that I am diminished, that ozers may begin to doubt me. I am using ze fear, ze anguish. Zey are a valuable tool and should always be treated as such. Zey are what you use to ensure zat such bad fortune never cripples you again. Moments of self-pity should be just zat. Moments, far and few between."

Barnaby nodded, completely in awe of such unrelenting strength.

"I'm not sure I can do that." He declared, aware that he may be sacrificing what little respect he'd gained.

"Zere is no being alive who cannot. Ze poets are right, in one respect. When one is tested, truly tested, zey will find a way to carry on. Ze are wrong in ze motivation, however. It is seldom love zat keeps one standing. It is usually zeir hatred of whatever zey're fighting."

Barnaby considered the deck below, pondering the swordsman's words.

"People could learn a lot from you." He eventually declared, giving Jacques a humble nod.

"No. Zey could learn a little from my words, and much from my mistakes. I know ze great secret, and still, my life is a failure."

"What?" Barnaby asked, frowning. "You're Jacques Beaufort!"

"And zat is all I'll ever be." Jacques shrugged. "Ze crew, ze people of the world, zey will never know me as anything more zan a swinger of blades. I have lost my leg, and all zey care about is whezer zeir money is safe."

Barnaby looked to the sky, its white clouds accompanied by a dozen circling Oracle-birds, their mirrored faces fixed on the *Blackbird's* patchwork deck. Jacques noticed them, as well.

"How many of zem were following you, prior to taking me aboard?"

"I'm not sure. We'd see one every couple of hours, I guess."

"A flock was following my ship from ze very beginning. Ze nobility, keeping tabs on zeir investment."

"You're famous, Jacque."

"Yes, as a fighter, a spiller of blood. I have seen how terrible zis world is, and my only contribution has been more pain. Is zat a great man, Barnaby? I do not zink so. A great man would take his suffering and turn it into beauty. For all my strength, my life is still solely about survival. I contribute nozing, I build nozing. I carry my steel and enable ze cycle. I am a failure. It is my hope zat you will walk a different path."

Barnaby considered the man beside him, his massive shoulders slumped beneath the weight of his words. He had no idea what he should say.

"Captain! The first gate is in view!"

Barnaby suppressed his sigh of relief. Thank you Sunniday. "How far?"

"I'd say three miles, give or take!"

Barnaby watched as Trigger strode across the deck, extracting the scope from his battered coat.

"Have you ever seen ze fixture?" Jacques asked, looking to Barnaby.

"No. Have you?"

"Twice." Jacques nodded, rising with a mild groan.

"It is always a great delight."

Chapter Nine

"Fu- "

Trigger glanced at Frank from the corner of his eye. The crewman understood, taking a moment to collect himself.

"My word, isn't that a large gate?"

"Indeed it is, Mr. Frank."

He couldn't blame Frank for his near slip, especially considering his own amazement. Each fixture rested behind a Great gate, their iron surfaces increasing in size as the race ventured on. The first gate was by far the smallest, standing at a mere hundred-and-fifty feet. Every inch of its surface was carved and crafted, depicting the history of a race long lost to time. The gates current owners could shed no light, the Vrachni having colonized the structures well after their makers had faded from existence. This discovery had proven valuable, giving the former nomads an almost unassailable control of the northern seas, one that the Tides served to somewhat remedy. After all, there was much business to be had by dealing with pirates, and when said dealings are sanctioned by the empire itself, well, only a fool would think to turn them down.

Trigger braced himself as they came to a halt, the shadow of the gate casting them into a miniature night. He could see several walkways winding between the carvings, yet not a single soul appeared on them, the gate standing still and empty, as it would have in the centuries before its rediscovery.

"Hello?" He called, raising his voice to its highest level. Beside him, Frank offered a mild wince.

The gates remained unmoved, the wind singing as it passed through thousands of hidden instruments. Trigger had often been told that the music was beautiful. At this moment, however, it merely added to the sense of total isolation.

"Hello!?" He repeated, this time causing Frank to take a step backwards.

"Yes, yes, we hear you! Calm the fuck down!"

Trigger was taken aback, his jaw snapping shut at such abrupt rudeness. The Vrachni had a reputation as blunt businessmen, yet he hadn't expected such outright hostility.

Upon the gate, a carving moved, swinging to reveal a narrow hall. The creature that stepped out was scabby and thin, its olive flesh covered in several red sores. It's lipless mouth was broad, yet puckered, filled to the brim with narrow teeth. Despite himself, Trigger couldn't help noticing that it vaguely resembled an arsehole, though much greater in size, and far more perilous.

"The fuck do you want?"

He preferred what came out of arseholes, as well.

"My name is Captain Trigger." He explained. "This is my vessel, the *Blackbird.* My crew and I were hoping that we- "

"Wait, Trigger. The navy Captain? The dickhead from the battle?"

Trigger took a breath, regaining his composure.

"Yes, I believe I'm the man you're referring to."

"Hahaha, really? Shit, are you sailing in the Tides? We've barely been following since Carnage came along. Bastard wins every year, and no one's ever game to try this route, anyway. Stay there, ok? I need to get the others."

The Vrachni vanished inside, leaving them floating in the lapping seas. Trigger was all-too aware of his embarrassed crew, who were taking measures to avoid his eye.

"How many others are there?" Frank asked. "We've lost a lot of time already, and can't really wait for a thousand gawking Vrachni."

"True, Mr. Frank." Trigger conceded. "Yet we are at their mercy. Turning back is not an option, and there is no other way through. It is best that we maintain our composure, and wait with as much patience as we can manage."

He was aware of Frank considering him, gaze filled with sly admiration.

"I know it's unpleasant, having a reputation like yours. Still, I just want you to know, that as far as I'm concerned, you're the greatest Captain to ever grace a deck."

Trigger allowed himself a smile, treating Frank to a grateful nod.

"Thank you, Mr. Frank. I believe they'll say the same of you, in your capacity as Quartermaster."

Frank's expression became one of confusion, deformed hand scratching at a peeling temple.

"We don't have a Quartermaster, Captain."

"We do now." Trigger replied, hoping Frank would understand. As with comedy, kindness lost its impact when it had to be explained.

Frank blinked.

Then he understood.

"Thank you, Captain!" He declared, jumping with excitement. "Do you mean it?"

"Aye." Trigger nodded. "A Quartermaster cares for the interests of the crew, and opposes the Captain when necessary. You have proven yourself in both regards. I am sure the others will be quick to agree."

"That we are!" Yelled Gary, leading the men in an enthusiastic cheer. Trigger had already informed them of Frank's promotion, and told them to be ready. As always, they did not disappoint.

"Gods, you're a noisy bunch, aren't you?"

Trigger looked to the gate as the Vrachni returned, accompanied by five others of his kind. Every one of them appeared equally decrepit, their frail bodies hunched and withered.

"Is this…all of you?" He asked, studying the group with mild surprise.

"Well, yeah." The leader spat. "This gate sits at the arse-end of nowhere, behind a legion of terrors that will kill anyone stupid enough to visit. Guarding it isn't really a priority."

They were old, Trigger realized. Too ancient to be of use, and thus shunted away to the darkest corner of their people's lands, where they could wither away in silence. It was an empty existence, a tragic end to any life.

At least it explained their attitude.

"You're right." He conceded, bowing his head. There was no point in being rude. They were miserable enough already.

"I can't believe you made it here." One of the Vrachni declared, shaking their leathery head. "Some of the greatest pirates who've ever lived grace the bottom of these seas. Yet here you stand, the most incompetent Captain in the empire's history. It's a funny old world, isn't it?"

"Oh, hysterical."

"You're younger than I expected." Another remarked, peering at him through a pair of bottle-bottom glasses.

"I get that quite a bit. I climbed the ranks with unusual swiftness. Had all the makings of a model major-general."

"Well, shit." The leader chuckled. "I bet they regret that decision!"

"Let him be." Shrugged the Vrachni with glasses. "He was young, brave and reckless. The time for all great mistakes."

"Ah, you're no fun." The leader sneered, waving a dismissive hand. "He knows we're just fucking with him."

Trigger scowled, his patience stretched to its limit.

"If you don't mind-" He began, rubbing his thumb against his finger. "-could you please desist from such language? It's disrespectful, and implies that you're lacking in advanced vernacular."

Silence. Dreadful, dreadful silence.

"Gods dammit, Captain." Frank sighed, putting his hand against his face.

The Vrachni leader regarded him with an astonished frown, clearly unsure how to proceed.

"What sort of pirate *are* you?" He eventually asked, looking to his companions.

"Clearly one of courage." Grinned the one with glasses. "And skill, considering that he made it here. Now, why don't we open the gate? Our clients won't be pleased if we fail to uphold our bargain."

"Clients?" Trigger asked, leaning forward. "What do you mean?"

His question was never answered, the sculpture snapping shut with a decisive clang. The Vrachni were gone, leaving them alone before the whistling gate.

"Temperamental bunch, aren't they?" Frank declared, scratching the back of his head.

"Aye, that they are." Trigger mused, resting his hand against his pistol. "Which begs the question, why exactly are they letting us through?"

"Are you sure that's what they're doing? Because the gate still looks awfully shut to me."

"A fair observation." Trigger replied, searching for some hint of movement. "Perha- "

Boom.

The sound struck before the motion did, their ship dropping downwards with frightening speed. Trigger's feet left the deck as the water rose, sealing them in a cone of towering blue. A sudden collision echoed below, and a moment later Trigger was back on deck, as were the rest of his startled crew.

"Captain, what is this?" Frank howled, clinging to the banister for all he was worth.

Trigger didn't answer. Instead, he took a calming breath, and began taking stock of the situation.

They were underwater, sunk beneath the tide like a falling stone. The sea was swirling all around them, the fish swimming by with unblinking eyes. Despite all this, they appeared completely unscathed, the water held at bay by some unknown force. Indeed, as Trigger continued to watch, he realized that he had never seen such perfect beauty, the sea-life around them proving more astonishing than he could ever have believed.

"Beautiful." He whispered, watching as a shark swam meters from his face. A school of fish followed in its bubbling wake, their scales throwing a symphony of color across the *Blackbird's* crowded deck.

"Ah, Captain?" Sunniday yelled.

"Yes?" Trigger asked, trying to restrain his growing grin.

Sunniday didn't answer with words. He simply pointed at the world above, which was rapidly vanishing behind the closing sea.

"There is nothing to fear." Trigger declared, adjusting his coat and standing tall. "I suspect that this is part of the process. If the Vrachni were trying to harm us, they would have simply denied us entry."

His men didn't argue, though they looked far from assured. He could hardly blame them.

Clank.

The ship jerked forward, almost sending him sprawling across the deck.

Clank.

"I don't like this!" Gary cried, holding the mast with tears in his eyes.

Clank.

Clank.

Clank.

The ship continued its jolting journey, progressing along the seafloor at a rough and measured pace. Dragging himself towards the prow, Trigger peered towards their hull, which was currently fixed between a pair of huge, metallic clamps. The clamps themselves were connected to an immense length of chain, which was dragging them forward with mechanical precision. How such a thing was possible, Trigger had no idea, yet the sheer number of weeds sprouting along its surface suggested that the chain was at least as old as the gate itself, if not quite as well maintained.

Clank.

Clank.

Clank.

The journey was slow-going, yet Trigger didn't mind. It allowed him time to admire the alien world around them, every nook and cranny holding another unknown wonder. He barely noticed as they passed beneath the gate, its dark frame extinguishing all light from the seas. For a moment, blackness ruled, yet the ocean had not run dry of marvels, a few tiny torches sparking into life, revealing the shadowed silhouettes of countless living lanterns.

"It's gorgeous."

Trigger turned to see that Sheridan had joined them, her white gown rendered green by the ethereal lights. He'd never seen her smile with such unrestrained joy.

"Indeed it is." He replied, as their vessel emerged from the gates great shadow, bathing once more in the distant sunlight.

Clank Clank.

Clank Clank.

Clank Clank Clank.

"Are we gaining speed?" Frank croaked, his voice made weak by nerves and fear.

"I believe we are." Trigger replied. "We also appear to be rising."

His words proved true, the sunlight growing stronger as their ship struck an incline, racing towards the surface at a growing pace. Sea-life flashed by as they barreled upwards, little more than blurs to Trigger's strained eyes. Eventually he was forced to stare directly ahead, his gaze fixing on the approaching surface, which had not yet bothered to open wide.

That could be a problem.

"It is going to open, isn't it?" Sheridan asked, wrapping a hand around the banister, whilst using the other to brace her wig.

Trigger studied the ceiling of blue, its shimmering form completely unmoved.

"No, Sheridan. I don't think it will."

He grabbed hold of the banister with a second to spare, saltwater filling his nose as they smashed through the veil, bursting to the surface in a spray of foam and fish. For several moments, the *Blackbird* swayed, rocking back-and-forth as the excess fluid drained from its decks. Trigger rode the movements as best he could, inspecting his crew for signs of harm. The journey had been kind, however, the worst injury belonging to Bearded Gary, who had been stung by a jellyfish that caught against his neck.

"Oh Gods." Gary groaned, cradling his swelling flesh. It was a rather nasty sting.

"Let me see." Said the doctor, his own beard plastered against his chest.

Reluctantly, Gary did as he was told, peeling away his fingers with a series of whines.

"It's nothing too severe." The doctor informed him, giving his knee an affirming pat. "I'll fetch you some ointments, and the pain should fade within the hour."

"No need!" Laughed Beer-bellied Bradley. "We all know what needs to be done! A bit a piss is the best thing for a jelly sting, and we've all got plenty to spare! Just put your head down on the deck, Gary. We'll handle the rest."

"That will be all, Mr. Bradley." Trigger declared, waving away the cackling crew. He had seen many horrors. His crew pissing on Gary would not be another.

"Take yourself below deck and rest, Mr. Gary." He ordered, carefully taking hold of the offending jellyfish. It was slick and slimy, yet he managed to keep his grip until he reached the banister, where he released it as gently as he were able.

"Should have let me stomp it." Growled Gary, cradling his neck.

"We were the intruders, Gary. Its reaction was fair. Stow your anger and focus on recovery. You'll want to be better when we reach the *Swaying Deck*."

Gary's expression shifted, his discomfort replaced by lustful glee.

"I thought we didn't have time to go aboard?"

"It will take at least two hours for me to organize the timber we need. I believe that will be ample time for most of the crew. Spread the word for me, will you?"

"Aye, Captain!"

He watched as Gary raced below deck, his frenzied shouts quickly drawing attention. After a few moments of explanation, the crew erupted into a wild cheer, the sound of their joy carrying through the *Blackbird's* countless wounds.

Smiling, Trigger approached the prow, fixing his gaze on the distant horizon. An enormous vessel marred its symmetry, its hull rocking with unusual ferocity.

"The *Swaying Deck*." Sheridan whistled, shaking her head. She'd somehow managed to keep her wig intact. "Never thought we'd be sailing there."

"Trust me, mine is the greater surprise."

Sheridan chuckled, dipping her head in concession.

"I'll not argue that. Can you see many other ships?"

"No." Trigger replied, running a hand through his sopping hair.

"Is that good or bad?"

Trigger peered through his dripping scope, studying the vessel's frenzied deck.

"Honestly? I have no idea."

****

"Three more cheers for the Captain!"

Barnaby leant his voice to the others, the crew managing only a single hoorah before Trigger cut them off, waving his hand in irritation. It was understandable. He'd sat through nine cheers already.

"Thank you, yet that is quite enough." He grinned, still somewhat damp from their recent adventure. "I would rather that you use this time to enjoy yourselves. Remember, it is limited. You are to be back on the *Blackbird* by sundown, and not a moment later. If you fail to do so, we will leave without you, and you will be forced to remain here until the next kind soul proves willing to take you aboard."

"I could live with that!" Roared Bradley, giving Barnaby a knowing wink. Barnaby laughed with the rest of the crew, managing to hide his growing fear. He'd heard thousands of stories about the *Swaying Deck*, and had found that through all of them, only two constants remained. The first was that the vessel would cater to any sin, so long as you possessed the coin. The second was that anyone who couldn't pay conventionally would be forced to in other ways, indulging the sins of others by way of recompense, generally without any choice in the matter.

"Settle down, settle down." Trigger instructed, once again motioning for silence. "Now, while I'm sure you're all eager to partake of the *Deck's* many...attractions, I would also ask that you keep your ears open for any information. If you can find our current position in the overall race, I would find myself feeling extremely grateful. Is that understood? Excellent."

Trigger nodded, studying them all with patience.

The crew looked to one another, waiting for him to continue.

"Well, what are you waiting for?" He suddenly declared. "The fun's in there, gentlemen!"

The crew bellowed its approval, surging towards the gangplanks in a tide of sweating flesh. Barnaby hung back, keeping close to Jacques and Magwa, who were regarding the display with mild distaste.

"I thought you'd be more excited." Barnaby ventured, studying them both.

"Magwa greatest hunter in tribe." The Kalyute shrugged. "Always desired by women. The thought of paying seems obscene."

It always struck Barnaby as odd that Magwa could make use of words such as 'obscene', yet apparently pronouns were quite beyond him. He often wondered if the savage was simply playing dumb.

"What about you?" He asked, turning to Jacques. The big man shifted on his wooden leg, suddenly appearing distinctly uncomfortable.

"The touch of ozers has never appealed to me." The swordsman replied. "It reminds me of more…unpleasant times."

Barnaby didn't press. There wasn't a need.

"Well then, did you want to stay on ship?" He ventured. "I don't have enough gold for a whore, and I'm sure we can find a way to entertain ourselves. I once spent a whole day following the cat, just watching it make its kills. You'd be surprised how fun it is."

Jacques considered him with what may have been dismay. Perhaps he'd shared a bit too much.

"No, I zink we should go aboard." Jacques declared. "Zis is a rare opportunity, and we would be fools not to take advantage."

"Magwa agrees." The Kalyute nodded, watching as the remainder of their crew vanished across the gangplanks. "He simply waiting for crowd to disperse."

"Well zen, should we proceed?" Jacques grinned, indicating that Barnaby should lead the way.

"Yeah!" Barnaby replied, his spirits buoyed by the show of respect. "I think we should!"

He raced towards the gangplank, springing onto the wood with something approaching grace. The timber proved more flexible than he'd anticipated, bending beneath his feet and nearly launching him skywards. Magwa saved him, however, his dark hand wrapping about his shirt.

"Cheers." Barnaby coughed, his joy subdued.

The others said nothing, allowing him to guide them across the flexing path. The wood groaned loudly as Jacques stepped upon it, the sound spurring Barnaby into a mild sprint. This placed him on the *Deck* with undue haste, his boots not yet prepared for the vessel's swaying motion. The sudden shift left him feeling light-headed, the impulse to vomit filling his skinny throat.

"Look to the horizon." Magwa instructed, patting his back. Barnaby did as he was told, fixing on the stable point. It calmed his stomach swiftly enough, the brief interval allowing Jacques to finish his crossing. Barnaby was amazed that the beam held his weight.

"Which way?" Barnaby asked, looking between the prow and stern.

"Up to you." Jacques grinned. "I have faith zat you'll find some fun."

Barnaby bowed his head, eventually deciding on a set of double-doors. There was no noise to serve as their guide, the vessel's unique timbers proving almost completely soundproof, to better hide its customer's various indiscretions.

"Ready?" Barnaby asked, seizing the polished handles.

"Always." Jacques beamed. Magwa simply nodded.

With a mighty flourish, Barnaby opened the doors, exposing the sights within.

They were not ready.

An ocean of sound crashed against them, a potent mixture of cackles, moans, clinks and scrapes. That was nothing compared to the lights, however, a rainbow of flames illuminating the bustling scene, each lantern tinted with bright and treated glass.

"Strange lights." Magwa growled. "Bad omen."

"Your people have a lot of zose." Jacques observed, shielding his eyes with a meaty hand.

"It is bad world."

"Can't argue wiz zat."

Jacques was the first to step inside, and the moment he did the noise practically doubled, every pirate present cheering his name.

"Captain Jacques, you beautiful son of a bitch!"

"Fuck me, it's Jacques Beaufort!"

"He lives, he fucking lives!"

After so many weeks with Trigger's crew, it was jarring to once more be among average pirates, their use of foul language almost exceeding their abuse of alcohol, or lack of personal hygiene.

"Hello, hello." Jacques waved, as a large crowd began to form.

"We caught your battle on one of the Mirrors!" An older pirate announced, his bleeding gums teeming with black-and-brown teeth. "Damn shame about your crew, but fuck me, did you teach them who's boss!"

"A worzless lesson, considering zey're dead." Jacques shrugged, trying to escape. The press was too strong, however, sealing him tighter than a hangman's noose.

"Bloody awful about your leg." Another pirate sighed, his face obscured by a lank and greasy fringe. "Do you think you can still take Hargrave? I've got thirty coins that say you can!"

"Zank you for your confidence." Jacques smiled, though the expression was extremely forced. "I am not what I was, yet I am swiftly gaining ground."

His words were met with a roar of approval, though Barnaby couldn't help but notice that several pirates appeared disappointed, glancing at Jacques remaining leg with a degree of hostile intent.

"It's that useless arsehole Trigger." Scowled a member of the crowd. "I knew you were fucked the moment he picked you up. Dickhead couldn't make it in the navy, what chance does he have as a motherfucking pirate?"

"I doubt zat Trigger has ever fucked a mozer." Jacques replied. "And I am certain zat wizout him, I would be long dead. If any of you win coin, it will be because of him. Which brings me to an important matter. Where is Hargrave, exactly? Has he arrived yet?"

"He anchored here yesterday." One of the pirates answered, running a hand across his grubby beard. "Pissed off early this morning. We all wanted him to wait for you, but apparently the bastard wants dramatic effect. He's going to reach the final fixture and set up shop there. Won't let anyone past until you two have your duel."

"Risky." Jacques frowned. "Trying to hold ze fixture alone."

"Oh, he's not alone." One of the crowd chuckled. "As soon as Carnage heard that you'd been picked up by Trigger, he signed on to help. No one's getting past that blockade."

Barnaby felt an unpleasant churning in the base of his stomach. How had he managed to join the one crew that every pirate wanted to kill?

"So, ze final fixture will be interesting indeed." Jacques mused, folding his arms.

"Fucking oath. Your leg means that they're changing the odds, as well. If you win now, well, a lot of us stand to make a shit-ton of gold."

"Well, I'd better win zen, hadn't I?" Jacques laughed.

"Fuck yeah!" Cheered a member of the crowd, raising a foaming tankard. Others joined, their celebrations weakening the circle enough for Jacques to push clear, the big man slick with sweat from the press of so many bodies.

"I hate crowds." Jacques declared, shaking his head.

"Magwa agrees. Suggests we find quiet corner, and try to stay hidden."

"I think that's a great idea." Barnaby nodded, glancing at a nearby stall. Its habitants were still studying Jacques with venomous intent, the daggers at their sides appearing awfully well-used.

Magwa led them through the crowd, treating it as dense vegetation. He chopped aside arms, hands, and more than a few half-empty drinks. A few men took issue, yet when they saw their attacker, they were swift to recant, the Kalyute's scarred frame warning against violence. Eventually they settled in a corner stall, its rickety frame providing protection from the pounding lights and music.

"Good find, Magwa." Barnaby declared, massaging his temples. The Kalyute ignored him, studying several scraps of parchment which had been pinned against the wall.

"So, who's drinking what?" Jacques asked, extracting a weighty coin-purse. "My treat."

"Thank the Gods." Barnaby laughed. "All I could afford is water."

"Zey charge for water."

"Air?"

"In a place like zis, who knows?"

Barnaby shook his head. This was a place for real pirates, not whatever the fuck he was.

"How many crews do you think are here?" He asked, as Jacques began counting coins.

"No more zan zree." He shrugged. "Any more and we would have seen zeir ships. I zink we have gained a substantial lead, despite our hardships. Few sail ze Howlers, yet zey are well worth the risk."

Thump!

The table shook as Magwa slammed down a piece of parchment, his dark hand obscuring the scrawled script.

"What this say?" He demanded, shoving it towards them.

"No idea." Barnaby shrugged. "Can't read."

"We'll have to change zat." Jacques declared, reaching for the parchment. Magwa lifted his hand, revealing the impressively detailed portrait his palm had been concealing.

"Is that the Captain?" Barnaby asked, frowning.

"It is."

"Why?"

Jacques didn't reply. Instead, his heavy eyes studied the parchment, before moving to the wall beside them. It was covered with similar documents, though none were quite so detailed or lengthy as the one in his grasp.

"Shit." Jacques whispered, running a hand across his face.

"What is it?" Barnaby asked, feeling a rising sense of panic. He seemed to feel that a lot these days.

"Zis is a bounty." Jacques explained, tearing the parchment in two. "One zat promises gold in exchange for your Captain's head."

"What!?" Barnaby asked, almost leaping to his feet. The table stopped him, bruising his knees and sending him crashing back down. "Who would ask for that? Is it Carnage?"

"No. It was posted by Roland Abernathy."

"Who the fuck is Roland Abernathy!?"

"He is no one." Jacques sighed. "A forgery. A name used by zose who wish to conceal zeir hatred."

"So, we have no idea who wants Trigger dead?"

"We have some clues."

"Such as?"

"Well, firstly, whoever zey are, zey really want him dead. Secondly, we know zat zey are very, very rich."

"How rich, exactly?"

Jacques pondered his reply, those large hands continuing to shred the parchment.

"Let us just say, were I not currently on Trigger's crew, I'd be hunting him down at zis very second."

The thought sent shiver's up Barnaby's spine.

"You've destroyed it though, haven't you?" He asked, the words a desperate plea.

Jacques crooked his head to one side, his expression mildly pained.

"Look at ze wall, Barnaby."

He did as he was told, scrutinizing the countless pieces of parchment. At least half of them bore Trigger's face.

"Oh." He murmured, feeling slightly sick. "Oh no."

Chapter Ten

"An excellent choice, sir! Though, are you certain I cannot interest you in one of our package deals? They come with a variety of perks and ext- "

"The timber will be fine, thank you."

"Very good, sir!"

The dealer waddled away, digging through his desk for the appropriate paperwork. Trigger took a second to enjoy the respite, the dealer's voice forever seared in his mind.

"Man could talk the arse off a donkey." Sheridan whispered, folding her arms.

"He does have a way with words."

"Oh, I agree. They're going to lead him six-feet under."

"Calm down." Trigger chuckled, running his fingers through his hair.

"When he offers you a job in the brothels, then you can tell me to calm down."

"Take it as a compliment."

"Have you seen the whores they have here? It's like they were dressed by autistic children."

"I've found that autists are often gifted with color."

"You know what I mean."

"I do, and I'm sorry. We won't linger much longer. Do you think the men have had enough time?"

"Our crew?" Sheridan snorted. "We could have been here a minute and they'd be fine. I keep trying to blind the buggers who peak into my room, yet by the time I reach the hole, they've done their business and left."

"That must make an awful mess." Trigger frowned.

"It does. I get Barnaby to mop it up. He's actually started chasing away some of the repeat offenders."

"He's gaining confidence." Trigger nodded. "Excellent."

"I'd say it's hard not to be confident with Beaufort at your back."

"I'd say you're right. The two have built quite the bond."

"Are you concerned?"

"Not really. Barnaby strikes me as loyal, and when push came to shove, Beaufort fought for the ship. He's already invested, and a relationship with Barnaby will help keep him in check."

"If you say so." Sheridan shrugged, her expression souring as the dealer approached.

"The paperwork is prepared, sir! Please, sign it at your leisure! The House could not be happier to enjoy your custom!"

Trigger suppressed the urge to roll his eyes.

"Thank you. I think I'll fill it out now, if that's ok. We're in a bit of a hurry."

"Of course, sir! Most of our customers are! That being the case, however, would you mind if I make a request of your stunning First Mate?"

"That is entirely up to her." Trigger replied, making for the desk.

"What is it?" Sheridan asked, folding her muscular arms. Her sleeveless gown accentuated the broadness of her shoulders.

"Well, madam, if you don't mind me saying, it is obvious that you are possessed of keen and sophisticated taste. Our vessel prides itself on catering to every need, including those of an aesthetic nature. If you will indulge me, I would very much like to introduce you to our broad range of fabrics and materials. Our position gives us a rather unique range, which I am certain you would find fascinating."

Trigger fought off a chuckle as Sheridan's expression changed, her hatred of the dealer grappling with her fondness for all things silken and fine.

"Captain?" She eventually asked, unable to make the choice.

"You've more than earned it." Trigger replied. "Purchase whatever you'd like. My only condition is that when you've crafted it into clothing, I'm the first one to see you wearing it."

"Deal." Sheridan beamed, turning to the portly dealer, who was regarding them both with a slimy grin,

"Excellent!" He exclaimed, heading for the door. "We shall return shortly, Captain Trigger. The papers are on the desk, as are a quill and ink."

"Have fun." Trigger nodded, taking a seat behind the desk. The dealer's buttocks had carved a particularly comfy groove.

Sheridan waved goodbye as she ducked through the exit, the door hinges squeaking as the dealer pressed it shut. Allowing himself a smile, Trigger turned his attention to the document, the flowing script written with impeccable skill. He would have admired it, were it not for the constant references to the House, and how grateful it was to be accepting his coin.

The House was a pantomime, of course, like so many things in the sprawling empire. They were the mysterious owners of the *Swaying Deck,* which appeared two years into the Tides existence. Its origins were never revealed, the exhausted participants too worn down to ever look beyond the smoke, mirrors, and whores. In truth, the *Swaying Deck,* and all its considerable profits, belonged solely to the royal family, who fed off the Tides as though they were starving leeches. When he had first learned this, Trigger had been supremely impressed. After all, the very creed of pirates was that they existed outside the institutions of polite society. Yet here they were, funding the very empire they sought to destabilize. When he had dwelled within that empire, Trigger found this deception a thing of beauty. Now that he lived beyond it, however, the knowledge appalled him. There was no escape, no real freedom. By fighting the empire, you only continued to feed it. There was no resistance. You were a part of the beast, whether you desired it or not.

The door swung open, hinges creaking in protest.

"You were quick." Trigger declared, looking up. "I've barely gotten sta- "

He cut himself off, watching as the quartet fanned across the room. He recognized none of them, not on a personal level, at least. He knew their kind, however, their sunburnt faces holding the unmistakably vermin-like qualities of genuine scum. These were the pirates that all good men fear, the kind who slit throats for a single coin, and break your fingers for nothing more than a refreshing ale.

"Hello." He nodded, setting aside the quill. Each of them was armed with a dagger and cutlass, all mercifully sheathed. Had they stormed into the room in a wild frenzy, his chances would be significantly worse. As it were, they had given him time to think and assess.

"Captain Trigger?" One of them asked, looking between him and a clutched piece of paper. Trigger didn't need to read it to know that it was a bounty, one which probably held his face.

"I am." He replied. "And you are?"

"Rusty Jones." The man proudly declared, exposing his teeth. Trigger wagered that their color is where he got the name.

"And your friends?"

"Part o'me crew." Rusty replied, swaggering towards the desk.

"The larger parts, I'd imagine."

"Yeah, they're big boys." Rusty winked. "Good for 'ard work, you know?"

"I'm certain they have their uses."

"'Oi'm certain they have dere uses'." Rusty parroted, in what Trigger believed to be a terrible impression. "You ain't half a fancy bugger, are ya?"

"I don't understand that question, and as such, I cannot answer it."

Rusty frowned, running his hand across the hilt of his cutlass.

"You givin' me cheek?"

"No, though, if you continue to advance in that fashion, I'll gladly feed you your teeth."

Rusty paused, raising an eyebrow and looking to his companions.

"He's got more balls than we thought!"

Trigger sighed, pushing his chair away from the desk. Rubbing his thumb against his finger, he considered his words, pondering whether a confrontation was truly inevitable. At this point, the answer was appearing rather dire.

"Gentlemen, I am not certain why you are here, yet I am sure I can hazard a guess. Before you make any decisions, however, I must ask you to consider a few simple facts. The first, and most pressing, is that whatever amount that bounty promises, it cannot be enough to justify what Carnage will do to you, should you deny him the pleasure of killing me. Secondly, and far less of a concern, I'll admit, is that I have no intention of being captured or killed. Now, while I realize that few people do, I also know that compared to most, I am far more capable of resisting these circumstances. This means that any attempts to harm me will be met with swift, and might I add brutal, retaliation. Therefore, I suggest that it is in your best interest to simply walk away, and forget this encounter ever occurred. I will happily do the same."

Rusty considered him for several long moments. It occurred to Trigger that his opponent may legitimately have failed to understand. Rusty didn't seem the brightest of stars.

"Yeah, that's a pretty bit o'speech." Rusty shrugged. "Good points, well said. Here's me reply."

Rusty threw the bounty onto the desk, sneering smugly as Trigger unfurled its crumpled edges.

"Oh." Trigger remarked, seeing the numerous zeroes that comprised the reward.

"Yeah." Rusty spat, hoisting up his belt. "Still think ya ain't worth it?"

"Regardless of my thoughts, someone else clearly does." Trigger sighed, setting the bounty aside.

"Well then, you understand." Rusty declared, shrugging apologetically.

"To a degree." Trigger replied.

"Gods, you're a cool one, ain't cha?"

"I'm in a bit of a rush, Rusty." Trigger announced, resting his hands on the desk. "If you're going to do this, please, don't dawdle."

Once more, Rusty looked to his men, scraggy face creased with astonishment.

"Aye." He replied. "Fair enough, then."

With a savage roar he sprung, scabby hand perched on the handle of his blade. He never got the chance to draw it, as with lightning speed Trigger seized the inkwell, slamming it into his temple in an explosion of ink, glass and blood. Rusty screamed as it seeped into his eyes, falling to the floor in a fetal heap. Unfortunately, his men were right behind him, leaping over their Captain in a wild stampede. Each was almost double Trigger's size, yet in the cramped confines this worked to his advantage, allowing him to bottleneck them around the desks edge. Ducking low, he swept underneath a questing fist, smashing his own into a stubbly jaw. His attacker stumbled back, great weight slowing his recovery and pinning a companion in place. The third assailant went around him, using his great height to reach across the desk and seize Trigger's collar. He allowed himself to be dragged, snatching his pistol from its holster and flipping it upside down. His assailant saw the movement, yet he had left himself completely exposed, allowing Trigger to slam the grip straight across his skull. There was a hollow crack of impact as the man's forehead split, his heavy body slumping down. The motion pulled Trigger with him, his remaining foes springing on the opening with a surprising amount of speed. One thick arm wrapped about his throat, hauling him backwards and denying him air. The other attacker circled around, two cannon-like fists crashing against his stomach and ribs. Had he continued, Trigger would have been done, yet these pirates were unused to an opponent who knew how to fight, and as such, open to making foolish mistakes. The crewman ceased his beating, attempting instead to unsheathe his sword. No easy task in such small quarters, especially when Trigger seized his wrist, stopping the motion halfway through. A sensible foe would have left it there, striking Trigger instead, yet the panic of combat was on them, and in a foolish move they persisted in trying to draw, wasting time, and allowing him to regain his bearings.

Leaping upwards, he planted both feet against the desk, propelling his strangler and himself straight into a bookcase.

Shelves broke and tomes tumbled as they collapsed to the floor, his attacker's grip loosening enough for Trigger to tear free. His other opponent used the opening well, finally drawing his sword with a victorious cry. He lunged towards Trigger with a fierce snarl, yet the noise became a whimper as Trigger raised his pistol, placing a bullet between his eyes.

"Carl!"

The crewman behind him had regained his senses, the death of his ally lending him strength. His bulging arms locked about Trigger's waist, hoisting him upwards and throwing him face-first into the sturdy wall. Lights flashed in Trigger's eyes as his skull bounced against the timbers, doubling in intensity as a fist cracked across his jaw. Trigger staggered, unable to block the next pounding blow. It took him under the chin, snapping his head upwards and providing him a marvelous view of the filthy ceiling. He would have fallen, given the chance, yet his attacker wasn't sated, lifting him by the hips and hurling him against the desk.

He really should have kept on punching. A disabled foe is no longer a threat. If you waste time merely causing them pain, you're giving them time to try and fight back.

Trigger slumped sideways, avoiding his opponents charge. The desk slid across the floor as his attacker slammed against it, throwing him entirely off-balance. Trigger enhanced the effect, driving his elbow into the back of their knee and crushing it against the heavy wood. The pirate bellowed and sank to one side, his screams increasing as Trigger took hold of his shirt, using it to haul himself up. His attacker threw a clumsy right, yet the angle was awful, allowing Trigger to catch his fist and lock it in place. The man sputtered as his own arm began to strangle him, and released a muted cry as Trigger kicked out his exposed ankle, leaving him gasping and kneeling on the floor. Using all his weight, Trigger drove his opponent forward, smashing his head against the desk. The impact broke his attacker's nose, leaving strings of snot clinging to the timber. Trigger tightened his grip, waiting until his foe was limp to release him, the big man toppling sideways and convulsing on the floor.

Panting for breath, Trigger retrieved his pistol and adjusted his coat, extracting a handkerchief from an inner pocket. He was bleeding from his nose, mouth, and a cut above his eye, yet for the most part he was relatively unscathed. He'd simply look dreadful tomorrow morning.

Dabbing at his wounds, Trigger made himself as presentable as possible, smoothing down his hair and making for the desk. He wasted no time in filling out the paperwork, though on one occasion he was forced to draw the quill across Rusty's face, as the ink on the floor had become too absorbed. When he was done, he stood once more above the weeping Captain, who was probing at his eyes with tender, shaking hands.

"Most of the glass is in your temple." Trigger assured him. "What you're feeling is primarily ink and blood. When your remaining men awake, have them fill a bowl of water, and submerge your face within it. If you can open your eyes, that should wash away most of the contaminates."

"You bastard." Rusty wept. "You've blinded me!"

"No, I haven't. I have killed one of your men, however, a fact which I deeply regret. I've killed enough for one lifetime and have no desire to keep adding to the tally. That said, I am also a man who believes in learning from one's mistakes and have no patience for those who cannot do so. Today, you made a mistake. Make it again, and you will see what I do to those who actually test my patience."

Rusty whimpered as Trigger stepped past, dropping his handkerchief into the pirate's palm.

"Now please, clean yourself up. That is no way for a Captain to behave."

He strode from the room, shutting the door with a gentle creak.

****

"Gods, how big can one ship be?"

Barnaby spun in awe, trying to take in the scope of the vessel. They had entered the markets, a thronging den of commerce and trade, vast enough to rival any city.

"Ze real question is, just what sort of waste are people willing to buy?" Jacques remarked, considering the stalls with boundless contempt. "Look at zese carvings. Zey may well have been done by a drunken chimp."

The merchant heard their words, yet if they were disgruntled, they made no show of it, instead treating them to a dazzling grin.

"You don't like? I have plenty more! I will make you bargain? Two-for-one? Pretty statue for pretty boy?"

"Is he talking about me?" Barnaby asked. He'd never been described as pretty. A vessel like this was not the place to start.

"No, zank you." Jacques declared, shouldering past the vendor with no small amount of force. Barnaby and Magwa followed, dwelling in the wake of Jacques' progress. His massive frame parted the crowd as though it were composed of children, his great height drawing attention to the only person who stood taller.

"Sheridan!" Barnaby called, racing toward the surprised First Mate. She was pressing a sheet of fabric to her cheek, the satchel at her side brimming with dozens of high-quality materials.

"Barnaby, Magwa, Jacques." She greeted, nodding at each of them in turn. "I'm surprised you left the ship. I'll take this, by the way." She added, turning to the portly man waiting patiently at her back.

"Excellent choice, madam!" He declared, clapping his hands with glee.

Barnaby loathed him already.

"Have you seen zis?" Jacques asked, offering her a copy of Trigger's bounty.

"No." Sheridan replied, stuffing the fabric into her bag. "What is it?"

"A bounty for our Captain. A large one."

"What?" Sheridan snapped, snatching the parchment. "For how much?"

"Much."

"Oh." Sheridan murmured, eyes widening as they studied the zeroes. "Oh my."

"Yes. Not many here would zink twice on seizing such a sum. Is ze Captain nearby?"

"I left him in the office." Sheridan replied, paling. "The dealer asked me if I…"

She trailed off, rounding on the chubby dealer, who was making a conspicuous effort to slip away.

"You knew about this, didn't you?" Sheridan snapped, tossing the parchment aside.

"Madam, the House cannot possibly keep track of how all its services are used. It would certainly never be complicit in taking advantage of such a service, either."

"You aren't the House though, are you?" Sheridan growled, taking hold of his sweat-soaked collar. "You're just a fat weasel, looking to score some coin."

"Now madam, this is poor behavior on your behalf!" The dealer whined, his greasy voice gaining a frantic edge. "I would hate to have to call down the guard, though I will if you continue to press me!"

Sheridan snorted, her other hand clamping about his throat.

"Go on then." She whispered. "Give us a scream."

With one deft twist she snapped his neck, tossing him aside without a second glance.

"Come on." She ordered, fixing her silken glove. "We need to check on the Captain."

They followed without a moment's delay. None of them had the balls to risk upsetting her.

Sheridan's long legs carried her faster than Barnaby could match, both he and Jacques falling behind as the First Mate and Magwa surged ahead. They lost sight of them as the pair rounded a corner, the sound of a rough collision sending Jacques' hands flying to his blades.

"Keep behind me." He declared, somehow faster than Barnaby, despite his missing leg.

"No problem there." Barnaby replied, hovering at Jacques rear.

They stepped into the well-lit hall, pausing to stare at the mass of limbs tangled against the wall. Sheridan had thrown someone against it, holding them there with an unbreakable grip. Magwa had joined in, his dagger poised against their pale throat. The pair must have reacted on pure reflex, a fact which Trigger clearly failed to appreciate.

"You may release me at any time, Ms. Sheridan."

Sheridan let him go with a sheepish mumble, her cheeks reddening with boundless shame.

"Sorry, Captain."

"No harm done." He replied, rubbing at his throat. "Though, I feel as though Magwa has given me a shave."

"Sorry, Captain." Magwa declared. He didn't look sorry. Judging by his grin, he was amused.

"There's a bounty on your head." Sheridan explained. "The dealer lured me away, and I suspect that there are men already on their way."

"They've already arrived." Trigger replied, indicating a cut above his eye. "Fortunately, they weren't the most competent murderers. Still, thank you for efforts. I appreciate a good rescue, even if it proves unnecessary."

"You're welcome." Jacques grinned, sheathing his swords.

"What became of the dealer?" Trigger asked, studying their group.

"I may have lost my temper when I first found out." Sheridan conceded, adjusting her wig.

"Understandable."

"You're not mad?"

"No. He attempted to have me killed, and worse, asked you to be a whore. I take no issue with his death."

"Oh. Wonderful!" Sheridan replied, smiling.

"What about ze timber?" Jacques asked, frowning.

"We may have to do without."

"Zat sounds difficult."

"Not as difficult as sailing from beyond the grave."

"A fair point."

"How we leave?" Magwa suddenly asked, deep voice startling them all. "Most men see bounty. Many between us and ship."

"Only if we go through the taverns and markets." Barnaby remarked, surprising himself. "If we go through the brothels, everyone will be too busy to notice."

The group stood in silence, pondering his plan.

"That's a fantastic idea, Mr. Barnaby." Trigger eventually declared. Unseen to the others, Jacques gave Barnaby an encouraging pat.

"Do we know where the brothels are?" Sheridan asked, gown swinging as she searched.

"Zey comprise ze majority of ze ship." Jacques announced, turning to lead. "Yet zere is a section two levels higher zat is completely dedicated to carnal delights."

"You know the way?" Trigger asked, falling into step beside him.

"Vaguely. It should not be hard to find. We will simply follow ze most lonely-looking souls."

"That's a bit grim." Barnaby mused, earning an indifferent shrug.

"It is accurate."

Surely enough, it was. They found the brothel in a matter of minutes, simply by following the dominant stream of traffic. People of all shapes hurried to the lude and painted doors, each of their faces wearing the same of expression of hunger, sorrow, and lust.

"This is depressing." Barnaby whispered, as they stepped through the swinging doors. The lights were dim and flickering, yet failed to hide the modified walls, which were fitted with several chains and portals. Various legs were fixed within them, spread-wide to expose their owners. At their side stood a woman of indescribable age, taking small amounts of coin from those who wished to have their way. It was a vulgar affair, devoid of passion or intimacy. It rather turned his stomach.

"For zose who can't afford a real connection." Jacques quietly explained, noticing his disturbed gaze. "At least, as real as it gets in a place like zis."

"We should set them free." Sheridan growled, fidgeting with her gloves.

"Nozing to set free. Most are zere by choice. It pays well, and zere is less chance of being beaten by an angry customer."

"That's awful."

"Zat's life."

Barnaby shook his head as they carried on, closing his senses to the grunts and thrusts around them. Eventually they passed through another set of doors, leading to a far more salubrious portion of the ship. Here the gold-taker was young and attractive, ushering her clients into sealed and private rooms. For a moment, Barnaby relaxed, yet as they made their way through the vast and thronging corridors, he realized that the difference between the two sections was completely aesthetic. The only difference were the doors and walls, their flat surfaces keeping the depravity from sight. They didn't make it better, they just ensured that it wasn't his problem.

He couldn't wait to leave this place.

Click.

Unfortunately, that was obviously going to take some time.

"It's Trigger, isn't it?" Asked the pirate, levelling his pistol at the Captain's chest.

"The likeness on the bounty is quite uncanny." Trigger replied, seemingly unfazed. "We both know there's no need to ask."

"Ah, I forgot you were a naval man." The pirate declared, taking a cautious step towards them. His hat was the most astonishing piece of headwear that Barnaby had ever seen, its rim wide enough to create a miniature eclipse. The feather at its peak was no less majestic, its plumage stretching farther than a maiden's hair. "It's a good thing to see. Resolve and courage are sadly wanting in most of our peers."

"You served?" Trigger asked, keeping his hands raised. The rest of them were doing the same, the pirate keeping himself just beyond their reach.

"Briefly, though, my career was nowhere near as…storied, as your own."

The pirate gave them a gold and silver grin, suggesting that his career as a scoundrel had proven far more lucrative.

"I don't suppose you feel a sense of loyalty to a fellow former serviceman?" Trigger asked, sounding supremely tired.

"None in the slightest, I'm afraid. I'm sure you understand."

"I do. The military often leaves a bitter taste."

"That it does." The pirate nodded, his great feather bobbing back-and-forth. "The lack of payment being a key ingredient. There's a lot a man could do with the bounty being offered for you."

"I'm certain there is. Though, you are at somewhat of a disadvantage."

"Indeed?"

"There's five of us, and you only have one shot. You may drop me, yet a moment later you'll be dealing with my comrades, three of whom are rather fearsome, if I'm being completely honest."

He didn't clarify who was the odd man out. It was polite, yet unnecessary. Barnaby knew where he stood, and he was more than happy in that position. Let the others lead the charge. It would give him time to run away.

"Ah, yes, your esteemed colleagues." The pirate nodded, studying each of them in turn. "I'm ashamed to say I can name only one. Mr. Beaufort, yes?"

Jacques nodded, the tendons in his neck as thick as Barnaby's arms.

"Zat is me. Who might you be?"

"Sharing names is dangerous business." The pirate replied, shrugging apologetically. "I try to cultivate an aura of anonymity. Makes grudges difficult, if you don't know who you're looking for."

"Clever." Trigger remarked, sounding genuinely impressed.

"Thank you." The pirate replied. "All you need to know is that I am well aware of your identities, and intend to profit from such information."

"You have a wager on my fight wiz Hargrave, don't you?" Jacques sighed, shaking his head.

"Most men do." The pirate shrugged. "Though, the majority placed theirs bets on you. Foolish, in my opinion. Even in your prime, Hargrave had your number. As you stand now? No chance."

Barnaby could feel the air tighten as Jacques' jaw clenched, the swordsman barely restraining a flash of rage.

"That said." The pirate continued. "I still need the fight to occur, if I wish to claim my winnings. Therefore, my proposal is simple. I kill Trigger, and claim the gold. The rest of us then part ways, never to meet again. I live my life, growing fat and wealthy, while you assume control of Trigger's crew. They'll follow you without question, I'm sure, and once you are in command, you can make your rendezvous with Hargrave, and try your best to prove me wrong. How does that sound? Before you answer, please remember that even if you all do leave here alive, it means that Trigger remains in charge. Considering his track record, I'd say that stacks the odds against you ever making it to the second fixture, let alone the third."

If he was insulted, Trigger barely showed it, a heavy exhalation his only response.

"You are suggesting zat we would be better off without ze Captain?" Jacques scoffed. "I would already be dead were it not for him. If you truly wish for me to have my duel, zen your best option is to send us on our way."

The pirate considered Jacques words, scratching thoughtfully at his stubbly chin.

"Then it seems we are at an impasse. I'm not going to let you leave with Trigger still alive, and if you try and rush me, one of you will certainly die."

"If we try and rush you, yes."

The pirate's pistol wavered, his eyes meeting Trigger's own.

"Meaning what, exactly?"

"That the door behind you opened the second you mentioned my name. Only a crack, mind you, yet I'd recognize that beard anywhere. I've been stalling for time, waiting for its owner to make his move, yet it's becoming clear that I need to force his hand."

Drops of sweat formed on the pirate's brow, his hand shaking as he fought the urge to glance at the door.

"You're bluffing." He smiled, though it didn't reach his eyes.

"I'm not." Trigger replied, with a face as cold as steel. "Though I *am* rapidly losing my patience."

"You're full of shit." The pirate declared, clearly rattled.

"I'm completely serious." Trigger scowled. "I'm also wondering if it's possible for crew to live off one-eighth rations."

"You're embarrassing yourself!" The pirate exclaimed, the tendons in his neck straining.

"I'm going to step towards you now." Trigger shrugged, keeping his hands raised. "Sheridan, if the men haven't subdued him by the time I'm in reach, by all means, kill them as well."

"Aye, Captain."

Barnaby couldn't see the door, and had no idea if he was actually bluffing. If he was, however, he was doing a damn good job.

"Stay where you are!" The pirate roared, thrusting his pistol at Trigger's heart. "I swear, take another step and I will gun you do- "

The door behind them exploded, its frame overflowing with four naked, sweating men. The pirate turned as they raced towards him, yet with fluid ease Trigger darted forwards, slapping the pistol from his hand. A moment later he was stepping back, allowing the men to indulge in a good old-fashioned beat-down. At first, Barnaby tried to watch, yet the sight of so many flailing members turned his stomach, the poor pirate groaning and moaning as he was steadily pummeled into the semen-stained timbers. Barnaby had suffered many indignities during his life, yet right here, right now, he had finally found a man that he could pity.

Eventually the men ceased, each of them panting as they stood before the Captain. Trigger wasn't averting his eyes, exactly, yet he was taking great care to maintain eye contact, his gaze never sinking below their chests.

"Well done." He commended, looking to each of them in turn. The quartet offered embarrassed nods, hands clasped to their genitals in a feeble attempt at modesty. "Though, you took longer than I expected."

"Sorry, Captain." Frank declared, clearing his throat. To his right, the others mumbled their own apologies, withering beneath Sheridan's judgmental gaze.

"You succeeded where it mattered." Trigger remarked, studying their unconscious foe. "We were lucky you were here."

"Why are you here, exactly?" Sheridan asked. "It's about time everyone returned to the ship."

"Ah, about that." Frank coughed, looking to the others. "Me and Gary were playing the wheel, and doing so well that they wanted us to stop. They gave us each two free vouchers for a turn with a whore, and sent us on our way. I gave my spare to Sunniday, while Gary gave his to Bradley. Thought we'd share the love, you know?"

"Very generous." Trigger replied, speaking above Sheridan's snort. "Though, I'm not sure why you were sharing a room."

"Ah, that." Frank nodded, every cheek swiftly reddening. "Well, none of us can read, you see. We didn't know that the vouchers were all for the same whore. It was already late when we found out, so we didn't have time to wait. We decided that if we all went at once; we'd have plenty of time to make it back to the ship."

"Oh, I bet you would." Sheridan chuckled, folding her arms.

"That's not what I mean!' Frank declared, raising a hand in outrage. The action exposed a testicle, which he was quick to cover anew. Beside him, his comrades sniggered, though they were quickly silenced by Trigger's voice.

"Leave them be, Sheridan. They saved us today, which warrants some respect."

"Aye, Captain." Sheridan pouted. "Fair enough."

"That said." Trigger began, a small smile gracing his lips. "You delayed greatly in performing the rescue, a fact which cannot be ignored. Normally, such hesitation would warrant severe punishment, yet in this case, you will be granted leniency."

"Thank you, Captain." Frank replied, treating Sheridan to a mocking sneer. "We'll just get dressed, and then escort you back to the ship."

"I said leniency, not absolution." Trigger announced, as the group began moving towards their room. "By all means, retrieve your clothing. You are only to carry it, however. Not a single piece is to actually be worn."

"You can't be serious." Sunniday replied, his booming voice subdued by fear.

Trigger smiled.

"I have never been one for jokes."

The naked group stood in stony silence, looking to each other in despair. All save Bradley, who merely shrugged, slapping his belly and exposing his dick.

"Stuff it, then. Let's give this ship a treat!"

He practically bounded into the room, his enthusiasm lending the others a degree of courage. They followed suit, returning to the hallway with scrunched bundles, each of which were pressed against their scrawny waists. Bradley had no such qualms, however, his own clothes thrown casually across his shoulder. Honestly, Barnaby couldn't help but feel a swell of respect.

"What about him?" Sheridan asked, prodding the pirate with a disdainful toe.

"He never told us his name." Trigger shrugged. "And he'll be lucky to remember it himself. Leave him be."

"Aye, Captain. Shall we return to the ship?"

"I think that would be best."

As one, they resumed their march towards the *Blackbird*, their path guided by the sight of Bradley's swaying cheeks. It was somewhat hypnotic, and utterly repellant.

"Your crew is razer...unusual." Jacques remarked, tearing away his gaze.

"Yeah." Barnaby conceded, with no small trace of pride. "They are."

Chapter Eleven

Trigger felt his spirit lift the moment the *Blackbird* came into view, the feeble moon lending a romantic air to its cracked and creaking timbers. Running a hand through his hair, he began to relax, the knowledge that they were departing easing his aches and pains. He had finally experienced the *Swaying Deck,* and had found its hospitality to be less than stellar.

"Alright men, you may dress yourselves, if you so desire."

His crewmen sighed with relief, donning their pants and shirts as swiftly as they were able. Their journey through the ship had been met with countless catcalls, jeers and whistles, yet while Trigger regretted the torrent of embarrassment his edict had heaped upon them, he had been pleased to discover that his plan had served its purpose, the sight of Bradley's naked form rendering the rest of them invisible by comparison. They had passed through the crowds without incident or challenge, moving unseen despite the numerous bounties bearing his face.

The crewmen finished dressing, the presence of clothing returning a familiar swagger to their bearing.

"Any other orders, Captain?" Frank asked, double knotting the rope that served as his belt.

"Aye. When you get on deck, report to the doctor as soon as you are able."

"Why?" Frank asked, raising a quizzical brow.

"Because you just spent time with one of the most used prostitutes this world has ever seen. To make matters worse, you were sharing her with Gary, who was inspecting himself for warts not so long ago."

He could have laughed at the expressions that stamped his crewmen's faces. It took all his will to suppress it, in fact. Sheridan was not so kind.

"You son of a bitch." Bradley growled, rounding on Gary. "Why didn't you remind us?"

"That's half-rations." Trigger warned, adjusting his coat.

"Sorry, Captain." Bradley nodded, seizing Gary by his collar. "We won't trouble you anymore."

Without another word the quartet departed, the three injured parties clinging tightly to Gary's extremely worried frame.

"Think they'll be gentle?" Sheridan asked, still chuckling.

"I doubt it."

Trigger led on, pausing at the gangplank and allowing the others to board. Magwa was the last to pass, the Kalyute clasping his shoulder with a firm and friendly hand.

"Magwa glad you survived."

"Thank you. I'm rather pleased myself."

Magwa grinned, once more revealing his filed teeth. Without them, his smiles might have been stunning. With them, however, they were more than a little disconcerting.

"Captain!"

Sheridan's voice sent them sprinting across the gangplank, the pair of them leaping to the *Blackbird* with a simultaneous thump. Trigger's hand was at his pistol, yet a quick scan sent his fingers into a slow and measured retreat. There was no danger, quite the opposite, in fact. The *Blackbird* was bustling, groaning beneath the burden of several timber deliveries. His crew were weaving about them, repairing their vessel's wounds.

"This is unexpected." Trigger remarked, as Sheridan approached from the starboard stern. An unfamiliar figure was at her side, his thin limbs appearing particularly frail beside Sheridan's broad physique.

"Good evening." Trigger greeted, as the figure halted before him.

The man made to reply, yet paused, turning his head and coughing into a silken handkerchief.

"It is." He eventually announced, treating Trigger to a wispy grin. His eyes were red and glistening, as though he were on the verge of tears. "Though, it has seen its share of tragedies."

"Do you represent the House?" Trigger asked, gesturing at the timber.

"I do. I oversee deliveries, and ship-to-ship transactions."

"We met your predecessor earlier today." Sheridan remarked, her voice sprinkled with threat.

"I am aware." The dealer replied. "His retirement was necessary. He had become neglectful of his duties, and no longer concerned himself with delivering a satisfactory experience. I am here to apologize on his behalf, and that of the House. As a token of goodwill, we have delivered the timber you requested, complete with a fifty percent refund of its original price."

The dealer extracted a pouch, offering it to Trigger as though the sight of it offended him. Trigger took it with a measure of caution, passing it to Sheridan for future inspection.

"Thank you." He nodded. "We appreciate the gesture."

"My predecessor did not represent the standards that the House has come to expect." The dealer replied. "While he was right to accommodate the posting of the bounty, he should never have allowed its pursuit upon our own premises."

Trigger frowned, confusion descending on his mind.

"You do know who posted the bounty, yes?" He asked, rubbing his thumb against his finger.

"We believe they used an alias." The dealer replied. "It is a common pract- "

"No." Trigger scowled, cutting him off. "No games. I served the empire, and know many of its secrets. The House is one of them. We both know who it was that put a bounty on my head, and just how much influence they hold. They aren't going to be pleased that you let me leave. Especially when they learn that you aided me, as well."

The dealer didn't reply for several moments, the handkerchief reappearing as he dapped at his lips.

"It is true, the individual who posted your bounty does hold considerable influence within the *Swaying Deck*. However, as with all great enterprises, this connection flows both ways. Your pursuer depends on us just as much as we depend on them, if not more so. Now, while they are free to protest our handling of this situation, rest assured that they are in no position to enforce, or demand, punishment. The House sees to its own affairs, Mr. Trigger. Today, you have profited from this arrangement. I suggest you appreciate this fact, and accept our gift without further reserve."

Trigger had been threatened many times in his life. It had never been done so politely.

"Very well." He nodded, knowing when to retreat. "You and the House have my thanks."

"Then our business is done." The dealer replied, shoes clipping the deck as he headed for the gangplank. "Please depart as soon as you are able. Other vessels will need to dock."

Trigger and Sheridan watched him go, sharing a look as he vanished from view.

"I think I preferred the old one." Sheridan declared, rubbing at her shoulder. "He may have made my skin crawl, but he didn't give me goose bumps."

"True enough." Trigger replied, feeling somewhat soiled by the encounter. "They honored our agreement, however, which is all that really matters."

"Maybe." Sheridan mused, studying him carefully. "Tell me though, what was all that about? You know who posted the bounty?"

"I can make an educated guess."

"Care to share?"

"I'm sure you can work it out. Which influential figure would like to see me dead?"

"Apart from Carnage?"

Trigger chuckled, bowing his head in concession.

"I have a knack for making enemies, I admit."

Sheridan extracted a fan from her bosom, whipping it back-and-forth as she pondered the suspects.

"Oh." She remarked, pausing mid-flap. By the expression on her lips, he knew that she'd arrived at the correct conclusion.

"Indeed." He sighed, running a hand through his hair.

"That could be a problem."

"It could."

"Should we even bother pressing on? If she's willing to put up a bounty, there's no guarantee that she'll honor the terms of the Tides. We could cross that finish line first, and still find ourselves swinging from the end of a noose."

"She'll honor the Tides." Trigger replied. "She's not above treachery and shadow-play, but directly ignoring established tradition? She'd rather die."

He tried to keep the bitter note from entering his tone. He failed, yet Sheridan was kind enough to ignore it.

"Well then, should we begin heading off?" Sheridan asked. "I've had more than enough of the *Swaying Deck*."

"That sounds like an excellent idea. Give the order, and see it done. I think I'm due for a wash and rest."

"Aye, Captain, on all counts." Sheridan grinned. "I've never seen you looking so rough. I could almost mistake you for a genuine pirate."

"That's the deepest wound I've received all day." Trigger laughed, making for his former cabin. He could see crewman rummaging about the splintered ruins, and was pleased to discover that they'd fashioned him a miniature replacement, its uneven ceiling resting an inch below his brow.

"Who designed this?" He asked, genuinely delighted.

"Tobey, sir." Came the nervous reply. Tobey himself stepped forward, clearly unsure whether he'd earned a reward or punishment. Trigger made a mental note to soften his tone. Uneasy men were inefficient men.

"Thought you'd like to have your space back, Captain." Tobey declared, indicating his quaint attempt. "Sorry about the size, though. It was bigger in my head, but something went wrong with the cutting."

"Aye, you let Howard do it." Scoffed a nearby crewman.

"I think it's fine." Howard grumbled, folding his arms.

"It is fine." Trigger announced, raising a hand for peace. "A noble and considerate effort. Each of you has my gratitude. Well done."

The crewman looked to each other, sharing several winks.

"Can I show you around?" Tobey asked, pulling open the door. It was about a foot too short for the frame.

Trigger investigated his quarters, which were now marginally smaller than the average outhouse.

"I appreciate the offer, yet I should be fine." He grinned, patting Tobey's shoulder. "All of you head down and tell the cook to see dinner prepared. We're about to set sail, and I'd wager that you could use a break. You've clearly been working hard."

"Aye, Captain." The men replied, giving him clumsy salutes. They departed with obvious excitement, whispering amongst themselves. With an amused chuckle, Trigger entered the room, pulling the thin door shut behind him. A moment later the cat was at his feet, strolling beneath the crack without a bended knee.

"Hey, boy." Trigger laughed, lying on his mattress, which occupied the entire floor. The cat leapt onto his lap, purring contentedly and clawing at his coat. He began patting it with a lazy hand, his bruised palm eventually falling still on it's warm and furry back.

He could hear Sheridan's voice thundering across the deck, calling the crew into frenzied action. It wasn't long before the vessel was moving, drifting from the *Swaying Deck* at an ever-growing pace. Closing his eyes, Trigger surrendered himself to his aching bodies will, a cloud of slumber descending on his exhausted mind. He knew he would have to wake soon, to plot their next course and see it followed, yet that was at least a few hours away, and in the meantime, he knew his crew would see him through.

They'd more than earned his trust and pride.

****

"So, what comes next?"

"Zat is up to your Captain."

"I know that." Barnaby scowled. "I'm asking what his options are."

"Ah. Zat is a difficult question."

"Why?"

"Because I am not completely sure. Ze path to ze second fixture is far less defined zan ze ozers. It has never been properly mapped or explored."

"Really?" Barnaby remarked, surprised.

"Ze sea widens, creating many more routes for passage." Jacques explained. "Zis is also when ze race begins to intensify. Ships battle, and do zeir best to maintain a lead. Zis is not an attitude zat encourages thorough documentation."

"So, we're sailing blind?"

"More poorly lit, zan blind."

Barnaby shook his head, glancing at the Captain's cabin. He and Sheridan had sealed themselves inside several hours ago, moving Trigger's mattress to fill the enormous hole made by Howard's dodgy craftsmanship.

"How long do you think it will take?" He asked, watching as the ships cat roamed up-and-down the deck. It was hunting, whiskers quivering as it stalked across the timbers.

"I have no idea." Jacques shrugged. "Your Captain is a decisive man, and knows ze seas well. He is also zoughtful, and measured in his actions. He could emerge in an instant, or in two days' time."

"You speak well of him." Barnaby declared, leaning back against his barrel. "Is that why you stood up for him, back at the brothel?"

"I explained my reasoning." Jacques shrugged. "None of it was false."

"Fair enough."

"None of zat is truly important, anyway." Jacques announced, a sly grin creasing his rugged features.

"What do you mean?"

"Your Captain and his First Mate. How close are zey, exactly?"

"Very, from what I've seen."

"Lovers?"

The question took Barnaby off-guard, summoning images of the pair in several compromising positions. He found them more than a little disturbing.

"Not as far as I know." He replied. "And if they are, well, I'm glad for my ignorance."

"It is a matter zat should concern you all." Jacques shrugged. "One should never mix command with emotion. It leads to hard choices, which often result in terrible decisions."

"The Captain knows what he's doing." Barnaby frowned. "Well, it seems that way to me, at least. Most people we've met seem to have a very different opinion, though I'm not entirely sure why."

"You don't know?" Jacques chuckled, eyebrows rising.

"No, I don't." Barnaby replied. "And whenever I ask, I always get a condescending remark, rather than an actual answer. It's extremely annoying."

"My apologies." Jacques nodded, sounding genuinely sincere. "One should never be punished for asking questions. What would you like to know?"

"His history. Why everyone treats him with such disrespect."

"Zat is a question with several answers." Jacques declared, weighing his words. "I am sure zat you have noticed your Captain's bearing, and how it differs from ze common man."

"He's a noble, I know that much."

"Indeed he is, and zis does him no favors. Pirates live to escape the shackles of polite society, and it does not sit well with zem when a member of this very elite attempts to insinuate himself amongst their ranks. To make matters worse, he is a former member of ze military, and has zerefore almost certainly fought against ze pirates he now strives to emulate. As far as most are concerned, he is a traitor and a hypocrite."

"Why did he leave, then?" Barnaby frowned. "Why give it all up for...well, this?"

"It was not by choice." Jacques shrugged. "He is just as hated by polite society. Ze only difference is zat a hated man can thrive on the sea, based solely on his wits and skill. Ze lawful world has too many restrictions, too many zreads to weigh us down. A single enemy can break you wiz nozing but a word, so long as zey know ze right ears to hear it. Trigger's enemy is powerful, and holds all ze right ears in ze palm of her hand."

"Her?" Barnaby asked, taken aback.

"Ze Empress." Jacques explained. "She despises your Captain, heart and soul."

Once again, Barnaby felt that crushing sense of sorrow and desperation, an overwhelming regret that fate had cast him on this cursed and broken deck.

"She's the one who posted the bounty?" He asked, his voice several octaves higher than usual.

"She would be my first guess."

Barnaby sat with his head in his hands, processing this new information. Jacques allowed him the time, patiently sharpening his dagger against a well-used stone.

Eventually, Barnaby rallied, deciding that he was ready to endure a little more.

"Are you ok?" Jacques asked, sheathing his blade.

"No, I'm terrified. Sadly, I'm stuck on this ship for the next few months, with no hope of escape or rescue. So, I may as well learn *why* I'm going to be murdered by the most powerful person in existence."

"Makes sense." Jacques chuckled. "And hints at ze beginnings of courage."

"Acceptance isn't courage. It's merely common sense."

Jacques smiled at his remark, yet made no attempt to address it.

"Our ruler's hatred of Trigger is relatively fresh, born from a battle zree years past. Did you hear about ze Bay of Breakwater, out on your little farm?"

"No." Barnaby replied, shaking his head. "Though, if it's bad news, we usually don't. The longer I'm out here, the more I realize that most of what we heard was simply propaganda. As far as my family is concerned, the Empress is a goddess, and the empire at large is utter perfection."

Jacques snorted, drumming his fingers against the barrel beside him.

"It must be delightful, to control history ze way she does." He mused. "I wonder how tall ze empire would stand, if her Oracle birds showed nothing but truth?"

"Probably just as high. What does my family care about a battle halfway across the world? We'll be dead before the enemy reach us, and in the meantime, the cows will always be feeding us milk."

"True enough." Jacques replied, sounding both angry and defeated. "Regardless, ze battle of Breakwater is one of the empire's greatest defeats, one zat Trigger oversaw."

"What happened?"

"Bad luck. Ze enemy had ze numbers, and ze maneuverability. Say what you will about ze Azrang, zey can build ships like no one else."

Jacques took a moment to clear his throat, eyes glistening as he pictured the scene.

"Breakwater is a gateway to many of ze empire's most vital regions, a center of trade and commerce. Ze Azrang knew zis, and made a ferocious bid to claim it. Warning was short, and only four vessels were able to arrive in time. Your Captain's was one of zem, while Prince Miguelle's was anozer."

"The Prince was at the battle?" Barnaby asked. "Isn't that…unusual?"

"Yes, zough ze Prince was renowned for being a headstrong fool. You know ze type. He fancied himself a story book Prince, one wizout fear, who led by example. With his sister actually running ze empire, he was more zan free to indulge his fantasies. He was beloved by all, of course."

"My mother cried when we heard of his passing." Barnaby nodded. "We knew that the plague was spreading swiftly, yet never thought it could touch the royals themselves."

"Plague?" Jacques frowned, studying him.

"The plague? Three years ago?" Barnaby ventured, suddenly feeling very stupid.

"Zere was no plague." Jacques spat. "Zere's never been any plague. Zree years ago was when the war was at its peak. Zousands lost zeir lives!"

"We were told that a plague had spread across the empire." Barnaby replied, horrified. "We were encouraged not to travel too far from home."

"You were lied to." Jacques snarled, shaking his head. "Zey told you to stay home so zey'd know where you were. Countless young men were pressed into service."

Barnaby suppressed a curse, caressing his forehead as several pieces fell into place. While no village could be described as 'nearby' to his home, he had heard reports of young men going missing from those which were closest, several of them vanishing from their houses with only the slightest trace of a struggle.

"That's horrendous." He declared, feeling an unusual bout of gratitude for his isolated upbringing. It may have saved him from a darker fate.

"Zat is ze nature of most great empires." Jacques shrugged. "Honestly, I must speak wiz your Captain about a reading program. Ze illiteracy on zis ship is utterly deplorable."

"So, if there was no plague, how did the Prince pass away?" Barnaby asked, trying to get them back on track. His curiosity was at its peak.

"Ze battle did not go well." Jacques explained, folding his arms. "Outnumbered as zey were, two of ze empire's fleet were swiftly destroyed, forcing ze Prince's vessel into close-quarters with ze enemy. It was a valiant strategy, an attempt to bottleneck zem until reinforcements could arrive. Sadly, ze Prince's men were overwhelmed, and he was captured by ze enemy commander. Trigger was left wiz an impossible choice. Surrender, and lose ze harbor, or fire on ze Prince's vessel, completing ze bottleneck, yet killing ze Prince as well. He had zousands of lives in one hand, and royalty in ze ozer. So far as I'm concerned, he made ze right choice."

"He fired?"

"Of course."

"So, that's why the Empress hates him." Barnaby mused. "He killed her brother."

"No." Jacques laughed. "Had he simply killed her brozer, she would have found a way to forgive him. Ze reason she hates him, is because he killed her brozer, and zen lost ze harbor anyway."

Barnaby's jaw dropped, and it took a very conscious effort to lock it back in place.

"How!?" He exclaimed. "Did they push past the bottleneck?"

"No. Trigger kept zem pinned for two hours. Regrettably, zis meant he missed ze troops who had circled round by land. Zey took ze city while his back was turned, slaughtering hundreds. It is one of ze greatest defeats ze Empire has ever suffered."

"But that's hardly his fault!" Barnaby protested. "They were outnumbered, and it was the Prince's decision to fight the enemy head-on. He would have known the risks!"

"Royalty rarely suffer for zeir mistakes." Jacques shrugged. "Zat burden falls to we lesser men."

"That's bullshit!"

"Zat is the way of zings. Ze Prince dies a selfless hero, your Captain is punished for confronting ze consequences. He was discharged from ze navy, and society in general. Outcast from his family, and branded wiz his current moniker."

"Trigger's not his real name?"

"No. After ze ordeal, he was branded as Captain Trigger-happy, due to his apparent eagerness to open fire. Eventually, it was shortened to Trigger. An achievement on his part, if you ask me."

Barnaby didn't reply, allowing this barrage of information to sink in. It explained the disdain their Captain often faced, yet as far as he was concerned, did little to explain the man himself. In his position, Barnaby would have buckled, giving himself entirely to depression, wine and whores. By contrast, Trigger seemed to have gained some kind of supernatural resolve, a drive that pushed him onwards, with faultless discipline and endless courage.

Barnaby had always been prone to admiration, yet usually it was reserved for those he had never met, people whose deeds had spread across the land, growing well beyond their storied champion. Now, however, he couldn't help but feel a small sense of pride in their fallen Captain, and his unwavering commitment to his cause and crew.

"Not many people smile after hearing zat story." Jacques remarked, studying his expression.

"They mustn't be listening, then." Barnaby shrugged. "From what I heard, there's every re- "

He was interrupted by the creak of Trigger's door, which swung loosely in its wonky hinges. Sheridan was first to emerge, stooping beneath the frame and groaning as she stretched to her full height. Trigger was right behind her, his bruised hand clasping a folded chart.

"Looks as zough we have our course." Jacques observed, gesturing at the map.

"Gentlemen, your attention!" Sheridan roared, raising a gloved hand. Today she had opted for a black and woolen affair, the smooth fibers stretching from fingers to forearm. They weren't her most attractive pair, but goodness did they look snug.

The crew ceased its activities, looking to their Captain and First Mate. Trigger offered Sheridan a quiet thanks, unfurling the map as he stepped to the fore.

"I thank you for your patience." He declared, showing them all the chartered course. "Sheridan and I did not make this decision lightly, yet we both feel that it is our best option, considering the information we acquired from the *Swaying Deck*."

Murmurs of concern rose from the crew, heads flicking as they discussed the choice. Their concern was not quite at the level inspired by the Howlers, yet more than a few appeared deeply uncertain, kneading rope between their fingers and shuffling on their feet. Barnaby himself was of two minds, yet for the most part found himself agreeing.

The map showed them heading north-west, through a stretch of sea regarded as the Pauper's Flip. The Flip was known to be risky, though in a very different way to most sections of the Tides. Those who sailed the Flip had but two possible outcomes, the results as different as night and day. You either passed through in record time, untouched by weather, sea or beast, or you never passed through at all. Countless ships had been lost to the Flip, vanishing from existence without record or trace. No one knew what terror stalked its misty waves, or could venture so much as an educated guess. Whatever it was, it had never left survivors, or even a distant, hidden witness. Still, more than half the ships that chanced it slipped through unscathed, and with Hargrave and Carnage already well-ahead of them, they needed to take a few beneficial risks.

"I know you have concerns." Trigger announced, holding up a hand and silencing the crew. "As always, you are free to voice them. However, we are losing time, and therefore must prioritize speed. It will be three days before we reach the Pauper's Flip, and we can alter our course at any stage before that point. Therefore, if you have a complaint, I ask you to please hold it for now, and instead focus on our tasks and bearing. When your work is done, you may take your complaint to Mr. Frank, who will present them all to me in a cohesive and comprehensive manner. If your arguments prove valid, I will reconsider. Am I understood?"

"Aye, Captain!"

"Excellent." Trigger nodded, flashing a grin. "Set to work, men. We've got exciting days ahead."

The crew offered a rowdy cheer, Trigger's confidence bolstering their own. Barnaby felt rather buoyed as well, and actually contemplated mopping some of the newly laid timbers.

Such enthusiasm faded as he spied the ships cat, which was shitting merrily on the starboard prow.

"Hey, Magwa!" He called, waving at the Kalyute.

"Yes?" Came the deep reply. Magwa was currently off-duty, and was napping in the shadow of their swaying mast.

"Is that a bad omen?" Barnaby asked, pointing at the cat.

"Probably." Magwa answered, without opening his eyes.

Chapter Twelve

Trigger waved a hand through the endless mist, watching his fingertips vanish in the seeping haze. He could just perceive the miniscule droplets that comprised the milky veil, the tiny pearls coating every surface with a fine sheen of freezing moisture. Most of his crew had spent the past week shivering, their clothing woefully ill-equipped to deal with such persistent saturation. Even below deck there was no relief, the mist seeping through the timbers without apparent regard for physical boundaries or limitations. More than a few of his men had fallen ill, their lungs swelling beneath the weight of unwanted fluids. His naval coat had served to protect him, while Sheridan had donated many of her garments in an effort to stem the flow of disease. The result had left him with the most oddly garbed crew the seas had ever seen, every able-bodied man swaddled from head-to-foot in silken dresses, scarfs and skirts. Frank had actually claimed himself a rather fetching brazier, which he had bound around his lips as a makeshift mask.

"I'm still surprised you gave him that." Trigger remarked, watching as Frank navigated his way across the mist-strewn deck.

"I've never worn it." Sheridan shrugged. "Didn't fit."

"And the rest?"

"Some of it I've worn too much, and needed to replace. Others I'll be wanting back, once we're through the mist. Not Gary's, though. We'll be burning that."

"Understandable."

The tapping of wood-on-wood alerted them to Beaufort's approach, Magwa and Barnaby in-tow. The trio had formed a bizarre friendship, one which had seen Barnaby's stock rising among the crew. Beaufort alone was a deterrent to bullying, yet with the Kalyute at his side, Barnaby was essentially untouchable.

"Fine day." Beaufort declared, gesturing at their obscured surroundings.

"Is it day?" Sheridan asked, shielding her eyes and glancing upward.

"We didn't walk into you, so I'd say it's likely." Beaufort grinned, hooking his thumbs through his belt.

"No one could walk into you; the noise you make with that thing." Sheridan teased, indicating his leg.

"In zis place, zat is a blessing." Beaufort laughed, patting the prosthesis.

"I'm glad you've adapted to it so well." Trigger nodded. "I've seen such a wound cripple many for life."

"Zey must have never had a reason to go for a walk." Beaufort chuckled, earning a smile from Barnaby. "As it so happens, we have one at zis very moment. Tell him, Barnaby."

At first the young man jumped, clearly unprepared to be summoned. He rallied quite well, however, only stuttering three times before the words escaped his lips.

"Well, Captain, you see, Jacques and I were thinking it would be a good idea if more of the crew learned to read. I mean, it would have helped you a lot, back on the *Swaying Deck*, and I'm sure it would come in handy further down the line. Frank's the Quartermaster, yet he can't read a word, or do any math that's bigger than his fingers, and, well, he's got less of those than most."

"Fewer." Trigger corrected, grinning.

"P-pardon?"

"He's got fewer fingers. We're talking individual units, not a singular mass. Were you more educated, you would know this, which is why I heartily endorse the plan."

Barnaby glanced at Beaufort, who gave him a subtle wink.

"He likes it." The big man explained.

"Oh! Great!" Barnaby beamed.

"The only issue is time." Trigger declared. "I'm not exactly in a position to give classes."

"I am." Beaufort announced, tapping his chest. "My duties are limited, considering my leg, and I would enjoy feeling somewhat useful again."

Trigger nodded, slowly, feeling his enthusiasm somewhat lessened. Yes, Beaufort had the time, and the knowledge. He had taught himself the finer arts, and would doubtless be capable of doing the same for others. Such a program would also give him boundless access to any crewmember interested, as well a subject over which they could bond. If it were a way to undermine him, while reinforcing his own position, it was a brilliant move indeed.

Trigger shook the thought away. Beaufort had vouched for him on the *Swaying Deck*. He had earned a measure of trust. Besides, Trigger would enjoy hearing conversations that consisted of something more than tits, ale and Gary's various growths. Honestly, it's as though the man were a sentient garden.

"A brilliant idea." He conceded, nodding in Beaufort's direction. The swordsman bowed his head, feigning modesty.

"It was all Barnaby's."

Trigger doubted this, still, he was happy to pretend otherwise. If the crew thought the boy had begun a program that benefited them all, they might be inclined to accept him for reasons other than his friend's physical might.

"You're oddly silent, Magwa." Sheridan observed, studying the Kalyute. Magwa gazed back at her, somehow appearing fearsome, despite the sequined dress he had swaddled about his core.

"Mist bad omen." He declared, wiping his shining skin.

"Your people have a lot of those." Sheridan frowned. "Do you have any good ones?"

"Not really. We come from place where everything trying to kill you. You make it to end of day, that good omen."

"Fair enough." Sheridan laughed, sweeping back her wig. It was clinging to her cheeks as though she'd been swimming for hours, the false hair threatening to slip from her skull.

The ship rocked slightly, as though touched by an abnormal wave.

"Sunniday, how is the sea faring?" Trigger asked, unable to see their lookout through the veil of mist.

For a moment, there was silence.

"I'm going to be honest Captain, I really can't tell. I haven't been able to see a thing for the past two days."

"Then what exactly have you been doing up there?"

More silence.

"Napping, mostly."

Trigger ran a hand through his hair, taking a calming breath.

"Mr. Sunniday?"

"Aye, Captain?"

"That's half-rations."

"Aye, Captain."

Accepting their current blindness, they waited patiently for several minutes, until yet another wayward spray thumped against their hull. Trigger attempted to discern if it was stronger than the first, yet eventually conceded that if it were, the difference was so slight as to be irrelevant. Still, in such perilous and unknown seas, it would be foolish to ignore any irregularity.

"Mr. Frank!"

"Yes, Captain?" His Quartermaster saluted, emerging from the clinging fog.

"The unusual waves. Have you been feeling them as well?"

"Aye. I was a bit worried at first, as they don't make a lick of sense considering the current. Still, the sea's always been a fickle bi- "

Trigger raised an eyebrow.

"Unpredictable." Frank corrected. "It's always been unpredictable."

"True, though I believe it merits inspection." Trigger replied. "You will work with Mr. Beaufort to record each collision, and the span of time that stretches between them."

"Me?" Beaufort asked, cocking his head to one side.

"Indeed. Consider it a test of your patience. If you're going to teach an entire crew how to read and write, you're probably going to need it."

"Can't argue wiz zat." Beaufort shrugged.

"Can I help?" Barnaby asked, his tone almost pleading.

"Are your other duties complete?"

"Aye, Captain. The cat is fed and the deck is clean."

Trigger blinked, running a hand through his sodden hair.

"Barnaby, are those the entirety of your duties?"

"Aye, Captain."

Trigger closed his eyes. Gods, give him strength.

"Mr. Frank?"

The Quartermaster gave a sheepish bow, twisting a hem between his fingers. Sheridan had loaned him a fetching red shawl, which Frank had adopted with surprising enthusiasm.

"Aye, Captain?"

"I believe it's time Barnaby was made a full member of the crew. Split the mopping between other crewmen, and assign him a few more complex tasks. Not too many, however. He is still responsible for the cat's wellbeing."

"I am?" Barnaby asked, sounding both disappointed and slightly relieved.

"You are. I've never seen anyone bond with him so quickly, or lay down their life so readily for his. You faced the Howlers for him, Barnaby. So long as you are on this ship, you will be his keeper."

"Yay?" Barnaby replied, his face the essence of confusion. Trigger fought hard to suppress a smile.

"Whoop!"

Another wave broke against them, this one wielding enough force to throw Sheridan from the banister. She caught herself on Trigger's shoulder, the brief contact serving as an effective reminder of both her size and power. His knees had been close to buckling.

"I believe that's a signal to begin counting." Trigger nodded, gesturing at Frank. "If they haven't ceased in the next three hours, report back to me with your findings."

"Aye, Captain."

Beaufort and Frank vanished into the mist, swiftly followed by Barnaby and Magwa. The Kalyute appeared even more unsettled, drumming his fingers against his axe in expectation of a fight.

"Do you think we should be worried?" Sheridan asked, peering over the banister. The sea below was completely lost, buried beneath near-solid fog.

Trigger stood beside her, contemplating the veil which had consumed their world.

"That's an excellent question." He replied, his mind making shapes in the swirling mist. "Unfortunately, I don't really know the answer."

Their vigil dragged on at a tedious pace, the arrival of night eroding even the most rudimentary sight. The deck was divided into fragments, isolated pockets of existence, a few stray lamps sheltering the shivering crewmen within. As for the waves, Trigger didn't need Beaufort's report to know that they were increasing in both size and frequency, the collisions tossing their vessel as though it were a ball between two children. He had dismissed the helmsman, opting to steer the *Blackbird* himself, just in case the capricious seas threw them entirely off-course. To lose their way in such shrouded conditions would be an absolute disaster, and he had no wish to burden any crewman with such a heavy responsibility.

"What in the God's names is this?" Sheridan growled, clinging to the banister as the ship lurched to one side.

"You'd have to ask them." Trigger replied, spitting the words through gritted teeth. The wheel was straining against his grasp, begging to be given free reign.

BOOM!

"Oh, good." Sheridan sighed, straightening her disheveled wig. "They're starting again."

If the savage seas weren't concern enough, fate had seen fit to supply another trial, the fire of distant cannons growing ever closer as they struggled through the swelling tides. At first, they had been simple whispers, yet as the combatants drew nearer their battle had become increasingly audible, the flash of gunpowder creating momentary stars in the infinite mist. Glancing over his shoulder, Trigger could see that they had somehow gained even more ground, the spark of their cannons no more than two miles distant.

"What wind are they catching?" He murmured, studying their own billowing sails. Further repairs had been made to their numerous tears, and he was certain that they were performing at peak capacity. Whatever was allowing their pursuers to gain so rapidly, it had nothing to do with the *Blackbird's* failings.

BOOM!

BOOM!

On and on the night crawled, intermittent cannon blasts accompanied by the ceaseless pounding of growing waves. Grappling with the wheel, Trigger was unable to give the combatants his full attention, yet Sheridan's eyes never wavered, tracking the battle with hawk-like focus.

"Only one of them is firing." She eventually declared, as the air was split by another thunderous volley.

"Pardon?" Trigger asked, holding steady against a particularly cruel wave.

"Only one of the ships is firing. Gods, I can't really see if there is another ship. All I know is that the cannon fire is coming from the same vessel, every single time."

"There's been no retaliation?"

"None that I can see. Also, there's been so much fire, yet no sound of a shot finding its mark."

"One could be excused for missing, in conditions such as these."

"That many times? Unless every man on that ship is blind, deaf and dumb, I find it highly unlikely."

"What are you proposing, then?"

Sheridan fanned herself, creating a spiral of mist around the thin wooden blades.

"That they're either terrible shots, or that there's something more here than a simple battle."

"Oh." Trigger sighed, stretching his aching shoulders. "Fantastic."

Whoosh!

Trigger crumpled as the shot streaked past, his lips almost kissing its iron surface. The passing wind threw his hair to one side, straining his eardrums to their absolute limit. For several moments his balance was destroyed, yet with a snarl of resolve Trigger kept their vessel steady, holding the wheel as tightly as he were able.

"You there! Swing to starboard! It's coming up on your port side!"

The voice cut to Trigger's core, despite the ringing in his ears. It was amplified to an inhuman degree, much like the Empress's had been at the beginning of the Tides. This made no sense, however, as Trigger knew all too well the complex sequences required to achieve such an effect, and was certain that such intricacies were impossible to recreate on the open seas.

"Who's there!?" He demanded, keeping the *Blackbird* on course. He wasn't going to risk his crew on the words of some ethereal madman.

"It doesn't fucking matter! Swing to starboard!"

"Explanations first!"

"Captain!"

Sheridan's cry disturbed him, such palpable fear completely unfamiliar from her powerful lips. He followed her shaking finger, watching as the mist unfurled to reveal a tall and skeletal mast, its swaying timbers embalmed by scraps of decaying sail.

"Oh Gods." He whispered, spying the black fungus which was thriving on the wood.

He wrenched the *Blackbird* starboard, their hull bouncing wildly on the furious waves. The skeleton ship followed as though it were a living creature, cutting through the tide like a serpent through grass.

"Arm the cannons!" He roared, as its blackened hull oozed towards their own. He could hear his men responding, doors banging and feet pounding as they raced to obey. Despite this, he knew they would be too slow, the abominations rapid approach defying all laws of nature.

"It's going to ram us." Sheridan declared, retreating from the banister. At first, the vessel seemed determined to fulfill her prophecy, bearing down on them with a hunger that set Trigger's heart against his chest. They would never survive such a crushing blow.

Tap.

It was the lightest sound of impact, a small puff of air that completely defied the enormous figure it served to announce. The giant leapt upon their vessel without a hint of effort or concern, springing from the mist as though conjured from a world beyond their own.

"Evening." The giant greeted, bowing his shaggy head. A second later he had darted across the deck, his hands outstretched towards their coming demise.

Sheridan lunged towards him, mighty arms tensed with brutal intent.

"What are you- "

Her words were cut short by an eruption of flame, the golden wall streaming from the stranger's gloved palms. It engulfed their pursuer, a raging inferno on the cold, dark sea. It completely dispelled a portion of the mist, blasting it aside and allowing Trigger an unimpeded view of the divine spectacle occurring right before his eyes.

"Who are you?" He asked, unable to contain his awe.

The giant looked to him with sapphire eyes, sweat-soaked face twisting into a cheeky grin.

"Someone you should listen to." He replied, his python-like arms beginning to shake. "Now, get us moving as quick as you can. This won't stop it for long."

Trigger studied the giant, and then chanced a glance at the small sun he had summoned.

Arguing did seem like a poor choice of action.

****

What the fuck was going on?

Barnaby hadn't bothered to descend when the others headed for the cannons. He was too weak to lift a cannonball, or to position the cannons themselves. He would just be another obstacle in an already crowded place, and he had sense enough not to make such a burden of himself. This meant that he was practically the only crewman on deck when the mysterious figure appeared, and that he had the best view possible of the display he was creating.

Sorcery. Genuine sorcery. Not some relic of ages long past, or a hidden secret of the royal family. This was a man who could spit fire from his fingers, and lay waste to an entire ship with a mere sweep of his arm.

Perhaps he was in the market for an apprentice?

"Fire!"

The deck shuddered as the cannons bellowed, spewing forth their cargo with a cacophonous crack. They tore into the flames and the ship they had restrained, though despite their accuracy not a single timber cracked, the shots apparently striking nothing but air as they flew into the fog.

"What are you?" Barnaby asked, shielding his eyes from the fires glare.

The flames shifted in reply, a bulge forming in their brilliant center. The growth swelled with every moment, the fire splitting like fabric as it grew too great to restrain, an enormous clump of wood and moss filling the entire sky above them. Barnaby staggered backwards as he observed its enormity, his gaze fixing on one particular point in the pulsing, swelling construct.

A robed and shadowed figure, its black eyes fixed directly on him.

"Oh, fuck." He whispered, searching for somewhere to hide.

At sea, your options are few.

The great hammer began to descend, collapsing towards their vessel with a hideous groan. Dropping to his knees, Barnaby didn't bother shielding his face. It's not like it would make any difference.

BOOM!

The shift in air pressure was catastrophic, popping his ears and sending tears blasting from his eyes. The *Blackbird* sunk beneath the weight of the impact, the wooden growth driving them down, down into the freezing sea. Water splashed at Barnaby's waist, chilling him to his very core, yet all he could do was rejoice, his jaw hanging wide as he marveled at the display above.

The giant had shielded them, somehow, someway. The colossal blow had been halted mere feet from their mast, crashing against a dome of pure sorcerous might. He could see their savior now, bent to one knee by the crushing strain, his ears and eyes bleeding from such astounding effort.

Sadly, their foe seemed ready to strike again.

The moss-strewn leviathan shifted, arcing upwards in preparation of its second blow. Without thinking Barnaby sprinted towards the prow, his feet carrying him faster than he'd ever moved before.

"The face!" He screamed, pointing at the figure in the wood. "Shoot the face!"

Any other Captain would have been lost. Fear would have left them deaf to his words, or crippled in their movement.

Not Trigger.

The Captain looked to him the moment he spoke, following his finger with uncanny precision. An instant later his pistol was drawn, the barrel swiveling towards their eldritch foe.

Trigger closed one eye, and took a deep breath.

CRACK!

The shot rang out across the deck, a clap of thunder followed by a hideous scream. The mass of timber and moss left the being within it almost completely shielded, yet Trigger had struck true. Black blood peppered the timbers as the creature veered sideways, sending chunks of wood and fungus plummeting towards their vessel. The club it had constructed was rapidly collapsing, threatening to bury them all beneath tons of festering debris.

"Hold on!" The giant boomed, rising to his feet and spreading his arms.

Barnaby looked desperately to either side. His choice of handholds was woefully few.

The giant's palms came together, releasing a burst of energy that set Barnaby's teeth on edge. The force propelled their vessel as though it were a leaf on a pond, caught in the fury of some rising tempest. Barnaby's feet were knocked out from underneath him, and as he fell he spied the final moments of the wooden construct, the bulk of its remains missing them as they blasted across the seas.

Not all, however.

The moss crashed down with the weight of sodden mud, crushing him against the deck. His mouth and nose were clogged by the smearing ooze, the sheer stench causing him to gag and retch. He fought desperately to pull himself free, yet their staggering speed impeded his already questionable balance, and it was not until their vessel slowed that Barnaby was finally able to peel himself clear of the clinging muck.

"Barnaby!"

He was pulled upwards by a firm and powerful hand, it's slender fingers swaddled in silk.

"Are you alright?" Sheridan asked, so concerned that she failed to notice the moss now clinging to her glove.

Barnaby was genuinely touched.

"I...I think I'm ok." He replied, attempting to wipe his hands. It spread the moss further across his shirt.

"Glad to hear it." The giant announced, swaggering towards them with a cheeky grin. "Shoot it in the face. That may be the best advice I've ever heard. And you-" He added, turning to the approaching Trigger "-what a fucking shot! Right between the eyes, in the middle of total insanity! I have to say, not many things surprise me, but this ship has certainly got me curious!"

"Curious?"

Sheridan practically barked the word, streaking across the deck and seizing the giant by his oversized collar. In a display of tremendous strength, she actually succeeded in lifting him high above her head, shaking him as though he were an insolent child.

"Who are you?" She demanded. "What was that...*thing*? Why did you lead it towards us?"

Despite his unfavorable position, the giant was clearly delighted.

"Put me down, and I'll answer all your questions." He declared, patting her thick arms. "Though, I insist you answer some of mine. Honestly, you're the quirkiest crew I've ever seen."

"Release him." Trigger ordered, rubbing his finger against his thumb. "We've seen what he can do. It would be foolish to try and force his hand."

Sheridan's face scrunched with distaste. Still, she did as she was told.

"Clever, too." The giant declared, nodding at Trigger. "That's good to know."

"Thank you." Trigger announced, folding his arms. "Now, if you would please answer her questions?"

The giant nodded, blue eyes flashing in the misty night.

"I'm a fellow Captain, or at least, I was. As you can see, the beast has left me without vessel or crew."

"What's your name?" Sheridan frowned. "What was your vessel?"

"Never had a chance to name it." The giant shrugged. "I woke up, hopped aboard, and started sailing as fast as I could. I knew that thing wouldn't be far behind, and was trying to gain some distance. It caught me, though. Always does."

"And your name?"

"Unimportant."

"I'm not inclined to trust a man who refuses to tell me his name. I've been down that road quite recently."

"Fair enough." The giant chuckled. "Though, tell me, was that man capable of summoning suns from thin air?"

Trigger unfolded his mist-soaked arms, letting them sink to his sword and gun.

"You move to threats quickly."

"Only when pressed." The giant shrugged. "Frankly, it saves a lot of time."

"Captain!"

Frank burst onto the deck, the rest of the crew in tow. Each one of them was armed to the teeth, their pistols levelled at the giant's head, chest and groin.

"Hey." The giant nodded, giving them a wave.

"Are we safe, Captain?" Frank asked, moving cautiously towards them. The others remained still, keeping their weapons ready.

"An excellent question, Mr. Frank." Trigger replied. "Are we?"

The giant cocked his head, squinting with thought.

"You're safe from me, if that's what you're asking. As for the creature we fought, that's a hard no. That thing will follow me to the ends of your world, and probably beyond. It'll be worse when it returns, as well. We've been playing cat-and-mouse for weeks, and I'd managed to severely weaken it. Your bullet would have been useless if it were at full-strength."

"That thing is following you?" Frank asked, studying the giant.

"It is."

Frank glanced over his shoulder at their assembled crew, his forehead creasing with iron resolve.

"Well then, I'd say our next step is pretty bloody obvious."

He cocked his pistol, aiming towards the giant's face.

"Mr. Frank!" Trigger roared, stepping between the pair. "That's half-rations, and if you fail to lower your pistol the instant I finish speaking, I will consider it outright mutiny. Am I understood!?"

"He just said that he's what the creature wants!" Frank argued, lowering his pistol. "I say we put a bullet in his head, and throw his carcass overboard! His life isn't worth our crew's!"

Murmurs of agreement followed his words, a fact of which Trigger was clearly aware.

"No one has suggested as much." He replied, adjusting his coat. "Yet that doesn't mean we should instantly resort to murder."

"I'd listen to your Captain." The giant shrugged. "The creature hunts me, yes, but it wants to capture me alive. If it found that someone else had claimed the kill, well, Gods pity that poor bastard."

"You're bluffing." Frank sneered.

"I'm not. I have no reason to. I could take you all, if need be."

This wasn't a lie. Of that, Barnaby had no doubts.

"Well then, what do you propose?" Trigger asked, meeting the giant's gaze. "We can't overcome you, and I won't ask my crew to sail with a man who brings such danger down upon them."

The giant scratched his shoulder, blue eyes fixed on Trigger's own.

"I've put you in a poor position." He declared, his uncanny features crinkling with what may have been pity. "I can see that. Balancing your people's welfare against your own moral compass. It's never an easy task. You have my apologies."

"Thank you, though, that fails to answer my question."

"I know." The giant grinned, giving their crew another curious glance. He settled on Barnaby, that cheeky smile growing as he beheld his moss-stained form.

"I won't stay." He announced, his voice rumbling across the deck. "Not if you don't want me to. Take a vote, and if you decide to cast me out, I'll go without complaint. All I ask for is a small vessel, and enough rations to return to shore."

"Thank you." Trigger nodded, visibly relieved.

"I vote he goes." Frank announced, raising his hand. "We don't know him, and we don't owe him. Give him what he wants, so long as he's far away."

Much of the crew roared in agreement, their own hands rising high.

Barnaby was surprised to see Jacques' among them. Apparently, so was the giant.

"You too, Beaufort?" He chuckled. "Were you not in my position, just a few short weeks ago?"

"No." Jacques replied, folding his arms. "I can honestly say zat I have never been pursued by a possessed and living ship. You represent danger, good sir, and I see no reason to invite you aboard."

The words struck Barnaby hard, the cold and practical dismissal clashing with the image he had developed of Captain Jacques Beaufort.

"Huh. Fair enough." The giant nodded, though a harsh edge had crept into his tone. "That seems to be a majority, Captain."

Barnaby watched as Trigger considered the hands, the Captain clearly struggling to contain his disapproval. His men had chosen cowardice, a decision which could never sit well.

"Are you all resolved?" Trigger asked, making one last attempt to redeem their valor. "Yes, this man brings danger, yet as we have seen, he is more than willing to combat that peril with bravery and skill. More than that, he is a being in need, one whom we possess the capacity to aid. Do you really wish to cast him aside?"

The crew looked to one another, considering their Captain's noble words.

"Yeah." Frank nodded, speaking for them all. "Fuck him."

Trigger raised an eyebrow, yet for the first time, Frank didn't recant.

"I'll take the ration cut." The Quartermaster declared. "It's worth it to keep my boys safe. We can see where you're coming from, Captain, and believe me, there isn't a man here who doesn't respect your compassion. Still, that same good nature is blinding you. This man is an unnecessary risk, and you charged me with looking out for the crew. That's what I'm doing. That's what we're all doing. We've come too far to let this stranger get us killed."

Barnaby blinked in surprise, impressed by both Frank's eloquence and passion. The deformed bastard genuinely cared.

Trigger's reaction was restrained, the Captain merely rubbing his thumb against his finger as he considered his crew's decision. The giant studied him in silence, completely unfazed by this turn of events.

It was Sheridan who took command.

"The crew's spoken, Captain." She declared, placing her hand on his shoulder.

The action seemed to wake him, Trigger standing tall as he turned to address their unwanted passenger.

"I will see that your every request is met." He promised. "You will have enough provisions to reach the shore, and our most stable dingy to accommodate the journey."

"That's more than fair." The giant replied, as a particularly vicious wave crashed against their hull. It was the first for several minutes, their sorcerous voyage having carried them clear of the unusually capricious seas.

"Does that mean the creature is returning?" Squeaked Gary, gazing around in fear.

"What, the water?" The giant frowned. "Oh, no. I haven't got a clue what's been causing that."

"You mean there's something else out here!?"

"Probably." The giant shrugged, giving Gary a cheeky grin.

The entire crew took a wary step backwards, studying the mist with renewed suspicion.

"On that note, I think it's time I depart." The giant remarked, looking once more to Trigger.

"I'd say it's for the best." Trigger sighed, considering his fearful crew.

It didn't take long for the preparations to be made, the cook assembling the rations with more haste than Barnaby had ever believed him capable. The whole crew pitched in to make the dingy sea-worthy, each of them regarding the giant as a kind of sentient curse, a peril that must be removed as soon as they were able. Less than an hour had passed before the giant was squatting in his dingy, regarding the rations with an easy smile.

"You *were* generous." He nodded, bowing his head in Trigger's direction.

"I only hope that they prove adequate."

"I'm sure they will." The giant replied, closing the sack and placing it between his massive feet. "Though, I don't think your crew would mind if I starved along the way."

Barnaby didn't doubt it. With the giant now minutes from departing, the rest of the crew had dispersed, essentially ignoring the problem until it went away. Even Jacques had averted his attention, teaching Gary how to spell as a method of distraction.

Not Barnaby, however. He had ventured as close as possible, a small part of him hoping that the giant would once again take notice, and offer him a place in that tiny, overburdened vessel.

"Barnaby should hang back." Whispered Magwa, appearing at his side.

"Why?"

"Darkness lurks beneath his eyes." Magwa replied, gripping the handle of his hatchet. "We have met two monsters tonight."

"You think everything is a bad omen."

"Yes. This time, Magwa mean it."

"Well, I think I'm ready to leave." The giant announced, looking to Magwa as though he had heard the exchange.

"Very well." Trigger replied, seizing the rope. "Once again, you have my apologies. Were it up to me, I would have allowed you to stay."

"I know." The giant shrugged. "You're a good man. That's a hard road to walk, especially as a leader. You're going to make few friends, and countless enemies. Trust me though, it's worth it, in the end."

"And why is that?" Trigger asked, lowering him towards the sea. As his face sank beneath the banister, Barnaby caught sight of the giant's expression, which had twisted into genuine sorrow.

"So few people end their lives being proud of who they are." The giant explained, voice fading as the rope dragged on. "They betray who they are for the most ridiculous of reasons. You know who you are, Trigger. Embrace it. Share it with those you love. Otherwise, you might just find yourself adrift, with only a sack of cheese and biscuits to keep you going on."

There was a mild splash as the dingy struck sea, followed by the slap of oars as they carved apart the waves. Barnaby joined Trigger at the banister's edge, watching the giant's departure with strained and narrowed eyes. He was gone from sight in a matter of moments, his powerful stroke driving him into the beckoning fog. He faded as suddenly as he'd arrived, a dark shadow collapsing into the endless, drifting white.

"Who was he?" Barnaby eventually asked, turning to his silent Captain.

Trigger ran a hand through his sodden hair, flicking the droplets to the ocean below.

"A phantom." The Captain replied, adjusting his faded coat. "Nothing more."

Chapter Thirteen

He'd had enough of mist. Of that, he was certain.

Trigger wrenched the wheel sideways at Sunniday's command, the column rearing up before them as though it were a surfacing whale. The *Blackbird* barely avoided its jagged surface, a few of the crewman reaching out to stroke its brittle edge.

"This one's hot!" Remarked Bradley, adding to the tally. At first the touching had been a show of bravado, the more reckless men placing themselves intentionally close to harm. A few of them had begun noticing inconsistencies, however, the temperature of the pylons ranging from ice-cold to unpleasantly warm. What's more, the sea had returned to its earlier raging, smashing against them from all sides.

"I'd say it was the hottest." Barnaby remarked, rubbing his palm.

"I'd say you're right." Frank acknowledged, looking at his own. "They've been getting hotter the further we go."

The statement was cause for concern, yet the conversation that preceded it brought a smile to Trigger's face. Frank had spoken to Barnaby with open respect, reflecting the mood currently permeating the crew. The young man's actions during their bizarre encounter had spread like wildfire, Beaufort using his gift for exaggeration to enhance Barnaby's achievements far beyond the reality. At this point, most believed that Barnaby had not only identified the strange ships weakness, but that he had personally guided Trigger's arm in making the impossible shot. Trigger didn't mind, however. The rumors had gifted Barnaby confidence without cockiness, and served to unite the crew. This newfound comradery was the sole reason for their continued existence, the sea's constant barrage having worn them all down both physically and mentally.

"Captain, swing to port!"

Trigger did as he was told, another shadowed colossus rising to his right. He spun the wheel as swiftly as he could, yet the savage waves denied him, driving their vessel onwards at a furious pace. With a hideous smash they struck the rugged pillar, splinters flying as each crewman struggled to keep their feet.

Most failed.

Trigger gritted his teeth as they bounced from the stone, cursing their ill-fortune. They had little timber remaining from their last round of repairs, and if the damage proved too extensive, there would be nothing they could do.

Crack!

Thud.

"Bugger me!"

Trigger glanced over his shoulder, attempting to discover the source of the shout. It proved to be Bradley, who was lying spread-eagle across the deck, his bulky framed pinned beneath an odd assortment of pale sticks. No, not sticks.

Bones.

"Sheridan, take the wheel." He ordered, stepping aside and racing from the prow. A small crowd was forming around Bradley, who was regarding his assailant with fear and disgust.

"Are you injured?" Trigger asked, pushing his way to the fore.

"Nah." Bradley replied, tossing the skeleton aside. "He just caught me by surprise."

"Where did it come from?" Trigger asked, bending to inspect the bones.

"Up there." Bradley replied, pointing. "I think they fell off that bloody pillar."

Trigger frowned, running a hand through his sodden hair.

"Are you certain?"

"Well, it was either that, or a pissed of seagull with a massive appetite."

"I doubt it." Trigger smiled, glad to see that Bradley was indeed unharmed.

"Sheridan! Swing to starboard!"

They all stumbled as Sheridan obeyed, barely avoiding another stone.

"What were the Gods thinking when they made a place like this?" Muttered Gary, crouching low.

Trigger couldn't reply. He was too busy racing towards the pillar, reaching out with a wild dive. He made contact by the tips of his fingers, yet even that was enough to feel the prodigious heat emanating from within.

"The sea is getting rougher." He pondered, staring at his hand. "While the stone is getting warmer…"

"What does it mean?" Asked Frank, attempting to gaze at the water below. Once again, the fog proved far too thick.

"One moment." Trigger declared, seizing a nearby rope. With one swift motion he threw himself overboard, using its length to control his descent. It didn't take long to reach the ocean, the shouts of his crew lost beneath its foaming waves.

"Gods." Trigger breathed, wiping his sweat-soaked face.

The sea was boiling, writhing and frothing as some unknown force heated them to extremes. In a moment of clarity, Trigger realized that the mist wasn't actually mist at all. It was steam, the result of a process which defied all logic and sense. With a tentative hand, he reached towards the writhing foam, tracing it with the tip of his finger. To say that it was scalding would be quite the understatement.

"Captain!"

He could barely hear Frank's voice over the raging water, it's furious hiss almost as draining as the heat itself.

"Yes, Mr. Frank!?" He replied, struggling to keep his composure.

"Hold on!"

"Pardon?"

The ship swung sideways, the shift so violent that Trigger was sent flailing outwards from the hull. His boots skimmed the sea as they twisted to port, desperately trying to avoid another steaming pillar. Unfortunately, the sea had different ideas, pressing them towards the stone with unrelenting force.

If the vessel struck, Trigger would be crushed between them.

With a grunt of effort he began to climb, his sweaty palms slipping on the soaking rope. For every inch gained, he lost another, the pillar growing closer with each moment. He could hear more shouting from above, and could feel the tug as they attempted to haul him upwards.

They wouldn't be in time.

Trigger braced himself for impact, weighing his few options. Sheridan may yet avoid collision, and he still had time to drop below the ship, trusting himself to the boiling sea. He would be burned, surely, yet there was a slight chance that he'd survive. Against the rock, however, he had no such odds.

"Captain!"

A powerful hand seized his sleeve, dragging him sideways with a savage yank. Trigger didn't fight it, letting himself be pulled towards Magwa's snarling face, the Kalyute's veins bulging with the strain of his weight. The savage was hanging from a damaged cannon-port, his feet hooked against its edge.

Trigger kicked against the hull as Magwa hauled him upward, their combined efforts sending them sprawling through the port. They cracked against the deck as their hull scraped the stone, a wash of splinters raining down as they huddled on the floor. Trigger winced as his ship received yet another wound, several timbers tumbling into the seething waters below.

The pair of them lay panting for a few hazy moments, the heat having risen to an unbearable degree.

"Thank you." Trigger nodded, rising to his feet. He offered Magwa his hand, which the Kalyute took without delay.

"Trigger die, we all die." The savage shrugged. "What Trigger find?"

"The sea is boiling."

Magwa opened his mouth to speak.

"I don't need you to tell me that it's a bad omen." Trigger interrupted. "I can see that for myself."

Magwa's jaw snapped shut.

"Come on." Trigger ordered, running a hand through his hair. "I'd say we're needed on deck."

****

Barnaby tried his best not to stare at Sheridan's cheeks, or the makeup-stained tears she wore upon them. They were the only sign of grief she was allowing herself to show, the First Mate devoting every portion of her being into keeping the *Blackbird* afloat.

"I can sail her." Jacques offered, moving towards the wheel.

"You couldn't make it through the Howlers." Sheridan replied, shouldering him away.

Jacques didn't argue, choosing to make a somber retreat.

"Sheridan!"

"Yes?"

Barnaby gripped the banister, hoping the next turn would not be too violent. He was beginning to feel awfully seasick.

"The mist is thinning!"

Half the crew raced to the prow, peering out with squinted eyes. Sunniday's words proved true, a clear patch of sky unfurling above the swirling white.

"We're almost out!" Barnaby cheered, beaming at Jacques. The swordsman returned his smile, before redirecting his gaze to the sea ahead.

"Wait." He frowned. "What is wrong wiz ze water?"

Glancing downwards, Barnaby saw the cause of his concern. With the mist parted, the sea was finally revealed, the once immaculate blue now a violent, writhing white.

"What does it mean?" He asked, directing the question to Sheridan.

"I have no idea." Came the murmured reply.

"Turn the ship!"

The voice emerged from death itself, Trigger's powerful words bringing them all to attention.

"Captain!" Sheridan cried, a new wave of tears springing from her eyes.

Trigger didn't respond, his coat billowing as he charged across the deck, leaping towards the wheel with frantic haste. Sheridan stepped aside with a puzzled expression, letting out a garbled wail as Trigger wrenched their vessel to port, desperate to avoid the mist-free sea.

"What are you doing?" She demanded, as the *Blackbird* twisted beneath their feet.

"I'm- "

The Captain never finished his explanation, as with a deafening scream the sea exploded, steaming droplets filling the air and burning Barnaby's skin. The heat and moisture blinded him, his eyes snapping shut in a feeble attempt to protect themselves. They were still shut when the *Blackbird* crashed, timbers snapping and cracking as the entire crew was slammed against the deck. Barnaby landed roughly, his skull bouncing across the sturdy wood. He wasn't certain if he blacked out, yet when he had recovered enough to open his eyes, he was certain he'd arrived in a different world.

The *Blackbird* was ablaze, crewman running back-and-forth to douse the flames. Trigger was still grappling with the wheel, barking orders to any man who had his hands available. They must have travelled a fair distance, as they were once again retreating from a towering pillar, this one larger and grander than any before. Barnaby could actually feel the heat radiating from its edge.

"How long was I out?" He asked, as Jacques offered his hand.

"About fifteen seconds."

"What?"

Barnaby glanced around, studying the sea. The mist-free region was completely gone, though he could see another resting several meters ahead.

"Ze pillar rose before our eyes. Had we been sailing over it, we'd have been torn to pieces by its peak."

Barnaby considered the steaming column.

"No." He replied, rubbing the back of his head. "Not possible"

"If you say so." Jacques shrugged.

As if in answer to his words, the sea erupted once more, spewing water into the sky and blasting heat across their deck. The empty ocean vanished, replaced by a spear of steaming stone, its visage distorted by the corrugated air.

"Oh." Barnaby murmured. "Oh."

"Yes." Jacques nodded. "It's quite ze sight."

This time, they avoided collision, Trigger's cunning mind having deciphered the signs that marked its approach. It was fortunate that he had, as the patches of faded mist started becoming more and more abundant, each one hurling forth a length of smoldering stone. Avoiding them was a scalding, laborious task, yet Trigger carried them through with expert precision, their vessel clearing the eruptions by an ever-increasing degree. Soon the mist was fading entirely, the sea calming and cooling as the force which heated it ebbed away. The rising pillars ceased their assault, replaced by their older, less mobile counterparts. The journey through them was almost pleasant, the clear sky displaying the worlds that had grown around and between their colossal heights. Complex bridges of moss and leaves, their lush lengths dotted with the homes of countless birds and mammals, the bizarre creatures having carved a life in this most isolated land.

"It's beautiful." Barnaby remarked, as they passed beneath another emerald bridge.

"Are you sure of zat?" Jacques asked, gesturing ahead.

"Oh." Barnaby remarked, leaning against the mast. "Oh wow."

Two pillars crossed against the rising sun, each of them spearing the same unfortunate ship. They had crashed against it from either side, pinning it between them and raising it high. Its battered hull sat rotting, aged timbers a forest of mushroom and moss. Hundreds of creatures moved amongst the wreckage, feeding and scavenging without concern. Dozens of eyes peered at them from cracks in the hull, wide and curious, yet devoid of fear.

"You sound impressed." Jacques declared, studying him with a raised brow.

"I am." Barnaby replied. "Aren't you?"

"No." Jacques replied, without hesitation. "All I see are ze ghosts of dead men."

"Really?" Barnaby asked, gazing in wonder as they passed the floating world.

"All I see is life."

Chapter Fourteen

"Hey, they're here! They're finally here!"

Trigger looked to Sheridan, who merely shrugged in reply. This was a very different greeting to the one they'd last received.

"Do you know how long we've been waiting?" Asked the gatekeeper, resting against a nearby statue. "A few of the pirates have been grumbling about moving on. If this fight wasn't worth so much, they probably would have!"

"Ze fight?" Beaufort asked, stepping forward. "Hargrave is here?"

"Oh yeah, said he couldn't be bothered waiting any longer." The gatekeeper shrugged. "He and Carnage have set up an arena, and the other crews have been more than happy to take the front-row seats. Shit, a few of the nearby natives have paddled over, and are selling their wares to all who'll buy. No one cares about the Tides anymore!"

"Fantastic." Beaufort murmured, caressing the handles of his blades.

Trigger could understand his uncertainty. He had recovered from his wound with astonishing speed, yet it was clear that he would never be the swordsman he was. True, he remained more capable than any member of Trigger's crew, yet compared to a warrior such as Hargrave, they were little more than children practicing with sticks.

Still, they had a race to win, and he couldn't jeopardize their odds for a single man.

"Well, if that is indeed the case, might I request you make our passage a speedy one?" He ventured, giving the gatekeeper his most charming grin.

"Sure, sure." The gatekeeper nodded, retreating from the statue. "Truth be told, it's getting to be quite the handful. We've never had so many humans lingering around the gate, and no offense, but you people make me a bit uncomfortable."

The gatekeeper vanished into the ancient barrier, slamming the door behind them with unnecessary force.

"That racist motherfucker." Gary declared, crossing his arms in outrage.

"Mr. Gary?"

"I know Captain, I know. I've been meaning to lose weight anyway."

The gate to the second fixture proved better maintained than the first, the entire process occurring in a fraction of the time. Before Trigger knew it, they were skating along the seabed, watching with wonder as dozens of sharks, fish and other undersea marvels soared above their heads. A few moments later they were rising upwards, though on this occasion the ocean saw fit to part, allowing them to emerge dry and unscathed into the gate's northern side.

"Oh my." Beaufort remarked, gazing at the sight ahead.

"Yes." Trigger agreed, running a hand through his hair. "They really were expecting you."

Beaufort's face sat larger than life, his visage painted across a sail of astounding height. Hargrave's rested directly beside it, the towering portraits serving as the doorway to the floating city beyond. At least a dozen vessels had taken anchor, forming a bobbing circle around Hargrave's legendary ship. At least a hundred smaller boats had been absorbed into their mass, their tiny hulls groaning beneath the weight of floating ovens, grills and other misplaced oddities.

Trigger scanned the ships for signs of the *Bloodbath*, and found it refreshingly absent. It had doubtlessly sailed further ahead, to ensure the event remained untainted. You could hardly host a duel if both combatants were struck by plague.

"Zis is madness." Beaufort observed, shaking his head as they drifted towards the makeshift arena.

"I don't disagree." Trigger replied, feeling a swell of pity for the man. All these people, just to watch him fight and die. He had many people invested in his own demise, yet still, at least it wasn't being made into a worldwide spectacle.

"You can do this." Barnaby declared, nodding with naïve confidence.

Sheridan and Trigger shared a look. They'd discussed it at length, and neither of them were quite so sure.

"Look! Look! It's the bloody *Blackbird*!"

The call spread throughout the bobbing vessels, their occupants swarming the decks for a chance to see their peg-legged champion. Someone sounded an old-fashioned war-horn, ensuring that their presence was known to every set of ears for at least three miles.

"You can do this, you one-legged bastard!" Encouraged a crewman from the nearest vessel, his aging skin covered in numerous black moles.

"You're going to die, Beaufort!" Sneered another, tucking his shin behind his knee and hopping back-and-forth. "You won't have any legs when Hargrave's done!"

"Ignore them." Trigger advised, earning himself a somber nod.

"I always do."

Their vessel occupied the final space in the floating circle, and with a gesture Trigger ordered the anchor dropped. The *Blackbird* was assailed as soon as it came to rest, the ships on either side tilting towards them as their crewmen leant in for a closer look.

"Oy Beaufort, good to see you've been keeping in shape!"

"Lemme' get a touch of yer sword! Come on!"

"Hargrave's waitin' for ya, boy. His sword's got ya name on it!"

To his credit, Beaufort didn't respond to a single taunt or jeer. He merely retreated below deck, accompanied by Magwa and Barnaby.

"What now?" Sheridan asked, speaking louder than usual. It was necessary to bypass the near-deafening crowds.

"Hargrave knows that Beaufort is here." Trigger replied. "I doubt he'll wait long to make himself known."

They waited in silence to see if he was correct, the banter around them fading as it became clear that Beaufort would not be ensnared. The taunts were swiftly replaced by calls for trade, several smaller vessels fastening to their own in the hopes of scoring coin. Trigger permitted the crew to interact, astonished by the variety of goods the natives had on-hand.

"Grilled seagull? Finest in all the sea!"

"Pretty pearls? Nothing like it in rest of world!"

"Fighting Beaufort action doll? Only two gold!"

"What?" Sheridan frowned, wandering towards the newest dealer.

"You want Hargrave instead? You want both? Two for three gold!"

Trigger followed his First Mate, and was amazed by what he found. The native had actually constructed tiny replicas of Hargrave and Beaufort, their limbs carrying misshapen miniatures of the swordsmen's famous blades. He'd even found a way to make their arms swing, if you squeezed their twiggy legs.

"Okay." Sheridan sighed, pinching her nose and scowling. "I think that's me done."

His First Mate excused herself, travelling below deck to speak with Beaufort.

"Captain!"

"Yes, Mr. Sunniday?"

"We've got a vessel approaching!"

Trigger moved to the prow, watching as the rowboat drew steadily closer. It had but one occupant, his broad shoulders and powerful strokes suggesting a degree of strength. Glancing at one of the wooden replicas, Trigger attempted to discern if it was Hargrave himself. If it was, the carving's resemblance was poor indeed.

"Good morning." He greeted, as the boat thumped softly against their hull.

"You Beaufort?" The man asked, stretching and standing. His hair was drawn back in a long and greasy tail, its ends swaddled with numerous beads. He wore no shirt or coat, exposing his chest with obvious pride.

Trigger didn't know him, yet he already felt a particular distaste.

"I am Captain Trigger." He replied, rubbing his finger against his thumb. "May I enquire as to your name and purpose?"

"Captain said I should speak to Beaufort." The man shrugged. "The rest of you don't matter."

Trigger took a calming breath, closing his eyes as he considered his response.

"Beaufort is currently a passenger on my ship, and therefore my responsibility. If your Captain wishes to speak with him, he must deal with me beforehand."

"Captain won't like that." The man replied, spitting into the sea.

"I'm not sure I care." Trigger replied, his patience at its end.

"I just rowed all this fucking way." The man sneered, gesturing at the tiny stretch of water he'd been forced to endure. "What do you want me to do? Row all the way back and fetch the Captain?"

"If you don't mind."

The man glared at Trigger with slack-jawed outrage, his dopey eyes filling with malice.

"Get me Beaufort." He growled, slamming his palm against their hull.

"I will happily do so, if you comport yourself with civility and respect. Otherwise, you are free to summon your Captain. I should point out, however, that if you ever strike my ship again, I will have you hanged without a moment's thought."

The man almost shook with indignant fury, a petulant child who had finally been refused. Trigger tried not to feel too much satisfaction.

He failed.

Eventually the fists unclenched, the man's muscles relaxing as he accepted defeat.

"May I please speak with Mr. Beaufort?" He asked, spitting the words from between his teeth.

"Of course." Trigger grinned, leaning against the banister. "Gary, would you please inform Mr. Beaufort that he has a visitor?"

"Aye, Captain."

Gary slipped below deck, leaving Trigger and his guest in relative isolation.

"Now sir, as we have returned to polite conversation, perhaps you would be willing to tell me your name?" Trigger asked, adjusting his coat. He was getting rather sick of people skipping introductions.

The man snorted, crossing his arms and scrunching his face. Still, he had enough sense to reply.

"They call me Tross."

"As in, Albatross?"

"Aye."

"May I ask why?"

"Because I'm big, and I dance well."

Trigger raised a curious brow. You can never see the hidden depths.

"You called for me?"

Trigger turned as Beaufort arrived, his scarred features twisted into an uneasy grimace.

"Ah, yes. Mr. Tross here wishes to speak with you, on behalf of Captain Hargrave."

Beaufort peered over the banister, studying the man below.

"How may I help you?" he asked, remaining civil despite his concerns.

Tross seemed to inflate beneath the weight of Beaufort's stare, puffing out his chest in a primitive display.

"You know why I'm here." He snarled, attempting to fill his voice with menace and power. "Captain Hargrave challenges you to a formal duel, to be fought on his ship at noon tomorrow. Do you accept, or is your stomach as weak as your right leg?"

"My right leg is fine, zank you very much." Beaufort replied, tapping his prosthesis. "Captain Trigger obtained me ze finest oak. As to ze challenge, inform your Captain zat I am most excited to meet him, and zat gutting him will be my sincerest pleasure."

Tross spat again, taking great care to avoid their hull.

"He's going to murder you." He sneered. "Our deck will run with your blood and brains."

"It would be ze first time brains touched your deck. Now please, leave us."

Tross opened his mouth in search of reply, yet swiftly closed it as he caught Trigger's eye.

"I believe that concludes our business." Trigger declared, as Beaufort turned and marched away. "Send your Captain my regards."

He said nothing more as Tross began his departure, sinking into his vessel with a murmured complaint. A few mighty strokes had him hurtling away, his features fixed into a hideous scowl.

"How'd it go?"

"Well enough." Trigger replied, turning to Sheridan. She'd obviously used the time to indulge in some shopping, her arms laden with silks and pearls.

"I'm glad you were able to take advantage." Trigger chuckled, admiring a length of vivid green fabric.

"I needed to." Sheridan replied. "What I loaned the crew was completely destroyed. Honestly, it's as though they'd never worn clothing before. Still, that's okay. I'm always glad for an excuse to expand my collection, and if I'm being honest, these natives have no concept of equivalent exchange. I practically robbed them."

"Well, you are a pirate."

"How long do we have until the duel begins?" Sheridan asked, considering her pile.

"It's at noon tomorrow."

"Not much time." She sighed. "Though, I guess I could prepare a fashionable scarf…"

"Would you be averse to finding dinner first?" Trigger asked, offering his arm. "I'm famished, and I could use something a little exotic."

"Well, you'd definitely find that here." Sheridan chuckled, hooking her elbow to his. "There's a boat selling marinated monkey."

"Really?"

"Aye. I've actually heard good things."

"Well then, by all means, lead the way."

Sheridan took him at his word, guiding him with friendly purpose. Trigger could feel himself relaxing with every thoughtless step, enjoying the sensation of simply being led. It was a welcome break from the demands of Captaincy, and one he knew he'd need. Tomorrow was only a few hours away, and it already promised to be a day to remember.

****

"Do you like it?"

Barnaby gagged in response, letting the half-chewed fish spill wetly from his lips. It hit the table with a soggy squelch, earning a round of laughter from Magwa and Jacques. It was the first smile the swordsman had worn since they passed into the fixture.

"That is fucking awful." Barnaby whispered, trying not to insult their host. Luckily, he was distracted, his hands blurring as they chopped and butchered another raw fish.

"How do people eat this?" Barnaby ventured, feeling as though his throat had been stuffed with wet cotton.

"I've heard zat it's a delicacy." Jacques shrugged, popping a piece between his lips.

"That just mean it expensive." Magwa declared. "Rich men eat it so they look rich. It about image, not taste."

"I'd say it looks pretty shit, as well." Barnaby muttered, prodding a pink and orange wad.

"Not Magwa's point."

"I know."

They continued rearranging their plates for what Barnaby considered a polite amount of time, eventually departing as swiftly as they could. They were already two boats distant when the chef moved to clean their table, his muttered insults still faintly audible in the late-night air.

"You've got this, champ!" Encouraged a drunken pirate, saluting Jacques with a foaming mug.

"Zank you." Jacques nodded, though his expression conveyed a different reply.

"Are you nervous?" Barnaby asked, trying to understand his state of mind.

"No." Jacques replied, giving him a friendly grin. "I've had too many fights to ever feel fear. Combat is my home, whezer it be on a street corner, or in ze middle of ze sea."

"I know that." Barnaby frowned, struggling to put his thoughts into words. "But this isn't just a random brawl. You're fighting Hargrave Longsteel, the only man whose reputation matches your own. Even worse, you'll be fighting with a substantial handicap."

"Do you want me to be scared, Barnaby?" Jacques asked, though not unkindly.

"No, of course not!"

"Zen why are you trying to convince me otherwise?" Jacques chuckled. "I know who Hargrave is. I know what people claim he can do, and believe it or not, I am well aware zat I am missing a leg. None of zis frightens me. On ze contrary, I believe my injury may provide me a distinct advantage, once our steel begins to sing."

"Jacques' have plan?" Magwa asked, glancing at his leg.

"Plans are useless in a duel. I have an idea, nozing more."

They continued weaving across the still-expanding arena, more and more ships arriving with each passing minute. The natives outnumbered the pirates now, having linked their vessels to create a floating marketplace, its timbers moaning beneath the burden of countless transactions. Jacques had been there less than a day, and through presence alone he'd provided enough gold to see these merchants settled for life.

"At least the natives are benefitting." Barnaby remarked, giving his satchel a tentative rub. His own purchase remained safe and sound, lodged firmly beside Jacques' bottle of rum. The swordsman had scoured the marketplace for this particular brew, claiming that it was the best spirit available when it came to celebration.

Considering how many victories he'd had, Barnaby was inclined to believe him.

"Hey, there he is!"

Jacques visibly tensed as yet another group approached them, their pale faces wide with excitement. The former captain raised his hands, preparing to ward them off, yet to Barnaby's surprise the group marched straight past him, pausing before Magwa with obvious delight.

"Are you Black Barnaby?" They asked, studying him closely.

"What?" Magwa frowned, reaching for his hatchet.

"We mean no harm!" The speaker declared, taking a cautious step back. "We've just been listening to some of Trigger's men, and they would not stop talking about all you've done! Did you really save Beaufort's life? And fire the shot that ended that evil fucking ship? We saw that thing on our way here, you know? It had caught another vessel, swarming across it like it was a damned octopus. We could hear the crew screaming as the timbers ground them down…"

The speaker paused for a moment, bowing their head in somber respect.

"Want him." Magwa announced, jerking his thumb at Barnaby.

The group turned towards him, regarding him with suspicious and disappointed eyes.

"But…you're not black."

"It's…it's a nickname." Barnaby began, looking to Jacques for help. "When we wounded the ship, I was covered in its moss."

"Oh, I remember the moss." Shuddered someone at the back. "Black as night, wasn't it?"

"It was." Barnaby nodded. "It stank, too."

"I never got close enough for a smell, and I thank the Gods for that!" Remarked the main speaker. "I can't believe you got close and survived! Do you know how many ships it's claimed?"

"No." Barnaby replied, rubbing the back of his head. "All I know is that it didn't claim our ours."

His words were born of honesty and panic, yet they were apparently a very good choice. The group gave an approving cheer, each of them flashing a wide-lipped grin.

"Bloody oath it didn't!" The main speaker boomed, clapping him on the shoulder. "It's a shame that the Oracle-birds couldn't see through the mist! I'd have loved to see how it all went down!"

"Probably best that you can't." Barnaby replied, once again attempting to speak only the truth.

"Aye, I bet it's too grisly for our virgin eyes." Laughed the speaker, wrapping an arm about his friend's neck. "We'd had enough from the glimpse we caught! I can't imagine what it was like to get so close."

He hung his head again, allowing the silence to emphasize his words. Barnaby suspected that he did it quite often.

"Anyway, me and the boys are heading off for more drinks, and we were wondering if you'd like to join us?" The speaker ventured, giving him an inviting smile. "The one thing these natives don't sell is a damn good story, and I bet you've got plenty just waiting to be told."

Barnaby looked to Magwa and Jacques, both of whom were suppressing enormous grins.

"I wish I could." He began, offering his palms. "But my friend has a duel tomorrow, and I promised that I'd help him prepare. Maybe another night, somewhere down the line."

"Not a worry." The speaker replied, seizing his hand. "A man like you is bound to be busy. Still, it was an absolute pleasure to make your acquaintance. Thank you for avenging all those men. We'll all sleep easier knowing that monster is dead."

"Ah, you're welcome." Barnaby replied, this time unwilling to reveal the truth.

"Well, we'll leave you to it." The speaker declared, giving them all a respectful nod. "Good luck with your preparations, and the duel. Hargrave's men have been crowing about this fight for years. It will be good if you finally shut them up."

"I intend to." Jacques replied, folding his arms.

"I bet you will." The speaker winked, he and his group retreating. "All the best, and good luck with the rest of the Tides!"

"You too!" Barnaby waved, watching as they were lost amongst the thronging crowd.

"What a lovely fellow." Jacques remarked, scratching at his chin.

"He was." Barnaby agreed. "Though, I think your stories have gotten out of hand."

"Zey're not my stories anymore." Jacques shrugged. "Zey're yours."

"I didn't make them up!"

"No, but zey are about you, and have grown beyond your influence. It is best to embrace zem now. You did an admirable job of it during zat very conversation."

Barnaby pondered this statement, and supposed it was true. That didn't mean he was comfortable. To be a famous pirate was no easy task. For every adoring fan, there was another man out there looking to make a name, usually by putting yours on a grave.

"A handful of drunks are easy to impress. What happens when someone tries to test the legend for themselves?"

"I suggest you run, as fast as you are able."

"You'd never run."

"I've only got one leg."

"You know what I mean." Barnaby frowned, trying not to chuckle.

"No, I would never run." Jacques sighed. "But you are not me, and I am certainly not you. Different bodies, different skills."

"Being a coward is a skill?"

"No, but staying alive is."

Barnaby fell silent, considering this statement.

"Fair enough."

They continued their swaying journey, the boats beneath them buckling before the growing swell. The necessary concentration kept them from speaking, none of them uttering a word until they had finally returned to the *Blackbird's* stable shores.

"Jacques' would really never run away?"

The question appeared to catch Jacques off-guard, mostly because it came from Magwa.

"No." He eventually replied. "I doubt I could live with such a smear on my honor."

"Honor's overrated." Barnaby shrugged. "I don't have a drop, and I'm doing pretty well."

"To live wizout honor is indeed a luxury." Jacques grinned. "One I have often wished for."

"It isn't hard." Barnaby chuckled. "Just think of the bravest thing you could do, and then perform the opposite."

"You two really are pirates, aren't you?" Jacques snorted. "Trying to talk a man out of his honor and self-respect. I mean, I'd expect it from you, Barnaby, but Magwa? I've seldom met a man wiz so much courage."

The Kalyute shook his head, his many scars glistening in the feeble light.

"Courage and honor are not same thing."

"You don't zink you're honorable?"

"Magwa knows he is not."

Barnaby and Jacques shared a curious look. They'd never heard the savage's story, or even come close to prising it from his lips.

"Why?" Barnaby asked, gazing at Magwa intently.

The Kalyute considered his hatchet, running a thumb along its obsidian edge.

"Reasons."

Barnaby and Jacques both swayed with disappointment.

"I may die tomorrow, you know." Jacques offered. "I would consider it a great tragedy, to die without having heard your tale."

"Good." Magwa declared, after a moment's thought. "Then Magwa promises to tell, after you've won. Consider it incentive."

Jacques and Barnaby shared a laugh, while Magwa offered a pointy grin.

"Fair enough, my friend." Jacques conceded, giving the Kalyute a nod.

"Fair enough."

Chapter Fifteen

Trigger winced as the crowd roared, the mass of bodies slamming him against Beaufort's muscular back. Hundreds of crewmen had crammed themselves onto Hargrave's groaning ship, the vessel sinking low as it struggled to bear their weight.

"Apologies." Trigger mumbled, pushing himself away from the swordsman's hulking frame.

"Zere certainly is a lot of zem, isn't zere?" Beaufort replied, studying the crowd with what may have been uncertainty.

"There is." Trigger nodded, running a hand through his sodden hair. The sheer volume of flesh was making it unbearably warm. "I'm surprised this ship is still afloat."

"It wouldn't be, if Hargrave hadn't put his foot down." Sheridan snarled, shoving away an opportunistic pirate, who had used the crowd as an excuse to venture towards her chest. "The damn ship was full, and people were still trying to climb aboard. Every vessel with a view is fit to burst, and I've never seen so many Oracle-birds."

Trigger glanced upwards and saw that this was true. The sky was almost lost beneath their steely wings, their polished faces capturing the scene from a thousand different views.

"The empire is watching." Trigger remarked, adjusting his coat.

"Zen I'd best not disappoint." Beaufort sighed, slipping into the ring.

"Good luck." Barnaby called, his voice cracking with concern.

Hargrave had spared no effort in the arena's construction, threading three ropes between four barrels, and positioning them in the shape of a square. Each fighter had been designated a corner, where they would rest in-between the numerous rounds. Well, assuming they made it past one, that is.

"What sort of fight takes place in a ring?" Sheridan snorted, studying the arena and shaking her head. "Ridiculous."

"Hargrave is a noble by birth, and this is how they compose their duels." Trigger shrugged. "How do your people settle their disputes?"

"You find the person you want to kill, and beat their head in with a rock." Sheridan replied, folding her arms.

"Well, less messing around, I guess."

"Frankly, I'd razer be zere." Beaufort grinned, glancing at them over his shoulder.

Any reply they might have made was lost beneath the crowd's deafening cheer, hundreds of hands clapping as the Captain's door slowly opened.

"Hargrave! Hargrave! Hargrave!"

The sea of bodies began to part, creating a corridor of flesh between the door and the ring. The man within it stood tall and proud, his chiseled features unmistakable, and twisted into a superior sneer.

"Hargrave! Hargrave! Hargrave!"

His long legs covered the distance in a handful of graceful strides, allowing him to step over the tightly stretched ropes. Without glancing at Beaufort he spread his arms wide, turning in circles and beaming at the crowd.

"Ladies and gentlemen, what a pleasure it is to see you all!"

The crowd released a thunderous cheer, which ceased the instant Hargrave raised his hand.

"I know what you endured to be here today, and I appreciate such commitment to the finer things in life! You have been patient, you have been hardy, and I promise you, you will be rewarded!"

Another round of furious ecstasy, once again silenced with a single gesture.

"Before you stand the two greatest swordsmen to have ever walked this world! Though admittedly, one of us walks a bit easier these days."

Hargrave pointed sadly at Beaufort's wooden leg, earning a round of laughter from the enraptured crowd.

"Ignore him." Barnaby whispered, as Beaufort's frown deepened.

"No." The swordsman replied, his shoulders rippling as he stretched. "It is better zat I remember."

"As such, it is my intent to provide each and every one of you the spectacle of a lifetime! I vow that I will fight to the last drop of blood, until the very last breath of my battered body! I can only hope that my esteemed opponent intends to do the same!"

"I do."

The crowd fell silent as Beaufort spoke, the swordsman rising from his corner as though he were violence made flesh. Two powerful steps brought him to Hargrave's side, their visages as different as night and day. Hargrave's spoke to a life of luxury, where gold and women flowed as freely as wine. Beaufort's told a different tale, one of broken bones and shattered dreams. Studying the pair, Trigger felt no doubts as to who was the better man.

Yet, for some reason, Hargrave wasn't showing the slightest trace of fear.

"Ah, he speaks!" The Captain declared, sneering directly into Beaufort's eyes. "When did they teach you that?"

Beaufort cocked his head to one side, betraying no anger at Hargrave's words.

"Zese people came here for a fight, you preening clown. Hurry up and give zem one."

This time the crowd roared for Beaufort, their excited stomps shaking the ship with the fury of a storm.

Hargrave must have read the mood, as he made no attempt at a witty response.

"Very well." He nodded, studying Beaufort. "Let us begin."

The crowd was cacophonous as the pair moved to their corners, each of them removing their shirts and hurling them across the deck. They were pounced upon with frenzied desire, blood spilling as people fought to claim a piece of their chosen champion.

"Well, this should be interesting." Sheridan remarked, observing the differences in the fighter's physiques. Trigger was inclined to agree.

Beaufort stood as he always did, tall, broad and heavily scarred. His muscles sat like anvils on his world-worn frame, every limb marked by violence and death. Hargrave, however, bore no such marks, his pale skin untouched by sword or club. He stood at least as tall as Beaufort, yet his shoulders were but a fraction of the width, his slender body devoid of any fat or weakness. He was a rod of steel, as long and lean as the sword he held.

"Captain Trigger!" Hargrave called, beckoning with a manicured hand. "Would you be so kind as to commence the bout?"

The crowd murmured at Hargrave's choice, shaking their heads as Trigger ducked into the ring. He was a little surprised himself.

"And please, try not to cock it up." Hargrave sneered, as Trigger took his place in the center of the ring. Suddenly his charity made a lot more sense.

"My good people!" Trigger began, uncertain as to whether the crowd deserved such a complimentary description. "Today's duel will be fought in the noble style, with set boundaries, restrictions and rounds. If either combatant willingly sets foot outside the ring, he is automatically disqualified, forfeiting both victory and honor. Blows to the groin are restricted, as is the clawing of eyes or ears. The duel will consist of five rounds, each lasting three minutes in length. Should a participant attempt to strike once a round has ended, they will also face disqualification. Combatants, do you understand?"

"Of course." Hargrave snorted, resting his sword against his shoulder.

"I do." Beaufort nodded, keeping his weapons low and ready.

"Very well." Trigger sighed, mentally wishing Beaufort the best of luck.

"Begin!"

****

Barnaby stepped aside as Trigger vaulted from the ring, swiftly making room for the circling swordsmen. Hargrave had finally abandoned his relaxed nature, his wiry arms tensing as he levelled his blade. By contrast, Jacques was keeping himself loose and low, swaying from side-to-side as if he were slightly drunk.

The crowd cheered madly, eager for the first blow.

"You've got this, Jacques." Barnaby whispered.

"He's a fucking dead man." Replied a nearby pirate, who'd overheard his murmured words.

"Neither of them seem particularly lively." Sheridan remarked, fanning her chest.

She wasn't wrong. The pair were still circling, neither one attempting to strike.

"Get on with it!" Yelled an unseen pirate, earning a roar of agreement from the frustrated crowd.

It must have been what Jacques was waiting for.

The big man lunged, stabbing at Hargrave's throat with his gleaming dagger. He may as well have been thrusting at the sea, as with a single step Hargrave avoided the blow, swinging his greatsword in an overhead sweep. Jacques barely avoided the blow, dropping low and slashing at Hargrave's twisting stomach. His opponent proved too swift again, dancing backwards and hacking at Jacques' outstretched arm. It almost made contact, yet at the last moment Jacques was able to parry, his short sword ringing as a large sliver was chipped from its polished length.

The pair retreated, each of them considering the other with dark and narrowed eyes.

"I think you need a better sword." Hargrave taunted, twirling his own.

"She is merely well-used." Jacques replied. "A few scars are to be expected."

"Is that how you explain them?" Hargrave taunted, nodding at Jacques' mangled skin.

"Zey need no explanation." Jacques declared, taking a cautious step. "You will understand zem well, once zis fight is done."

"I doubt it." Hargrave spat. "Dead men tell no stories."

The Captain vaulted forward, sweeping his sword at Jacques's feet. The swordsman sprung sideways to avoid the blow, yet with expert precision Hargrave struck with his foot, kicking Jacques knee and buckling his leg. The move put Jacques off-balance, allowing Hargrave to smash the pommel of his sword against Jacques' cheek. Blood flew as the swordsman reeled, barely parrying a stab from Hargrave's thrusting blade.

"That's round one!" Trigger roared, slamming his fist against the nearest barrel.

Hargrave ceased his attack, pausing mid-slash with a mild sigh. Jacques himself was frozen mid-parry, his blades crossed to catch the attack.

"Return to your corners." Trigger ordered, a declaration which both seemed eager to follow.

"Are you alright?" Barnaby asked, as Jacques rested heavily against his barrel. Hargrave's blow had split his cheek, a trace of pearly white bone visible amongst the glistening red.

"It is nothing." Jacques replied, clapping a rag against the wound.

"He's...he's fast." Barnaby ventured, restraining himself. What he really wanted to do was plea for a forfeit.

"He is. He also has great reach, and ze skills to make use of it. His reputation is well earned."

Jacques removed the rag from his face, passing it gently into Sheridan's hand.

"What are you going to do?" Sheridan asked, washing the rag in a waiting bucket.

"Drive him into a corner, and break down his guard." Jacques replied. "I must match his speed wiz strength and power. If I wear him down, I slow him down."

"And if you can't?" Sheridan asked, voicing the question Barnaby was scared to ask.

"Zen Barnaby can have my swords." Jacques grinned, giving him a nod.

Once again, Barnaby had no idea what he was supposed to say.

"Combatants!" Trigger cried, once more in the center of the ring. "Are you ready for the second round?"

"More than ready." Hargrave boasted, barely out of breath from his earlier exertions.

"I am." Jacques nodded, his face spewing blood onto the polished timbers.

"Very well. Begin!"

Trigger darted from the ring as the duel flared to life, the pair's earlier caution thrown to the wind. They met in a clash of furious steel, each of them bearing the savagery of a charging bull.

Jacques swung high and low, his sword and knife striking at Hargrave's chest and thighs. The Captain avoided them both with astounding speed, his footwork immaculate as he weaved across the ring, hacking and slashing at every opening. It was here that Jacques' prosthesis revealed its shortcomings, hampering his lunges and slowing his twists. It was a fractional delay, yes, but for a man like Hargrave it was a world of opportunity, allowing him to dash across the ring almost completely at will, completely in defiance of Jacque's valiant attempts.

"He can't catch him." Barnaby whispered, receiving a glance from Sheridan.

"No." She sighed. "He can't."

Clang!

The crowd cheered as Hargrave ceased his dodging, catching Jacques' blade against his own. A moment later his elbow was flying, crashing into Jacque's cheek and opening his wound an even greater degree.

"That can't be legal!" Barnaby gasped, almost averting his gaze.

"It's not his balls or eyes." Sheridan replied. "So it's still fair game."

Barnaby watched in horror as Jacques was forced to retreat, falling victim to his own strategy as Hargrave assailed him again. The Captain's blade was huge and heavy, yet he wielded it as though it were an extension of himself, using it to batter Jacques across the ring and straight into the waiting ropes.

"Come on, Jacques!" Barnaby cried, as the swordsman slumped against them. "Get up!"

His friend never had the chance, as an instant later Hargrave was on him, that great blade arcing towards Jacques skull. He caught the strike against his crossed swords, yet the sheer power sent him reeling, the ropes burning his side as he staggered along their length.

"Jacques!" Barnaby screamed, his voice turning hoarse. "Jacques, move!"

The swordsman simply couldn't, his huge frame panting as Hargrave struck again and again, each blow creeping closer to Jacques' sweat-stained flesh. It was all he could do to keep Hargrave at bay, his sword and dagger a blur as they parried and deflected, slowing slightly with each titanic blow.

"Just a few more seconds." Barnaby murmured, his clenched fists turning white. "Just a handful more."

Boom!

Jacques buckled as Hargrave kneed him in the gut, the explosive move catching him completely off-guard. Barnaby watched in horror as his best friend folded, exposing his neck to Hargrave's blade.

"It's done." Sheridan whispered, shutting her fan.

With contemptuous ease, Hargrave readied his sword, hoisting it overhead. Jacques made no attempt to defy him, cradling his stomach and slumping against the ropes.

Hargrave held his blade high, and waited.

And waited.

And waited.

"The round is over!" Trigger roared, slamming his fist against the barrel.

"What?" Barnaby asked, pleased, yet utterly perplexed. Hargrave had stood within inches of the win, yet he'd abandoned it without a care. Even now he was grinning, retreating to his corner with obvious good cheer.

"What the fuck was that!?" Screamed a voice from the depths of the crowd, who obviously shared in Barnaby's confusion. The question seemed to increase their ire, many of them hissing and booing at Hargrave's ridiculous behavior.

Thud.

The barrel rocked as Jacques crashed against it, letting the wood support his gasping frame. The swordsman was completely exhausted, yet a mischievous spark still lingered in his bloodshot eyes.

"Are you alright?" Barnaby asked, offering him a water-filled flask. Jacques emptied it before he replied.

"He is stronger zan I anticipated." He panted. "And far too quick on his feet. I cannot restrict his movement, and he can match my power blow-for-blow."

"You have to forfeit." Barnaby declared, fear robbing him of all restraint.

Jacques snorted, shaking his heavy head. The simple motion sent an arc of blood spraying across the deck.

"No, I cannot. My name would become a joke, a convenient insult to all cowards and weaklings."

"But you'd still be alive." Barnaby begged, tears rolling across his cheeks.

"A life of disgrace is no life at all." Jacques replied, accepting a rag from Sheridan.

"Then do you have a plan, at least?" Barnaby asked, desperately searching for a source of hope.

"Keep away from ze ropes." Jacques replied. "And avoid a direct exchange."

"That doesn't leave you with…well, anything." Sheridan frowned, taking back the blood-soaked rag.

"No, I guess it doesn't." Jacques shrugged.

Barnaby hung his head, before turning his gaze towards the jostling crowd. Most of them were still murmuring in outrage, shaking their head at Hargrave's mercy. Many had placed bets on a second-round win, and were rightly feeling cheated of their glory and gold. It was a turbulent sea of disgruntled faces, which made the man weaving between them all the more conspicuous. His features alone were narrowed with focus, his lean body twisting and turning as he made his way to Hargrave's corner.

He'd been standing behind Barnaby only a few moments before.

"What is it?" Jacques asked, noticing his concern.

"I'm not sure..." Barnaby frowned, watching as the man bent towards Hargrave's ear, whispering softly with urgent haste.

Trigger was back in the center of the ring.

"Combatants, are you ready for the third round!?"

"Salivating." Hargrave sneered, levelling his blade at Jacque's heart.

"I am." Jacques nodded, though his battered frame suggested otherwise.

"Very well." Trigger nodded, studying Jacques with obvious concern.

"Begin!"

Jacques never even managed to leave his corner.

Hargrave covered the ring in two broad steps, turning the second into a savage stab. Jacques twisted to deflect it, slapping aside the blade and sending it wide. With breathtaking skill, Hargrave turned this to his advantage, spinning on his heel and slamming his elbow into Jacques' exposed skull. The force sent him reeling back into his barrel, the sturdy wood cracking as he crashed against it. Hargrave's blade came thundering down, attempting to cleave Jacques in two. The swordsman caught it by the barest degree, his crossed weapons singing as the steel smashed against them. The force drove Jacques to one knee, leaving his face open to Hargrave's own. The blow snapped his head back in a wash of blood, propelling him once more into the waiting ropes.

Barnaby tried to suppress the vomit rising in his throat. He wasn't certain that he'd succeed.

Hargrave swept low, trying to open Jacques' torso from navel-to-throat. Again, the swordsman managed to parry, yet the act left him open to Hargrave's stinging headbutt, which bloodied Jacques' nose and sent him staggering sideways. Hargrave pounced on the opening, swinging his sword at Jacques' stumbling thighs. This time, the blow struck home, Jacques' desperate twist failing to avoid the blade entirely, leaving him with a gash across his right.

"Come on, Captain! Finish the bastard!"

Hargrave's crew began to chant as he continued his frenzied assault, every strike aiming to leave Jacques maimed. Again and again he was denied, however, Jacques' bleeding form somehow managing to maintain a feeble defense, repelling each blow by the barest degree. Both combatants were panting now, Jacques' back rubbed raw from the merciless ropes. Hargrave's body remained completely unscathed, yet the frustration on his features was clear to see, his attack's growing wilder with every deflection. Gone was the perfect symmetry between man and blade, the strain of his weapon finally manifesting in one slow and labored swing.

Jacques saw the moment from a thousand miles away, slipping to one-side and slashing Hargrave clear across his brow.

The crowd went ballistic as the Captain's blood spilled, dropping from his skull in thick, fat drops. Barnaby himself cheered as Hargrave retreated, pressing the wound with obvious shock.

"You cut me." Hargrave spat.

"I did." Jacques nodded, moving away from the biting ropes. He appeared to have a spring in his step.

"You think this will win it?" Hargrave sneered. "You think this matters?"

"I zink it is inconvenient." Jacques grinned, as blood trickled into Hargrave's eyes.

The tiny distraction served as the swordsman's signal, his massive body a blur as he darted across the ring, his blades streaking towards Hargrave's blinded form.

"Yes!" Barnaby roared, throwing his hands high. Many of the crowd joined him, while others held their breath in anxious anticipation.

Clang!

"Aw!"

Their excited shouts had been the warning Hargrave needed, the Captain shifting to one side as he parried Jacques' blow. He replied with one of his own, driving the pommel of his sword towards Jacques' chin. The swordsman saw it coming, slipping sideways and slashing at Hargrave's extended wrist.

"The round is over!"

Jacques pulled his strike, his blade less than an inch from Hargrave's sweating flesh.

"Come on!" Demanded the crowd, booing at Trigger's interruption. Barnaby was tempted to join them.

"Fair is fair." Sheridan snapped, cuffing him around the ear. "Hargrave isn't the only one who's been saved by an ended round."

"Yeah, yeah." Barnaby muttered, rubbing the side of his head. His pain was quickly forgotten, however, as Jacques strolled calmly to his side of the ring.

"You got him!" Barnaby cheered, practically leaping to his side.

"I wounded him." Jacques replied. "Zere is a difference."

Barnaby looked to Hargrave's corner, where the Captain's crew were desperately working to patch his leaking wound. Gone was the earlier bravado, Hargrave's easy confidence replaced by exhaustion, pain, and more than a little fear.

"You've worn him out." Barnaby declared, returning his gaze to Jacques.

"His sword did zat." Jacques replied, shaking his head. "I just hope it will be enough."

The swordsman's words were humble, yet Barnaby could still detect a trace of mischief hiding behind his eyes. Jacques was being coy, yet for the life of him, Barnaby couldn't decide why.

He knew better than to waste time asking.

"So, what's your plan now?" Barnaby ventured, as Jacques dapped at his cheek with the increasingly stained rag.

"He is tired now, which makes him slower and weaker. Now is when I drive him to the corner, and tear apart his guard."

"Sounds good." Barnaby grinned, trying to suppress the hope swelling in his chest.

"Aye." Jacques nodded, handing him the rag. "I zink so."

As his friend turned towards the center of the ring, Barnaby noticed a commotion brewing in the crowd to his left, many of them snarling insults as a slender pirate forced his way between them.

It was the same pirate who'd been behind him last round, and once again, he was on his way to Hargrave's corner.

"Jacques!" Barnaby hissed, trying his best to appear unconcerned. "Jacques!"

"Yes?" The swordsman asked, glancing over his shoulder.

"A spy! Hargrave's been using a spy! He's known what you've been planning!"

Jacques studied him for a quiet moment, his heavy features crinkling into an amused frown.

"You mean it took you zis long to notice?"

"What?"

"Combatants, are you ready for the fourth round!"

"I am." Hargrave spat, stepping forward and twirling his blade.

"I am." Jacques nodded, treating Barnaby to a subtle wink.

"Very well. Begin!"

Jacques responded to the call as though he were a man aflame, screaming in fury as he charged across the ring. An unprepared man would have faltered or retreated, yet Hargrave's informant had made his report, and with a victorious cheer Hargrave lunged to meet his foe, the tip of his blade driving towards Jacques' chest.

It never came close, as with an easy step Jacques' danced around it, dragging his dagger along Hargrave's arm.

The crowd cheered as Hargrave staggered, pulled on by his own incredible momentum. The Captain tried valiantly to recover his stance, yet Jacques denied him, slamming his shoulder into Hargrave's ribs. The savage blow sent him sprawling across the deck, his sword slipping from his hand as he rolled violently beneath the ropes, his limp form pausing outside the ring.

"Yes!" Barnaby screamed, leaping into the air. "He did it! He fucking did it!"

"That's half-rations." Sheridan declared. "And no, he didn't. A ring-out only counts if your opponent is attempting to flee. Getting shoved out merely pauses the round."

"Oh." Barnaby sighed, his shoulders slumping.

"Though, I have to admit, it's damn entertaining to watch." Sheridan added, flashing him a grin.

"Yeah." Barnaby nodded. "It is."

The crowd parted as Hargrave attempted to rise, his large hands searching for his fallen blade. It was one of his crew who finally retrieved it, pressing the handle into his bloody palm.

"Thank you, Tross." Hargrave murmured, refusing a hand up and climbing to his feet.

Jacques regarded him silently from the ring, occupying its center as though it were his personal fort.

"Well struck." Hargrave conceded, stepping across the ropes. He winced mid-way, clutching his side with shaking fingers.

Jacques made no reply. He merely raised his sword, levelling it at Hargrave's heart.

"Combatant, are you ready to continue?" Trigger asked, his battered coat blowing in the growing wind.

"Aye." Hargrave nodded, lifting his blade. "I am."

"Very well. Continue!"

Jacques was moving before the word had faded, his dagger striking at Hargrave's throat. The Captain avoided it with a nimble step, throwing his elbow at Jacques' face. It missed as Jacques sunk beneath it, slashing savagely at Hargrave's thigh. His steel struck the deck as Hargrave threw himself away, kicking at Jacques' side with a heavy boot. The swordsman caught the blow against his forearm, scowling as it drove him three steps across the ring. He had barely regained his balance before Hargrave struck, his greatsword arcing towards Jacques' chest. Metal screamed as three blades clashed, Jacques' pinning the weapon between his own.

"You are good." Jacques whispered, his voice so low only Barnaby could hear.

"As are you." Hargrave conceded, the pair so close that their lips might touch. "Crafty, as well."

"I need to be." Jacques snarled, his arms shaking from the enormous strain. "It's the only way to fight scum like you."

Jacques threw his head forward, breaking Hargrave's nose with a sickening crunch.

The Captain staggered, weakening enough for Jacques to force his weapons forward, driving their points into Hargrave's chest. The Captain snarled as the steel tore his flesh, yet responded with a wild punch, his knuckles cracking against Jacques' jaw. Most men would have folded, yet Jacques wore it as though it were a mother's kiss, slamming the pommel of his dagger across Hargrave's bloody scalp. The Captain buckled, his legs wobbling unsteadily beneath him, before crumbling entirely to a savage kick from Jacques.

"Now it's over." Sheridan remarked, as Hargrave slammed against the deck.

The entire crowd had lost its mind, with even those who had bet on Hargrave cheering for Jacques and his massive upset. The only dissenters were Hargrave's crew, who were studying their Captain with disappointment and concern. He was making a valiant attempt to rise, yet his shaking limbs could no longer hold his weight, let alone that of his enormous blade. It was Jacques himself who recovered it from the timbers, levelling its point at Hargrave's face.

The crowd fell silent, each man leaning forward in hushed anticipation.

Hargrave raised his eyes, meeting Jacques' own with pure admiration.

"You have... beaten me." He coughed, nodding at the blade. "I can see that. You defeated me, and you weren't even at your best. I am bested, Mr. Beaufort. I forfe- "

His concession died between his lips, impaled on the end of his own blade. With ruthless efficiency Jacques drove it forward, smashing through Hargrave's skull. The sheer force impaled Hargrave to the rapidly reddening timbers, the hilt of his sword pressed to his bent and broken nose.

"Sorry." Jacques declared, stepping away from the crimson mess.

"I didn't catch zat last part."

Chapter Sixteen

"Oh, Gods."

Trigger glanced at Sheridan, who was covering her mouth with a satin-gloved hand. Her horror was obvious, as was that of the muttering crowd. Apparently, they had been unprepared to witness such brutality, despite their earlier remarks. Trigger could hardly blame them. To watch one man slay another, should never be met without appall.

In this particular venue, however, such empathy could lead to violent results.

"What the fuck!?" Roared Tross, leaping into the ring. "He'd surrendered! The fight was done!"

Jacques regarded the pirate without regret, unsheathing his dagger with deliberate intent.

"He cheated!" Screamed another of Hargrave's crew. "He murdered the Captain!"

The deck began chiming with the ring of unsheathed blades, Hargrave's crew preparing to take its revenge.

"Gentleman, please!"

Trigger wasn't certain what he intended to say, or why he'd leapt atop a barrel. All he'd done was make himself an obvious target.

"Yes, it is true, Beaufort did strike a somewhat…dishonorable blow."

"You're fucking right he did!"

"However!" Trigger pressed, as the crew crept closer to Jacques' waiting form. "His actions were in line with the rules of the contest. Hargrave never completed his concession, nor did any member of his corner. As such, Beaufort was within his rights to strike a killing blow."

He could hear what he was saying, yet even he didn't really believe it. What Beaufort had done was a cowardly act, as close to legal murder as a man could ever come. Trigger himself was disgusted, and knew that his opinion of Beaufort would never recover. Still, the swordsman had won the duel in a viable fashion, which did not merit death from an angry mob.

"He cut the Captain off while he was trying to surrender!" Tross snarled, brandishing his cutlass in Beaufort's direction. Considering the skills the man had so recently presented, Trigger considered this a rather courageous challenge.

"A tactic that the duel in no way forbids."

"Hargrave spared his arse in the second round!" Whined a nearby crewman, waving his pistol with a concerning lack of control.

"Beaufort was making no effort to concede." Trigger replied. "And we all know that Hargrave's leniency had nothing to do with mercy. He'd bet on himself to win during the course of round three, and was trying to ensure he received full pay."

Many of the crowd gasped at this revelation, their shock taking Trigger completely by surprise. This had been a fight to the death, staged on a pirate ship in the middle of lawless seas. Why had they expected fair play?

"I bet on that bastard to take the first round!" Roared a burly member of some unknown crew. "You mean he was stalling?"

"Fuck your first, I'd bet on the second!"

Trigger glanced to where Sheridan was standing, her muscular arm resting around Barnaby's shoulder. She motioned with her eyes that it was time to leave. Trigger was inclined to agree.

"Your Captain was a filthy cheat! And a shit one at that!"

"Hargrave was better than a dozen men!"

"Really? Because one man just put him in the ground, and he's missing half a leg!"

"I'll put you in the ground, you stinking bastard!"

"Come on then! If you fight like your Captain I should be- "

BOOM!

The gunshot thundered, followed by a thump as a body collapsed.

"You fucking cunts!"

Trigger watched from his barrel as all fell to ruin, the ring imploding as dozens of pirates crashed against its boundaries, eager to butcher the other side.

"Beaufort!" He cried, watching as the swordsman was swarmed.

"Beaufort!"

The warrior had vanished, pulled beneath the tide of wrestling flesh.

"Get Barnaby to the ship!" Trigger ordered, drawing his pistol.

"Aye, Captain." Sheridan replied, flooring an attacker with one bone-crushing punch. A moment later she had Barnaby's shoulder, guiding him through the mob as a parent would their child.

"What about the Captain?" He heard Barnaby ask, before the pair were lost behind the roaring crowd.

An excellent question.

Trigger looked to where he'd last seen Beaufort, that section of deck now occupied by dozens of swinging, bloodied fists. Of the wounded swordsman, there was no discernible sign.

Trigger sighed, using his pistol to form a makeshift club.

Pirates. Such an undisciplined lot.

Trigger threw himself forward with a wild cry, diving headfirst into the brawl. A mass of bodies caught his weight, at least four men crumbling as he crashed against them. A fair few uttered murderous threats, yet swift blows silenced them all, the butt of his pistol leaving them either dazed or completely unconscious.

"Beaufort!" Trigger roared, ducking below a dripping cutlass. "Beaufort, can you hear me?"

A heavy figure pressed against him, forcing Trigger deeper into the growing violence. It had gone beyond a simple disagreement, many of the pirates realizing that this was the perfect opportunity to dispatch a hated rival, or to thin out the competition for the remaining race ahead.

"Beaufort!" Trigger snarled, smashing his pistol against a chin. "Beauf- "

A punch from nowhere caught his cheek, sending him crashing to his knees. The instant he was down the cowards converged, stomping and kicking at his fallen form.

"Shameful." Trigger spat, catching a leg as it streaked towards him. With a brutal snarl he twisted it back, snapping the shin with an ugly crack. His attacker's scream must have served as a warning, the others parting enough for him to find his feet.

A large hand found his shoulder, dragging him sideways with ludicrous ease.

Trigger knew of only three people who possessed such strength.

"Are you alright?" He asked, as Beaufort released his formidable grip. The swordsman had taken a few blows, his face a swollen mass of gashes, wounds and cuts.

"I'm fine." Beaufort replied, slashing the stomach of a nearby foe. "Zank you for finding me."

"My pleasure." Trigger declared, avoiding a grappling pair. "Shall we leave?"

"Aye."

Beaufort led the way, clearing a path through the thinning crowd. Its anger had been completely expended, replaced by desperation and fear. Bodies littered the deck as though they were freshly caught fish, while all around them splashes could be heard, the impacts of those who had decided that the sea presented a safer choice.

"Here." Beaufort nodded, cutting down a cowering young man. He couldn't have been older than Barnaby.

The swordsman had led them to a narrow boarding plank, one connected to a small native canoe, bobbing gently a few meters below.

"Well-spotted." Trigger remarked, trusting himself to its unstable length. He hadn't even noticed it.

"I found it last night." Beaufort replied, moving along at an astonishing pace. "I couldn't sleep."

"Nervous?" Trigger asked, surprised at the admission. Still, he could hardly blame the man.

"I was." Beaufort nodded, studying him for a short moment. "I still am. Zis battle will only worsen, especially once everyone has reached zeir vessels. Ze *Blackbird* must leave soon, if she wishes to avoid ze conflict."

"I'd say you're right." Trigger replied, attempting to gain his bearings.

"It is zis way." Beaufort informed him, rushing towards a connecting plank.

"Is it?" Trigger frowned, running a hand through his hair. It struck him as slightly off, and while he had no doubts as to Beaufort's abilities with a blade, his sense of navigation was still up for debate.

"Yes." Beaufort replied, his features creased with agitation. "I told you, I came zis way last night."

Trigger studied the sea around them with a critical eye. It *could* be the correct path, in a somewhat circuitous way.

"Lead on." Trigger declared, deciding that the swordsman had earned a measure of trust.

Beaufort nodded, darting across the planks with only mildly hindered grace. Trigger followed, regretting his decision with every step. Beaufort clearly had no idea.

"This isn't the way." He eventually sighed, pausing. Beaufort greeted his words with a snarl of irritation, his prosthesis shrieking as he slid to a halt.

"It is."

As respectfully as he were able, Trigger gestured at the surrounding vessels.

"These are all bars and floating taverns. We were surrounded by merchant ships. Silks and carvings."

Beaufort folded his arms, gazing around with curious eyes. Eventually he nodded, his broad shoulders sinking in defeat.

"You're right." He conceded, scratching at his cheek. "We're nowhere near the ship."

"It's back that way." Trigger announced, gesturing with his thumb. He could hear the sounds of cannon fire, and could see that the smaller vessels were beginning to drift free, the owners banishing their customers without ceremony or thought. The floating market was breaking like glass, and they would soon be left with no vessel or path.

"You're certain?"

"Yes." Trigger replied, preparing to turn. "Now come on."

Beaufort caught him by his coat, holding him in place with that iron grip.

"Zere's no need to panic." Beaufort declared. "We boz know your crew will be fine. Zey are capable, and you have trained zem well."

"Thank you, but this really isn't the time." Trigger frowned.

"It is." Beaufort nodded. "You need to know how highly I regard zem, and zat I will do my best to keep zem from harm."

Trigger stared into Beaufort's eyes, attempting to find the meaning behind his cryptic words.

"What- "

He didn't see Beaufort move. All he felt was the crash of his elbow, like an anvil dropping against his chin. His vision faded, the world vanishing behind flashing lights. Eventually those lights became darkness, a freezing void without time or sensation.

On instinct alone, Trigger tried to breath. It felt as if his lungs had burst into flame.

He came up gasping, hacking water from his lungs in ragged gasps. The sea around him was shrouded in smoke, the black clouds clawing harshly against his stinging throat.

"Beaufort?" He mumbled, speaking around his swollen jaw. A heavy wave slapped his cheek, filling his nose with water, and conjuring yet another bout of agonized rasps.

Closing his eyes, Trigger allowed the sea to take him, sinking into its depths without a struggle. The world above was too chaotic, too distracting, and he desperately needed a moment to think.

He had been struck, most likely by Beaufort. The traitor must have hurled him overboard, where he'd drifted for no small amount of time. He could hear the sound of cannon fire blasting in the distance, which suggested that the gathering had already disintegrated, devolving into a running battle that would see thousands dead.

This knowledge left two main questions. The first was whether his crew had managed to escape, and if so, had Beaufort been among their ranks? The second, and far more pressing, was how far away had they managed to travel, and how, exactly, was he going to catch them?

Trigger surfaced, taking a deep and calming breath.

"There, Captain!"

The voice that sounded behind him was impossibly deep, as coarse and rough as a granite mace. The one that followed was even worse, though only because Trigger could identify its owner.

"Captain Trigger. I must say, it is a pleasure to see you again!"

Trigger turned, finding himself gazing into a small wooden hull. Glancing up, he saw that the boat held two occupants, each one of them the mass of at least three men.

"Carnage." He sputtered, meeting the Thrallkin's yellow eyes. "How have you been?"

Carnage's crimson features split into a grin, his great hand descending towards Trigger's throat.

"Better than you, Trigger. Better than you."

****

"Where are they?"

Barnaby scanned the ships around them for some sign of the missing pair, his vision obscured by gunpowder and smoke. At least half-a-dozen ships were entirely aflame, including Hargrave's once glorious vessel. Many more were being smashed to pieces, the formation of the arena having left them wide-open to the cannons of their rivals.

"We can't wait forever!" Frank declared, as a cannon thundered close to port.

"We'll wait as long as we need!" Sheridan replied, her wig askew from their retreat. Returning to the ship had been a brutal affair, the knuckles of Sheridan's gloves now torn and bloodied. Still, they were in a better condition than the men who'd bloodied them.

"No, we won't."

Frank drew his sword, as did Sunniday, Gary and Bradley. The cannon fire grew louder, smothering the screams of the dying and wounded.

"You can't be serious." Sheridan snarled, tossing aside her wig. "He's our Captain!"

"He is, and he's a damn good one." Frank replied. "Which is why I'm obeying his orders. My duty is to see that the crew is protected, something I can't do if we stay here. The Captain would want us to leave. The crew wants us to leave. You don't have the authority to stop that."

"What about Jacques?" Barnaby pleaded, putting himself between them. "You're not just abandoning Trigger. You're leaving him behind, as well."

"I know, and I'm sorry." Frank declared. "I really am. But I'm doing this for the sake of our crew. We can't risk dozens for just the two. It isn't fair."

His companions nodded, though none of them appeared pleased with this turn of events.

"This is mutiny." Sheridan growled, taking a step towards them.

"It isn't, and you know it." Frank replied. "Now please, stand down."

A cannonball crashed down as she considered her choice, spraying them all with freezing drops.

Slowly, Sheridan lowered her fists, stepping aside and exposing the wheel.

"Fine." She sighed, sounding utterly defeated. "Go."

Without another word, she turned, making her way towards the ships edge.

"Where are you going?" Barnaby asked, as Frank took hold of the *Blackbird's* wheel.

"They're free to leave." Sheridan replied, hoisting one leg across the banister. "That doesn't mean I have to."

Barnaby watched in shock as Sheridan threw herself overboard, only to halt a moment later. A large hand had caught her waist, stopping her fall and sending her sliding back to the swaying deck.

"Jacques!" Barnaby cheered, as the swordsman's battered features appeared. Sheridan was less excited, hoisting Jacques aboard with a fearsome snarl.

"Where's Trigger?" She demanded, as Jacques struggled from her grip.

Jacques' expression crumpled, as though he'd been dealt a mortal blow.

"Your Captain was a noble man." He replied, as Sheridan studied him with rising horror.

"What do you mean!?" She barked, raising her fist and stepping towards him.

"Ze crowd turned to madness." Jacques replied, making a measured retreat. "Trigger found me in zeir clutches, and fought his way zrough. I was freed, yet it caused ze mob to turn on him. I was wounded and outmatched. Zere was nozing I could do."

"You left him!?" Sheridan shrieked. "After he came back for you!?"

"He was great man." Jacques declared, his mighty shoulders slumping. "I am so sorry zat- "

Sheridan struck, slamming him face-first into the moistened deck.

"I don't care." She snarled, with murderous intent.

"Sheridan, please!" Barnaby begged, throwing himself against her. "There was nothing he could do!"

His new position afforded him a view of Frank and the others, who were watching the scene with obvious despair.

"Well, that settles it." Frank muttered, mostly to himself. "Hoist the sail, men! We're leaving!"

"Aye, Mr. Frank!"

The ship rocked forward as they caught a stiff breeze, carving through the water with mounting haste. The cannons were still firing with pace and regularity, making every moment in the fixture a dance with death.

"Get off me." Sheridan snapped, grabbing Barnaby's collar and tossing him aside. Jacques had risen to his feet, and while he had yet to unsheathe his blades, it was clear that he was more than ready to start putting them to use.

"I did all I could." Jacques declared, wiping at his bleeding lips. "And I am sorry for your loss. Understand, however, zat I will make no more apologies, or tolerate another blow."

"You're a coward." Sheridan spat, clearly undaunted by the threat.

"Your Captain knew what he was risking." Jacques replied. "It was a brave and admirable act. You dishonor his memory wiz such petulant behavior."

For a moment, Barnaby feared that Sheridan would strike again, yet after a handful of seconds she turned away, retreating to Trigger's quarters without another word.

"Are you alright?" Barnaby asked, racing to Jacques' side.

"I'm fine." He replied, still dabbing at his lips. "She is angry, and full of grief. She will regret her actions in ze coming weeks."

BOOM!

The explosion of a nearby ship sent them both dropping to their knees, the screams of the fallen indiscernible from the cheers of the triumphant.

"Swing to starboard!" Sunniday roared, having retaken his position at the peak of the mast. Frank followed his directions as best he could, navigating through the dozens of vessels that were obstructing their path.

"There's a ship to port that's showing her broadside!" Sunniday declared, as a vessel before them burst into flames. "She's gaining fast!"

"We're already at full sail!" Frank replied, his voice made high by rising fear.

"They're preparing to fire!"

"Well, fire back!"

"We'd never hit them from this angle!"

"What the fuck do you want from me!?"

BOOM!

Barnaby stayed low as the enemy fired, the ship shuddering beneath him as iron smashed against its hull. He could hear crewmen screaming from somewhere below deck, their fragile bodies pinned between crushing metal and shredding wood.

"Fuck's sake, Frank! Do something!" Sunniday screamed, clinging to the crow's nest as it trembled back-and-forth.

"Do what!?" Frank replied, huddling feebly beside the wheel. "I've never even steered a ship, let alone captained it!"

"Zen get out of my way."

Jacques marched fearlessly towards the wheel, ignoring the cannons and their endless barrage. Splinters flew as he shoved Frank aside, gripping the wheel between blood-stained hands.

"Prepare to drop anchor!" He cried, his powerful voice ringing throughout the ship. "And on my mark, be ready to fire!"

"We can't drop the anchor!" Frank protested, as crewman scurried to obey. "We'll be statues in the water!"

"No, we won't." Jacques replied, his features twisting into a madman's grin. "Maintain full sail as ze anchor drops! When I give you ze word, severe its ties to our ship!"

"Wait, what!?" Frank asked, clearly horrified with Jacques' demand. Even so, the crew were following his instructions, embracing the discipline Trigger had so efficiently enforced.

"We need our anchor!" Frank pleaded, as yet another volley crashed against their stern.

"Zis is a race, Mr. Frank." Jacques declared, muscles bulging as he squeezed the wheel. "I see no reason why we'd wish to halt."

Frank gazed at Jacques as though he were mad. Maybe he was.

At this particular moment, Barnaby couldn't see a more capable choice.

"Drop anchor!"

The steel plummeted, scraping the ocean floor with a barely audible thunk. It caught a heartbeat later, the chain pulling tight as the *Blackbird* strained against it. Barnaby tumbled as the vessel was sent into a wild swing, aiming its cannons squarely at their panicking foes.

"Fire!" Beaufort roared, his bellow eclipsing the cannons themselves.

The crew obeyed, filling the skies with iron rain. The enemy ship was torn to shreds, their prow and sails obliterated beneath the explosive assault.

"Captain, we're spinning back towards the battle!" Screamed a crewman from below, his words enhancing Jacques' grin.

"Loose the anchor!"

Timber cracked as the men set to work, severing the anchor at the peak of their arc. As the chain fell away the *Blackbird* sailed on, veering from the battle at a thunderous pace.

"You did it!" Barnaby cheered, as the battle faded to meaningless smoke.

"He did." Frank conceded, wiping his brow. His tone was filled with obvious doubt.

Jacques made no reply as he leant against their wheel, his scarred features the essence of humility.

As the sounds of conflict faded, more and more crew emerged from below, surveying the deck with tentative joy.

"Did we escape?"

"Where's the Captain?"

"Yes. Where is the Captain?"

The last question came from Magwa, who burst through the crowd with axe in hand.

Jacques looked to Barnaby, his great chest heaving as he gave a sigh.

"I am sorry." He announced, indicating to Frank that he should take the wheel. Frank did so, allowing Jacques to face the crew.

"Your Captain was a great man, a noble man. He came back for me when ze battle began, and in doing so, he saved my life. Sadly, against such overwhelming odds, he lost his own."

The crew gasped, many of them staggering as though physically struck.

"No."

"Not a chance."

"That can't be right!" Roared a particularly boisterous crewman, his rugged beard crusted with ale and stew. "The

Captain's carved his way out of a fucking sea-monster! You think anyone back there could bring him down?"

"Aye!"

"We have to go back!"

Barnaby started as a large presence occupied his right, Sheridan's heavy frame pressing roughly against his shoulder. She was nodding, clearly touched by the crew's display of loyalty.

"I saw him die." Jacques replied, shaking his wounded head. "Zere's nozing to go back for."

Several crewmen muttered disbelief, yet many more took Jacques at his word, their faces sinking with the realization that their Captain had been lost. Barnaby could barely accept it himself.

"Beaufort saw him fall?" Magwa asked, gesturing at Jacques with his hatchet's edge. "He is certain?"

"I did." Jacques nodded, broad shoulders slumping.

Magwa's hatchet hovered, as though the Kalyute were weighing the swordsman's claim, measuring its truth. Eventually, he judged it worthy, lowering his hatchet with a weary sigh.

"To lose Captain is a terrible omen." He declared, sheathing his weapon and shaking his head.

"Forget your fucking omens!" Snapped a member of the crew. "Without Trigger to lead us, we'll be long dead before any bad luck steers our way!"

"Wouldn't dying be considered bad luck?"

"Piss off, Terry. You know what I mean."

"You raise a valid point." Frank declared, interrupting the pair with a wave of his hand. "Few of us can navigate, and even fewer can read. We can't plan for shit, and when it comes to a fight, we're about as useless as a whore without holes."

The crew regarded him with interest, clearly intrigued to see where he was going. Barnaby was quite curious himself.

"We're going to need a new leader, and we're going to need them quickly." Frank continued, his words punctuated by the boom of countless distant cannons. "Someone who can take our lack of experience, skills and intelligence, and use them in a way that creates a functioning ship. Trigger made it look easy, and I'm willing to bet that there isn't a soul alive who can use us half as well. The Captain was truly one-of-a-kind."

The crew released an admiring roar, though all Sheridan produced was a disgusted snort.

"He was the best." Frank nodded, folding his arms. "So, we owe it to him to find a worthy successor. Someone who will lead us to the win he deserved."

"Jacques!"

"Sheridan!"

"You can do it, Franky!"

"Black Barnaby!"

Barnaby started as his name was called, and was even more surprised to see a few appreciative nods. Had Jacques' stories spread so far?

"Please, keep your suggestions to yourself!" Frank declared, raising his hands for silence. "Tradition holds that we wait at least one day before announcing a new Captain, and as far as I'm concerned, it's a tradition we'll obey. Tomorrow I'll place a barrel directly beneath the mast, and hand each man a scrap of paper. You will mark this paper with the name of the crewman you believe best suited to the task."

A tentative hand rose.

"Yes?"

"What if we can't write?"

Frank blinked rapidly as he considered the question, his democracy destroyed through simple ignorance.

"Right." He replied, rubbing the bridge of his nose. "New plan. We all meet here tomorrow at noon. I'll call out names, and if you think they suit the job, just give a yell. Sound good?"

"Aye!" Cheered the crew, apparently choosing that moment as the right time to practice.

"Unbelievable." Sheridan murmured, her dark eyes fixed on Jacques. The swordsman had declined to join the cheer, yet he did appear pleased by Frank's declaration.

"Alright then!" Frank roared, waving his deformed hand. "That's it for today! See to your duties and tend to your grief. We've got a big day tomorrow, and a larger race ahead!"

The crew gave a few coarse grunts in reply, whispering amongst themselves as they dispersed.

Barnaby was silent, however, completely unsure as to how he should proceed. He wanted to offer Sheridan a few words of comfort, yet his mind and tongue were proving extremely uncooperative.

"You should tend to Beaufort." Sheridan announced, glancing at him with an odd mixture of contempt and predatory curiosity. "Get him to the doctor. I'd say he needs it."

Barnaby's lips quivered as he sought out a reply, yet Sheridan cut him off long before one came.

"Don't worry about it" She declared, placing a slender finger right across his lips. The shock of contact froze him, leaving him as helpless as a scruff-held kitten. "See to your friend, make sure he's okay. I'll talk to you privately, tonight, in Trigger's old quarters. Do you understand?"

Barnaby nodded, completely forsaking his attempts at speech.

"Excellent." Sheridan nodded, removing her finger and marching away.

Barnaby stood alone for several awkward moments, attempting to decipher what exactly had occurred.

He didn't have a fucking clue.

Chapter Seventeen

"Captain Carnage, dinner, about five hours, and aboard my ship, the *Bloodbath*."

Trigger's eyelids flickered open to glaring candlelight, the ringing in his ears almost eclipsing his addresser's bizarre sentence.

"Pardon?" He asked, feeling as though he were still underwater. Too many blows to the head, in far too short a time.

"I'm answering your basic questions. Who, what, where, when and why."

Trigger forced himself to focus, pushing past the pain in his skull.

He was seated, though in no way restrained. His sword and pistol had been removed, yet his coat, scope and other effects remained intact. Before him was an immense and well-varnished table, its surface reflecting the sumptuous feast adorning its considerable length. It also reflected the face of his companion, red features twisted into a patient grin.

"Carnage." Trigger nodded, the action sending a wave of agony rippling down his spine. "I missed you at the duel."

"I can juggle horses." Carnage shrugged, leaning back into his chair. "Two humans brawling holds little appeal."

"Fair enough." Trigger conceded, adjusting his coat.

"Drink?" Carnage asked, motioning to the shadows. A member of his crew emerged, red skin completely bare, save for the chef's hat perched precariously on his scalp. Trigger tried to avoid staring as the Thrallkin lumbered towards him, filling his wine glass with a humble bow.

"Thank you." Trigger ventured, taking a grateful sip. Whatever tortures Carnage had in store, he doubted he'd resort to simple poison.

"I apologize for his lack of uniform." Carnage began, tucking his arms behind his head. "One encounters chefs quite rarely at sea, and the hat is all we've been able to find."

Trigger considered this statement, and the crimson penis swinging inches from the table.

"I believe I may be dreaming." He declared, downing a thoughtful sip.

"Do your dreams often consist of giant red cocks?"

Trigger pondered the question, unsure of the best response.

"Do you mean red *exclusively*?"

Carnage studied him a moment, yellow eyes narrowed to sparking coals. A moment later he was chuckling, his great chest pumping like a blacksmith's bellows.

"You are *ice*." Carnage declared, shaking his head. "Completely unarmed on an enemy ship, and still you manage to crack a joke. I admire you Trigger, I really do."

"Thank you." Trigger replied, finishing his wine. He'd had far worse.

"Refill?" Carnage asked, raising a crimson hand.

"Thank you. That would be delightful."

If he was going to die, he may as well be drunk.

The naked Thrallkin reappeared, filling his cup with unnecessary flourish. He clearly enjoyed his current role.

"You may eat, as well." Carnage urged, gesturing at the food. "Ajak spent hours preparing this feast."

"And it looks incredible." Trigger replied, nodding at the chef. "I merely require a moment to recover, if you don't mind. I swallowed some seawater before you found me, and it has left my throat feeling rather dry."

He took another sip, using the pause in conversation to further assess the room. It was a surprisingly tasteful affair, its walls occupied by countless leathery tomes. As collections went, it was rather remarkable.

"I see you are an avid reader." Trigger announced, indicating the burdened shelves. Carnage followed his gaze, smiling as he studied the aging covers.

"I am, though sadly, many of these remain unread. My education consisted of very little reading, and I am not as swift as I would otherwise prefer."

"I see." Trigger replied, unsure how to proceed. He knew what composed a Thrallkin's education, and was well-aware that Carnage would soon be using it on him. He needed to delay that for as long as he were able, at least until he had something resembling a plan.

Carnage studied him with those yellow eyes, his smile receding slightly as Trigger failed to converse.

"Well then, I guess we should see to business." The Thrallkin declared, propping his cheek against a fist.

"I guess so." Trigger replied, cursing his hesitation. Glancing at the table, he saw that he'd been provided cutlery, a rather fetching set of gilded silver.

Against Carnage, they may as well be toothpicks.

"You can stop that right now." Carnage announced, gesturing at his knife and fork. "You're not going to need them, unless you decide to eat. I'm not going to hurt you, Trigger."

Trigger ceased his machinations, suspicious of the Thrallkin's claims, yet also highly optimistic.

"What is your definition of harm, exactly?"

"The same as yours." Carnage replied, delicately seizing his fork. "Which is the reason why we're speaking."

"Indeed?" Trigger remarked, snatching up his own. The turkey before him smelt quite divine.

"Yes." Carnage nodded, grinning as Trigger began to eat. "You've been to war, and seen its horrors. Few pirates can claim the same."

Trigger considered his reply, helping himself to a serving of steaming mashed potato. It had been fluffed to utter perfection.

"War tends to be a military affair." He eventually declared, dabbing at his lips. "Pirates and the military rarely consort."

"True." Carnage shrugged. "I never met a pirate while I was on the front lines. Then again, I scarcely met a soldier, either. A human one, at least. Have you ever been to the front lines, Trigger?"

It was an odd question, mostly because Trigger wasn't aware of a 'front line'. He'd always known the war to be a fragmented affair, unplanned battles that flared into life, before fading away into ashes and death.

"No. I can't say I have."

"Do you know where they are?"

Trigger frowned, annoyed more by his ignorance than Carnage's tone.

"No."

"Do you know who we are fighting?"

"I believe I do, though I'm beginning to suspect that I may be wrong."

"You catch on quickly." Carnage grinned.

"It aids others in reaching their point." Trigger replied, setting aside his fork.

"Fair enough." Carnage laughed, propping his feet against the table. "I guess I'll get to mine. Your empire is a lie, Trigger. A corrupt, festering wound, spreading its taint across our world."

"It's not my empire." Trigger scowled, sipping at his wine.

"I know." Carnage nodded, clapping his hands in glee. "I've heard your story, and what a story it is. Honor, duty and sacrifice, all capped off by a marvelous betrayal. Your life should be a play, Trigger."

"It feels like it, at times." Trigger replied, glancing at the naked chef.

"Then consider this the beginning of a new act!" Carnage declared, sitting up straight and spreading his arms. "A brighter one, filled with purpose and righteous retribution!"

"You should finish more of these plays." Trigger advised. "They have much to say about the topic of revenge."

"The first thing I ever read was one of these plays." Carnage replied. "Believe me, there is a point where fiction and reality must forever part ways."

"What is it you want from me, exactly?" Trigger asked, once again surprised by the Captain's eloquence.

"To lead us." Carnage announced, grinning from ear-to-ear.

Trigger blinked.

"Pardon?"

"I want you to serve as our Captain." Carnage elaborated, gesturing for more wine. "To guide our actions over the coming years."

This conversation had taken many odd turns. This one left Trigger almost entirely mute.

"May I ask why?"

"Because you are a leader, a pirate, and a warrior." Carnage replied. "A combination that leaves you perfectly equipped to forge the new world."

Trigger rubbed his finger against his thumb, considering this wild proposal.

"What would this role entail? And why would you have me lead, rather than yourself?"

Carnage's grin began fading, his yellow eyes affecting a distant stare.

"I know your story, Trigger. What do you know of mine?"

"That you escaped the Empire's clutches. That you fled the war and seized the first ship you found."

"So, you know nothing." Carnage chuckled, shaking his head.

"Apparently."

Carnage snorted, the distance in his eyes lengthening by countless strides.

"I was born on a farm, as all my people are. My birth was commissioned due to growing demand, the press of enemies having driven my people to the precipice of extinction. Reinforcements were necessary, and so the Empire delivered. My mother was restrained, raped, and forced to carry me for however many months my people require. The instant I was born, I was taken from her arms, and sent off to war."

"Barbaric." Trigger declared, feeling a swell of pity.

"Quite the opposite." Carnage replied. "It is high-level manufacturing. After all, my people are simply a product of war. One they have refined to a staggering degree."

Trigger thought on this, shaking his head in horror at the Empire's cold and indifferent gears.

"Where is this Front line?" He asked, struck by a sudden notion. "It must be distant indeed, if you were old enough to fight by the time you arrived."

"It is distant, though not so far as you would think." Carnage replied. "My people age quickly, and within two years we can match any human youth. Within two more we can challenge a man, and with every year after that, we grow further and further beyond you."

"And how old does that make you?" Trigger asked, studying the behemoth before him.

"Seventeen." Carnage shrugged, his shoulders wider than two men across.

Trigger raised an eyebrow, yet managed to restrain his surprise.

"A young age to have seen war."

"It is not unique amongst my kind." Carnage replied. "Every member of my race may claim the same. What makes my crew unique is that we managed to escape."

"How?"

Carnage rapped his fingers against the table, his expression made heavy through unwelcome thoughts.

"Our skin is reddened through necessity." He began, holding up his hand for further inspection. "It is our camouflage amongst the corpses, our greatest way of remaining unseen. It is how we approach the enemies' citadels and strongholds. We crawl towards them on our bellies, using the fallen as our well-paved paths."

"Gods." Trigger breathed, remembering his own military past.

"As we struggle forward, the Empire's watchdogs rest at our heels, murdering and maiming any brave fool with the temerity to flee. This is rare, however. My people have been bred and broken for at least three hundred years, and the training runs deep in our blood. Few have the resolve to work against it."

"You do." Trigger nodded, feeling a hint of admiration.

"I do, as does the rest of my crew." Carnage replied. "We are all of an age, and thus shared everything as we grew to adulthood. The deaths, the beatings, the hatred and the fear…"

Carnage trailed off, yellow eyes filling with a lifetime of rage. It took several moments for the sensation to abate, moments in which Trigger remained silent and still. He had seen that fury in his father's favorite hounds, their lean features devoid of mercy as they ached for the next hunt and kill.

"I spoke to them as we grew." Carnage continued, gathering himself. "I whispered the thoughts swirling about my mind, questions as to what we were doing, and why were we doing them? At first, I was ignored, but over the months I wore them down. They joined my ponderings, yet even with all of us working together, we could never find an answer. We were fighting, we were dying, for absolutely nothing."

"A common trait of any war." Trigger sighed.

"And one that even we could see." Carnage snarled. "A group of uneducated beasts, bred solely to fight and die. We tried spreading our message, yet the others were unreceptive, too indoctrinated or feral to consider our words. They died by the cartload, and we were forced to watch, all while struggling to keep ourselves alive against an enemy that cannot be defeated."

"So, you left." Trigger nodded, the picture forming in his mind.

"We did. Our watchers had grown complacent, believing us to be the same cattle as our brainwashed brothers. We turned on them in the night, bending our cages and snapping our shackles." He shook his head, forehead creasing with frustration and despair.
"My people could walk away from that war without the faintest trace of effort. The only thing that holds them is what they have been taught, and it is a more effective prison than any fashioned from stone or steel."

"I'm sorry." Trigger declared, running a hand through his hair. "I never knew."

"Few do." Carnage replied. "Your Empire excels at keeping secrets, especially those the public might reproach."

"Of that, I am well-aware."

"I know." Carnage grinned. "One doesn't climb as high as you did without learning a few sordid details."

"An apt choice of words." Trigger conceded, cocking his head to one side. "My time in the navy taught me more than I ever cared to know."

"Do you regret it?" Carnage asked, rubbing thoughtfully at his chin.

"No." Trigger replied, folding his arms. "When I think of the man I was, the ignorance that he endured, I am disgusted."

"I knew I liked you." Carnage chuckled, studying Trigger with boundless glee. "The moment you shot Falcon, I knew. You were the one we needed, a man who can make the hard choices, who can take the shots that no one else would dare to make."

The sentence was intended as a compliment, yet it merely drew Trigger's memory to the cruelty of that day, the insane barbarism of Carnage's actions. The sympathy he had developed faded in an instant, replaced once more by steely contempt.

"What happened to Falcon was a tragedy." Trigger declared, linking his fingers. "It was needless brutality, which debased all who took part. I do not look back on that day with any fondness or pride."

"Nor should you." Carnage shrugged. "I certainly don't."

Trigger's eyebrows rose once more, the movement born from disbelief.

"It's true." Carnage replied, reading his expression. "I was a maniac. I still am, a fact which returns us to your original question. I want you to lead, Trigger, because I know that I cannot. Not objectively. I was raised in a blood-soaked trench, with no name or morals to call my own. My first lesson was to slaughter my enemies, with as much savagery as I could muster. This makes me an effective fighter, but a terrible Captain. All our raids, our infamous, horrifying attacks, were attempts at revolution. Feeble, misguided attempts, sprung from a mind that is not entirely sane. Falcon's death was a symptom of that. I encountered him at a tavern, and slighted him, as is my way. Being a man of courage, he insulted me right back. My response was…disproportionate."

"You could say that." Trigger frowned, completely unsure as to how he should proceed. After all, Carnage had just declared himself an utter lunatic.

"You're uncertain about my offer." Carnage nodded, his ropey hair bouncing against his chair.

"I'm uncertain about many things." Trigger replied. "As conversations go, this was a rather…intense affair."

"That is fine." Carnage announced, raising a magnanimous hand. "I would have been concerned about betrayal if you'd leapt at the chance. Doubt means that you're considering it, and that your reply will likely be genuine."

"And if my reply is no?" Trigger asked, fully aware of the risk he was taking.

"A question to be answered at a later date." Carnage shrugged, resting his palm against the table. "After all, you're not exactly going anywhere, are you?"

Trigger studied the room around him, from its groaning shelves to its crimson Captain.

"No." He sighed, gesturing for more wine.

"I guess I'm not."

****

The deck was silent as Barnaby approached, the crew having adopted their grief with the same enthusiasm they placed in every task. What drinking there was seemed entirely somber, no songs or shanties escaping their lips. No dice rolled across the sea-worn timbers, and every deck of cards sat nestled in their holster.

Knock!

Knock!

Knock!

Barnaby winced as his knuckles struck the door, shattering the near-ceremonial silence. Every head turned to look as he waited for a reply, Sheridan taking her sweet time to move across Trigger's tiny quarters.

Boom!

The door swung wide on its fragile hinges, drowning the knocks that had come before. Sheridan took its place in the slanted frame, illuminated by a flickering light.

She was almost naked, her breasts and groin covered by a handful of silk.

"Get in here." She ordered, her voice low and lustful. At least, Barnaby assumed that was the case. He'd never been addressed with lust before.

The decision was never his to make, as Sheridan seized him a moment later, dragging him inside with a powerful tug. The door snapped shut behind him, leaving them alone in the ill-lit room.

"What are yo- "

Sheridan threw him on the mattress with an audible thump, knocking the wind from his lungs and leaving him gasping for air.

"No talking." Sheridan instructed, removing his pants with one skillful tug. She threw them towards the poorly built door, one pant-leg slipping beneath the considerable gap.

As her waist descended towards his own, Barnaby gained some idea of what was about to occur. He wagered that he should probably feel at least a trace of arousal. All he could manage was panic.

Sheridan tore the silk from her waist with one mighty twist, sliding it beneath the door without a second glance. From his lower position, Barnaby was able to follow its passage, the delicate material vanishing beneath a scramble of questing hands. The crewmen knew what was happening inside, and he was certain that it would only take a moment for one of them to gamble a perverted glance.

The concern vanished as Sheridan's skin touched his, her thighs warm and smooth against his own. Gasping from surprise, Barnaby made to look at her, yet Sheridan forced his gaze away, driving his cheek into the comfortable mattress. It kept his eyes towards the crack in the door, affording him a spectacular view of the curious crew, who had pressed their stomachs to the deck in an attempt to see.

Gary was giving him an immense thumbs-up.

Sheridan started grinding, driving his pelvis downwards and wriggling her own. She moaned and gasped as though she were enjoying it, yet at no stage had Barnaby actually entered her. The crew responded to the sounds with frantic excitement, wriggling like snakes in an effort to witness Sheridan's joy.

The crack was too narrow, however, and all that they could see was Barnaby, a fact which caused many to cease their attempts. Still, they were whispering and laughing as dispersed, glancing back at him with admiration.

"How many are left?" Sheridan whispered, bending towards his ear.

"What?"

"How many of the crew are still watching?"

"Only a few." Barnaby mumbled, her grip too strong against his jaw.

"Well, they get a reward for dedication." Sheridan replied, pitching them into a sudden roll. The movement swapped their positions, exposing her thighs to the gawkers outside. A few stray cheers greeted their appearance, bringing a smile to Sheridan's lips.

"What now?" Barnaby choked, her palm still clamped against his throat.

"Hold on." Sheridan replied. "And act like you're enjoying this."

Her hands snaked downwards with astounding speed, clamping his buttocks with painful force. A moment later her arms were pumping, driving Barnaby into a rhythm that he could never have managed alone. The mattress wailed beneath their writhing, accompanied by the whispers of those still following their false display. They sounded impressed, which was something, at least.

Sheridan pumped him for Gods know how long, until even the last straggler had retired to their bed. By the time she was finished his thighs were rubbed raw, the pounded skin swelling to a hideous bruise.

"Good work." She whispered, giving his arse a squeeze. "Now, get out, and tell everyone that you gave me the ride of my life. I'll be doing the same."

With casual ease she tossed him aside, sprawling across the mattress with a deafening yawn.

"What…what just happened?" Barnaby asked, wincing as he stood to put on his pants.

"Just do what I said." Sheridan asked, allowing him a view of her marvelous groin.

For the first time that night, Barnaby's manhood stood fully erect. It was a bit fucking late, unfortunately.

"Not bad." Sheridan nodded, as he quickly covered up.

Barnaby wasn't certain as to how he should reply. His lips answered for him, forming an awkward chuckle that would put a donkey to shame.

Turning red from foot to face, Barnaby exited the quarters, limping slightly as he did.

He awoke to a legion of eyes, a sea of crewmen surrounding his hammock.

"How was it?" Gary asked, leaning in with a hungry gaze. His closeness disturbed the slumbering cat, which was curled across Barnaby's lap. It had wandered in seeking warmth, and by the Gods, had his crotch been holding some heat.

"How was what?" Barnaby replied, rubbing at his sleep-filled eye.

"Don't play coy!" Gary chuckled, giving his shoulder a friendly slap. "We all saw, and boy, did we all hear!"

"Never thought you'd have it in you." Bradley declared, scratching at his considerable waist. "I never thought you'd have it in *her*."

"Oh." Barnaby muttered, unsure how to play this particular game. "You're talking about Sheridan."

"You're damn right we are!" Gary exclaimed, leaning toward him with a conspiring grin. "She's been talking about it as well. Staggered out of her quarters this morning, with a smile so wide it could replace the moon! Frank had the balls to ask her what happened, and God's above, you should have heard the praise!"

"I still don't believe it." Bradley murmured, shaking his head.

"Well, tough luck, Bradley. We all heard it, and more than a few of us watched it. Shit, I even won a prize."

Gary held up a wrist, revealing the strip of silk he had carefully tied around it.

"You're a seedy bastard." Bradley frowned. "You know that, right?"

"Aye, I do." Gary nodded, giving the fabric an obvious sniff. A few of the crewmen cheered, while others shook their heads in disgust. Barnaby approved of the latter display.

"Anyway." Gary began, lowering his swaddled wrist. "You haven't answered me. How was it?"

All faces fixed on Barnaby, eyes wide with lustful intrigue.

He considered his words carefully, all-too aware that defying Sheridan was never a viable option. He had experienced her strength first-hand, and had no desire to feel it again.

Well, maybe a little bit.

"It was…violent."

The crew stared at him for what seemed an age, filling him with doubt. If he'd failed to convince them, well, Sheridan would not be pleased.

And he'd probably be dead.

"I fucking bet it was!" Gary roared, seizing his thigh and squeezing it tight. Barnaby tried to smile as the crew carried the cheer, yet Gary's fingers were pressing against his bruise, and it was all he could do to restrain a scream.

"You old dog, you!"

"Cheeky little bugger!"

"She must prefer 'em small, it's why none of us have ever got a look!"

Barnaby blushed beneath their adulation, his hammock swaying from their constant slaps and shoves. The movement proved the final straw in breaking the cat's patience, as with a faint meow it leapt away, clawing at his groin as it slipped to the floor.

Barnaby wished he could join it.

Ding! Ding! Ding!

The crew fell silent as the bell rang out, regaining some composure as they rose to their feet.

"Time to get up, young stallion." Gary grinned. "It's voting time!"

"What?" Barnaby frowned, rolling from his hammock without a trace of grace. "How long was I asleep?"

"Thirteen hours." Gary chuckled. "We thought you needed it."

Barnaby failed to reply as the crew dispersed, heading towards the stairs in an orderly press. Bradley led the charge as they ventured from the room, huffing slightly as he pushed Barnaby aside.

"Don't mind him." Gary whispered, patting his shoulder. "He's been carrying a candle for Sheridan since he first stepped aboard. Poor bastard can't stand that you got there first."

"Oh." Barnaby muttered, feeling himself deflate. Another enemy. How wonderful.

Gary laughed as he guided Barnaby upwards, the pair of them blinking as they stepped out on deck. The sun was reaching its peak, forming shimmering walls of scorching heat.

"Crewmen, are you ready!?"

Frank's voice rang proudly from the stern, capturing the attention of all onboard. While some were still seeing to their necessary duties, most had taken up position before Frank's feet, their boot-swaddled heels bobbing with excitement. Sheridan was standing among them, positively resplendent in her best wig and gown. She spotted Barnaby the moment he emerged, beckoning him over with a girlish wave.

"Your woman calls." Gary whispered, giving him a playful shove. "You'd best answer."

Barnaby marched across the deck, trying to still his pounding heart. Sheridan looked almost playful as she studied his approach, fanning at her chest with a patterned fan. It was completely at odds with the sexual barbarian he had experienced last night, and merely added another layer of confusion to his already turbulent mind.

"How are you feeling?" Sheridan whispered, pulling him close. He could hear the crew chuckling amongst themselves.

"Sore." He croaked, his voice breaking beneath her stare.

"Did you do as I said?"

"Yes."

"Good boy." She replied, giving his buttocks a commanding squeeze. Behind him, he could hear Gary utter a supportive cheer.

"Is this everyone?" Frank asked, counting the crew with his mottled hand.

"It is." Jacques declared, rising from his seat at the fore of the crowd.

"Good, good." Frank nodded, clearly unwilling to question his math. "Then we can finally begin."

"When the time comes, vote for yourself." Sheridan commanded, whispering into his ear.

"What? Why?"

"Because I told you to."

She gave his buttocks another squeeze, this one decidedly less friendly.

Barnaby swallowed nervously, preparing to raise his hand.

"Alright, we'll be doing this alphabetically." Frank declared, unfurling a list of poorly inked names.

"What does that mean?" Bradley frowned, his bad mood extending to all he surveyed.

"That we'll call out your names based on their order in the alphabet."

"The alphabet has an order?"

"What the fuck is the alphabet?"

Barnaby watched as Jacques' covered his face. His lessons had not extended to most of the crew.

Frank gave them all a withering look, before returning his attention to the hastily scrawled list.

"Abraham, John."

No hands were raised. John didn't complain.

"Angsley, Wolfgang."

Again, no hands. Wolfgang appeared to be slightly relieved.

"Beaufort, Jacques."

A third of the crew raised their hands, cheering at Jacques' name. The swordsman had raised his own, his head cast downwards in apparent humility.

"No surprise there." Sheridan growled, her fanning increasing to a rapid pace.

"He is the best choice, after you." Barnaby ventured, fearing for his life, or at least his fragile cheek.

"He's a liar and a traitor." Sheridan replied, shooting him a contemptuous glance. "You'll see it for yourself, soon enough."

"Alright, alright, settle down. We've plenty more to go through."

Frank's voice calmed the cheering crowd, drawing Sheridan's attention back to the stage. Barnaby was grateful for the reprieve.

"Burges, Huey."

"Cartwright, Jackson."

On and on the names rolled, their syllables losing meaning in the constant drone. Not a single finger answered the cries, not even when Sheridan was finally called.

"Really?" Barnaby asked, studying the crew with confusion and fear. He was worried that Sheridan would be angered, yet her features told a different tale. The First Mate was beaming from ear-to-ear.

"Well, alright then." Frank shrugged, also taking note of the evident snub.

"Hews, Bradley."

"Fuck yeah!"

Bradley raised his own hand, looking to others for support. None came.

Frank pressed on, ploughing through the list until his own name was reached. It was met by a smattering of friendly cheers, and a handful of eager votes. Not enough to conquer Jacques. Not even close.

Barnaby looked to Sheridan. Her grin had spread further, cracking the make-up around her eyes.

"Come on." She whispered, her grip increasing with each uttered name. "Come on!"

"White, Barnaby."

Sheridan held her breath, throwing her hand up high. Barnaby did the same.

As did more than half the crew.

Frank gazed at the sea of digits, his astonishment a match for Barnaby's own.

"Well, that's it then." He declared, rolling the parchment with a casual shrug. "No one's beating that. Gentlemen, say good morning to your new Captain!"

Those who had voted for Barnaby cheered as Sheridan drove him towards the stern, shoving him up the stairs with more than a little force. To be fair, he was resisting quite a bit.

Eventually, Barnaby stepped out onto the stern, and looked into the faces of his brand-new crew.

Jacques was nowhere to be seen.

"Uh, hi." He began, waving a timid hand.

From the back of the murmuring crowd, Gary gave a supportive thumbs-up.

Chapter Eighteen

"Captain, your services are required!"

Trigger sighed as he opened his eyes, the voice cutting through his dreams as though it were a blade through reeds. He hadn't adjusted to Carnage's crew, their theater-based education leaving them with a rather grandiose manner of revealing their intent.

To be honest, he should fit right in.

Donning his coat and belt, Trigger stumbled to the door, another night of wine and feasting having left him with a cracker of a headache. Carnage had apparently taken a liking to his company, making time to see him at every evening meal. Trigger had been expecting more revelations, or at least some sort of pressing towards Carnage's proposal, yet the Captain seemed happy enough to discuss his collection of plays, a topic which Trigger quite enjoyed.

"Yes?" Trigger asked, wincing at the sunlight as he opened his door.

A chiseled set of abs sat waiting, the hot skin inches from his narrowed eyes. Gathering himself, Trigger redirected his gaze at the face two-feet higher than his own.

"Yes?" He repeated, adjusting his coat.

"The Captain wants you on deck." The Thrallkin declared. Insensitive as it was, Trigger was unable to remember his name. Their manufactured features all appeared the same, and were it not for his hair, even Carnage would be indistinguishable from the rest of his crew.

"Of course." Trigger nodded, waiting for his addresser to move.

He didn't.

"Are you going?" The Thrallkin asked, clearly puzzled by his inaction.

"I will." Trigger replied, giving his companion a friendly grin. "Though, you'll have to go first, if you don't mind. No offence, but you take up an awful lot of space, and my doorway only has so much."

The Thrallkin cocked his head, studying the door and then himself.

"Oh." He chuckled, patting his great frame. "Yeah."

The Thrallkin stepped aside, allowing him to pass.

"Thank you." Trigger nodded, moving as quickly as he could. He had swiftly discovered that Thrallkin intelligence was as varied and nuanced as mankind's own, and that while Carnage possessed an intellect to rival any so-called prodigy, many of his crew were far less gifted. Coupled with their enormous strength, Trigger was inclined to believe that this enhanced their threat. Stupidity backed by power is a terrible thing.

His journey across deck was no less impeded, the hulking frames of laboring Thrallkin constantly forcing him to readjust his course, lest he be felled by a swinging elbow, or carelessly thrown hand. The labyrinth of motion delayed his progress, and by the time he finally reached the bobbing prow, Carnage had clearly begun losing his patience.

"You called for me?" Trigger asked, making a wary approach.

"What took you so long?" The Captain demanded, his heavy features twisted into an imposing scowl. Gone was the friendly countenance Trigger had slowly been warming to, the good cheer replaced by a seething rage, a lust for violence that was barely restrained. Rubbing his finger against his thumb, Trigger willed himself to remain calm, and once again made note of the fact that for all his wit and charm, Carnage remained a savage lunatic.

"Your ship and crew are rather large." Trigger ventured. "And I am rather small."

Carnage paused his approach, great chest heaving up and down.

A small grin split his fearsome scowl.

"Hah, fair enough." He chuckled, cocking his head to one side. "Though, I have to admit, if you think we're big, well, you're not as worldly as I thought."

"And what's that supposed to mean?" Trigger asked, as Carnage gestured towards the prow.

"Take a look at the horizon." Carnage ordered. "And see if you can guess."

Trigger obeyed the cryptic command, studying the sky for signs of change.

There was no sky left to see.

"Gods." Trigger breathed, gazing at the heavens with wide-eyed wonder.

A mountain range sat heavy before them, weathered and chipped by the sea's cruel winds. Despite this battering, and the countless scars adorning its length, the peaks sat higher than any he'd seen, their worn crests flecked by sprinkling snow. They were a humbling, beautiful sight, one that paled in comparison to the fortress upon them.

"*This* is the path you chose?" Trigger asked, astonished that Carnage would take such a risk.

"Thodurk and I are actually old friends." Carnage shrugged. "Besides, it's the fastest route, if he decides to let us pass."

"And if he doesn't?"

"Well, then there isn't much we can do about it, is there?"

Trigger nodded his concession, gazing in awe at Thodurk's abode. He had heard the tales of the giant's lair, the whispered warnings and fearful accounts. He had seen too much to dismiss them entirely, yet he had always assumed an exaggeration, a partial lie on the speaker's behalf. Surely, nothing in the world could be so grand.

Clearly, he was wrong.

The fortress was a match for the mountains themselves, even half-vanished amongst the clouds. Its chiseled length spanned the entire range, guarded by cannons of staggering size. A single shot would eclipse their ship, shattering their vessel with a simple graze. The core foundation was even larger, an impenetrable mansion of stone and steel. The Empire's fleet could fire upon it, and barely scratch the front-door varnish.

Trigger tore his gaze from the towering sight, directing it to the grinning Carnage.

"Are you impressed?" He asked, reading Trigger's expression. "Most people are. I think it's a bit tacky, personally."

"Oh, really?" Trigger asked, raising his brow. "Perhaps you should tell Thodurk. He might consider redecorating."

Carnage chuckled, crossing his arms and shaking his head.

"I'm glad you think speaking with him is such a viable option." Carnage replied. "It is the reason we're here."

"Pardon?" Trigger asked, hoping he'd misheard.

"Well, we're also running a bit behind." Carnage added, mostly to himself. "We need the extra days, if we're ever going to retake the lead."

"We're going to speak with Thodurk?" Trigger asked, tapping his fingers against the prow. He was not very comfortable with this turn of events.

"Maybe." Carnage shrugged. "If he's in the mood. That's why we're waiting. I want something to offer when we make our approach."

"An offer?"

"Aye." Carnage laughed. "An offer. Thodurk's at his best when he's had a good meal."

Trigger pondered this declaration, his misgivings increasing with each moment.

"What are we waiting for, exactly?" He asked, unsure why he was wasting his time.

"Please." Carnage snorted, tossing aside his hair. "You already know."

Trigger did. Unfortunately, there was nothing he could do to stop it.

"Ahoy there!"

The ship had been drawing closer for the past half-hour, its approach as cautionary as sense would allow. Under normal circumstances, Carnage's vessel would be unmistakable, the corpses and chains a surefire sign. In its current state, however, it appeared perfectly innocent, the crew having swabbed and scrubbed until every trace of blood was stricken from the deck. It had been done for Trigger's benefit, as he would have been stricken down the moment he came aboard, had the *Bloodbath* been decorated with its usual attire.

This knowledge galled him, leaving him well-aware that were it not for his presence, the men on the approaching ship may have stood some chance of escape. As it was, they had ventured blindly into the Thrallkin's clutches, and with Carnage's hand about his lips, he couldn't even give a shout of warning.

He watched through a narrow slit as the vessel lay anchor, it's Captain peering at their deck with a scarred and squinting eye.

"Anyone aboard?" The man repeated, nervously fingering his still-sheathed sword.

Beside them, Trigger could feel the Thrallkin shuffling, their bloodlust rising with the promise of death.

"Not yet." Carnage ordered, his voice low.

"See anything, Captain?" Asked the vessel's First Mate, their scalp swaddled in bloodied rags.

"No…" The Captain began, rubbing at his chin. "Send a small party aboard. If we see movement, we leave."

"Aye, Captain."

Trigger admired the man's restraint. He hoped it would be enough.

Four men grunted as they emerged from below, their hands wrapped about a sturdy plank. They lay it between the vessels with a round of groans, one of them holding it steady as the other three crossed.

"Not yet." Carnage whispered, as his crew quivered with mounting frenzy.

The plank buckled slightly as the men trod its length, drawing their weapons and keeping low.

"On my word." Carnage grinned, holding up a massive fist.

The men completed their crossing, dropping to the deck with tiny thuds.

"Now." Carnage hissed, releasing his fist with a wild swing.

The Thrallkin burst from their cover in a wave of crimson blurs, streaking towards the crewmen with astonishing speed.

The men barely managed a cry before the they were upon them, snapping their wrists and crushing their skulls.

"Drop the plank!" Screamed the panicked Captain, his arms waving in mindless fear. "Drop the fucking plank!"

It was far too late for that.

Five Thrallkin were already upon it, covering its length in three massive strides. They landed on the enemy ship with thunderous booms, the deck itself trembling beneath their weight.

"Kill them!" Ordered the Captain, brandishing his sword. "Kill them, and drop the bloody pla- "

A Thrallkin fist collided with his jaw, snapping the bone in two.

Trigger watched in horror as the Thrallkin battled their prey, sinewy limbs a whirlwind as they weaved between bullets, hammers, and manically stabbing blades. The crimson warriors made no use of their weapons, subduing the crew through fist alone.

"You're impressed." Carnage grinned, reading his features once again. "That's okay. This time, I'd say it's deserved."

A wooden dunk punctuated the screams, followed by a heavy splash.

"Oh, good for them." Carnage chuckled, watching the plank as it bobbed away. A valiant crewman had succeeded in removing it, cutting of the Thrallkin's access to their already gore-filled deck.

"Loose the grapples, boys!"

Four Thrallkin stepped forward, each of them twirling a length of rope. Thick iron hooks were fixed to the end, and with practiced ease their wielder's let fly, hooking the enemy banisters with flawless precision.

"Pull!" Carnage ordered, once again raising that mighty fist.

The Thrallkin bulged as they tore at the rope, their muscles as large as Trigger's head. With a spine-chilling groan the enemy vessel shifted, gliding towards their own.

"Pull!"

The banister snapped and buckled, the timbers breaking beneath the hooks. Still, the ship was drawing closer, the gap between them lessening with every second.

"Alright, boys!" Carnage roared, hefting his savage axe. "Let's get over there!"

Trigger studied the space between their ships. It remained fifteen feet, at least.

With a howl of excitement, the Thrallkin charged, covering the void in a single bound.

"I'll be back soon." Carnage grinned, offering Trigger a friendly wink. Then he too was off, bridging the divide with a casual leap. The whole vessel shuddered as he crashed against the deck, cleaving a man in two without pausing for a breath.

The conflict that followed was brutal and swift, fueled by the screams of butchered men. Their bones broke and their flesh tore, the rhythm of their pain so consistent that the Thrallkin crew began to sing, their voices made light with laughter and joy.

Hack, cut, stab, slash!
Gonna grab some booty, grab some gash!
Gonna add that booty to my stash!
Hope it doesn't give me a nasty rash!

It was a popular shanty; one Trigger had heard in many a tavern. He hoped to never hear it again.

The slaughter was done in a handful of minutes, the captured vessel awash with blood as the Thrallkin secured it to their own. The creatures were also completely drenched, yet the nature of their skin left the gore almost completely invisible, blending seamlessly into their crimson hue.

"Alright, boys, are we ready to move?" Carnage called, as the last of the ropes were fastened in place.

"Aye, Captain."

"Good, good." Carnage beamed, wiping his hands with a filthy rag. "Full speed ahead, then. Hopefully Thodurk heard the commotion."

"Where are we sailing to, exactly?" Trigger asked, studying the mountains with a curious eye. So far as he could see, there was nothing but stone for a hundred miles.

"It is hard to see, if you've never used it before." Carnage conceded, placing a hand on Trigger's back. He guided his gaze towards a nearby tunnel, one almost hidden by the mountain's bulk. It was large enough to accommodate a fleet of ships, yet perched as it was beneath such colossal mass, it amounted to little more than a mouse's door.

"How many passages are there?" Triger asked, as they sailed towards its beckoning width.

"That's the only one." Carnage replied, wringing the blood from his shaggy locks. "You either go around the mountain or sail directly under Thodurk's feet. His family is old, you see, and knew what they were doing when they had this place built. This is their sea, regardless of what the Empire says."

"What about their vessels?" Trigger frowned. Where are they docked? How do they pass through?"

Carnage snorted, his finger's moving deftly as he weaved a freshly claimed skull into his already laden hair.

"What ships? Giants have no need for ships. The bastards just go for a slightly-damp stroll."

"You can't be serious."

"Oh, entirely." Carnage replied. "Trust me, you may think this is grand, but once you meet Thodurk in person, well, you'll gain a little perspective."

Trigger considered this information as they sailed towards the pass. He believed it was perspective he could do without.

"Alright." Carnage beamed, as the shadows fell across their ship. "Here we go."

The tunnel was incredibly vast, all sunlight forbidden by its stony walls. The only illumination were the widespread entranceways, pinpricks of white in the chilling dark. It was an awful place, a corridor of night and death, its only redeeming feature being the pounding winds, which funneled their vessel forward with impressive force.

"Lower the sails." Carnage ordered, his voice almost lost in the howling gale.

Trigger attempted to give him a quizzical look. He couldn't see a thing in this pitch-black void.

"Why are we stopping?" Trigger asked, his voice echoing off the distant walls.

"Because this is where we need to be."

Trigger listened carefully as Carnage moved to the stern, his footsteps heavy against the deck.

"Oy, Thodurk! Raise the net, you great bloody oaf!"

Trigger closed his eyes, praying for the God's to extend his patience. He could hear Carnage pacing, clearly annoyed by the lack of reply.

"Thodurk! Thodurk, can you hear me!? You fucking should, with ears as big as yours!"

They all stood in anxious anticipation.

Silence.

"Perhaps insults were a poor way to start?" Trigger ventured, running his fingers through his hair.

"I don't know, Captain." Declared a Thrallkin somewhere to his left. "I'd say it's more likely that he didn't hear. Those rocks are awfully thick."

"I'd say you're right, Bodi." Carnage replied, ignoring Trigger entirely. "It's understandable, I guess. Thodurk's getting on in years."

There was a pause as the Captain considered his options, his fingernails scraping against his chin.

"Bodi, be a good lad and fire the cannons. That should be enough to gain his attention."

"Aye, Captain!"

The deck wobbled slightly as Bodi sprang away, barking his orders left-and-right.

"I don't think this is a good idea." Trigger declared, trying his hardest to sound respectful.

"Why not?" Carnage snapped, apparently feeling hostile to contrary opinions.

"Oh, I'm sure you'll work it out." Trigger replied, taking great care to cover his ears.

BOOM! BOOM! BOOM! BOOM! BOOM!

The cannon fire thundered throughout the cave, amplified and echoed by the sea-smoothed walls. The result was deafening, an explosive symphony of bangs and cracks. Several Thrallkin yelped as the cacophony peaked, the whole ship creaking as they slumped to their knees. Trigger's skull was also ringing, despite his attempts at muffled protection. He could only imagine what they were feeling, with their superior hearing and unguarded ears.

"You…you knew that would happen." Carnage accused, long after the chaos had passed.

"I did. I also tried to warn you."

Carnage was quiet as he digested this thought, a fact which left Trigger feeling distinctly unsettled. While his eyes were slowly adjusting, his vision remained far from ideal, and it would be nothing at all for Carnage to slither up behind him, and snap his neck with a single twist.

"Heh, fair enough." The Captain declared, his yellow gaze glinting in the dusky light. "You see, that's why we need you. You're clever. You think ahead."

"Well then, I guess I should tell you that meeting with Thodurk is a terrible idea."

"You aren't Captain yet." Carnage chuckled, as the waters beneath them began to shift. "Besides, it's out of our hands now!"

The ship lurched sideways as the water rose, closing about their hull with wicked force. Their captive vessel was affected as well, rolling towards them with an ominous groan. It was all Trigger could do to keep his feet, barrels and boxes smashing as they slid freely across the deck, crashing into the banisters with near-lethal force.

"I'd hold on to something!" Carnage cackled, his voice quite close to Trigger's ear. He did as he was told, searching desperately for any purchase. Eventually he found a sodden rope, one pulled tight by the pressure of restraining their ship.

A net. They had been snagged and captured by a giant net.
CRUNK!

His stomach sank as their vessel rose, the net hoisting them up with irresistible force. A moment later the cavern was lit, the abyss above parting to reveal a candlelit cellar, its wine casks as large as a nobleman's manor.

"Try not to look so morbid, Captain!" Carnage declared, waving at Trigger with a corpse's arm. The Thrallkin was grinning like a madman, perched between the masts of their helpless ships.

"There are worse ways to go than being eaten by a giant!"

"Name one." Trigger replied, as the net drizzled seawater across his scalp.

"Hah." Carnage chuckled, letting the corpse drop to the deck below.

"You've got me there."

****

"What about this? This looks look safe."

"That's the way we came."

"Oh, right. What about here?"

"That would take us west. Our destination is to the north."

"Oh, yeah. What about here?"

Frank sighed, rubbing at his eyes with his mangled hand.

"Barnaby, do you actually know how to read a map?"

Barnaby swallowed, caressing his scalp with a nervous palm.

"Would it be a bad time to reveal I don't?"

"Gods." Frank muttered, turning from the table with a look of despair.

"Go easy on him." Sheridan declared, giving Barnaby's shoulder a supportive pat. "Everyone has to start somewhere."

"Yes, they do." Frank replied, turning to them with a frustrated gaze. "They start at the bottom, and through merit and hard work, rise to a position that befits their talents. They don't get made Captain after a few months of mopping, just because you convinced the crew that they're a stallion in bed!"

He finished his rant with a bracing breath, regaining his composure with surprising ease.

"If you believe that's how the world works, you haven't been paying much attention." Sheridan shrugged, seizing the map and adjusting her wig. She'd been a redhead since the day of Barnaby's election, the fiery strands matching her boundless will. It was Sheridan who'd managed to keep their vessel afloat, in spite of Barnaby's boundless incompetence. What's more, she had somehow managed to keep anyone else from noticing, the rest of the crew congratulating Barnaby on how well he'd acclimated to the roll. Only Frank had noticed the truth, and he had already realized that it was best for the others to keep believing Sheridan's lies. No man wanted to doubt their Captain.

"We'll take this route." Sheridan nodded, stepping towards Frank and extending the map. He followed her finger, his tired eyes crinkling with mild suspicion.

"Not a very daring passage, is it?"

"Trigger put us in danger so we could gain a lead, something we actually achieved. There's no sense in crippling ourselves further, if it's something we can easily avoid."

"True." Frank conceded, taking the map from Sheridan's hands. "Yet there's something to be said for boldness. We can risk a little danger, if it further cements our lead."

"What do you propose, then?" Sheridan asked, folding her arms. "Would you like to take a run at Thodurk's Pass?"

"I said a little danger." Frank scowled. "Not suicide."

The Quartermaster studied the map, his malformed hand tracing the various routes.

"What about this?" He asked, spreading the parchment across the table. "The Maiden's Thighs. It's nothing we can't handle, and swift enough to keep our edge."

"The Maiden's Thighs?" Barnaby frowned, scratching at his scalp. He was trying to see the resemblance, and frankly, he was coming up blank.

"The passage is named for its content, not its shape." Sheridan informed him. "You'll see when we get there."

"So, you agree it's the best route?" Frank asked, looking to them with hopeful eyes.

"It is faster." Sheridan conceded. "And if we guide the ship correctly, the danger should be minimal."

"Wonderful." Frank nodded, turning to Barnaby with a sarcastic smile. "Of course, none of this matters if the Captain disagrees."

"I don't." Barnaby replied, his voice breaking beneath Frank's gaze.

"Then it's settled." Sheridan beamed, clapping her hands. "I'll inform the helmsman."

"Ah, shouldn't I do that?" Barnaby ventured, trying to salvage a drop of pride.

"It isn't your place to be running simple errands." Sheridan declared, giving his shoulder an affectionate pat. "I'll handle this. You head to bed, and try to get some rest. You'll be addressing the crew come morning, so we'll need you at your best."

"Oh, yes." Frank muttered. "We wouldn't want to miss another dazzling display."

Barnaby withered, his cheeks burning with growing shame. His first address had not gone well.

"Good night, then." He murmured, turning towards the door.

"Good night." Sheridan replied, rolling the map with a chipper grin.

"Night." Frank grunted, picking at his teeth with an untrimmed nail.

Suppressing a sigh, Barnaby exited the room, shutting the door behind him with a gentle thud.

"Squeak!"

A streak of grey surged across the floor, squeezing itself into a nearby hole. He might have doubted that he saw it at all, were it not for the droppings it had left smeared across the timbers. Not two meters distant, the ship's cat lay resting, watching the scene with a half-closed eye.

"Really?" Barnaby asked, crouching beside it and shaking his head. He knew the creature was grieving, yet he never thought it would be hit this hard.

"He wouldn't want this, you know." He began, patting its side with his calloused palm. "You have a reputation to uphold. He wouldn't want you to throw it away, just because he isn't here."

The cat's head shifted the mildest degree, so that's its sorrow-filled gaze was fixed on him.

"Yeah, I miss him too." Barnaby cooed. "He was a good Captain. Better than me, that's for sure."

He might have imagined it, yet Barnaby could swear the cat nodded in agreement.

"Thanks." He chuckled, scratching beneath its chin. The creature offered a small purr, which Barnaby accepted as a sign of approval.

"He likes you."

Barnaby jumped as the voice appeared at his shoulder, startling the cat and making it rise.

"Well, he should." Barnaby replied, turning to Jacques with a sheepish grin. "I've fed him enough."

Once again, he was reminded of Jacques's incredible bulk, the swordsman having halted only a few paces away. He towered over Barnaby, though it wasn't his height that was most remarkable. It was the way he carried his weight, the menace behind his every motion. He forgot it so often that he assumed Jacques controlled the effect, summoning it at a moment's will. That couldn't be the case, however, as right now he was feeling completely intimidated, and Jacques had no reason to be threatening him.

Did he?

"We haven't had a chance to speak, since you were named Captain." Jacques declared, giving him an easy smile. It didn't seem to reach his eyes.

"I know!" Barnaby replied, throwing up his hands in exasperation. "I always assumed that Trigger did jack shit. Now, I can't he found time to piss."

"I see you aren't maintaining his rules on swearing." Jacques observed, folding his arms.

"What? Oh, no, I guess not."

"A great shame. I found ze civility to be quite refreshing."

"Well, I can enforce it, if you like." Barnaby shrugged. "I don't mind either way."

Jacques smiled again, though this time, it was completely genuine.

"I zank you." Jacques nodded, the menace fading from his massive limbs.

Barnaby wasn't sure what he'd done, yet he was bloody glad he'd done it.

"So, what have you been up to, while I've been kept busy?" He asked, trying to steer them from Sheridan's door. Things remained tense between the First Mate and Jacques, and he had no desire to see a late-night brawl. Those were usually reserved for Monday and Wednesday. The cook made sausages. It was nice.

"Nozing much." Jacques replied, following him as he crept down the hall. "I am still teaching ze crew to read, and have been learning the various knots."

"Good luck." Barnaby chuckled. "Gary tried to teach me once, and I almost managed to lose a finger."

"...How?"

"Tied a knot around it, couldn't get it undone. Damn thing went blue before it was free."

Jacques pondered this story for several moments, before finally giving a careless shrug.

"Sounds as zough you tied an exceptional knot."

They turned the corner, finding themselves in the dwindling pantry. This surprised Barnaby, as he'd been under the impression that he was guiding their progress. Apparently, he was wrong.

Jacques closed the door, barring it with his bulging frame.

Barnaby refrained from wetting himself. Barely.

"Why are we here?" He ventured, making a subtle attempt at backing away.

"To speak." Jacques replied, spreading his arms in a peaceful display. "Nozing more."

"We were speaking."

"Yes, in a corridor filled wiz prying eyes."

"Prying eyes?" Barnaby echoed, scanning the room for possible exits.

There were none to be found.

"Zose sympathetic to Sheridan's cause." Jacques explained, keeping his voice low and level, as though Barnaby were a skittish hound.

"What cause? What are you talking about?"

Jacques closed his eyes, his nostrils flaring as he took a breath.

"You must have noticed ze zings she's done. Ze way she's seized control."

"She's done no such thing." Barnaby scowled. "She fought tooth and nail to make me Captain."

"And since you were elected, has zere been a single decision in which she did not hold sway?"

Barnaby didn't reply. There wasn't a point.

"She has made you her puppet." Jacques continued, taking his silence as encouragement. "One zat will take ze blame the moment she makes a mistake."

"That isn't Sheridan." Barnaby snapped, more defensively than he should. Truth be told, Jacques' words were ringing true, answering several of the questions he'd been posing to himself.

"Really? Zen tell me, what reason would she have to want you as Captain? She was zere for all our battles. She knows how everyzing occurred. She cannot have been swayed by our tales. She knows that you lack any knowledge or experience, and we all know that you have never slept with her, regardless of her paltry zeatrics. So, I ask you again, tell me what her motives are."

Barnaby bit his lip, struggling to speak before the swordsman's demands.

"To… to spite you." He declared, raising his chin in surprising defiance. Well, surprising to him, at least.

"Perhaps." Jacques nodded, his casual demeanor catching Barnaby off-guard. "Zough, zat seems a bit…excessive, does it not? Endangering ze entire crew, merely to undermine me?"

"Maybe." Barnaby grumbled, feeling a tad insulted. He may not be the most qualified Captain, yet he wouldn't say that he was a *danger* to the crew.

"And ask yourself zis." Jacques pressed, closing the gap between them with a carefully measured step. "Had Sheridan been elected, how long could she have held her post?"

"Pretty bloody long, I'd wager." Barnaby shrugged. "She actually knows what she's doing, and there isn't a man on this ship who could throw her out of power."

He knew the last remark was a sting at Jacques' pride. He didn't regret it, however. This whole conversation had soured his mood, which had already been dour for the past few days.

"Not a man, no." Jacques conceded. "Yet ships are sailed by crews, not a single man. And in ze end, ze crew will always have zeir say."

"And you doubt that Sheridan could keep them in line?"

"In a more… tolerant world, I have no doubts zat she could." Jacques shrugged. "Sadly, zis is ze one we live in. Our crew might find her acceptable, yet countless ozers would not. Zey would jeer, mock, and demean ze crew, until zeir pride demanded zat she be removed. After all, who wants to be ze man zat's commanded by a wench?"

"I've known many men who answer to their wives." Barnaby frowned. "Most of them, in fact."

"Those men know how to swallow their pride." Jacques grinned. "A talent which escapes your average crew."

Barnaby scratched at his sweating neck. He couldn't argue with that.

"So, you're saying I'm her decoy, then? The rest of the world believes I'm in charge, while she runs things behind my back?"

"Yes, essentially. Zough, 'behind your back' is a bit unfair. She's been doing it right in front of you. I don't zink she respects you much."

The remark hurt, for a multitude of reasons. Mostly because he knew it was true.

"Is there a point to this?" Barnaby scowled. "Yes, I'm useless. Yes, I'm her puppet. I know it, you know it, she knows it. None of that matters, as there's nothing I can do."

"Of course zere is." Jacques snorted. "You're Captain. She is yours to command."

"You think Sheridan would obey me, if I tried to give her orders?" Barnaby scoffed.

"Yes. She is part of zis crew, and a crewmember follows zeir Captain. If Sheridan refuses to do so, well, she is not really one of ze crew."

Barnaby studied Jacques, attempting to grasp the motive behind these poisonous, somewhat alluring thoughts.

Knock.

The sound startled them both, though Jacques' reaction was far more violent. His swords were drawn in a heartbeat, their chipped steel reflecting the light.

"Captain?"

Magwa's accent was unmistakable, as was the timbre of his voice. Jacques sheathed his blades with a sheepish grin, opening the door to the Kalyute's curious face.

"This is odd." Magwa observed, considering them both with narrowed eyes.

"Just seeking some privacy." Jacques replied. "It's surprisingly hard to find."

"Oh." Magwa remarked, studying them with a now mischievous gaze. "Magwa didn't realize."

"Not like that." Jacques grinned, catching Magwa's line of thought.

"Magwa no judge." The Kalyute shrugged. "His people never understand the fuss. It just going in a different hole. No chance of baby, either."

"That's…one way to look at it." Barnaby conceded.

"Best way." Magwa replied, tapping his hatchet with a dark-skinned palm. "You done?"

"We never started." Jacques chuckled. "But yes, I'd say we've finished our conversation."

"Have we?" Barnaby asked, his mood darkening again.

"Yes." Jacques repeated. "I've said all I care too."

"Want to get drunk?"

They both considered Magwa's request, his offer accompanied by a pointy-toothed grin.

"Definitely." Jacques beamed, hooking his arm around the savage's shoulders.

Barnaby studied the smiling pair, remembering the days before all the intrigue, when all they'd do is drink and labor, struggling to survive through Trigger's latest adventure.

Simpler times. Better times.

A night of drunken reminiscing was exactly what he needed. Tomorrow's address could hang itself, with ten-ton stones around its feet.

"Yeah." He nodded, steering them all from the pantry's shadow. "Ale sounds like a fucking delight."

Chapter Nineteen

Trigger watched the sun rise, its golden rays piercing the oppressive gloom. They must have been here for at least a day.

"Does it normally take this long?"

"Well, it's not as though we can leave." Carnage replied, pacing the deck with impatience.

He wasn't wrong.

Trigger leant against the banister, once again studying the cavernous room. The net had deposited them in an ungainly heap, beaching their vessel on a colossal floor. No enforcer had been present to prevent them from escaping, the sheer scale of their prison proving deterrent enough. They could have left the ship at a moment's notice, yet the only exit sat at least an hour's march away, a titanic door that put all to shame. They could hack at its timbers for seven days, and still not breach their woody depths.

BOOM!

Trigger raised a curious brow, unsurprised by the deafening sound. They'd been hearing it all night, in various stages of intensity.

BOOM! BOOM!

"This one's close." He observed, as the deck beneath them began to quake.

"They are." Carnage grinned. "And I think they're getting closer."

BOOM! BOOM! BOOM!

"I believe you're right." Trigger replied, his sense of calm receding.

BOOM! BOOM! BOOM! BOOM!

The whole ship was trembling, as though it were a cornered beast, surrounded by his father's hounds.

Trigger despised hunting.

BOOM! BOOM! BOOM! BOOM! BOOM!

The shaking ceased, replaced by the scream of a rusty lock.

"Finally." Carnage remarked, folding his arms.

The enormous door swung open, the wind striking their vessel with hurricane force. Trigger's coat billowed in the blinding gale, flecks of dust sealing his vulnerable eyes. He opened them to a waking horror, a sight that his mind could scarcely define.

A giant stood before their ship, his boot-straps higher than their greatest mast.

Trigger craned his neck, attempting to discern the titan's face. Such vision was beyond his reach.

The giant moved, his mountainous knees folding as he stooped towards their vessel, reaching for them with a monstrous hand. Societies could have settled on that palm, establishing a village, crops, and even a road, were they so inclined. As it was, the great appendage seized their ship, the other claiming their captive vessel with an equal amount of ease. Without a grunt of effort, the giant lifted them high, carrying their weight as if they were a child's model.

"This...this is Thodurk?" Trigger asked, his voice made feeble from awe.

"What? No." Carnage chuckled, shaking his head. "This is just the butler."

Trigger studied the leviathan, his shoulder's so broad they could carry a country.

"The butler?"

"Yes. The butler. Thodurk's much more impressive."

Trigger held his jaw in check. Barely. It seemed ridiculous, yet as he gazed harder at their captor's dress, Carnage's words began making sense. While the threads of the fabric were as large as Trigger himself, the giant's jacket was unmistakably a servant's, its tailed ends conjuring whirlwinds as they trailed in his wake.

BOOM! BOOM!

The giant increased his pace, strolling from the room that had ensnared them. Trigger counted his tread, and realized that an hour's journey was but three steps to their captor.

"Wait a minute." Carnage snarled, as the giant turned into an endless hall. "He's taking us to the fucking kitchen!"

"That sounds perilous." Trigger ventured, as the Captain balled his fists.

"Trepa!" Carnage barked, storming across the deck. "Fire a few of the cannons, port side only!"

"Aye, Captain!"

"Are you sure that's wise?" Trigger asked. He was still somewhat deaf from their last cannon-based adventure.

"It's necessary." Carnage replied. "Which is all that matters."

A moment later the cannons were firing, most of the shots striking their captive ship. A few collided with the fortress walls, tiny specks on its ancient stone. One or two shattered against the giant's fingers, earning a curious rumble from his bell-tower throat.

The ship shuddered as he hoisted it high, bringing the deck level with his questioning eye. Trigger could see its film of moisture, and were he so inclined, could probably have swam in its sticky depths.

"Yes?"

The voice was so deep it clutched Trigger's stomach, vibrating through him as a solid blow.

Carnage himself took a moment to reply, his own voice weakened by the jarring sensation.

"It's Captain Carnage, you colossal imbecile! Take me to Thodurk!"

Even the Thrallkin seemed pathetic in such awesome surrounds, his threats robbed of menace by their utter enormity.

Their vessel shifted as the giant leant close, studying their deck with that terrible eye.

"Carnage." The voice boomed. "I didn't recognize you. Your ship actually appears halfway respectable."

"That's because we have a guest!" Carnage replied, forcing Trigger forward.

"Oh. Is he an appetizer?"

"No." Carnage chuckled. "He's my new partner. The other ship is Thodurk's meal."

Trigger's stomach sank as the giant lowered their vessel, raising the other ship for inspection. He studied it for several moments, considering the corpse-riddled deck with an appreciative gaze.

"Not bad." He conceded. "There's almost a whole meal here. Fairly fresh, as well."

"I only bring the best." Carnage declared, performing a mock-bow.

"I'll take you to the master." The giant replied. "Though, I can't promise that he'll be receptive. The Empress sent a shipment only a few months ago, and we're still working through the remaining dregs."

"Well, there's no dregs in there." Carnage beamed, pointing at their captured prize. "Every man was fit as a fiddle, until we broke their spines."

"You shouldn't have done that." The giant announced, resuming his thunderous march. "The master enjoys hearing them crack."

"Ah." Carnage remarked, tugging at his too-small collar. "I'll remember that for next time."

"If there is one." The giant smirked, winking as they reached a door.

KNOCK! KNOCK!

The pounding set Trigger's teeth on edge, despite its prim and practiced pace. Each knock echoed with the force of a storm, rumbling through the halls in a deafening wave.

"Enter."

The voice that summoned them was oddly piping, yet no less booming than that of their captor. Shifting them to his opposite forearm, the giant waited a moment before turning the knob, swinging the door open on its silent hinges.

"What is it?" Asked the piping voice, as the butler returned them to his hand.

"You have a guest, my lord. Mr. Carnage, I believe."

"Captain Carnage." The Thrallkin grumbled, though, not too loudly.

"Really? How long has he been waiting?"

"About a day or two, my lord. He brought you a gift."

Bowing, the butler extended the captured ship, its butchered crew stinking in the humid air.

The room trembled as his master approached, his great frame finally squeezing into Trigger's gaze.

So this. This was the mighty Thodurk.

He stood at least a head taller than his towering aid, his shoulders barely contained by their sky-blue coat. Trigger measured his arm span, and realized that if he started his ascent at dawn, and did not stop for rest, he might just cover their length before the moon had risen. The butler seemed almost feeble in comparison, even his titanic limbs appearing malnourished before such colossal girth.

And yet, for all his awesome size, it was Thodurk's fashion that surprised Trigger most.

A woolen wig adorned his well-shaped skull, while his rugged features were smeared with a cloud-white paste. A false mole rested mere meters from his lips, so large and solid that it could crush a dozen men, were it to tumble from its painted perch.

"Not what you were expecting?" Carnage asked, keeping his voice low.

"No." Trigger replied, doing the same. "Is that a cravat?"

"Yes. Thodurk is from noble stock, and takes his heritage rather seriously. You should get on well."

"Gods, I hope so." Trigger replied, as Thodurk plucked their gift from his vassal's palm.

"Hmm. Not a particularly interesting design." He remarked, studying the vessel from stern-to-prow. "Though, I see you have stowed some treats on board. That was thoughtful."

With skillful fingers he removed the corpses, placing them in his butler's hand.

"Prepare these for supper, and fetch us a decent wine. Oh, and place Carnage over by my desk. There's a good man."

He dismissed the butler with a wave of his hand, turning towards a distant shelf. Trigger followed his movements as the butler ferried them on, watching with awe as the giant lord paused, considering a display of staggering dimensions.

It was a model battle, a savage contest between two fleets, carefully positioned in their allotted roles. You might have found it in a wealthy child's chambers, were it not for the fact that every vessel could fit at least three dozen men.

Dunk!

Their ship lurched to one side as it touched against the desk, sending them sprawling across the deck.

"Gently, Mavis." Thodurk chastised, setting down his gift with deliberate care. "They are guests, remember."

"My apologies." Mavis declared, offering a heartfelt bow. Without another word, he exited the room, leaving them alone with his colossal master.

DOOM! DOOM!

Thodurk's footsteps were twice as bad, his extra-weight producing truly horrifying force.

"So, Carnage." Thodurk began, slipping softly into a monstrous chair.

"What brings you to my home?"

****

"Are you sure?"

"Well, they've been gaining for two days, and don't appear to be changing course."

"This is a race." Barnaby ventured. "They may simply be trying to overtake us."

"Maybe." Sheridan replied, fanning at her face. "Though, they may also intend to remove some competition. News would have spread about Trigger's death, and that means the vultures are about to descend."

Barnaby glanced upwards, watching as an Oracle-bird swooped overhead.

"What are your orders, Captain?" Sunniday asked, closing the scope with a decisive snap.

"We- "

"We should prepare for battle." Sheridan interrupted. "Let them get close, then show them our cannons. Cripple their sails, or, failing that, destroy their vessel entirely."

"We don't know that they're a threat." Barnaby frowned, annoyed by the interruption, and the pointless savagery.

"This is a race, Captain. Everyone is a threat."

Sheridan's words held many truths, yet her disregard for his authority left him blind to any point. She was proving Jacques correct with each passing day.

"We maintain our course for now." He declared. "Try and increase our speed. If they gain further, and start appearing hostile, I'll reconsider our options."

"Aye, Captain."

"I don't think- "

"I don't care." Barnaby replied, leaving the crow's nest without a goodbye. He regretted it a moment later, as this placed him squarely in the precarious rigging, with no First Mate to prevent his fall. Gods, after what he just did, she may be the one to cause it.

"Wave!"

Barnaby paused, clamping his palm around his lips. At this height, there was little danger of the water reaching him, yet he had already seen six crewmen fall to the sea's insidious touch, and had no desire to join them in the overcrowded brig.

SPLASH!

The crimson tide struck in an explosion of red, staining their deck the color of blood. The crew below did their best to avoid its foaming spray, clinging desperately to the rags they had swaddled about their faces. A single touch to the mouth or nose had proven damaging enough, the mysterious waters leaving their victim in a state of lust-filled delirium, one where their basic sense of decency and restraint were all but abandoned.

Commanding pirates was difficult enough. When they were high as fucking kites, and trying to bugger everything that moves, it was practically impossible.

He waited a moment to complete his descent, only touching deck when the waters had stilled. The crew had already set to work, mopping at the poison with a fearful vigor. Each one of them was careful to avoid contact, draining their mops and buckets with the utmost caution. It almost made Barnaby smile. A few short weeks ago, and he'd have been the one who was mopping it up.

"What's the decision?" Frank asked, stepping around a crimson puddle.

"We're holding to course."

"Risky. Is that your plan?"

"It is." Barnaby replied, folding his arms.

"Good." Frank nodded, giving him an encouraging grin. "Very good."

Jacques sidled up beside him with surprising stealth, having adapted to his new leg with his usual composure. Magwa was right behind him, the Kalyute being the only crewman immune to the Maiden's tainted seas.

"You're sure you don't want a rag?" Barnaby asked, tapping at his own. "Just in case?"

"Red river runs beside Magwa's home." The Kalyute smirked. "He and his wife make use when children are away. It make nights interesting, to say the least."

"If you're sure." Barnaby replied, as Frank offered a helpless shrug.

"Your home is razer distant." Jacques declared, fidgeting with his rag. "How can you be certain zat ze effect is ze same?"

"Magwa can't. Though, he has no problem with finding out."

"Fair enough." Jacques conceded, as Sheridan dropped to the sodden deck.

"That ship is still gaining." She informed them, lifting her hem with a silk-gloved hand. "They're faster than us. Considerably."

"Maybe we should lose some weight." Jacques ventured, giving Sheridan a meaningful stare.

"Maybe we should." She replied, meeting his gaze with a disdainful sneer.

"My Gods."

A mop clattered against the timbers, carelessly discarded by Bradley's shaking hands.

"You are gorgeous." He crooned, steeping towards Sheridan with hungry eyes. His pupils were widened to a hideous degree, the white almost swallowed by their glinting black.

"Not another one." Sheridan sighed, touching a finger to her temple. During their journey through the Thighs, she had found herself the subject of the deranged crewmen's advances. The only exception had been Slippery Joe, who'd tried his luck with a slumbering Gary.

They were still picking his teeth from the nearby wall.

"I want you." Bradley announced, clutching at his groin without shame or reserve.

"I can see that." Sheridan replied, attempting to keep things civil. "And I'm flattered. Unfortunately, my heart belongs to another."

"Who is he?" Bradley demanded, foaming at the lips, and probably from other places. "I'll gut him! I'll gut him like a pig!"

"Charming." Sheridan murmured, extracting her fan and flaring it wide. "Though, I'm afraid the answer remains a forceful 'no'."

"You think you have a choice!?" Bradley roared, sinking so low his knuckles scraped the deck.

"Always." Sheridan replied, fanning herself without concern.

"I'm going to have you, bitch!" Bradley screamed, charging her with a wild howl.

"Bradley, stop!" Frank ordered, unsheathing his sword in a heroic, yet clumsy, display.

Bradley paid no heed, his lunge carrying him forward with furious force. Magwa put himself in the madman's path, yet sheer mass and ferocity left him woefully ill-equipped, Bradley's excess bulk throwing him aside as though he were a bundle of half-snapped sticks. This same momentum carried him straight past Jacques, who didn't raise a finger to end his assault.

Then again, he didn't really need to.

Sheridan floored Bradley with a single blow, his jaw cracking as he slumped to the deck.

They all took a moment to study his form, a few stray twitches being the only sign of life.

"We've got another for the brig!" Sheridan roared, summoning crewmen to carry Bradley down.

"Well done." Frank declared, as the workers shuffled past. As they did, Barnaby made a mental note to inspect Bradley's quarters. Considering their rations, there was no way he should be that fat.

"Thank you." Sheridan replied, resuming her fanning with a graceful shrug. "Though, I have to admit, I'm getting rather tired of my would-be suitors."

"So long as zey can see you, you will remain zere target of choice." Jacques declared, resting his hand on the hilt of his sword.

"And I'm guessing your suggestion is to lock me away?" Sheridan replied, her tone heavy with hate.

"If need be."

Barnaby took a moment to brace his nerves. He knew what was coming next.

"Perhaps we should ask the Captain?" Sheridan snarled, closing her fan with a savage snap.

"An excellent idea. Unusual for you." Jacques replied, narrowing his eyes.

Gods dammit.

"What should we do, Captain?" Sheridan asked, directing her gaze towards his face. Jacques did the same, and for an instant he was remined of his childhood, the day he'd wandered off at the harvest festival. He'd stumbled into the bullpen, and, idiot-child that he was, attempted to walk along the fence that separated the beasts. The fence had broken, dropping him directly between the pair, who were far more interested in each other than they were in him. He was just a helpless child, doomed to be crushed between raging beasts. It was a terrible feeling; one he was experiencing at this very moment.

"Umm…" He murmured, chewing at his lip. Truth be told, he had no idea. In the past few months, he had solved every crisis by coming to either Sheridan or Jacques, a policy which left him woefully incapable of solving this dispute. After all, where do you turn to when your saviors are the ones putting you in strife?

"I don't know." He mumbled, lowering his gaze.

"You're our Captain." Jacques declared. "You have to know, or at least pretend you do."

"You'd certainly know about that." Sheridan snapped. "Pretending is all you've ever done."

Jacques chuckled, though his smile stopped short of his eyes.

"Zis is ridiculous." He announced, massaging his nose between finger and thumb. "It has been weeks, and still you blame me for Trigger's passing. It is irrational, and has made you a danger to ship and crew."

"I'm the danger?" Sheridan roared, stepping towards him. "You murdered our first Captain, and now you're trying to corrupt the second!"

"I am not ze one who spreads her taint across his every word."

"That is one thing I'll give you." Sheridan replied, her voice made breathless by growing frustration. "You're better at this than I'll ever be. You play the part of friend, spread your subtle lies, and plant your festering tendrils in all the necessary ears. And then, once they're so clogged with shit that they no longer hear the truth, you set about your business, killing and destroying whatever you will."

"I am a people person." Jacques shrugged. "Zis is no crime. A First Mate bullying her Captain, however, is a far greater offence, particularly when she is leading him to perilous mistakes."

"What mistakes?" Sheridan demanded, narrowing her eyes.

"And even worse, you are a First Mate who deceives the crew she has sworn to protect!" Jacques yelled, pointedly avoiding her query.

"Wave!"

Sunniday's cry went mostly unheard, lost beneath the fury of Jacques' reply. The debate had enraptured the crew, who had gathered around the pair in a curious circle.

"Jacques, Sheridan, please." Barnaby began. "We need to mo- "

"I have done nothing but protect this crew!" Sheridan spat, gloved fists rising towards Jacques' face.

"By lying?" Jacques sneered. "Do you really zink zat's what ze crew requires? Zey should have chosen a Captain who was fit to lead! Instead, you tricked zem into voting solely wiz zeir cocks! It was a pazetic ploy, one I can- "

"Wave, wave!" Frank interrupted, as the towering tide rose high overhead.

Barnaby looked for refuge. There was none to be had.

The water washed over them in a pounding rush, sweeping crewmen from their feet with primordial ease. Barnaby watched as his people went under, their eyes wide with shock as the wave folded their limbs. When Barnaby's turn came, it was a graceless and blundering affair, his ankles blasting out behind him as he tumbled towards the deck, slamming face-first into the blood-red pool. It took him a moment to regain his bearings, his protective rag hanging wetly from his lips. Coughing, he rose unsteadily to his feet, studying the vessel for signs of life. The first he saw was Sheridan.

And damn, was she looking fine.

Chapter Twenty

"Carnage. Has it been a year already?"

"It has. You seem to be doing well."

"I am, thank you. The Empress is trying rather desperately to get me involved in her war. Her tributes are becoming quite... exorbitant."

"I'll bet." Carnage sneered.

"Ah, yes. I forget how distasteful you find her. We shall move the topic along. Tell me, who is your little friend?"

"I am Trigger, Captain Trigger." He declared, stepping forward and adjusting his coat.

"A naval man?" Thodurk remarked, studying his dress. "Are you a prisoner? I'm surprised, Carnage. You never struck me as the sort to take enemies alive."

"I'm not. He's a guest." Carnage replied. "A very important one. Do you remember our last conversation? I promised you a fleet commander, one without peer in strategic wit."

"And this is he?"

"It is. Trigger was considered the finest in the Empire, until he turned to a life of glorious piracy."

"Odd, for a man of your stature to abandon that world." Thodurk observed. "What's more, you have the bearings of nobility about you. No, don't try to hide it. It's in the way you hold your jaw, the way you set your shoulders. It is unmistakable, and means that there can be only one reason for your current career. You failed, and were cast from your home in disgrace."

Trigger considered his words, unsure how familiar he should make his reply.

"That is correct, yes."

"Ah, honest as well." Thodurk nodded. "A respectable quality. Good show."

Trigger glanced at Carnage, still somewhat convinced that he was being deceived. Thodurk had the size, certainly, yet his demeanor didn't match the legends.

Their conversation was interrupted by the return of the butler, his thunderous steps shaking their vessel. He was clutching wine, and a bowl of what appeared to be prunes. This was not the case, however, their appearance a deception of perspective. The withered black husks were far too large, their brittle forms proving quite irregular.

They were corpses. Crisped and blackened on some colossal stove.

Taking a breath, Trigger did his best to restrain his distaste.

"Thank you, Mavis." Thodurk grinned, as the butler filled his enormous cup. "Some for our guests, as well, if you please."

The butler nodded, reaching across the deck with a titanic limb. If he overbalanced even slightly, and caught himself against the wood, he would crush their vessel into a thousand pieces.

Trigger sighed with relief when the great arm retracted, pillar-like fingers clamped around a seemingly tiny chest.

"My apologies." Thodurk nodded, as Mavis guided the chest towards their ship. "I know it is improper to have a guest pour their own refreshments, yet our difference in size makes your cups rather difficult targets."

Trigger could see his point. A man could drown in Thodurk's cup.

The chest thumped loudly as it struck the deck, its true size revealed as it left the butler's grasp. It was almost as large as Trigger himself, its timbers thicker than Carnage's arm. The hinged lock was loosely secured, unable to fasten around the contents within.

"By the Gods." Carnage chuckled, throwing back the lid. "Your collection has grown."

Trigger took a step forward, restraining his amazement for the wealth on display. The chest was overflowing with diamonds and gold, a fortune to rival the Empire's vaults.

"Tokens, from your Empress." Thodurk shrugged. "They are of no use to me, yet still, it would be rude to refuse."

"I'll take them off your hands." Carnage remarked, studying a chalice with shameless greed.

"It would also be rude to give them away." Thodurk chuckled, sipping his wine with a deafening slurp.

"We're planning to kill the Empress, aren't we?" Carnage ventured. "Insults should be of no concern."

"*You're* planning to kill the Empress." Thodurk corrected, seizing a handful of crispy corpses. "I've merely offered my help, if you succeed in winning my favor."

He devoured the bodies with a graceful chomp, fitting at least six cadavers in his waiting jaw. Trigger could hear their bones snapping with every eager chomp, their charred flesh staining Thodurk's teeth a fearful shade of black.

"And how I am doing so far?" Carnage asked, apparently unfazed by the grisly display.

"Fairly well." Thodurk replied, as Mavis placed a thimble of wine at the center of their stern. It held more liquid than a tavern's casks. "Though, your new commander seems rather shy."

He grinned as he spoke, the gaps in his teeth stuffed with shattered limbs.

"My apologies." Trigger declared, setting aside his reserve. "This is my first time encountering a man of your... stature, and I find that it has caught me off-guard."

"Understandable." Thodurk replied, downing another serve of ash-black flesh. "Though, I assure you, you have nothing to fear. The Empress has left me quite well stocked. Even these are more for Carnage's benefit. Which reminds me- "

With effortless poise, Thodurk seized a handful of corpses, depositing them neatly on the *Bloodbath's* deck.

"-enjoy." He declared, giving them all a magnanimous nod.

"Thank you." Trigger nodded, adjusting his coat. "Though, I may abstain, if it causes no offence."

"Your loss." Carnage remarked, his lips already blackened by a meaty thigh. "Mavis has a gift for spices."

"He really does." Thodurk agreed, giving the butler a respectful nod.

"He is a master, I'm sure." Trigger replied, trying to ignore the smell.

"My, you are proper, aren't you?" Thodurk giggled, dabbing at his chin with a pavilion-sized hanky. "Good show. Most would have lost their nerve by now."

"That's why I chose him." Carnage beamed. "Unflappable, like a cast-iron cunt."

Trigger considered the compliment, deciding that it may have been the strangest he'd ever received.

"These men." He asked, gesturing at the gory feast. "You say they were supplied by the Empress. Who were they? Convicts?"

"Oh, no." Thodurk replied. "Convicts are usually healthy, excellent for labor. These are the poor, starving and diseased. I believe you call them undesirables."

"They have committed no crime!?"

"None of which I'm aware."

"That's appalling!" Trigger exclaimed. "Why not send you livestock? Pigs, cattle? The Empire has more than enough!"

"It probably does." Thodurk shrugged. "Yet those are things for which the Empire has a use. Our crispy companions can make no such claim."

He emphasized his words with another mouthful of limbs, dabbing at his lips with that cursed handkerchief.

"The Empress commands this?" Trigger asked, a coldness forming in his chest.

"That's not all she commands." Carnage chimed. "Tell him about the arrangement, Thodurk."

"Gladly." The giant beamed. "You see, there is a reason the Tides run past my keep. Your majesty's ancestors arranged it with my own, as a way of ensuring us a steady supply of food and entertainment. It was meant to deter us from invading, should we find ourselves bored or hungry. It works rather well, I must say."

Thodurk motioned to his butler, who swept across the room with three primly measured steps. With a practiced flourish, he seized a nearby curtain, drawing it back with a dramatic swing.

A vast mirror sat resting on the hidden wall, its surface made a sapphire by the reflected sea. A battered ship marred the illusion as it battled across the waves, its sails reduced to tatters by some unknown foe.

"Perhaps your Empire's greatest gift." Thodurk declared. "My window to the world, and what a world it is."

Trigger studied the mirror with astonishment, watching as the image shifted from one scene to another, capturing the sights of the Oracle-birds' gaze. Of his own vessel, there was no sign, the *Blackbird* proving absent time-and-time again.

"It is quite amazing." Trigger conceded. "I wonder, have you seen my former ship? It goes by the name of *Blackbird*."

"Ah, yes!" Thodurk replied, appearing rather pleased by this revelation. "Easily the most interesting vessel this year! I didn't realize you were her former Captain! You all look rather alike to me. Your stunt with the sea-vermin was rather dashing, I must say."

It took Trigger a moment to understand the reference. When finally he did, it was an understandable remark. From the giant's perspective, the sea-monster was indeed little more than a ferocious rat.

"Thank you." He nodded. "I have always considered the safety of my crew to be paramount. Do you know how they are faring?"

"Oh, I'm sure they'll crop up sometime soon." Thodurk replied. "The last I saw, they were heading into the Maiden's Thighs. An interesting choice."

"We sailed the Thighs once." Carnage remarked, picking his teeth with a corpse's finger. "Things got weird."

"Oh, I bet." Thodurk chuckled. "You're a rambunctious lot to begin with."

"Yeah." Carnage beamed, glancing at his feasting crew. "We do get a little wild."

Trigger ignored their banter, focusing his attention on the shifting mirror. Vessel after vessel flicked across it, each of them in various states of repair. One or two were quite far ahead, their battered hulls having traversed the seas with almost preternatural speed. Catching them would be quite the challenge, if Trigger ever managed to reclaim his ship.

"Oh, here we go" Thodurk nodded, as the mirror altered once again, the sapphire waves replaced by a raging sea of blood.

"My ship." Trigger grinned, leaning against the banister with childish excitement. He hadn't realized how much he missed her glorious sails, or the pristine sheen of her hull.

"Oh, my word." Thodurk declared, dabbing at his lips. "Is that poor man aflame?"

Trigger's joy evaporated as the image increased in clarity, unveiling a display of remorseless savagery.

"No." He whispered, watching with horror.

"Damn, Trigger." Carnage snorted, chewing thoughtfully at a wrist. "Looks like that ship is a fun place to be."

****

Filthy mangy cunts. They were stealing his woman. His!

Barnaby howled as the bastard crashed against his thighs, slamming them both against the deck. He punched and clawed at his attacker's face, trying to break the fucker's nose. The cunt was stronger, however, laughing stupidly as he shrugged off the blows. His meaty fist struck Barnaby's jaw, sending an explosion of lights across his altered vision. It was as though a red veil had been thrown across the world, one that opened his eyes to the depravity of his fellow man, and the divine, sexual appeal of the opposite sex. He needed to have one, and right now, this bastard, and so many others, were standing in his way.

Barnaby drove forwards, slamming his forehead against the nose. Blood splattered as the appendage broke, covering Barnaby in a mask of red. He laughed as it trickled into his waiting mouth, seconds before he struck again, biting his opponent at the base of the jaw. The weak fucker howled as his teeth sank deep, rolling away in a panicked escape. Barnaby let him go, rising and searching for his desired prize.

She was nowhere to be found.

"She's mine!"

Barnaby ducked, watching as the flaming chair sailed overhead. A few of his competitors had started a fire, and were now attempting to throw each other in, burning their wrists as they grappled before the flames.

Crunch!

The sound came from Barnaby's ribs, the plank of wood striking with devastating force. He hit the banister with a clumsy stumble, coughing and gasping as the air left his lungs.

"Where is she!?"

Barnaby threw himself sideways, barely avoiding a strike that would have surely crushed his skull. He was showered with splinters as the weapon shattered, leaving his foe clutching a brutally jagged stake.

"Where is my woman?" The bastard asked, seizing Barnaby by his collar. "Where are her juicy thighs?"

The fucker dragged the stake across Barnaby's face, tearing his skin from scalp-to-chin.

"She's mine." Barnaby sputtered, speaking around his severed lips. He flailed weakly at his captor's grasp, yet the bastard was too big, throwing Barnaby aside with a bull-like snort.

"No, she's not!" The heavy cunt roared, raising the stake above his head. A moment later his eyes were crossing, his knees giving way as he collapsed to the deck.

"Apologies." The new foe declared, addressing the unconscious prick. This one was different from the others, his skin as black as the midnight sky, raised and puckered by countless scars.

He was clearly a threat, and Barnaby hated him for it.

"You can't have her." Barnaby spat, staggering slowly to his feet. "She's mine!"

"Magwa doubts that Sheridan agrees." The black bastard replied. "Though, Barnaby is free to try. Plenty of others have. All are now unconscious, and destined to be sore."

Barnaby snarled, striking at his foe with feral swings. The motherfucker avoided them all, weaving around his wrists as though they were dancing. Eventually he tired of the movement, catching Barnaby's forearms with a vice-like grip.

"If Barnaby calms, Magwa will take him to Sheridan."

"I hate you!" Barnaby spat, writhing against the bastard's hold.

"Magwa knows you don't mean that."

"I will murder you!"

"Magwa would like to see you try."

The cunt steered him through the rapidly thinning crowd, the strong culling away the weak with astonishing efficiency.

"Such devastation." The black bastard remarked, shaking his head. "This is why Magwa's people start when they are young. Keep's the trips from getting too bad."

"You!"

The timbers shuddered as an attacker emerged, his shoulders drenched with spray and blood. He was missing his leg below the right-knee, though the prosthesis had clearly seen use as an improvised weapon. Half its length was covered in gore.

He was big. Bigger than the rest. Perhaps he would kill the black attacker.

Then Barnaby could murder him.

"Magwa means Jacques no harm." The black one declared, releasing his grip on Barnaby's wrists.

The big bastard didn't even look at him. His gaze was fixed on Barnaby.

"You took what was mine!" The brute declared, thumping his chest. "You took it all!"

Barnaby didn't understand. He'd yet to take the woman, though, he was certain that he would… either way, he didn't care. If he was upsetting this overgrown cunt, well, that was his problem.

"Fat old prick." He taunted. "Smelly great bastard."

"Barnaby, please." The black one implored. "Not helping Magwa's cause."

"Fuck you."

The black cunt sighed, just as the big one began to lunge.

The attack took Barnaby off-guard, the huge bastard shoving aside the black one with hilarious ease. Barnaby struck out as the fucker drew near, yet his own knuckles broke on that stubbly chin, a heavy fist to his stomach folding him in two. A moment later he was airborne, the huge fucker hoisting him upwards by the folds of his shirt.

"Traitor." The big bastard snarled, shaking him as though he were a mangy dog. Barnaby spat down at his opponents snarling features, aiming a kick at his unprotected chest. His foot thumped uselessly against the muscle-ridden flesh, twisting the ankle into an awkward position.

"You are nothing!"

The bastard slammed him down, smashing him into the timbers with devastating force. His shoulder popped as it took the brunt, his arm bending inwards at an unnatural angle. Barnaby screamed at the pain, his vision darkening as consciousness fled. Desire kept him fighting, however, his lust for the woman eclipsing all other needs. She would be his.

Barnaby turned, slamming his fist into his attacker's balls. The bastard grunted, bending forwards with a muted snarl. His great palm struck out an instant later, pinning Barnaby's skull in place.

"Pathetic. Little. Wretch."

Each word was emphasized by the bastard's fist, striking his stomach over-and-over as though it were tempering a piece of steel. Eventually it grew too much, a stream of vomit erupting from Barnaby's slit lips. Most of it fell on his own face, his opponent's palm deflecting it downwards, while his savage blows conjured more and more.

HISSSSSSS!

The big fucker screamed, reeling backwards as something white and crimson clawed at his rapidly reddening face.

"Get off!" The huge bastard screamed, trying and failing to remove his furred opponent. The creature was stubborn, however, lashing out with a fury that eclipsed Barnaby's own. Claws and teeth flashed in a hurricane of frenzy, spattering the deck with the big cunt's blood.

"Get! Off!"

The bastard spun, punching madly at his own skull. The creature would have been flattened, yet with astonishing grace it avoided the blow, leaping to safety and racing away.

With a groan of agony, Barnaby rose, watching as his opponent cradled his eyes. The creature had almost blinded him, his forehead and cheeks dripping from a thousand cuts and bites.

"You're mine." He growled, stepping towards him with murderous intent.

"Apologies, Barnaby."

His legs were swept with practiced efficiency, sending him sprawling. His chin was the first thing to touch the timbers, the sudden jolt leaving him dazed and confused. A shadow leapt across him an instant later, racing along the deck with fantastic speed. His blinded foe never had a chance to defend, that huge frame falling to three sweeping blows.

"Apologies, Beaufort."

The black cunt. He was still alive.

"You…you won't take her from me." Barnaby rasped, attempting to rise. He had taken too much damage, however, his broken body refusing to move.

"Magwa doubts he will be taking anything." The black prick replied, raising his hands in submission. "He doubts the Captain will be, either."

"…Wha?" Barnaby asked, unable to form words.

"Stay where you are!"

A gun barrel pressed between his eyes, the cold steel soothing his battered flesh.

"You, savage! Cast aside the axe!"

The black bastard was suddenly surrounded, a whole horde of cunts appearing on deck.

"Magwa cannot." The black prick replied, shrugging defiantly at the bastard horde.

"You won't have her." Barnaby gurgled, seizing a leather-clad ankle. "She's mine."

"They've all turned, Captain." Remarked one of the bastards, turning to another. "All except the Kalyute, and the coward in the crow's nest."

The other cunt nodded, turning to the black one with a sneer of distaste.

"You, savage. Who is the Captain?"

The black one nodded at Barnaby, who spat at them all with a bloody snarl.

"Gods." The sneering cunt declared, shaking his head. "Tie him up, and get him inside with the others."

"Aye, Captain."

Two cunts seized him about the arms, dragging him upwards with coughs and gags.

"He stinks."

"Yeah, and look at his face. He's not going to be happy when he sobers up."

"Fuck you!" Barnaby roared, attempting to bite a flexing shoulder. They shrugged him aside with ease, looking to the leader with imploring eyes.

"You're a sorry replacement." The cunt declared, stepping towards him and shaking his head.

He struck Barnaby across the jaw, knocking all thought from his addled mind.

Chapter Twenty-One

"Thank you for doing this yourself. We appreciate the lift."

"Nonsense, Carnage. I enjoy a good stroll, and I believe your champion needed the air."

He wasn't wrong. After what he'd just witnessed, Trigger was feeling sick to his stomach.

"I'm sure your crew will survive." Thodurk encouraged, giving him an uncertain grin. "Well, some of them, at least."

"Shame the mirror cut out early, though." Carnage remarked. "That little guy was about to get stomped."

"Some empathy, Carnage, please." Thodurk scolded. "Consider your guest's emotions."

"You're right." Carnage conceded, playfully hanging his dread-locked head. "I was being insensitive. I'm sorry about your crew, Trigger."

"Thank you." Trigger replied, gathering himself as he adjusted his coat.

"Still, I hope this hasn't diverted your attention from the more pressing matters at hand." Thodurk declared, crunching boulders into gravel as he sauntered across the mountain. The journey would have taken Trigger at least a week to complete, yet for Thodurk it was simply an afternoon wander, a relaxing climb around his titanic abode. "Yes, your former crew is in peril, yet the world at large is in far more dire straits."

Trigger considered this statement, watching as the ocean loomed into view. From this height, the waves themselves were lost to the blue, their mighty crests reduced to shimmers of white.

"He's right, Trigger." Carnage agreed. "Think about what you saw today. Those are innocent men, women and children, and the Empress feeds them to Thodurk without a second thought. Even the Tides is another design, one that has cost thousands of men their lives. Your crew may well be joining them."

The words stung at Trigger's conscience, creating a swell of contempt for his own inaction. He had allowed himself to be deceived and captured, taken from his crew when they needed him most. Worse than that, however, he had tolerated the existence of a regime that saw fit to destroy countless innocent lives, simply for the profit of an entitled minority. A minority to which he had once belonged. One which had already shown him its evil, and thoughtlessly cast him aside. And what had he done in reply? He had allowed it to continue prospering, and even contemplated ways in which he might return.

He was a coward, and a wretch. No more.

"My crew will have to fend for themselves." Trigger declared, rubbing his finger against his thumb. "The three of us have work to do."

Thodurk and Carnage shared an exuberant glance, their faces splitting with unfettered glee.

"Excellent form." Thodurk nodded, giving Trigger a supportive wink.

"I knew I chose right." Carnage cheered, pointing at Trigger with intense satisfaction.

"I do have terms, however."

"They always do." Thodurk chuckled.

"Let's hear them." Carnage nodded, rubbing his hands together. "The sooner they're said, the sooner they're met."

"The first is for you, Thodurk. From this day onwards, you are to turn away all tributes from the Empress, be they human, livestock or otherwise. You have an ocean at your feet, and all the means to construct a rod."

"Done." Thodurk beamed. "I already have a rod, truth be told, and quite enjoy the occasional whale. Fishing is actually a proud tradition of my family. The Snoufflepousses built their lives on the sea."

"The Snoufflepousses?"

"Yes. My ancestral name. I am Thodurk Sebastian Snoufflepousse, and I am very glad to be at your service."

Trigger glanced at Carnage, who offered him a tiny nod.

"He's not kidding."

"Very well." Trigger nodded, deciding to let it go. "My second request is rather similar. I ask that you cease feeding on the ships that dare your keep. You will open up this passage, loosening the Empire's grasp on the ocean and trade."

"Sounds reasonable."

"My last request is simple. I desire an explanation."

"As to what?"

"Why are you helping us? You clearly place little value on human lives, and your dealings with the Empress have left you quite comfortable. What do you stand to gain?"

"Insightful." Thodurk remarked, his great knees bending as they reached the shore. He placed them in the water as a child would a toy, the impact causing them all to stagger.

"You are completely correct, of course. I am comfortable, and the lives of your people hold no sway on my own. Yet, I am also an entity of reason, and as such, know my place in the world. I have studied it from end-to-end, wandering its fields with shameless awe. It is a beautiful gem, Captain. One that will fade, if things continue as they are."

"What do you mean?" Trigger asked, as Thodurk sat on the pristine sand. The movement created a mild spray, coating the deck in golden grains.

"The Empire unifies nothing. It creates only suffering and slavery, and blinds you all to your potential. It imprisons even those who exist beyond it, as they are forced to define themselves through their fruitless defiance. It is breaking the world, and thus must be destroyed. Especially if we are to face the enemy that comes."

"What enemy?" Trigger asked, frowning.

"You haven't told him." Thodurk sighed, glancing at Carnage.

"I've been easing him in. I'd say it's safe, now that he's committed."

"This is all rather cryptic." Trigger declared, folding his arms.

"My apologies." Thodurk replied, bowing his head. "However, experience has taught us both to exercise a certain level of… restraint, when speaking about this topic. It is often met with disbelief."

"You're a thousand feet tall, and he's bright red." Trigger replied, raising an eyebrow. "How fantastic can it be?"

"Well said." Thodurk conceded. "Tell him, Carnage."

The Thrallkin took a moment to respond, his yellow eyes darkening with unwanted thoughts.

"It's hard to describe." He began, shrugging his powerful shoulders. "You know about the Empire's wars. Gods, you've fought in them. I've told you about the Front Lines, and the horrors my people have faced. What I haven't told you, is that they mean nothing compared to what is coming from the Jaw."

"The Jaw?" Trigger asked, astonished by the tone in Carnage's voice. It wasn't just fear. It was terror.

"The Empire isn't at war with invaders." Carnage replied, scratching at his crimson chin. "It's simply repelling refugees."

"Pardon?" Trigger asked, blinking.

"The creatures at the Front Lines... I don't know what they're called. I don't know how they're made. All I know is that they hunger, and that on our best days, even my people are barely a match."

Trigger thought back to the battle, the way they had taken that ship without spilling a drop of Thrallkin blood.

"And our enemies...they're fleeing this menace?"

"Yes. Scurrying away, desperate to find safety. The Empire stands as their greatest hope. It kills them the moment they tread on its shores."

"And I'm guessing that few but the Empress know this." Trigger sighed, running his fingers through his hair.

"Only her most inner-circle." Carnage nodded. "Few men see them and live to report. My people alone can venture that far and survive long enough to recount what they find."

Trigger didn't bother replying. He didn't doubt their words, or the callousness of his former home. Another atrocity he must add to the list. It was getting long indeed.

"These creatures you speak of. Are they a match for you, Thodurk?"

The giant took a long moment to reply, dabbing at his lips with that sail-sized handkerchief.

"One, two, maybe a hundred, and I could swat them down as though they were simple men. Yet I have wandered the Front Lines, further than even Carnage can claim. I stood in their midst, and watched the horizon falter beneath the burden of their ranks. Had I remained a moment longer, I would have been devoured. Great as I am, I cannot face them alone."

Trigger considered the giant, every facet of his colossal form.

"So, that's why you need us." Trigger frowned. "To fight a war that you can't win."

"I consider my people to be your shepherds." Thodurk replied, shrugging without apparent shame. "For the most part, we leave you to your own devices. Let you eat, let you sleep. Occasionally we take you for food, though we always make sure to leave the herd intact. Now the wolves are coming, however, and what is a shepherd without his sheep?"

"You're no better than the Empress." Trigger declared, his anger dismissing his sense of restraint.

"Why, of course I am." Thodurk chuckled. "I'm honest."

"He's not wrong." Carnage chimed, leaning against the banister with a mischievous grin.

"You would say that." Trigger replied. "It isn't your people that he intends to consume."

"Well, that's more a matter of taste, than anything else. He tried eating one of us on our first visit to his keep. Apparently, our flesh is a bit too gamey."

"He ate one of your crew? And still you formed this alliance?"

"Of course. Why let one life dictate the many? I saw a chance to reshape the world, to make it into something better. Only a selfish fool would throw that away, just for the sake of his own moral comfort."

Trigger wished he could have argued. That he could declare the pair of them madmen, insane radicals without reason or rhyme. Unfortunately, he knew how often those labels were applied, and how unfounded they often were. In many cases, there was only one difference between a madman and a hero.

Who won.

"The sun is setting." Thodurk remarked, stretching his neck with a deafening crack. "You really should be on your way. You have a race to win, after all."

"That we do." Carnage replied, nodding his shaggy head. "Would you mind giving us a slight advantage?"

"Anything for you, good sir."

Thodurk's great hand descended, gripping their stern with pillar-like fingers.

"Farewell, my friend." Thodurk beamed. "I look forward to hearing of your success. Captain Trigger, it has been an absolute pleasure."

"Cheers." Carnage replied, giving the giant a half-hearted salute. "I'll be seeing you soon."

"Thank you." Trigger replied, truly unsure how best to reply. "It's been an… enlightening experience."

"Enlightening." Thodurk chuckled. "I like that."

The whole ship lurched as the giant drew them backwards, his bicep bulging against a well-made sleeve.

"Now, I really suggest that you hold on."

Trigger braced himself against the banister, suddenly aware of the giant's plan.

"Relax." Carnage laughed, a demented edge entering his eyes. "It's actually quite fun!"

Thodurk's arm shot forward, propelling them across the sea at an astonishing pace. Their vessel actually gained some air, bouncing across the tide like a skimming stone. Trigger fought back a scream as the world whipped by, the clouds themselves a blur as they travelled mile after mile. The timbers groaned and the mast swayed, the wind slashing at their faces with an audible howl. Finally, after what seemed years of motion, their strained ship slowed to a reasonable pace, one that allowed for unbraced limbs.

"Get those sails up, boys!" Carnage roared. "I can feel a good wind, and I want us riding it before our push fades!"

The Thrallkin hurried about their duties, scaling the rigging with preternatural speed. Their enhanced physicality made them the perfect crew, able to function where others could not.

They could be an incredible asset, were one inclined to put them to use.

"So, what did you think?" Carnage asked, turning to Trigger as the sails flared wide. "Fun, or no?"

Trigger took a deep breath, still uncertain as to the nature of his day. When it came to Thodurk's push, however, his thoughts on the matter were completely resolved.

"Marvelous." He replied, giving Carnage a friendly grin. "Absolutely marvelous."

****

Oh, Gods. Pain. So much pain. How could one man be in so much pain?

Barnaby groaned, a low, wet gurgle that hurt all the more. His face felt as though it had been pummeled with stones, the kind chefs used to keep their meals warm.

Reducing the intensity of his groan, yet not ceasing entirely, Barnaby attempted to open his eyes. His left failed, while his right formed a slit that allowed some semblance of vision.

He kind of wished it had just stayed shut.

"He's awake, Captain."

"Yes, Bill, I'm aware. He wasn't exactly being quiet."

Bill bowed his head in apology, yet didn't lower the rifle he had pressed to Magwa's skull. Gods, the whole room was bit too rifle-to-the-heady, almost every person present having a barrel near their brain. Barnaby himself was no exception, though admittedly, his own guard seemed rather relaxed. He must have assumed that Barnaby was no real threat.

Eh, fair enough.

"Can you speak?" The strange Captain asked, his countenance appearing oddly familiar.

"Does he look like he can?" Snapped Sheridan, who was seated opposite Barnaby's bed. Her guard seemed to be rather concerned, the rifle trembling in his battered hands.

"I was speaking to him." The strange Captain declared. "Now, boy. Speak if you can."

Barnaby opened his mouth. It felt as though a trail of hot ash were spilled across his face.

"I'll assume that's a no." The Captain nodded, as Barnaby gave an agonized yelp.

"Astonishing." Sheridan snorted, rolling her eyes.

"I have no reserves about gagging a woman." The strange Captain replied. He frowned as he spoke, the twist in his features jogging Barnaby's mind.

"He…Hen'y…Falc'n." He rasped, his swollen jaw refusing to move.

"You know me." Falcon nodded. "Good."

"We were all present at the starting line." Sheridan declared. "And you weren't an easy sight to miss."

"Yes." Falcon nodded, tapping his fingers against the desk. "That was not my finest hour. Still, it remains the reason for my presence, and my motive for your rescue."

"Oh, this is a rescue?" Sheridan remarked, gesturing at the rifle mere inches from her face.

"Indeed, it is." Falcon scowled. "Where it not for my arrival, your 'Captain' would be dead, and you would have been raped to pieces by a drug-addled crew."

It was no easy feat to make Sheridan bite her tongue. Still, that just about did it.

"Th'nk…you." Barnaby grunted, making a feeble attempt at maintaining good relations. He had a sneaking suspicion that Falcon already disliked him. He must be an excellent judge of character.

"You are welcome." The Captain replied, his tone somewhat approving. "Though, my actions come from duty, not kindness. I owe Trigger a debt, and I intend to repay it, regardless of the…undesirables, this might force me to encounter."

He gazed directly at Magwa as he spoke, his lip curling slightly with obvious disgust.

"Your arrival would have meant nothing if Magwa wasn't here." Sheridan declared, leaping to the Kalyute's defense. "Barnaby and I would be corpses on the deck."

"I have no doubts that Trigger raised him to be an effective pet." Falcon frowned. "He seems a prudent man."

"Trigger would never make Magwa pet." The Kalyute announced, giving them a pointy grin. "Magwa not house-trained."

Sheridan chuckled at the Kalyute's remark, while Barnaby gave him points for sheer balls.

"Trigger considered him a valuable crewman." Sheridan explained. "And saw fit to punish all those who denied it."

"Yes, well." Falcon shrugged. "Every man has his flaws."

Barnaby wasn't certain that a lack of racial intolerance counted as a flaw. Still, he was in no state to argue.

"Is there a point to all this?" Sheridan snapped, gesturing around the room. "I mean, you already think that you saved us. That should clear your debt, shouldn't it?"

"My debt is to Trigger." Falcon replied. "And he is not yet saved."

A somber mood prevailed as Sheridan hung her head, her ruby wig askew from the exertions of the day.

"Trigger's beyond saving." She eventually declared. "We lost him at the fixture."

"You lost him, yes." Falcon replied. "That doesn't mean he can't be found."

Both Sheridan and Magwa raised their heads, while Barnaby managed a minor twitch.

"What do you mean?" Sheridan asked, a terrified, hopeful plea.

"Your Captain isn't dead." Falcon announced, showing them all his very first grin.

"I knew it!" Sheridan cheered, almost flipping the table as she bolted to her feet. "Where is he? What happened?"

Falcon considered the First Mate with a contemptuous scowl, clearly unimpressed by the emotional outburst.

"Sit, please." He requested, gesturing at her chair.

His sorrowful tones beat heavy against Sheridan's joy, and with a fading smile she reclaimed her seat, careful to avoid the rifle still training at her face.

"What happened?" She repeated, regaining her former composure.

"I am not yet privy to the entire tale." Falcon replied, his thin features twisting with simmering rage. "Though I will be, after a brief interrogation. All I know is what I saw. I was at the duel, you see. Well, the arena, at least. We arrived late, and as I've never been one for crowds, I decided to avoid the match entirely. Instead, I ventured to one of the floating taverns, one of the few not operated by those filthy natives."

Barnaby glanced at Magwa. He seemed unoffended. Sheridan was doing the same, a fact which did not escape the Kalyute's notice.

"Oh, Magwa is fine." The savage shrugged. "The Captain is right. They are a filthy bunch. Magwa's people tried to skin them, but they smelt too bad to make a tent."

"Fair...fair enough." Sheridan conceded, bowing her head. Across the table, Falcon gave the tiniest shudder.

"I was at this tavern when relations broke down. We were quite far removed from the arena, allowing me to watch the chaos from a relative point of safety. The most interesting sight was your Captain and Beaufort, who were fleeing along a pathway that led nowhere near your ship. Beaufort appeared to be leading."

Sheridan cracked her knuckles, each one popping like a distant shot.

"They paused to argue, presumably because Trigger realized the deception. Sadly, he was far too late. Beaufort struck him unawares, and threw him into the churning sea."

"That bastard!" Sheridan snapped, slamming her fists against the desk. "That two-faced, treacherous cunt!"

"Quite." Falcon nodded, frowning at the interruption.

Barnaby merely lay in silence, struggling to digest the Captain's words.

"I would have mounted a rescue, yet conditions were worsening by the moment, and I had my crew to consider. We made ready to depart, hoping that we could catch you before Beaufort returned. We were delayed, however, by several unwarranted attacks. There was providence behind this mishap, however, as it allowed us to observe Trigger's next bout of misfortune."

"Which was?" Sheridan asked. "Was he harmed?"

"…Captured." Falcon hesitated.

"By whom?"

Falcon exhaled, gripping the sides of his chair with barely suppressed rage.

"Carnage."

Barnaby felt a shiver of dread, ignoring the pain it caused his limbs. He knew that Trigger had it far, far worse.

"Gods." Sheridan whispered, turning pale with horror and fear.

"I know." Falcon replied. "It's a fate I'd not wish on any man."

"All this time." Sheridan murmured, her eyes growing distant. "He's had him all this time…"

"Yes, I imagine your Captain has endured the most terrible pain. Carnage is a sadistic and vile creature. Still, just this once, that works to our advantage. It means that Trigger may still be alive."

"Then we have to find him." Sheridan declared. "As soon as we are able."

"I agree, and I have some idea where he might be. I would enjoy some corroboration, however."

"Beaufort." Sheridan growled. "If he dealt with Carnage, he might know where the bastard's heading."

"My thoughts exactly."

Falcon clapped, a short, precise motion, which was met by a groan from the door's rusty hinges. A pair of unfamiliar crewmen backed carefully into the room; their rifles trained at Jacques' shackled form. Two more men were swift to follow, creating a perfect square of restriction.

Not that it stopped Sheridan. She was up and moving before her own guard could blink, swatting aside the procession as she seized Jacques by his throat.

"We saved you!" She screamed, dragging him across the room. "We spared your miserable life!"

She slammed his face against the table, opening the countless scratches etched across his face.

"We should have left you to starve on that fucking bank!"

Again and again she threw him down, smearing the timbers with a portrait of blood. Falcon observed the display without judgement or emotion, waiting several moments before he finally raised his hand.

"That's enough."

The guards placed their rifles against Sheridan's chest, shoving her away from Jacques. His swollen features had almost doubled in size, yet the swordsman was simply laughing, as though the pain was nothing more than a tickle.

"I take it you told her about my deal?" He chuckled, squinting at Falcon through a swollen eye.

Falcon nodded, and with quiet efficiency a guardsman struck, slamming the butt of his rifle against Jacques' cheek. Barnaby winced in sympathy, the day's revelations not enough to undo their several months of friendship.

"You will speak when spoken to. Understood?"

Jacques spat a tooth onto the floor, rolling his shoulders with obvious contempt.

"Compliance would be wise."

Falcon nodded again, and with a fearsome crack another guardsman struck, sending Jacques slumping towards the floor. He caught himself against the desk, palms slipping in his own pooling blood.

"Why?" He snorted. "I am captured, and know ze penalty for my actions. I am to die, and personally, I would prefer to pass knowing zat I spited my foes, razer zan bowing to zeir childish whims."

"If you know your fate, then you also know that there is no reason for us to make your end comfortable. We can stretch it out for days, or weeks. Break you in ways you never knew possible."

"Break me?" Jacques chuckled. "I was broken decades ago, in ze stinking basement of a perverted beast. I do not fear your torture. I have endured far worse."

Falcon considered the swordsman, his face revealing admiration for such bold-faced bravado.

"Put his hands on the table."

The guardsmen seized Jacques' wrists, pinning them against the desk.

"I'm going to ask you questions." Falcon declared. "You will answer, honestly. Each time you don't, I will take a finger."

Jacques didn't reply, or struggle.

"Your deal with Carnage, what was it?"

Barnaby stared at Jacques with mounting fear. The swordsman's lips were tightly sealed.

Answer, you crazy motherfucker.

Falcon waited several moments, before releasing a weary sigh.

"Very well."

His dagger was out in a silver flash, arcing towards the table with precision and speed. It removed Jacques' finger with a sickening crunch, embedding itself in the ruined wood.

Jacques grunted in pain, recoiling with enough force to wrench his hands free. Still, he didn't scream.

"I do not bluff." Falcon remarked, sweeping the finger aside. "Now, I will ask you again. Your deal with Carnage. What was it?"

Jacques didn't reply, breathing heavily as he cradled his blood-soaked palm. Then, with a maniacal grin, he sat himself forwards, placing his hands on the table.

"I've got ze patience for nine more times." He sneered.

"Have you?"

Chapter Twenty-Two

"Just a couple?"

"No."

"One or two, that's all I'm asking."

"How do you think they'll react to that, exactly? 'Hello, my name is Captain Trigger, the laughingstock of our whole nation. This is my companion, Captain Carnage, widely regarded as the most fearsome murderer the world has ever known. Would you care to join our fleet? Oh, and while you're at it, could Carnage and his crew have a few of you to nibble on? They're terribly hungry'."

"Hmm." Carnage mused. "Fair point. Though, you aren't a Captain anymore, you're an Admiral."

"Not until I have a fleet." Trigger replied. "Which will be a long-time coming, if we try and eat our new recruits."

"Fine, fine." Carnage conceded, raising his hands in defeat. "We're taking their ale, though."

"What about the wine?" Trigger frowned. "What Thodurk gave us could drown a horse."

"It's gone off."

"How? It hasn't been two weeks!"

"Some of the crew fell in."

Trigger sighed, rubbing his finger against his thumb.

"How?"

"They wanted to know if they could drink from the thimble while doing a handstand on the rim. They can't."

"Evidently. Though, surely that doesn't bother you?"

"Normally it wouldn't, but they were holding a raw chicken when they fell in."

Trigger restrained himself from asking why. It would only lead to further questions.

"We will take a portion of their ale." He declared, studying the distant ship. "If they agree to join us."

"And if they don't?"

"We allow them to proceed, without doing them harm."

"What if they try to harm us?"

Trigger considered Carnage, studying the Thrallkin's massive form.

"Then I pity them, and question how they got this far."

"Can't argue with that." Carnage chuckled, tapping at his too-small hat.

Trigger didn't reply, focusing instead on their growing target. He recognized the flag and build, the pair marking the vessel as the *Dragon's Breath*, a rather infamous man'o'war. Thirty-two cannons on either side and manned by a crew of retired soldiers. Trigger wasn't surprised that they had made such progress, their reputation as hardened combatants being undeniably deserved. Every man was a veteran, while their Captain, Julius Conyack, had been sailing the seas before Trigger was born. They'd come second in the Tides on several occasions, losing primarily to Carnage's crew. It was a fact that would doubtlessly become a point of contention, and a stern reminder that for all their power, the Thrallkin came with plenty of baggage.

"Raise the white flag!" Trigger ordered, gesturing to Carnage's… no, *his* crew.

The fabric rose with measured speed, catching the wind with a serpentine flow. Trigger watched as the *Dragon* replied, hoisting a series of flags with astonishing pace.

"They're asking who we are." Trigger announced, folding his arms.

"I know." Carnage replied, giving him a sideways glance. "I can read a set of fucking flags."

"Half-rations." Trigger declared.

"What?"

"Foul language will never be tolerated when you are standing on my deck. Should you or any of the crew feel the need to use it, you will find your rations cut for the duration of the week. Am I understood?"

Carnage turned to Trigger with an uneven grin, clearly unsure if he was part of a joke.

"You're serious, aren't you?" He finally asked, as Trigger refused to acknowledge his doubt.

"I am. You wanted me for discipline. Now you have it."

Carnage took a bracing breath, clearly restraining the anger within. Trigger could see it raging behind his gaze.

"Very well." He declared, spitting the words. "How will you have the crew respond?"

It was an excellent question. If he announced that they were Carnage's crew, the *Dragon* might fire on principle alone. Yet if they didn't reply, they were likely to fire out of sheer distrust.

"Unfortunately, there's no flag for Thrallkin." Trigger began, taking a moment to adjust his coat. "Would you care to stand with me on the prow? I doubt they'll mistake you for anyone else, and my presence at your side should arouse their curiosity."

"Or they snipe us."

"That is a possibility, yes."

"One you're willing to entertain?"

"I am. We've already put them on edge. To keep them waiting further would be a terrible mistake."

"A greater mistake than being shot in the head?"

"I'm surprised you're so worried. Would that even kill you?"

"Maybe. Even if it doesn't, it would fucking hu- "

Trigger raised his eyebrow, and folded his arms.

"It would be most uncomfortable." Carnage snarled. "And I suggest that you let this one slide. We're still rather new to civility."

"I'll give you a month." Trigger replied, as they made their way towards the prow. "After that, I expect you to enforce it with the utmost zeal."

"Of course, Admiral." Carnage nodded, taking his place at Trigger's side. A telescope flashed on their target ship, its glass training towards their forms.

"Here we go." Carnage winced, tilting his chin towards the deck. If the enemy did fire, the bullet would strike his densest bone. It was a rather clever defense, though, one that Trigger could not employ.

"What are they doing?" Carnage asked, attempting to peer under his crimson brow.

"Constructing a reply." Trigger declared, watching as they adjusted their row of flags.

"Any idea what it might entail?"

"Yes." Trigger grinned, watching as a field of white was hoisted high. "Good news, I believe."

"Huh." Carnage shrugged, sounding mildly disappointed. "I was kind of hoping they'd shoot."

"Wanting to test your limits?"

"Essentially."

"Well, the day is young." Trigger replied. "You may still get your chance."

Their vessels converged at a hesitant pace, an awkward dance between virgin mates. The *Dragon* proved to be slightly larger, its flush cannons an obvious warning. They were willing to talk, yet not afraid to fight.

"Good morning!" Trigger called, as their broadsides paralleled. Several crewmen studied him from their elevated deck, squinting eyes filled with mistrust. He could hardly fault them.

"Good morning."

The greeting came from a one-eyed scoundrel, the empty socket bared without patch or bandage. It was an old wound; the scarred flesh having faded to a simmering maroon. His close-cropped hair was salt and pepper, pitch-black barbs sprinkled with grey. He didn't seem pleased to be having this meeting.

"I hope the day has found you well." Trigger began, giving a respectful nod. He'd never met Captain Julius, yet this man certainly seemed to fit the rank.

"Whether I'm well or not, the days always seem to find me, and they usually bring a shit-head for company. Who are you, and what do you want?"

The Captain's men didn't chuckle at his barb. They seemed a miserable bunch in general.

"My name is Admiral Trigger, and I have called this meeting to propose an idea. Am I correct in guessing you are Captain Julius?"

"If you're an Admiral, where's your fleet?" The man asked, completely ignoring Trigger's request.

"It's under construction." Carnage replied, his deep voice rolling across the waves.

"Ah, Carnage." The man replied, leaning against the banister of his over-sized ship. "How are you faring? I didn't recognize your ship without the bodies and bones."

"I'm well, thank you." Carnage declared, his yellow eyes flashing with mischief. "We've actually been redecorating. New me, new ship."

"New pet?"

"I'm no pet." Trigger announced, rubbing his thumb against his finger.

"Really? Because I don't see you putting Carnage in a cage, and that's the only way to deal with his kind."

Trigger heard the cocking of several dozen guns, their barrels appearing over the *Dragon's* edge.

"Untrue." Trigger replied, giving them all his most charming grin. "Dialogue has proven to be quite successful."

"He's right." Carnage chimed. "When you get to know us, my people are lovers, not fighters."

"Oh." Julius sneered, looking between them with obvious disgust. "So, it's like that, then."

Trigger repressed the urge to cover his face, while Carnage glanced at him with appraising eyes.

"I'm down if he is." The Thrallkin shrugged. "Though, he seems a bit reserved to swing that far."

"May we please come aboard?" Trigger sighed, missing Sheridan with all his heart.

Julius looked to his men, who held their weapons without shudder or shake.

"You and Carnage. The rest stay behind, on deck and in-line. You fuck up, we shoot."

"Acceptable terms." Trigger replied. "I promise, my crew will behave."

"You're sailing with monsters." Julius declared. "Your promises mean jack-shit."

"Yes." Trigger conceded, rubbing at his eyes. "I'm beginning to see that. Men, please, form a line."

The deck rumbled as his crew replied, falling into rank without complaint. He was actually impressed, as were their potential allies.

"They listen to you?" Julius frowned, as his men lowered a sturdy ramp.

"They are my crew."

"How did you swing that?"

"Carnage asked me."

Julius looked to Carnage, who nodded in affirmation.

"This fucking world." Julius murmured, shaking his head. "Getting weirder every day. Come on, then."

Carnage and Trigger boarded his ship, the beam bending beneath the Thrallkin's weight. As soon as they touched deck the plank was removed, stranding their crew on the timbers below.

"Nice ship." Carnage remarked, studying the *Dragon* and its bristling crew. They'd clearly never seen him at such close range, the enormity of his form casting their weapons in doubt.

"Aye, she gets the job done." Julius declared, leading them to his spacious quarters.

"Well, mostly." Carnage grinned. "She could stand to be a little faster."

Uncomfortable silence. Trigger silently cursed the Thrallkin.

"Yes...I suppose she could." Julius scowled, taking a seat at his battered desk. Though large, his quarters were furnished with a practical scarcity, unadorned by trinkets or decoration. The Captain had a bed, a desk and a chair to seat him. There wasn't even a pitcher of water.

"May I have a chair?" Carnage asked, gazing forlornly at the dusty floor.

"No."

Carnage frowned, chorded muscle twitching with barely restrained rage. Trigger understood his anger. It was an unnecessary snub, one intended solely to annoy. A dangerous game, particularly with Thrallkin.

"You said you had an idea." Julius ventured, propping his forearms against his desk. "Speak it."

"The fleet we're constructing." Trigger replied. "We'd like you to be part of it."

Julius stared at him, long and hard.

"No."

"I understand your misgivings." Trigger began. "I know this offer comes from an unusual part-" "Nothing unusual about you." Julius replied. "You're a posh wanker, backed by a ton of savage muscle. You're every would-be-conqueror the world has ever seen."

"We're not conquerors." Trigger frowned. "We have no intention of oppressing or dominating. We- "

"You intend to liberate, to do away with the old and usher in a bright new age." Julius sneered. "I've been around a while, boys. I've heard it all before."

"Then you should know that the world needs change."

"Nothing ever changes. People die, kids go hungry. The rich don't give a fuck, and the poor dream of the day that they don't have to. That day comes when they die, for most. The ones who do get rich? Well, they dive right in to shitting on the poor."

"Gods." Carnage remarked. "That's bleak."

"That's life." Julius shrugged. "Though, I'm not surprised it shocks you. You've destroyed enough to make it foreign."

Trigger ran his fingers through his hair. This was not going well.

"Have I slighted you in some way, old man?" Carnage growled.

"Your existence slights me. Your ill-conceived notions offend me."

"Our 'notion', is to cast down a tyrannical empire." Trigger frowned, hoping that Carnage could keep his calm.

"It can never be cast down." Julius scoffed. "There isn't a name for what you're fighting. It's more than a twisted ruler, or a council of greedy souls. It cannot be destroyed, because the moment you think you've won, you've become the entity you fought. Even in defeat, it will always consume."

"Are we still talking about an Empire?" Carnage remarked, tugging at his hat.

"We're always talking about an Empire. Old or new, it's always the same."

Trigger wanted to argue, to oppose the old man's speech. Unfortunately, it resonated all-too strongly with what he had come to know. The Empire always profits, even from those who seek its end.

"There's nothing here, Trigger." Carnage snorted, regarding the Captain with intense disdain. "His conscience is as withered as his dusty old cock."

"Aye, you might be right." Julius replied, his eye narrowing in a fearsome scowl. "I agreed to meet with you, after all."

"Fuck you, old man, I'm trying to fix the world!" Carnage roared, taking a step towards the ancient desk.

"Easy!" Trigger ordered, placing his hand on Carnage's chest. "Think of the crew!"

"You value your men, at least." Julius observed, turning his gaze to Trigger. Despite the tenseness of the situation, the old man had maintained his composure. "A redeeming aspect for a deplorable reputation."

"You know who I am, then."

"I do." Julius nodded. "A mistake like yours is not often overlooked."

"Then you know the decision I made. That I chose the people, and not the prince."

"A bold choice, and a commendable one. However, were you choosing the people, or victory?"

"They were one and the same." Trigger replied, adjusting his coat.

"Lucky for you. That isn't always the case. I'm curious to know what you'd decide, if the two were separate."

"I'd choose the people." Trigger announced, without a hint of hesitation.

"Then you're destined to lose."

"You'd rather I chose victory?"

"No. That's the tyrant's choice."

"Gods, he can't win then, can he?" Carnage interrupted, raising a hand in anger.

"I told you that earlier." Julius shrugged. "It's not my fault you've failed to listen."

"Oh, you're full of answers, aren't you?" Carnage sneered. "All mouth and no balls."

"I'd fight for a cause, if it were worthy." Julius replied. "It just so happens that none of them are."

"Yo- "

"Carnage, please." Trigger declared, cutting off the Thrallkin's rant. "The Captain is entitled to his opinion. We cannot demand that he follows our cause."

Carnage glared at him, that cavernous chest swelling with frustration.

"He doesn't even know what he's talking about." Carnage replied, his tone becoming lethal and low.

They needed to leave. Soon.

"I truly think he does." Trigger announced, giving the Captain a friendly nod. "Thank you for your time, sir. I hope the remaining voyage finds you well."

"You're both going to die." Julius replied, ignoring his attempt at parting civility.

"We're all going to die." Trigger shrugged. "From what I've gathered, it's all you're looking forward to."

He didn't waste words on more pointless goodbyes. He simply exited the cabin, listening to the steps as Carnage followed.

"What sort of pirate can think like that." Carnage grumbled, simmering quietly at Trigger's back.

"An experienced one."

The *Dragon's* crew observed their progress, half their rifles turning to poke at Carnage's face. Three men scurried away, returning a moment later with the boarding plank in tow.

"No, that's bullshit." Carnage frowned, his voice rising with every word. "You are pirates! You live outside the developed world, because you see it for what it truly is! Now, when someone offers you the chance to fight, to really fight, you turn tail and run! Is it a lie!? Your philosophy, your rebellion, is it all a cover? Cheap words, to excuse the raping and pillaging!? Are they merely a veil, to hide your eyes from your own base nature!?"

"You've read too many stories, boy."

Julius strode out of his chambers, the sword at his hip now partially unsheathed. It was an odd weapon, far shorter than the blades to which Trigger was accustomed. It belonged in a battlefield trench, not on the seas.

"Why?" Carnage replied, flexing his shoulders. "Because I still hope for a better world?"

"Hope is fine." Julius shrugged. "Just never expect that it will happen."

"No." Carnage whispered, balling his fingers into a fist. "That's just what you people want us to think."

Trigger studied the Thrallkin, astonished by his passion. Carnage believed in what they were doing. He believed in it with all his heart.

"You're not too bright, are you boy?"

The question came from a nearby rifleman, his greasy hair slicked to the point of solidity. His fellow crewmen looked to him as he spoke, their expressions mirroring Trigger's own thoughts.

This man had sealed their fate.

Carnage lost control, bounding across the deck at a terrifying pace. The crewman attempted to fire as the Thrallkin seized his face, yet Carnage knocked the rifle aside, sending the shot into polished wood.

Trigger didn't bother with a call for restraint. He knew that moment had already passed.

With a sickening crunch Carnage crushed the man's skull, tearing it from his body with a soggy squelch. The meaty spine remained attached, the many joints bending as he waved it overhead.

We can save this. Trigger whispered to himself. *We can-*

Carnage used the spine as a whip, slashing it across a crewman's face.

Trigger sighed, restraining the urge to massage his eyes. So much for that.

"Fire!"

The Captain's roar was deafening, yet paled beneath the cracking guns. The crew opened fire with defiant zeal, the majority aiming for the Thrallkin crew, while a few dared Carnage's heaving chest.

None were successful.

The Thrallkin treated the bullets as though they were merely irritating bees, their crimson limbs a blur as they raced towards the gap. The distance between decks meant nothing, their powerful leaps carrying them upwards with no regard for gravity. Those who were struck simply grunted at the pain, their dark blood polluting the sea below.

"Is that it?" Carnage roared, slapping away a rifle as it fired at his groin. The bullet crashed beside Trigger's foot, coating his boot with splinters.

Steel rang as swords were drawn, the Thrallkin having closed the divide, robbing rifles of their worth. A handful were used as makeshift clubs, the wooden butts useless against the Thrallkins' mass. Many were snatched from their owner's grasp, the Thrallkin chuckling as they hurled them aside, or used the barrels to spear their foes' skull. To their credit, the *Dragon's* crew maintained their calm, holding rank as they unsheathed their blades and readied their smaller, more manageable guns. It was an admirable display. Truly, each of them was a man of iron.

They would be a grievous loss.

The Thrallkin ploughed through their defenses as though they were made of straw, snapping and bending with obvious glee. Flesh tore and bones shattered; the crew rendered fragile in the Thrallkin's great hands. Carnage attacked with needless savagery, gouging eyes and tearing jaws. It was his face that disturbed, however. The unabashed joy in his yellow gaze. The Thrallkin was having the time of his life.

Swish!

Trigger dove sideways, feeling the wind as the blade missed his back. He landed with grace and rose, turning to face his oncoming foe. Their identity came as no surprise.

Captain Julius, his one good eye made wet with tears.

"You boarded our ship on the pretense of peace." He snarled, sinking low. "And this? This is what you bring?"

His words were almost lost beneath the snapping of bones, the screams and gurgles of his dying men.

"I didn't want this." Trigger replied, raising his hands defensively. "I didn't know."

"I said that you were travelling with monsters." Julius spat. "That no good could come from your childish thoughts. Look now, boy. This is what your war will bring!"

Julius lunged, sword sweeping at Trigger's throat. He ducked beneath it, slamming his fist into the Captain's jaw. The old man took it well, kicking Trigger's stomach with a furious snarl. The force sent him reeling, yet Trigger kept himself upright, refusing to bend before the rising pain. It saved him from a finishing slash, one which would have opened his scalp if he'd moved to caress his wound.

The Thrallkin hadn't trusted him with a pistol or sword. Right now, that was proving to be a terrible mistake.

Trigger ducked to the right, barely avoiding an overhead swing. Julius followed with a surprise elbow, his body flowing with a lifetime of experience. Trigger couldn't dodge, yet he lessened the impact by turning, avoiding a broken nose by the barest degrees He responded with a punch of his own, striking the Captain on his missing eye. It wasn't an honorable act, yet neither was hacking at an unarmed opponent.

"Bastard." The Captain snarled, slamming his pommel into Trigger's chest. The blow sent him staggering across the deck, its surface made slippery by the ever-increasing blood. A moment later he was leaping, an awkward, one-legged hop, that barely removed him from the Captain's slash. He landed with even less balance, teetering on his heels like a drunken lout. He couldn't move, and his opponent knew it all too well. The Captain lunged, his sword-point fixed on Trigger's chest.

Trigger twisted at the hips, raising his elbow and deflecting the blow. His chest was torn by the razor-edge, yet the length of the blade had been his salvation. A few inches longer, and he wouldn't have been able to judge its approach. The weapon had been made for the press of the trench, not a vast and open deck.

Trigger seized his advantage, shoving the Captain with all of his might. The man went flying, failing to hold his footing on the saturated deck. He crashed into a nearby door, which buckled beneath his considerable weight. He fell through the timbers with a gasp of surprise, a series of thuds suggesting that he'd landed on stairs.

Trigger didn't care. He raced across the deck, pausing only to snatch up a pistol. A second later he was at the door, peering down into an unlit room. He could barely make out the Captain, his body a tangle at the base of the stairs.

He could hear shuffling at the fringes of the room.

"I know you're there." Trigger declared, aiming his pistol at the shadows. "Your fellow crew are dead, and your Captain is defeated. There's no sense in maintaining the fight."

More shuffling, accompanied by an unusual squeal. A strange clinking merely added to the puzzle, the slow drag of chain on wood.

"Stay…stay where you are." Julius spat, apparently still conscious. With an agonized wince, he turned towards the dark, swinging his sword at the shapes within.

Prisoners. Of course.

"He can't hurt you." Trigger declared, beginning a measured descent. "What are your names?"

A bizarre clicking, followed by pops and whistles. They seemed familiar, yet he had lost his recognition in the fog of combat.

"Step into the light." He ordered, pausing halfway down the stairs. "You will be treated fairly, I swear."

"He promised me the same." Julius snorted, blood leaking from his shattered nose. "His word is as worthless as you are! Monsters wait above!"

He made an odd click of his own, one which was met by wails. Julius laughed at the sound, before sighing in some form of content.

"They'll never trust you now." He chuckled. "Superstitious fools, this lot."

"This lot?" Trigger murmured, finally placing the unusual sounds. It was a language, one spoken only by the most isolated of tribes. Magwa's own tongue was a close relative, yet still not so alien as the one he heard.

Trigger plumbed the recesses of his mind, searching desperately for the word he required. Eventually he found it, his lips performing the whistle for 'friend'.

The wails and whimpers eased, though didn't completely cease. Wetting his lips, Trigger repeated the whistle, trying to keep it loud yet gentle.

The shadows shifted, chains clinking as their owners moved. It took a while, yet slowly the captives stepped into view, their brown eyes struggling against the foreign light.

Children. Half a dozen of them. Stripped of clothing, and judging by the bruises, any trace of innocence.

Rubbing his finger against his thumb, Trigger hefted his pistol, aiming it at the Captain's skull.

"Such disgust." Julius snorted. "Awful lofty, for someone who keeps such company. They're monsters, boy."

Trigger lowered the pistol, taking a moment to correct his aim.

"Aren't we all?"

****

"Water back to normal."

"Aye. Took its bloody time."

Barnaby and Magwa studied the waves, the last traces of crimson having faded from the foam.

"Barnaby okay?" Magwa asked, after several moments of peaceful silence.

"Not really." Barnaby replied, shifting in his makeshift chair. He still couldn't stand for any period of time, and had ordered the removal of all polished surfaces. Seeing his face was a bit too much.

"It not that bad." Magwa declared, watching as Barnaby traced the wound. "It marks Barnaby as man."

Barnaby glanced at Magwa's flesh, following the intricate labyrinth of mottled scars.

"Don't feel like one."

"Few ever do."

Barnaby groaned, putting his weight against the banister. The wind was rising, the cool breeze soothing his swollen cheeks.

"They tell stories about Barnaby, though." Magwa remarked. "Say he fought Jacques to a draw."

"Jacques is missing two fingers, and he's still feeling better than me." Barnaby snorted. "Where'd they get such a stupid idea?"

"Jacques. Apparently, he tells the tale to all he sees."

"Even now, he lies?" Barnaby frowned. "Why?"

"Magwa unsure. He thought Jacques hated you."

"I thought we were friends." Barnaby murmured, feeling the object he had stashed in his belt.

"Magwa thought that too, at first. The red water doesn't lie, however. It makes us honest, sends us after our greatest desire. For most, it another's touch. Not Jacques. He never tried for Sheridan, or anyone else. He tried to kill Barnaby. That is all."

"I'm not surprised." Barnaby sighed. "He doesn't seem the type to be controlled by sex. Neither do you, really."

"Oh, Magwa was at full mast." The savage grinned. "He just knows the water. Controls his urges."

"A valuable skill." Barnaby acknowledged, sinking back into his chair.

"Very. Now, are you ready for Magwa to take you down?"

"Not really."

"Well, the choice is no longer yours." The Kalyute declared, seizing his chair and hoisting it up. Magwa wasn't large, yet his strength was beyond question, the savage barely panting as he carried Barnaby's weight.

"Sorry, Captain!" Gary bowed, cautiously ducking around them. He avoided looking at Barnaby's face. It was becoming a common choice.

Repairs to the ship had been laborious, the fire having damaged a large section of deck. Surprisingly, the loss of life had been rather small, the crew's incompetence in combat having saved them from disaster. Even at their most feral, they'd failed to land real blows.

"You should try walking. You'll never recover, if you're too scared to push yourself."

Magwa set Barnaby down, watching silently as Falcon approached. The Captain regarded him with his usual distaste, as though he were an urchin who had pissed on his shoes.

"Soon." Barnaby replied, cradling his battered ribs. "I'll be ready for the third fixture, I promise."

"Then I hope you're a man of your word." Falcon declared. "Few will stand for a moaning cripple."

Barnaby frowned at that. He was hardly moaning.

"Magwa believes in his Captain's strength." The Kalyute nodded, blind as always to Falcon's hate. "In the meantime, Magwa happy to carry."

"Unsurprising." Falcon sneered. "It is your proper place."

"It is." Magwa beamed. "When friend cannot stand, it is friend who should carry them. Important rule of my people."

Falcon considered Magwa with contempt, attempting to discern if the savage was mocking. Even Barnaby wasn't quite sure.

"Your face is healing well." The Captain announced, choosing to ignore the Kalyute riddle.

"No, it isn't." Barnaby replied. He'd lost any patience for meaningless prattle.

Falcon regarded him, a trace of approval filling his gaze.

"Well, it makes you fearsome, at least."

"Yes. I'm sure many people will flee at the sight of me. Women and children, mostly."

"Self-pity is a useless trait."

"And yet, it's all I have left."

Falcon sighed, glancing over to his bobbing ship, which was following theirs at an even pace.

"I can see you're in a mood, and there is still much to prepare before we reach our destination. Continue about your business, and find me when you are less despairing."

"Gods, how long do you intend on sailing?"

Falcon ignored his jibe, striding across the deck without a backward glance.

"Bye, Captain!" Magwa cheered, waving.

Falcon didn't reply, though Barnaby was certain that he shook in distaste.

"I like him." Magwa announced, lifting Barnaby high.

"You're the best of us, Magwa."

"Magwa knows. Now hold still, the stairs are tricky."

They ventured deep into the ship, the fire having stained the walls with its clinging scent. Down, down they journeyed, into the very base of the swaying hull. With a grunt of exertion Magwa released him, mere feet from the stinking brig.

"The smell is awful." Barnaby gagged, crinkling his nose.

"It is, isn't it? Zey do try to keep it clean, yet ze cat, he does not like me. He pisses on ze bars ze moment zey are done, and shits on ze floor when I am asleep."

Jacques chuckled at this twist of fate, seating himself before the bars. Inches of steel held his mass at bay, yet still Barnaby felt unguarded, as though Jacques could escape at any moment, and snap his aching neck.

"You're in good spirits." Barnaby frowned.

"I have never been prone to melancholy." Jacques shrugged. "Regardless of how…justified."

He considered his limbs as he spoke, his hands and foot swaddled with rags. Falcon had taken the ring finger from each, and removed the matching toe. They'd stopped after that, as Jacques had still been laughing, while the guards who held him were retching with disgust.

"You deserved what happened to you." Barnaby scowled. "You aren't the victim here."

"Oh, I know. Besides, I imagine my ordeal has only begun. Zis Falcon, he seems a…vengeful man."

"That he does." Barnaby replied. "An honorable one, too. He's going to help me assemble a fleet, and then, when our numbers are great enough, we're going to find Carnage, and make him pay for all he's done."

"Ah. Good." Jacques nodded, leaning against the bars. "Zen I won't be in here long."

"Why's that?"

"Because Carnage's crew will eat you alive."

"He'll be outnumbered, out-gunned."

"Each of his men can juggle horses. Your guns and ships will mean nozing."

"You really believe that he's so fearsome?"

"You know me, Barnaby." Jacques shrugged. "You know what I can do. So, you should listen when I say zat Carnage is my better. No, not my better. Zat implies some point of relative comparison. Ze truz is, he operates on a level I could never conceive."

Barnaby bit back his reply, astonished by the swordsman's words. It was possible that Jacques was simply striking at his resolve, yet Barnaby knew him to be a prideful man. He would never underplay his skill, not unless there was a valid reason.

"You've seen Carnage fighting?" Magwa asked, leaning against a nearby wall.

"I've seen his opponents dying." Jacques grinned. "Zough, Carnage himself was merely a blur."

"You're full of shit." Barnaby scowled, mostly for the sake of his mental peace.

"Believe what you will." Jacques shrugged. "You're ze one Carnage is going to eat."

"Why did you do it?" Barnaby demanded, deciding it was best to change their focus.

"Do what?"

Barnaby squeezed the object in his pocket, trying his best to break it in half. It was annoyingly resilient.

"Make a deal with Carnage. Lie to us all. Betray your Captain, betray your crew!"

Jacques gazed back at him, scabbed features devoid of regret.

"I lost my ship." He shrugged. "And yours happened along."

"That's it!?" Barnaby exclaimed. "All those hours of false friendship, the loss of your leg, the battles and the brawls…and that's your reply?"

"You need somezing more?"

"You were our friend." Barnaby frowned. "Our brother. I can't believe that you'd just…throw it away."

"And when did I do zat, exactly?" Jacques laughed. "I betrayed Trigger, yes. I do not regret zat decision. Serving beneath him chafed, and I wished to regain my former stature. Had I been allowed ze captaincy, zere would have been no issue. You would never have discovered my treachery, and I would have led us all to riches and glory. Instead, you allowed yourself to be manipulated, to be used for Sheridan's little schemes. Had you been stronger, the rift between us would never have formed."

"So, it's my fault?"

"Fault is a concept for ze simple and weak." Jacques shrugged. "A way of fitting the world into zeir narrow minds. I am stating facts, nozing more."

"Facts that ignore your contemptible flaws."

"I ignore nozing." Jacques grinned. "Nor do I hold a trace of remorse. All men seek to better zeir station. To put zemselves above ze rest. Ze only difference is zeir level of restraint. Most are content with minor triumph, imagined victories, such as ze color of zeir skin, or ze validity of zeir Gods. Ze great require more, however. I believed myself ze superior Captain, so I used my might to dispose of Trigger. I would have died where I shipwrecked, so I used my cunning to board your ship. I needed allies, so I forged a friendship with ze outcasts and freaks."

Barnaby leant forward, preparing to hurl abuse. Jacques pre-empted him, raising a hand in dismissive contempt.

"You rage now, because you believe my actions false, or somehow shameful. You zink it invalidates ze laughter we shared, ze joy. Zis is foolish. I offered you my company to benefit myself. You accepted for ze exact same reason. Zat I admit it, does not make me lesser zan you. It makes me more honest."

Barnaby sat back, studying the swordsman from head-to-toe. For the first time, he saw how diminished the man had become, his huge frame weathered by their countless trials.

"I'm ready to go." He declared, giving Magwa a friendly nod.

The Kalyute didn't speak. He simply sauntered over, and lifted Barnaby's chair.

"I've hurt your feelings." Jacques remarked, attempting an expression of sorrow. "Zat was never my intention."

"You haven't hurt a thing." Barnaby replied, as Magwa carried him towards the stairs.

"Goodbye, Beaufort."

He didn't look back as they exited the room, even as Beaufort cried out his name. He remained silent for their entire ascent, until the sea was once more in view.

"Could we move to the banister, please?"

"Of course."

Magwa took him to starboard, placing him down with a mild groan.

"That went poorly." The savage announced, rubbing his spine and flexing his hands.

"I don't know." Barnaby shrugged, emptying his pocket of the figure inside. It was a near-perfect replica of Beaufort, one he'd purchased at the floating duel. At the time, he'd thought it was amazing. It even swung the weapons when you squeezed on its legs. Now?

"It was educational, at least."

He tossed the figure overboard, watching it sink beneath the waves.

Chapter Twenty-Three

"Can we eat them?"

"No, Bodi."

"Why? We ain't got no use for them."

"We promised to stop eating people."

"Kids ain't people."

"I'm sure Trigger disagrees." Carnage replied, though he still looked to him with a hopeful glance.

"Yes, children are people." Trigger declared, somewhat appalled that it had to be said. Not exactly surprised, however. Even in polite society, he was sure you'd find people who'd gladly disagree.

"Well then, what do you propose we do with them?"

"They'll stay aboard the *Dragon*. I'll see to their needs, and we'll return them to shore as soon as we're able."

"You don't mean that." Carnage snorted. "We both know that they'll be re-enslaved as soon as they touch land. You aren't going to risk that."

Trigger couldn't argue. The Thrallkin had seen right through him.

"We'll return them to their people." He replied. "We'll have to pass those lands at some point."

"That's months away, maybe years. You're basically adopting them."

Trigger glanced at the nearby table, where the children were feasting with chaotic glee.

"If that is what I must do to keep them safe, then so be it."

"Ugh." Carnage remarked, extending his tongue in distaste. "You're a moral creature, Trigger. It's part of what drew me to you. Still, at times, I find you sickening."

"I'll wear that as a compliment."

"Wear it how you like. Just make sure that these children don't distract you from our goal."

"Quite the opposite, I imagine." Trigger replied, glancing at the laughing youths. One boy had missed his mouth, covering his chin with chunky stew. "I believe they'll help me stay on target."

"Hmm." Carnage mused, tapping his hand on a pile of books. The Thrallkin had raided Julius' quarters, and chosen them as his spoils of his war.

"Anything of worth?" Trigger asked, gesturing at the hefty tomes.

"All knowledge is worthy." Carnage replied, resting his palm against the covers. "Though, I hurled his journal overboard."

"Why?"

"It recounted his days at sea, in very…intimate, detail."

Carnage glanced at the children, his yellow eyes saying more than enough.

"You did the right thing, then." Trigger nodded.

"I know." The Thrallkin snorted. "I don't know why you gave me so much grief over what happened with the crew. As far as I'm concerned, we did the world a favor."

"In this particular case, I don't disagree." Trigger replied. "Yet, we had no idea what they were when you started your attack. As far as we knew, you were butchering potential allies."

"He'd already turned us away."

"Yes, and had you let him live, he would have told others of our plans, and your good behavior. We'd have gained some respectability."

"From a kiddy-fiddler."

"That isn't my point, and you know it." Trigger frowned. "Killing this crew was valid, we both agree on that. However, if this ever going to work, you must find a way to restrain yourself."

"You shot Julius in the dick!"

"After he tried to kill me. The next crew might be more reasonable, and completely innocent of any wrongdoing."

"They'll be pirates." Carnage laughed, tugging at his hat.

Trigger massaged his eyes, wearying of the Thrallkin's banter.

"You're exhausting."

"The voice of dissent should always be valued." Carnage shrugged. "I'm your partner, not your yes man."

Trigger ran his fingers through his hair, considering the validity of the Thrallkin's words.

"Very well." He conceded, raising his hands in defeat. "I'll say no more on the matter. What we should be addressing are our plans for the *Dragon*."

"Oh, that's easy. We'll keep it as your flagship."

"My flagship?" Trigger repeated, studying the vessel with an appraising glance. "Wouldn't you rather the *Bloodbath* have that honor?"

"Nah." Carnage replied, shaking his head. "*Bloodbath* is mine, always will be. I've grown too attached. Besides, the *Dragon* is better suited. Bigger, more guns."

"Guns alone don't make a ship."

"No, the crew does." Carnage nodded. "Which is why you're taking half of mine."

"You're trusting me with my own ship?"

"Well, I'm going to have to, aren't I? Can't wage a war if I'm always worrying you'll betray me."

Trigger nodded, though he couldn't help but notice the duplicity of the Thrallkin's words. Yes, he'd given Trigger his own vessel, yet by placing so many of his people upon it, he had given himself a means of instant control. Trigger was still on a leash. It had simply lengthened.

"Well, I'll considered this matter resolved, then." He declared, knowing defiance would gain him naught.

"Cranking them out today, aren't we?" Carnage remarked, downing a swig of ale. The *Dragon* had been extremely well-stocked.

"We have one more to consider." Trigger informed, adjusting his coat.

"Which is?"

"We're almost at the final fixture. What are our intentions?"

"Press on, I'd say." Carnage replied. "If we pause, that gives every vessel sailing a chance to overtake, and lets any ahead of us further cement their lead."

"Does that matter, though?" Trigger replied. "We are substantially ahead of most; the very people we need to recruit to our cause. If we wait at the fixture, we can stop them as they arrive, and spread our influence to a greater degree."

"And the race?"

"Does it really matter? If we triumph in our war, it will be abolished. If we lose, well, we'll be dead."

"Fair enough." Carnage chuckled. "Though, we'll be catching the dregs, if we follow this plan. The more fearsome crews will be matching our pace, or maybe slightly ahead. That day at Thodurk's cost us. Honestly, you'd think he'd be more punctual, considering his heritage."

"We need the ships, more than we need the men." Trigger declared. "At this stage, at least. There's no point having an army if we lack the means of transport."

"True, though, having a few men of quality would put my mind at ease."

"Really?" Trigger remarked, raising a curious brow. "This ship men held of quality, and your crew decimated them. I'd say you'll more than balance a numerical disadvantage."

"Against humans? Definitely. What happens when we become a genuine threat, however? When the Empress recalls my people from the cursed Front line? How do you think we'll handle a few thousand of my kind?"

"These Thrallkin, they would be led by humans, yes?"

"Yes."

"Who would treat them badly, and sacrifice their lives without a moment's hesitation?"

"Yes." Carnage replied, yellow eyes flashing with the beginnings of rage.

"Then we simply need to speak with them. If they see how far you've come, what you have achieved, well, I doubt they'll return to the Empire's yoke."

"You'd be surprised." Carnage declared, his tone made bitter. "We met many of our kind as we fled the Front lines. Very few would hear my words."

"Your words have improved since you hit the high seas." Trigger replied. "And now they are backed by action and fact."

"You think it will be enough?"

"You've convinced me."

"True." Carnage grinned, looking around the room. It was a different smile to his usual fare, one that spoke of the Thrallkin's age. He was simply a young man, doing his best in an indifferent world.

In this moment, at least, Trigger was proud to be at his side.

****

"I think we're making them nervous."

"Good. They should be."

Barnaby leant against the banister, studying the vessel they had pincered in place. He couldn't argue with that.

"You should say something." Sheridan remarked, folding her arms. "Before Falcon does."

"Why?"

"Because they're going to assume that the speaker is our leader. You want that to be you."

"Do I?" Barnaby snorted. "Leading people hasn't treated me kindly."

"Ahoy there!"

"Too late." Sheridan sighed, as Falcon appeared at the prow of his ship.

"My name is Henry Falcon, Captain of this fine vessel. My companion is Captain Barnaby, or Black Barnaby, as he is otherwise known. We wish to speak with your Captain!"

There was a commotion on the deck of their captured ship, the crewmen shuffling back-and-forth as they drove their leader to the fore.

"Say something." One of them hissed, giving the man a forceful prod.

"Ah...umm...greetings?" The man ventured, his feeble words near lost on the wind.

"You are their Captain?" Falcon asked, his tone revealing immense regret.

"I...I am."

Barnaby watched as Falcon sighed, clearly exhausted by their latest recruit. Their fleet was almost eleven strong, yet not one of those crews seemed worth a damn. They'd been hoping this one would hold more steel. Apparently not.

"What is your name?" Falcon demanded, studying the man with growing contempt. The Captain took a fair stretch to reply, his own gaze fixed on Barnaby's face.

"Captain...Captain Thunderbrass, my lord."

Sheridan snorted, shaking her head at the ridiculous name.

"Captain...Thunderbrass." Falcon repeated, swilling the word around his gums. He didn't seem to enjoy the taste.

"Aye...Thunderbrass."

"A bold name. I imagine it's why you chose it."

"That's...that's right, my lord."

"Not a lord."

"Sorry, your honor."

Barnaby chuckled. The other Captains had been wretched, yet Thunderbrass made even him look brave.

"How'd you come by this ship, *Captain* Thunderbrass?"

Barnaby didn't know if Falcon had intended to make the question offensive, yet that had definitely been the result.

"In...inherited it. My dad was a pirate."

"You were raised on the sea?" Falcon asked, suddenly perking up. A lifetime of experience could be valuable.

"N...no." Thunderbrass replied, shaking his head. "Raised...raised on land by my mother. She sold turnips. Got a letter when my father died, saying that...that he'd left me the ship."

"So, you took it? Brave man."

"Didn't...didn't want it." Thunderbrass choked. "Mumma made me take it. Said she was sick of holding my hand."

"Gods." Falcon remarked, closing his eyes. Thunderbrass didn't reply, hanging his head in shame. Still, his story had Barnaby's interest.

"Why does your crew follow you?" He asked, putting more of his weight against the ship. He had recovered enough to stand, yet not without considerable aid, and a hefty dollop of discomfort. The agony twisted his features into a perpetual scowl, one which accentuated his hideous scar.

"They…they…they said I was my father's son, and…and that they owed it to him to see me safe."

Loyalty. He could respect that, at least.

"Who's your First Mate?"

"That would be me."

The man who stepped forward resembled a bear; his considerable girth coated in a curly-black pelt. Barnaby had never seen such a hirsute form.

"And you would be?"

"Name's Florence." The bear-man replied, gut exposed by his too-small shirt. "Though, the crew call me Latrine."

"…Why?" Barnaby asked, thoroughly perplexed.

"Hit a man with a latrine once. At first, they called me Florence and the fighting latrine. Then, Florence and the latrine. Finally, they settled on just Latrine. They're a lazy lot."

"Can't be that lazy, to have gotten this far."

"Lazy isn't incompetent, however hard the nobles try and make it seem."

"I'll drink to that." Barnaby grinned. The expression did nothing to improve his visage. He could see Thunderbrass quivering with fear.

"I imagine there isn't much you'd not drink to." Florence declared, folding his arms. "You've a wild reputation."

"Do I?"

"Slaying sea-monsters, fighting ghost ships, bedding giantesses…way the world tells it, you're a dangerous man indeed. You look like one, I've got to say."

"The scar is from his latest feat." Sheridan chimed, placing her hand on Barnaby's shoulder.

"Which was?"

"Our crew fell to madness in the Maiden's Thighs. During the chaos, Barnaby fought Beaufort himself."

"He give you that scar?"

"He did."

"And where is Beaufort now?"

"In the brig." Sheridan replied, her voice filled with ingenuine pride. "Recovering from his wounds."

The captured crew murmured at this declaration, studying Barnaby with increasing awe. He really wished people would stop lying on his behalf. Well, their behalf, really.

"We all saw his duel with Hargrave." Florence declared. "To best Beaufort is no small feat."

"It was really more of a draw." Barnaby shrugged, deciding it was best to play along. He may hate the lies, yet they were the best chance they had of rallying the fleet.

"Even so, I doubt any man here could claim the same."

"I'm glad you're impressed. It might make you inclined to hear our offer."

"Inclined or not, I doubt we have a choice." Florence replied, indicating the vessel's encircling their ship.

"True enough." Barnaby nodded, leaning against his cane. His legs were beginning to tire, and he was eager to resolve this conversation.

"Our offer is simple enough. Our former captain, Trigger, has been captured by Carnage."

"Aye, we suspected as much. I recognized your ship from the harbor and thought it odd when Trigger failed to appear. He brought it on himself, however. Only a fool would challenge that monster."

"He was sparing my brother from terrible pain." Falcon declared, clearly angered. "His actions were noble, and incredibly brave."

"I never said that they weren't. They were still fucking foolish."

Barnaby shook his head, barely suppressing a chuckle. He didn't disagree.

"Be that as it may, we seek to rescue him."

"Then you are also fools."

"Is your entire crew composed of cowards?" Falcon sneered, slamming his hand against his ship.

"I'd say it's about fifty-fifty." Florence replied. "And the brave half have common sense."

"We aren't alone." Barnaby ventured, gesturing at their modest fleet. "We have the numbers."

"Aye, you have ships, and men." Florence nodded. "Carnage is a bastard, and he's made many a foe. I'm sure you'll find plenty of souls willing to take a shot. That isn't my main concern."

"And what is your concern, exactly?"

"Can you win?" Florence shrugged. "Can you use your fleet well enough to overcome their power? Remember, each member of his crew is worth twenty of yours, and his ship has more cannons than any vessel here. You're going take losses, and when you do, I think you'll find that your allies falter. It's easy to run in when you think you have the numbers, but once reality sets in, and the stench of death is on the air, well, a lot of that courage turns to wind."

"You think they'll fail to honor their word?" Falcon asked, furrowing his brow at the First Mate's claim.

"I think they're pirates, and you're asking them to die for no real gain."

"As you said, many of them are fighting for vengeance."

"Which is all well and good, until it gets you killed."

"You're not going to join us, are you?" Barnaby sighed, stating what Falcon couldn't accept.

"No, we're not. It's a damn stupid cause, with little-to-no appeal. Much better to sail on, and take advantage of your battle. While the rest of you bleed, we'll be sailing across that finish line, to a life of rest and easy plunder. We wish you luck, however. It does take balls to try what you're doing."

"And what if we blow you to splinters and ash?" Falcon sneered. "How will you sail to victory then?"

"On the current, or in the bellies of fishes." Florence shrugged. "Though, can't say I fancy either."

"Well, I suggest you rethink your position."

Florence shook his head, turning his back on Falcon. He focused instead on Barnaby, having recognized him as the reasonable party.

"Is that how you're doing this? Strong-arming others into service?"

"We aren't the Empire." Barnaby replied, giving Falcon an even gaze. "If you don't wish to join us, then we aren't going to force you."

"Thank you." Florence nodded, offering him a grateful bow.

"Don't thank me." He sighed, tapping the head of his cane. "Yes, we're not going to kill you. That doesn't mean you're free to go."

"What...what do you mean?" Florence asked, appearing nervous for the very first time.

"You aren't the first ship to turn us down. I doubt you'll be the last. What all of you've had in common is a focus on the Tides. You want to win, which is more than fair. We all entered with that very intention. Sadly, while Trigger is our fleet's main goal, we'd still like the pardon as a potential consolation. If that's to be the case, well, we can't have you winning, can we?"

Groaning slightly, he lifted his cane, pointing it at Florence's ship.

Cannon-fire boomed as half their fleet fired, chain-shot whistling as it spun through the air. It struck the vessel with a thunderous crack, shattering the mast and sails. The crewmen screamed as the rigging collapsed, crushing a few beneath the ropes and wood.

Barnaby lowered his cane, informing the fleet that its duty was done.

"I hate doing that." Sheridan remarked, fanning herself with a scowl of distaste.

"As do I."

"Yet, you're the one who gives the order."

Barnaby glanced at her, despising every inch of her beautifully garbed form.

"I've done a lot of things I hate over the past few months." He spat. "You become accustomed to it."

"Maybe you should have fought harder." Sheridan shrugged. "Become defiant, not accustomed."

Barnaby didn't respond. She wasn't wrong.

"You bastards!"

Florence emerged from a fallen sail, his forehead split by some unseen collision. His words were accompanied by the groans of his crew, many of them pinned and dying.

"It was this, or your entire ship." Barnaby replied, feeling dirty as he spoke.

"You have only your cowardice to blame!" Falcon declared, clearly unconcerned by the damage and death.

"I have you to blame, you fatherless cunts! I curse you both, for now and all time! May your lives be long and terrible, and your endeavors set to ruin!"

Barnaby didn't believe in curses. He knew most pirates did, however, and that Florence was giving them the greatest insult he could ever conceive.

Which was fair, really. They'd blown his mast to pieces, crushing his crew in the process. Were Barnaby in his position, he'd be hurling curses too.

"I'd say we're done here." Sheridan remarked, inserting her fan between her cleavage. "Damn shame, really. Thunderbrass might have been weak, yet Florence had his head on straight."

"Aye, he did." Barnaby nodded, signaling the fleet to raise their sails. He observed that Falcon was doing the same, his keen eyes fixed on their subservient Captains. Fewer than half were looking to him, while the rest had focused on Barnaby, following his orders with dutiful swiftness.

"I think I was wrong." Sheridan declared, clearly noticing as well. "You've developed a knack for this. Must be the scar."

"Must be."

Barnaby braced himself as a wave struck their hull, his cane sliding on the well-polished wood. Mastering it had proven an exhausting task, yet he had quickly found that it leant him an air of authority, as though he were a grizzled old man who'd aged beyond reproach.

"This will be interesting." Sheridan remarked, restraining her shawl against the wind. Her gaze was fixed on the gathering fleet, taking note of the positions their companions took. The majority were settling behind their own vessel, while two strays had drifted behind Falcon's. It was a contest now, an anxious wait to see who would fall in line.

"He's coming up on our broadside." Sheridan remarked, as Flacon's prow drew level with their stern. "Should we allow him to pass?"

Barnaby inhaled, weighing his options and tapping his cane. He'd had enough of falling in line.

"Full speed ahead!" He roared, turning his gaze to Frank. The Quartermaster nodded, giving him the slightest grin.

"Aye, Captain! You heard him, men! Full speed ahead!"

The *Blackbird* leapt as the wind took its sails, carving through the waves at a cracking pace. Falcon matched them for as long as he could, yet eventually he was forced to relent, his vessel vanishing behind their stern. Barnaby spared him less than a glance, their eyes meeting for the shortest time. His fellow Captain seemed quite unimpressed.

He didn't give the slightest of fucks.

"How many more can there be?"

"Who knows? We had a substantial lead, yet the duel cost us several days. Plenty could have overtaken us."

"True, though it's just as likely they were blown to bits."

"I guess. We're also coming up on a fixture, the last place to rest and restock. A few will have berthed to make repairs."

"Could Carnage be one of them?"

"Maybe, though it's unlikely. Thrallkin don't need much, so supplies aren't really an issue. Trigger wouldn't have taken much, either. The man eats like a teenage girl, one who's worried about their figure."

"That's if they're feeding him at all."

"Aye." Sheridan sighed, directing her gaze to the cabin wall. "If they're feeding him at all."

"Which I'm sure they are." Barnaby declared, attempting to recover his thoughtless words. Yes, he was sick of being walked on, yet that was no reason to act like a dick.

"Magwa knows Trigger will be on his feet." The Kalyute announced. "He survived being eaten by the Great Green Eyes. A man with red skin is no threat."

"Carnage is more than a man with red skin. He's eight-feet tall, for starters."

"Good. Trigger excellent shot. Big target is easy target."

"If he has a gun."

"Trigger resourceful." Magwa shrugged, giving them a friendly grin.

"Well, I'm glad you're feeling so confident." Sheridan remarked, contemplating her gloved hands.

"The future never certain. Better to entertain the good, than dwell on the bad."

"I like that." Barnaby nodded, swilling his cup of wine. "Which probably means it's bullshit."

"You people, can't drink wine without getting sad, can't drink red water without going insane. Magwa glad he not part of your tribe."

"I wish you were. Maybe Falcon would keep his mouth shut." Sheridan shrugged. "Though, I think he finds me only a touch more appealing."

"Probably the tits." Magwa declared. "It the reason Magwa likes you."

"I think they might be part of the problem." Sheridan chuckled. "Still, I'll take the compliment."

"What if Carnage *is* at the fixture?" Barnaby asked, unable to shake the thought. "Could we take him on with just seven ships?"

"In a purely naval contest, yes." Sheridan replied. "We have too many cannons, too many angles. Unfortunately, our goal is to save Trigger, which we can't do if he's been shredded."

"So, we'll have to board?"

"That we will."

"Which is far more dangerous."

"That it is."

"Is it something we can manage? Seven crews to Carnage's one?"

This time, there was no reply. The silence was heavy, and brought a new thought to his brimming skull.

"Sheridan?"

"Yes, Barnaby?"

"What if Falcon decides that revenge is his goal?"

"What?"

Barnaby sat up, placing his cup on the swaying floor.

"What if he decides that saving Trigger puts the fleet at too much risk? What if he gives the order to fire?"

"He...he wouldn't. He gave his word. He owes a debt."

She didn't sound very sure.

"Carnage tortured his brother, and while Trigger spared him pain, he was the one who eventually killed him. What would matter more to you? Killing the beast that tormented your family, or saving the man who shot them dead?"

"Well, when you put it like that..." Sheridan frowned.

"Falcon seems honorable to Magwa." The Kalyute shrugged.

"When a man treats those different to himself with outright hate and loathing, that is a bad omen." Sheridan declared. "It's how I knew Trigger was truly noble. He never cared what I was. Never cared what you were, either."

"He even take on Barnaby." Magwa nodded. "So accepting."

Magwa was being sincere, so Barnaby ignored the insult. Barely.

"Aye, he was always willing to give you a chance, no matter your color or creed. It's why our crew is so bloody incompetent."

Barnaby chuckled at that, his laughter earning Sheridan's glance. She smiled at him, genuinely. It was a refreshing sight.

"Wonder if Trigger be so accepting, once we manage to get him back?"

Sheridan's smile vanished, smashed to pieces by Magwa's thought.

"Well, he'll probably be sick of Thrallkin." Barnaby ventured, attempting to make light of the morbid possibilities. "Though, that doesn't matter much. They're pretty rare, and everyone's allowed one racist inclination."

"Gods, he'd probably still be willing to give the bastards a chance." Sheridan remarked. "I've never met a man so foreign to a grudge."

"Trigger might hold one against Beaufort. Magwa would."

"Trigger will follow the law of the sea, though I can't imagine he'll take much pleasure in it."

"Well, we'll have to take it for him."

Barnaby drank as the others pondered his words, frowning at their hate-born tone.

"You're taking his betrayal hard." Sheridan observed, tapping the rim of her half-drained wine. "Good."

Barnaby measured his reply, unsure how candid he should really be. He and Sheridan were back on semi-friendly terms, yet her recent manipulation had left a sour taste, one the wine could not completely remove.

"He was my friend, and our crewmate. We saved his life and embraced him as one of our own. He spat on that without a moment's thought, all for the sake of self-profit. Now, the man who saved him is at Carnage's mercy, suffering through Gods-know what. Yes, I am taking his betrayal hard."

There was a moment of quiet as the others registered his words, sipping at their drinks with furrowed brows.

"What would Carnage have done to him?" Magwa asked, looking to them with questioning eyes.

"I don't want to think about it." Sheridan replied, scowling.

"The thought must be present."

"Aye, it is. Constantly. That doesn't mean I wish to acknowledge it."

"Whatever it is, it doesn't matter." Barnaby declared, tapping his cane against the deck. "We all know Trigger. Whatever they've done, however they've torn him apart, he'll find a way to bring himself back."

"I'll drink to that." Sheridan declared, raising her cup. Each of them finished their wine, the toast made somber by unspoken dread.

They lowered their cups, silence reigning for a too-brief time.

"But…what would they have done to him?"

"I can't imagine, Magwa. I truly don't want to."

Chapter Twenty-four

"Cannonball!"

Trigger and the children clutched at their faces, shielding themselves from the twenty-foot spray.

"Chain-shot!"

A few girls screamed at the terrifying sight, Thrallkin limbs flailing through the air.

"Inverted duck!"

Trigger laughed at that one. He was rather partial to inverted duck.

The Thrallkin whooped as they leapt from the deck, posing mid-fall for a variety of effects. They had begun the practice at sunrise, and spent the day perfecting it into a marvelous display. They had developed a name for every position, the more aerodynamic members flipping and twirling with the grace of an acrobat, their crimson bodies shining as they dropped into the sea. Some were leaping from the very top mast, the sounds of their collision almost painful to the ear. It was an impressive display, one that brought the children joy, though it was a distant second to the Thrallkin's primary method of juvenile care.

"You ready?" Bodi asked, hoisting Stub above his head. The little girl clicked and whistled with delight, clapping her hands as Bodi tested her weight.

"You ready, Captain!?"

"Aye, let her fly!"

Bodi ran for all he was worth, red muscles bulging as he covered the deck. Stub released a scream of joy, one which doubled as Bodi spun on his heel, hurling her skyward with a deafening roar. Stub soared upwards in a spiral of limbs, flailing and laughing as she enjoyed her ascent. The laughter was quick in becoming a scream, gravity snatching her down at a horrifying pace.

Trigger hated this part.

"You better move, Captain!" Bodi yelled, as Carnage weaved across his ships deck.

"Yeah, yeah, I'll get her! Not so much spin next time!"

Stub's screams intensified, her tiny frame plummeting towards the sea.

She couldn't swim.

Carnage suddenly bolted, his frame a blur as he dove from the banister, reaching out with two tree-trunk arms. They caught Stub in a near-loving embrace, the Thrallkin twisting to take the fall. They hit the water with a drawn-out splash, sliding across the surface for several meters, before sinking beneath the waves.

A moment later, Carnage reappeared, clutching Stub to his saturated chest. The little girl was laughing, eyes wide with delight. It was an expression all the children had worn, an odd mixture of wondrous joy, and total surprise at remaining alive.

"Well, alright." Bodi nodded, clasping his crimson hands. "Who's next?"

Every child leapt at his shins, attempting to climb into his waiting palm. Trigger merely chuckled, shaking his head at the bizarre display. It wasn't the safest of games, yet they were happy, and frankly, that was enough for him.

Their vessels had been anchored for almost a week, drifting side-by-side in the desolate fixture. All life was scarce in this part of the world, the few natives who met them proving suspicious and grim. They'd traded a few paltry supplies, then vanished into the surrounding lands, their thin canoes blending into the curtain-like scrub. They had yet to see another vessel, and while Trigger was glad for the idyllic reprieve, a few stray worries were beginning to creep.

"They'll show."

Trigger glanced to his right, unsurprised that Carnage had approached undetected. The Thrallkin was huge, yet moved like a cat when the occasion demanded.

"I hope so. A fleet demands more than a pair of ships."

"Ah, but what ships they are!" Carnage grinned, gesturing at their bobbing hulls. "Two men o' war, each of them brimming with Thrallkin might. How many harbors could hold us at bay?"

"Many. All they'd need is a solid fort."

"And how many ports have those?" Carnage snorted, waving his hand.

"Twenty-six, at least."

"Shit. Really?"

"Oh yes." Trigger replied. "The Empire is well-equipped, especially when it comes to defending its shores."

"Can't be that well-defended." Carnage frowned. "I mean, you were there when a harbor was taken."

"I was. It was the most vicious battle I have ever seen, with staggering losses. There was no fort present, and the Empire was outnumbered by at least five-to-one. Still, were it not for their numerical advantage, the Prince and I would have stopped them cold."

"Ah, but you'll be on our side, this time." Carnage grinned.

"Yes, I will. And I'm telling you that without more ships, we don't stand the slightest chance."

Carnage sighed, folding his arms behind his head.

"You're not the most cheerful leader, are you?"

"I am when it's merited. Our current situation is tenuous, however, requiring a degree of contemplative restraint."

"Well, don't tell them that." Carnage nodded, as another child soared towards the distant clouds. "Gods' know when they last had fun."

"True enough." Trigger murmured, watching as a Thrallkin caught the boy. The children had been in an awful state, their dark skin stretched across fragile bones. They'd fed them as soon as they were freed, yet the sudden nutrition had proved too much, causing most of them to vomit within hours of consumption. They'd taken it slow after that, building up the meals at well-rounded intervals. It had proven far more successful, strengthening their spirits and limbs. Most of them seemed healthy now, though all of them bore scars from their ordeal, a constant reminder of their captors' misdeeds. Sometimes Trigger would see them, and feel a sense of satisfaction for the dea-

"We have movement!"

Trigger abandoned his thoughts, moving to the crowded stern. His entire crew had gathered with astonishing speed, their broad shoulders blocking his ascension of the stairs.

"Out of the way, you curs!" Carnage roared, slapping the heads of those in his way. "Your Admiral's trying to see!"

The crew mumbled apologies, sheepishly forming a well-made line. Trigger strode past them, nodding his thanks to Carnage. The Thrallkin didn't reply, focusing instead on the towering gate, and the sea bubbling beneath its frame.

"Who do you think it'll be?" Carnage asked.

"I have no idea. Though, I know who I'm hoping for."

"I'll be impressed if it's them. Things were looking pretty grim."

Trigger merely nodded. The Thrallkin wasn't wrong, yet still, he felt inclined to hope.

"Here they come!"

The ocean split as a vessel emerged, its long prow spearing from the shimmering waves. The hull and mast were soon to follow, each of them coated in dazzling drops. It leant the ship an ethereal edge, one well-suited to the flag it wore. Trigger could have sworn that it came from a dream.

"You're kidding me." Carnage remarked, smiling in disbelief.

The *Blackbird* drifted on the gentle waves, its crew scurrying to adjust the sails.

"They made it." Trigger beamed, unable to contain his delight. "They made it!"

"Not even that burnt." Carnage observed, his keen eyes narrowed as they studied the deck. "You must have been carrying a fair chunk of wood."

"We used the majority for repairs." Trigger replied. "They must have stopped for more."

"Stopped where? There's nothing out here."

Trigger frowned. That was an excellent point.

"We've got more coming!"

The lookout's words caught them by surprise, as did the *Blackbird's* restraint.

"Shouldn't they be moving?" Carnage asked. "Dangerous to stay that close. The other ship is likely to fire, especially this late in the race. Though, I suppose they might be intending to attack. Take advantage of the enemies' confusion."

"I doubt they were fighting. We would have heard the cannon fire."

"True." Carnage conceded. "Could they be allies?"

"We'll just have to see." Trigger frowned, adjusting his coat against the wind.

A few moments later, the next vessel emerged, bursting swiftly from between the waves. Surely enough, it made no attempt to assault the *Blackbird*, choosing instead to drift to one-side.

"We got another one!"

Trigger and Carnage shared a glance. Two ships were strange. Three at once was completely bizarre.

The third ship appeared, as did a fourth, a fifth, a sixth and a seventh. Only the *Blackbird* was bearing its flag, the others rallying beside its hull. None of them offered so much as a shot, their crews interacting with harmonious accord.

"Alright, I'm lost." Carnage shrugged, scratching beneath his molding hat.

As one, the vessels turned towards their own, sails bulging as they caught the wind. They had adopted a military formation; one which Trigger was quick to discern.

"Carnage?"

"Yes?"

"Get back to your ship."

****

"They've taken Julius!"

Barnaby didn't know who Julius was. Still, Falcon sounded concerned.

"That's bad, I take it!?"

"Julius could kill two men while sitting on his hands!" Falcon declared. "And his ship could level a small town!"

"We still have the numbers!" Sheridan roared, her figure resplendent in a close-fitting dress. The outfit was undeniably fashionable, yet practical enough to drive home the point. Sheridan was here for blood. Nothing else.

"Do you see Trigger!?"

Falcon's question was a good one. All Barnaby could see was a deck of red, the Thrallkin as huge as his nightmares recalled. His vision had always been shit, however, and he would rather defer to more accurate eyes.

"He's on the *Dragon*!" Sunniday roared, pointing at the red-strewn deck. Squinting, Barnaby tried to follow the lookout's gaze, yet his pupils proved unequal, failing to identify their captured Captain.

"Is he harmed?" Sheridan asked, the concern apparent in her wavering tones.

"He seems unharmed, yet surrounded. That's not all, though. I can't be sure, but I think there's children aboard!"

"What?"

Barnaby frowned, praying for eyes that could properly function. His prayers went unheeded, yet eventually he discerned the tiny forms, the children made ants by the scale of their captors.

"They're moving them all to the *Dragon*!"

Sunniday gestured at the foaming seas, where several of the Thrallkin were beginning to appear. They had been occupying the space between vessels, their black hair concealing them in the deep blue waves. A few had children clinging to their necks, the poor wretches shivering from the cold and fear.

"Gods!"

The cry came from many, Barnaby included, as a flash of red streaked between ships. A Thrallkin had leapt the incredible span, his broad shoulders bulging as he caught the *Bloodbath's* edge. Even with his inadequate eyes, Barnaby could recognize that ridiculous hat.

"Carnage." Sheridan growled, squeezing the harpoon she had claimed as her own.

"He left Trigger on the *Dragon*." Frank observed. "Why?"

"It gives him leverage. We attack him, his crew kill Trigger. We attempt a rescue, he slinks away."

"Cunning bugger." Frank conceded, whistling between his teeth.

"Not cunning enough. We're here for Trigger. Now, we only have to fight half a crew to get him."

"Half a Thrallkin crew." Barnaby declared. "And that's if Falcon is willing to comply."

They all glanced at the scowling Captain, who was assessing the scene with a critical eye. He didn't seem pleased. Then again, he rarely did.

"Falcon, what's the plan?"

The Captain didn't reply, though his gaze was fixed on Carnage. The Thrallkin vessels were beginning to shift, preparing to depart the perilous fixture.

"Falcon, we need to move!"

The Captain turned to Sheridan, his features twisted by hate.

"Damn." Barnaby whispered, as the Captain raised his sword.

"Forget the fucking plan!" He roared, his voice carrying across the sea. "A thousand pieces to the man who sinks Carnage! Full sail ahead!"

A cheer rose from the members of their fleet, every vessel surging towards their fleeing foe.

"Bastard!" Sheridan roared, slamming her fist against the ship.

"He used us." Frank sighed. "Just like Beaufort."

"He is a pirate." Barnaby shrugged. "We shouldn't be surprised."

"Well, we don't need his bloody fleet!" Sheridan snarled, hoisting her harpoon high. "Full speed ahead! Aim for the *Dragon's Breath*!"

"You're kidding, right!?" Frank exclaimed, as the *Blackbird* followed the bristling fleet. "Most of our men can barely fight! A single Thrallkin will hand us our arse, let alone twenty!"

"Trigger is in our sight!" Sheridan roared, slamming her harpoon against the deck. "We can't just let them slip away!"

"We're outgunned, and outmanned!"

"And they're down a Captain! Without Carnage to lead them, they're nothing!"

"They're eight-feet monsters who catch bullets with their teeth! Organized or not, that's more than we can take!"

Barnaby ignored their bickering, focusing instead on the unfurling scene. The fleet was swiftly gaining, the size of the Thrallkin vessels hindering their speed. Strangely, however, the fleeing ships made no attempt to separate, their hulls almost kissing as they raced across the sea.

"Both of you, be quiet." He ordered, catching the pair off-guard. They fell silent, looking to him with questioning glares.

"They're staying together." He declared, pointing at their prey.

"That doesn't make sense." Sheridan frowned. "Carnage is a bastard, yet his men are loyal. They'd be happy to sacrifice themselves, and I doubt he'd think twice about letting them die. Why isn't he trying to lure us away?"

"Magwa thinks this strange." The savage announced, scratching at his scalp. "Many bad omens."

"Magwa's right. There's something we don't know."

"Well, let's hope we're enlightened soon." Sheridan spat, as their fleet grew closer to Carnage's own. The Thrallkin had closed on the fixture's end, and if they made it through the pass, well, the battle that followed could see them all dead.

"Falcon's almost in range." Frank observed, sounding supremely hopeful.

"He is, but the rest of them aren't. Carnage won't buckle from his shots alone."

Barnaby didn't partake of the talk, his concerns lying with the passage ahead. In all their plans, they had never expected to face Carnage there, in the perilous depths of the Spiraling Void. If their vessels tumbled into those cascading jaws, he doubted that any would wash out alive.

"Falcon's in range!" Sunniday cried, his words made redundant by the fire that followed. Smoke billowed as Falcon unleashed, his cannon balls smashing the *Bloodbath's* stern.

"He's insane." Frank whispered, shaking his head.

"No, he's not. He knows what lies ahead, just as well as we do. He's hoping to keep Carnage here, where we can use our numbers to the greatest advantage."

"Think it will work?"

"On a sane man? No. On a lunatic like Carnage? Maybe."

The Quartermaster sighed as he met Barnaby's gaze. They both hoped the First Mate was right.

"Fire!"

Falcon's voice was barely audible, yet his men must have heard it. Another bombardment escaped their hull, slashing the *Bloodbath* with boulders of steel. They were joined by another vessel, the *Kraken's Feast*, which was taking its chances at the *Bloodbath's* port side. This left it dangerously exposed to the *Dragon's Breath*, yet the other vessel was fixed on escape, offering no shots to its vulnerable foe.

"They're not going to stop." Frank moaned. "Carnage isn't a fool."

"No, but he's a petty, unstable cunt. He'll stop. Just one more volley, you'll see."

Barnaby gritted his teeth, clinging to the handle of his trembling cane. He certainly hoped so.

"Fire!"

This time the cry was louder, the devastation more complete. The vessels had gained more ground, their shots striking the length of the hull. A few Thrallkin roared in pain, their deep cries shaking through Barnaby's bones.

"Alright, you cunts! I'll show you what a ship can do!"

The voice was unmistakable, boundless in bloodlust and endless in rage. Carnage appeared at the stern of his ship, which flushed out its cannons as it started to turn.

Barnaby watched as Sheridan beamed, her eyes wide with unfettered glee.

"He did it!"

Her joy was feeble before Falcon's own. Barnaby could just make out the Captain, his features made foreign by an unusual grin. Carnage had made himself an easy target, and already Falcon's cannons were beginning to adjust, fixing themselves on the Thrallkin's frame.

"Fire!"

The blasts were premature, launched before the cannons had truly found their mark. One had, however, a man-made meteor of hideous force. It struck Carnage, spinning the Captain on his crimson heels. For a silent moment, they thought it was done, yet silence became gasps as Carnage stood tall, his thick legs twisting on the *Bloodbath's* deck. Around and around he went, extending his arms to their impressive full length. The ball was clasped between his hands, the weight restrained as though it were air.

"By the Gods." Frank whispered. It was appropriate enough.

Carnage finished his rotation, releasing the shot with a wild yell. The metal soared towards Falcon's ship, striking its prow in an explosion of splinters. The bowsprit was snapped from the ship, a few jagged barbs its only remains.

Barnaby glanced at Falcon, reading the terror on his face. He'd underestimated Carnage, both in his strength, and in his brilliance. The Thrallkin had made himself a target on purpose, drawing the fire away from his crew. It had given them time to slink below, to prepare their own cannons for a retaliatory blow.

Carnage grinned, his yellow eyes flashing with demented joy.

"Fire!"

The world trembled as the man'o'war struck, dozens of cannons blazing from its scratched and pummeled hull. Falcon vanished amongst an onslaught of steel, his smaller vessel screaming as its deck was torn to shreds. The *Kraken* was treated to just as much wrath, its crew reduced to slush by the metallic rain.

"Come on!" Carnage taunted, his frame concealed by the rising smoke. "Who will test me next!"

"Fire!"

Falcon's voice came as a complete surprise, as did the volley that escaped his ship. A new wave of fire struck Carnage from his perch, obliterating the banister of his battered ship.

"Tough bastard, I'll give him that." Sheridan remarked, eyeing Falcon's vessel for some sign of life. It appeared in the form of a shambling mess, Falcon's chest and back coated in a fine wash of blood.

"He's hurt." Barnaby whispered, squeezing tightly against his cane.

"Who cares? He's done it!" Frank cheered, gesturing at their swarming fleet. They had almost encircled Carnage's ship, pinning the vessel in a circle of death.

A tiny shiver of elation danced through his spine, yet Barnaby's joy swiftly faded, replaced once more by dread and despair.

"I wouldn't be so sure." He declared, gesturing at a point beyond their small fleet. Sheridan and Frank followed his gaze, seeing the vessel that had caused his concern. The *Dragon* had abandoned its attempt to flee, and was currently turning to engage their fleet, every cannon flaring from its considerable ports.

"We...we can take 'em." Frank croaked, a valiant effort at stalwart resolve.

"Ah, Captain!?"

Sunniday sounded worried, yet also oddly confused.

"Yes, Sunniday?"

"The other ship, there's, ah, there's something you should see!"

"Is it Trigger!?" Sheridan demanded, already scaling the perilous rigging. "Have they harmed him!?"

"No, no. He's fine. He's ah, he's the one who's steering them!"

Barnaby glanced at Frank, who began shaking his head as he made for the mast.

"This fucking crew." The Quartermaster complained. "This ridiculous fucking ship."

Barnaby didn't fault him for swearing. He was feeling so inclined himself.

Chapter Twenty-Five

"Bodi, can you get through to Carnage's ship?"

"Aye, Admiral."

"Can you do it unnoticed?"

"Aye, Admiral!"

"Then go, swiftly! Tell him that I'm going to create an opening, and that he needs to take it as soon as he is able!"

"Aye, Admiral!"

No more was spoken as Bodi dove from the deck, slipping into the sea without a ripple or splash. The Thrallkin never surfaced, his mighty lungs sufficient to carry him the distance.

"All hands, prepare to fire! Aim for their masts, not the hull! We want these men alive!"

His words seemed ludicrous, particularly as the fleet resumed firing. Carnage's vessel was assailed from all sides, almost a hundred chunks of steel crashing against its hull. To the Thrallkin's credit, they wore the blows without panic or fear, returning fire in a glorious blaze. Falcon's ship shuddered as its timbers snapped and groaned, Carnage concentrating fire on the leader of his foes.

"Admiral, shall we fire!?"

"Not yet!" Trigger replied, studying the *Blackbird* for some trace of intent. They had refrained from attacking, holding position at the circle's edge. They were the only ones to notice his vessels approach, the crow's nest swaying as three familiar figures crammed into its width.

Trigger extracted his scope, putting it to his eye as he studied their frowning faces. Their gazes were fixed on him, and judging by the words on their lips, they weren't particularly impressed. If he ever retook the *Blackbird*, he'd have to dock Sheridan at least a month's worth of rations.

Sighing, he closed the scope. They were abstaining from the fight, and if they continued to do so, he may just be able to explain one day. It would not be this day, however.

A new clap of thunder split the smoke-filled sky, every vessel firing at the *Bloodbath's* hull. Countless holes dotted the smoking wood, showing streaks of red as the Thrallkin moved to reply. Many of them were covered in blood, each new volley summoning a chorus of cries.

"Would Bodi have reached them yet?"

"Aye, Admiral. Bodi's quick in the water!"

"Very well." Trigger murmured, squeezing the wheel tight. "All hands, fire!"

The Thrallkin roared, their voices joining the cannons as they exploded into life. Their volley struck the target with near-impeccable aim, shattering the mast in an avalanche of wood. Tigger heard the crewmen screaming as the rigging crushed their skulls, and felt a swell of despair for the lives he'd destroyed. He believed in the cause, however, and knew that Carnage would be needed. This was simply their first battle, and it was his task to ensure that victory was theirs.

He adjusted the wheel a few degrees, angling their cannons towards the next ship. Confusion had settled amongst their foes, the unexpected fire ceasing their assault. Carnage was taking advantage of the lull, his massive frame charging towards the shattered stern. He was ready to move, Trigger simply needed to keep the door open.

"Fire!"

His crew cheered as another volley soared, striking their new target with a murderous crack. The damaged mast buckled beneath its own weight, ropes and rigging flailing as it crashed to the sea.

"Go now, go!" Trigger whispered, as Carnage grappled with his half-smashed wheel. The thing had been reduced to splinters, each turn costing the Thrallkin at least a thimble's worth of blood. He ignored the cuts, however, while his crimson crew tended to the swaying sails, guiding the fabric with calloused hands. Their efforts proved successful, propelling their vessel forward at a ponderous pace. Confusion still reigned, however, the members of the fleet unsure as to whether they should press the attack, or see to Trigger's vessel first. It was a hesitation that cost them, as it ensured that none would be swift enough to bar the *Bloodbath's* passage.

"Admiral, there's movement in the fleet!"

Trigger had expected as much. While the *Bloodbath's* escape was all-but inevitable, it was still possible for the fleet to strike a handful of blows, one of which could cripple the vessel, or at least slow it down. What he wasn't expecting, however, was for Falcon to have raised his every remaining sail, directing his prow at the *Bloodbath's* stern.

"Determined." Trigger frowned, watching as the vessel dashed across the waves. It was half the *Bloodbath's* size, and all the quicker for it. There was no way Carnage could avoid it in time.

Trigger seized the *Dragon's* wheel, turning with all his might. He aimed between the ships they had crippled, locking in the rudder with a decisive click.

"Full speed ahead!" He roared, watching as the sails flared into life.

"Aye, Admiral!"

The *Dragon* groaned as the wind caught its wings, carrying it towards the disorganized fleet. He could see the misgivings in his crew's eyes, yet appreciated their lack of questions. It was a dangerous gambit, yet Carnage's only shot at survival was to abandon his ship, and if Trigger didn't close the gap between them, the Thrallkin stood no chance at avoiding the enemy guns.

CRASH!!!

The sound of impact was deafening, the two vessels screaming as they tore each other's hulls. Falcon had used his broken prow to the utmost advantage, driving its jagged remnants deep into Carnage's stern. It had shattered the rudder to glorious effect, robbing the Thrallkin of any control. They could only hope it was an act of suicide, one that had removed the fleet's most capable Captain.

"Don't worry about us! Just fire on the enemy!" Falcon roared, voice muffled by bloody debris.

Trigger sighed. No such luck.

He watched as Falcon dived from the deck, followed by the remains of his decimated crew. The whole fleet moved to fulfill his orders, their cannons turning to the *Bloodbath's* corpse. If the Thrallkin remained, they would be reduced to sawdust and paste.

"Carnage, get out of there!"

The sides of the *Bloodbath* erupted, bleeding as the Thrallkin tore through its hull. Many of them were clasping cannons to their chest, lighting the fuses as they fell through the air. It was a final act of defiance, a brutal farewell from the ill-fated ship. It was also hideously effective, their freakish strength allowing them to direct the cannons at will, sending the blasts directly into any desired foe. Countless pirates screamed as the steel tore through their flesh, leaving them as nothing more than streaks on a deck.

"That's it Captain, bleed the buggers dry!"

Trigger admired his crew's enthusiasm. He was almost inclined to share it.

"Prepare to fire!" He ordered, swinging the wheel to port. It directed their broadside at a major portion of the fleet, that which was closest to Carnage's crew. The vessels were swarming with rifles and men, each one desperate to bag a Thrallkin head.

"Fire!"

Their cannons struck while the crews were distracted, mowing men down with ruthless effect. The survivors reacted as Trigger knew they would, ducking for cover and shielding their heads.

"Full speed!" He ordered, turning the wheel once more. "Full speed!"

"Aye, Captain!"

The *Dragon* shrieked as it spun to port, setting their stern towards the fleet. The panic they had caused would last a minute at best, yet Trigger was certain it would be enough time. He had seen the Thrallkin swim, and knew that Carnage would catch them. The primary concern was now the enemy, and gaining some distance from their cannons.

"Admiral, the fleet is moving to pursue!"

Trigger nodded, willing the *Dragon* to gain some pace. He had expected the fleet to dawdle, to waste a few minutes in rescuing Falcon's crew. Apparently, their loyalty was at an all-time low.

Then again, they *were* pirates.

"Admiral, we've got Carnage coming aboard! He's got wounded with him!"

"Find a few men to help them up! Ropes, poles, anything they can hold!"

"Aye, Admiral!"

A handful of Thrallkin raced about the deck, aiding those too injured to scale the vessel's hull. Glancing over his shoulder, Trigger took note of the wounds, most of which were surprisingly minor. Still, he supposed it made sense. For a wound to stop a Thrallkin, it needed to be fatal.

"Help him, not me!"

He recognized the voice as soon as Carnage his spoke, his gruff tone made rougher by the splinters in his throat.

"Take the wheel." Trigger ordered, waving at a passing Thrallkin. "Keep our current heading. Deviate, and we're all dead. Understood?"

The Thrallkin nodded, taking the wheel between enormous, somewhat-uncertain hands. He was a member of the not-too-bright. Still, desperate times.

Trigger sprinted across the deck, studying those who had clambered aboard. He halted at Carnage's side, the Thrallkin on his knees as he tended to a crewman.

"Carnage, are you harmed? How many did we lose?"

"A moment, please!" Carnage snarled. His patient was on his back, torso torn from belly-to-throat.

"Will he survive?" Trigger asked, studying the gaping wound. It seemed a bit unlikely.

"Possibly." Carnage grunted, flexing his mighty fingers. "It depends."

"On?"

Carnage didn't reply. Instead, he drove his hands into the Thrallkin's wound, blood and bile flying as he probed the crewmen's chest.

"It depends…on whether or not…I can find…this!"

Carnage extracted his prize, raising it high for all to see. The steel-shard sparkled as it caught the sun, its wicked curve measuring at least half-a-foot in length.

"There, you'll heal." He declared, giving his patient a friendly pat.

"Thanks...Captain."

The Thrallkin closed his eyes, drifting away into a peaceful rest. He'd certainly earned it.

"He can heal from that?" Trigger asked, awed by the size of the Thrallkin's wound.

"He can now. Would have been impossible with the shrapnel."

"How many did we lose?"

"Eight. They had a lot of cannons."

"I'm sorry." Trigger declared, putting his hand on the Captain's back.

"My fault." Carnage frowned. "Got carried away. Should have stuck to the plan. You did well getting us out of there. Even if the cunts did break my ship."

"I'll let that curse slide." Trigger nodded, preparing himself to retake the helm. "It's your limit for the day, however."

"Eight of my people just died in my arms."

"Then honor them with action, not useless words."

Carnage snorted, his yellow eyes flashing with rage.

"Fair enough." He conceded, following Trigger towards the stern. "What do you propose I do?"

"Get the crew secured, and ready for close-quarters combat."

"You think they're going to catch us?"

"Not exactly. Though, there's a rather strong chance they'll land on us."

"Pardon?"

"The Void, Carnage. We're there."

The pair of them turned to face the prow, studying the expanse that raged beyond.

"Ah, well." Carnage grinned, tugging at his too-small hat. "This should be fun."

****

"They've gone over." Sheridan spat, slamming her fist against the ship.

"Pursue them." Falcon rasped, his throat rubbed raw from the salt and smoke.

Barnaby considered the water before them, its waves made daggers by the unmatched flow. It had already seized their hull, dragging them towards the Void at an ever-increasing pace. They didn't exactly have a choice.

"Full sail ahead, and keep our prow fixed to the port-side channel!"

"Will that work?" Barnaby asked, as the first of their fleet were consumed by the Void. The ocean itself buckled where the passage began, forming a near-vertical drop into the chaos below.

"It's where the *Dragon* was aiming." Sheridan shrugged. "And it's the safest route. Though, that isn't really saying much."

"We should take the starboard." Falcon croaked. "Rush ahead, and use the Peacock's Tail to board their ship."

Barnaby closed his eyes, willing the Captain to expire or sleep. His conscience had forced him to save the drowning crew, yet it was a decision he had started to regret.

"And tumble prow-first into the Void?" Sheridan sneered. "No, we'll take our chances with port. Once we're past the Void, we'll have them outpaced on the open sea."

"We thought we had them back there! Carnage is too dangerous, and now he has Trigger helping him! We aren't going to win if we don't take risks!"

"Trigger isn't helping him." Sheridan growled. "I don't know what he's doing, but Trigger would never aid that beast."

"He keeps savages as pets, and takes a woman aboard his ship." Falcon snapped. "These are not the markings of a worthy mind!"

Sheridan struck, flooring the Captain with a single punch.

"Gods, what a twat." Frank exclaimed, studying the man with immense distaste.

"Frank?"

"Hey, twat isn't swearing. Where I come from, only posh people use twat."

"Yeah, the rest of them use donkeys!" Gary sniggered, earning a chuckle from the rest of the crew. The laughter quickly faded, as the last of the fleet fell over the edge. They could hear its crewmen screaming as they were carried down the slope, the voices becoming distant at an all-too hectic pace.

"Anyone hear actually ride the Void before?"

"Nope."

"No."

"Not me."

"My granddaddy did!"

"No, he didn't. Fuck off Joel."

"You fuck off! He did!"

"How did we make it this far." Frank sighed, closing his eyes.

The precipice loomed before their prow, the heavy wood swinging slightly to starboard.

"Dammit Bradley, I said keep it steady!" Sheridan snapped, turning towards the helm. "Bradley?"

They all turned to look, Barnaby's guts turning to gravy as he beheld the untouched wheel. Bradley was standing more than two meters distant, his large frame restrained by Falcon's arms. Apparently, he'd taken the punch better than they thought.

"Get the wheel!" Sheridan roared, racing towards the stern. Most of the crew followed, yet Barnaby didn't bother. He knew he was too slow, and that it was already far too late.

The prow of the *Blackbird* entered the void, the hull beneath them dropping as it bent towards the slope. For a moment, the Void stood revealed in all its glory, a complex network of channels and tracks, suspended above a gaping abyss. A single missed turn, or overshot edge, and your vessel would tumble without break or reprieve, until time itself had come to an end.

The raging current took them, throwing them all to the spray-covered deck. The world howled as their vessel gained speed, bouncing and shaking as the sea clawed at its hull.

Barnaby was one of the last to their feet, his slender cane struggling to fix on the wood. The spray was so vicious it might have been rain, the razor-sharp droplets assailing his cheeks.

"Captain, we're veering towards the starboard pass!"

He'd never heard such panic in Sunniday's voice. Looking at the path before them, he understood why.

"Everyone, brace!"

The entire vessel shuddered as it crashed into the pass, the new current double the strength of the first. Some poor bastard screamed as he slipped from the deck, his words swiftly drowned by the thundering tide. Several more bellowed as the *Blackbird* gained speed, reaching a pace that no ship could hold.

"Loose the anchor!" Barnaby screamed, as a terrible bend appeared in the path. "Try to slow us down!"

"We don't have a fucking anchor! Beaufort cut it off!"

"Oh." Barnaby muttered, his eyes going wide. "Oh fuck."

"The sails, Captain!"

He turned to Magwa, who was studying the bend with unabashed fear.

"The currents too strong for that! No wind will right us!"

"No, use main sails as an anchor!"

Barnaby frowned, considering the fabric high overhead. "What?"

Magwa merely rolled his eyes, not bothering to explain as he unsheathed his axe. A moment later he was hacking away, splitting the rigging with haphazard blows.

"What are you doing!?" Frank screamed, watching as the savage assailed his ship.

"Saving lives." Magwa spat. "Magwa would appreciate help!"

"Get your hands off me, you contemptible wench!"

Barnaby glanced to the helm, where Sheridan had Falcon pinned by the throat. Her fist was raised to finish the fight, yet the ships wild motion cost her the blow, jolting her sideways as she swung at his face. It gave Falcon an opening, one he used to brilliant effect. One second, Sheridan was pinning him. The next, she was flat on her back, struggling to rise as Falcon unsheathed his sword.

"Barnaby! Move!"

He looked back to the mast, where several of the crew were now lending their aid. Their weapons were flashing as they slashed at the ropes, desperate to beat the oncoming bend. It was getting awfully close.

Barnaby grimaced as he sprung into life, hopping towards them as the final rope tore. An instant later the sail was falling, swinging into the sea with a marvelous splash. They had left its length fastened by a handful of rigging, which went taut the moment the sail touched down. The *Blackbird* responded with a hideous groan, shifting its heading the slightest degree.

"Sheridan, grab the bloody wheel!"

The First Mate responded with astonishing speed, kicking Falcon aside as she conquered the helm. Spinning the wheel with all her might, she sent their ship into a pendulous swing, their hull scraping on the edge of the bend and sending splinters and sea into the endless abyss.

"Cut the ropes, now!" Magwa ordered, leaping for the remaining strands. "Before they throw us off course!"

Glancing at the chords, Barnaby could see that the danger was real. They were already pulling tight, threatening to hurl them at the next vicious bend.

"Move!"

The call came from Gary, who was raising his pistol with one squinted eye. A second later he fired, splitting each rope with a single great shot.

The crew paused, admiring the man and his still-smoking gun.

"Yeah." Gary conceded. "I'm surprised too."

"Will one of you please restrain this bastard!"

They turned back to the helm, where Sheridan had resumed her conflict with Falcon. She had driven his body against the wheel, holding him in place as she directed the ship. It was an impressive bit of multitasking, yet not one she should be undertaking, considering the circumstance.

"Magwa, if you will?" Barnaby asked. "Put him in the brig. And good thinking on the sail."

"Not that good." The Savage replied. "There many turns, and very few sails."

"He's got a point." Frank declared, as the next fearsome bend began to appear.

"Right." Barnaby sighed, gritting his teeth.

"We need something heavy!" Sunniday called, gazing at them all from up in his perch.

"Well, do you see anything heavy!" Bradley asked, rubbing his head.

"Only your fat arse!"

Barnaby covered his eyes. This crew. This useless Gods-damned crew.

"What *can* you see!?" Frank asked, glaring up at Sunniday.

"The ships ahead are fighting Carnage. There are points where the paths converge, and some of the mad bastards are using it as an opportunity to fire. Gods, some of them are actually attempting to board!"

"That's practically suicide." Barnaby frowned, shocked by the lengths they seemed willing to go.

"Well, a thousand pieces is a fair bit." Gary shrugged. "I'd probably try it."

"Aye, it's a heavy sum, and right now, that means I wouldn't think twice about *throwing it in the fucking sea*!" Frank roared. "Focus, will you!"

Chastised, Barnaby gazed at the edge of their hull, contemplating the water below. The rapid spray was still coating his face, yet was mitigated somewhat by the gun ports between.

"The cannons." He grinned, turning back to his panicking crew.

"What?"

"We use the cannons!"

"The cannons weigh a bloody ton!"

"Exactly!"

"No, I mean, how the hell do we get them out?"

"Ah." Barnaby remarked, losing his joyful grin. "Well, I have an idea, but I doubt you're going to like it."

"Eh, whatever." Frank sighed, shoulders slumping in total defeat. "At this point, I'm up for anything."

"Good." Barnaby nodded, tapping his cane against the deck. "Then organize a gun crew, and head below. We're going to take a page from Trigger's old book."

"Oh." Frank exclaimed, eyes going wide as he realized the plan.

"Oh damn."

Chapter Twenty-Six

"This, this is fucking ridiculous!"

Trigger didn't disagree, watching Carnage dispose of yet another charging fool. The Thrallkin were swatting aside their foes as though they were children, their powerful strikes launching them straight into the sea. Well, the lucky ones, at least. A few of them were propelled even further, their screams lost to time as they sailed across the Void.

The enemy had proven most persistent, captivated by the promise of plunder and revenge. Those who had followed their path were boarding via ropes, while those who had taken the starboard route were travelling high above them. Unfortunately, the passages intersected enough to allow assaults from overhead, a combination of cannon fire and gunshots spraying across their deck. Even now, a particularly courageous party had descended from above, sinking to their rigging like spiders from the sky.

"Trigger, your left!"

The warning came not a moment too soon, as a nearby pirate attempted a shot. Trigger was already ducking as the gunpowder lit, poor aim and manufacturing sparing his life. He charged his opponent as the grizzled man cursed, tossing aside one pistol while drawing another. He was preparing the shot when Trigger struck, tackling his grime-covered chest. They hit the deck in a tangle of limbs, yet his foe smashed his head on the spray-covered wood, losing his focus and breath. Trigger was on him a moment later, releasing a flurry of punches, and prying the pistol from his grasp. Gathering his senses, the man attempted to fend him off, ramming his palm against Trigger's cheek. It did him no good, as Trigger wrenched his arm aside, slamming the gun against his face. Blood flew as the man's cheek tore, his body going limp between Trigger's thighs. There was no reprieve, however, as a rock-solid boot took him square between the ribs, knocking him flat against the deck. Trigger knew what was to follow, and on instinct he swung the pistol, deflecting a sword blow against the barrel. Three of his fingers were cut in the act, yet he considered it a small price to pay, ignoring the pain as he kicked out a leg, sending his new foe down to one knee. It left his face exposed, and an instant later Trigger was firing, putting a bullet between his eyes. He paid no heed to the gore that followed, snatching the cutlass his opponent had dropped. The chaos on the deck was easing, yet every few seconds their vessel would shudder, its unguided hull grinding the edge. That was something he would need to address.

Without pausing for breath, he began a hard charge, avoiding all blows that came for his skull. There were Thrallkin nearer the helm, true, yet Trigger knew that their value lay in combat, and that for each foe he slew, they would drop ten. It made more sense for him to steer, so that his crew could attend to what they do bes-

A hand seized his ankle as he raced up the stairs, slamming his chin against the crest of the stern. He felt the skin split as it slid across the wood, while the wound on his chest was opened anew. Turning, he barely deflected an oncoming stab, the cutlass grazing his shoulder and arm. His opponent pressed the advantage he'd made, using his sword to keep Trigger down. He was bigger and stronger, and with a black-toothed grin he squeezed Tigger's throat, driving his thumb into buckling flesh. Trigger's mind raced for answers as his vision went dim, eventually settling on the edge of the stairs. The ship had no rail between stair and deck, as such designs were unfitting for a vessel of war.

Using his legs, Trigger pressed against the nearest stair, rolling them both across the edge. They fell eight feet to the merciless wood, with Trigger's foe bearing the brunt of the blow. He lost a black tooth as his jaw struck the deck, and lost many more as Trigger kicked his stunned face. This time, he did pause for breath, though, it was an admittedly brief one. An instant later he had ascended the stairs, taking the wheel between bloodied hands.

Peering out across the sea, he realized he'd arrived a few seconds too late.

The enemy vessels were gathering, forming a line that spanned the whole pass. At first glance, this may have been helpful, as it restricted crewmen from swinging aboard their ship. Trigger could sense their intent, however, and knew that they were planning a far deadlier assault.

"Carnage!"

"What!?" The Thrallkin roared, tearing the head from his struggling opponent.

"They're going to ram us! Drive us over the edge!"

"Well, you should fucking move then, shouldn't you!"

"No chance! The *Dragon's* too slow! And that's half-rations!"

Carnage let out a weary sigh, snapping the arm of an oncoming foe.

"What's the plan, then!?"

An excellent question. The *Dragon's* size ensured that no single ship could alter its path, yet three working in unison would certainly succeed. They needed a way to repel the blow, to push back against the enemy hull...

The nearest Captain twisted his wheel, steering his ship towards Trigger's own. The others were swift to follow, their crewmen bracing for the collision.

"How many enemies remain on ship!?"

"About seven, no, make that six. Five, actually. Well, down to three now- "

"So, we're winning, good! Carnage, gather your ten strongest men, and have each of them hold a sturdy rope. Send the others below deck and order them to ready our port side cannons!"

"Aye, Admiral!"

The crew had heard his words, and were already racing to fulfill the command. The strongest seemed quite keen to obey, flexing their muscles as they picked up the rope.

"Men, do you see those enemy ships!?"

"Aye, Admiral!"

"They intend to throw us, to hurl us all to an endless grave! It is your mission, your duty, to see them denied! The moment that hull draws near, you need to put yourselves between us, and push it back with all your might!"

"Aye, Admiral!"

Trigger was impressed. Many would question such a lunatic demand. Not the Thrallkin, apparently. Gods, they seemed to thrive on them.

It explained how Carnage held such control.

Adjusting his coat, Trigger watched their opponents draw near. His contemplation was silent, while the Thrallkin jeered and thumped at their chests. If they were doubtful or frightened, they had no intent of making it known. When the moment of truth arrived, Trigger ensured that he did the same.

"Alright men, are you ready to prove your unyielding strength!?"

"Aye, Admiral!"

"Then make the leap and make our foes weep!"

The Thrallkin cheered at his poetic attempt, hurling themselves between the two hulls. Red muscles flexed as they spread themselves wide, bracing their bodies between shifting wood. They took the first ship with laughter and mirth, their opponents astonished by the inhuman display. It distracted them, causing them to forget their allies charge. The second vessel struck in an explosion of curses, knocking both crews flat on their faces. The Thrallkin's laughter faded as they took the extra weight, a few groans emerging from their stressed and straining forms.

"Just a little longer." Trigger murmured, as the *Dragon* shifted beneath his feet. "Just a few moments more."

The whole deck shuddered as the third vessel collided, many Thrallkin screaming as their muscles gave way. The *Dragon* lurched sideways with a calamitous groan, its massive hull scraping across the thin edge.

"Trigger...if you have a plan...use it!"

"When the cannons go, push for your life!" He replied, knuckles whitening as he twisted the wheel.

"All gun crews, fire!"

The Thrallkin responded with astonishing speed, firing a volley of glorious steel. Smoke billowed port-side as the Thrallkin pushed hard, the blast enhancing their efforts just a tiny bit more.

"Reload, and re-fire!" Trigger ordered. "Every cannon at the exact same time!"

"Aye, Admiral!"

BOOM!

The bullet missed him by the barest degree, his left ear buzzing as the shot sailed past. Trigger dropped low, his keen eyes settling on the space between hulls. The enemy crewmen had bridged it, using a plank to cross the small gap. It wasn't a large force, yet one look told Trigger that they knew how to fight, and that their reason for crossing was simple enough. Take out the Thrallkin gunners, and turn the cannons towards Carnage's team.

"Very well." He sighed, using his belt to secure the wheel. He was awfully sick of life-and-death fights.

He vaulted from the stern with a moderate shout, brandishing his blade as he fell to the deck. He landed with a nimble roll, barely avoiding a trio of shots. He was on his feet a few moments later, sprinting towards a quartet of foes. They discarded their guns with a mixture of sneers, clearly referring to butcher up-close. This was fine with Trigger, as it gave him the chance to snatch up a gun, and empty its barrel between a foe's cheeks. The deck was littered with such discarded weapons, and if he wanted any chance at survival, he'd have to make use of all he could see.

The pirates gazed at their fallen friend, anger twisting their bloodshot eyes.

"He shot Kevin! Gut the fucking prick!"

They rushed the deck with a chorus of snarls, their bare feet tapping across the wet wood. Trigger didn't try to engage them. Instead, he leapt on the banister, using the extra height to spring clear overhead. His opponents seemed confused, yet that shifted to rage as he slashed the boarding plank, destroying their bridge to home and safety.

"All gun, fire!"

His crew responded instantly, a new volley lending Carnage some strength. His team bellowed loudly as they made use of the force, shifting their foe a few inches aside. It was a small achievement, yet the *Dragon's* hull no longer touched the edge, while an upcoming turn ensured that if the fleet maintained its position, at least one of the vessels would be hurled from the pass.

"You've lost!" He declared, as his opponents advanced. "All fire crews, reload!"

"Way I see it, we kill you, they follow soon after." Sneered the shortest of the men. "It's your little tricks that have spared 'em the edge."

"Carnage is wiser than you'll ever know. Slay me, and all you achieve is earning his wrath. There is an alternative, however."

"Doesn't he talk pretty." Chuckled the largest, a heavyset man with a potato-like nose.

"You can put down your weapons, and speak with your fleet. Tell them to stand down, and listen to my words."

"Why the fuck would we do that?"

"Because *fire!*"

The *Dragon* shifted as the cannons blared, throwing his foes across to one side. Trigger was ready, however, using the movement to aid his assault. He struck the largest straight in his nose, reducing the potato to a purple mash. The big man buckled, tears streaming from his eyes, leaving an opening that Trigger was swift to fill, slamming his elbow across the smallest man's jaw. His last foe recovered quickly, however, slamming his shoulder into Trigger's side and driving him across the deck. Trigger grimaced at the considerable pain, the blow widening his already oozing wound, while also bruising at least two of his ribs.

His opponent pursued his stumbling feet, swinging his hatchet towards Trigger's face. He was barely able to parry, catching the weapon's handle across the length of his blade. The impact destroyed what balance he held, allowing his foe to hurl him backwards, straight into the banister of their still-groaning ship.

"Get him, Adrien!" Roared the enemy crew, as their own vessel moaned under the stress to its hull. The bend was growing closer, a fact of which the enemy had finally become aware. Every Captain was at his helm, ordering the crew to lower their sails, and trying their best to disperse the fleet. On one hand, this was excellent, as it meant an end to their attempts to drive the *Dragon* edgeways. On the other hand, Trigger had locked the wheel in place, and if he didn't release it soon, their own vessel would sail prow-first to the Void.

He threw himself sideways, hearing the thunk as the hatchet broke wood. Lashing out, he struck his opponent across the cheek, knocking him back at least a good step. He followed the blow with a kick to the knee, bending the joint out-of-place. The pirate screamed as he sank to the deck, cradling his leg with calloused hands.

Trigger didn't waste time on apologies. He was already racing towards the helm, struggling to stand on the now-quaking deck. Two of the fleet had retreated, leaving only the first vessel pinned to their side. The weight of the collisions had almost fused their ships entirely, the twisted timbers linked in a broken embrace.

He took the steps three at a time, nearly losing his footing on more than one occasion. Reaching the stern gave him no time to rest, as with a terrible shudder the last ship pulled free, sending them veering towards the bend's edge.

Triger didn't waste moments grappling with his belt. He simply cut it in two, feeling a slight pang of regret for the waste of good leather. Then, he seized the wheel and wrenched to port, fixing their prow once more on the sea.

"You brilliant little man! You did it!"

Trigger turned to watch as Carnage retook the deck, scaling the side with a wince and groan. His crewmen were swift to follow, their hefty bodies swollen from exertion. That they could move at all was astonishing, which is why Trigger was doubly surprised when Carnage sprang to his feet, the Thrallkin Captain grinning as he paced towards their conquered foes.

"Oh, you've been captured on the wrong ship." Carnage chuckled, flexing his fingers as the smallest crewman screamed. Potato-nose had woken as well, his broken appendage weeping as he backed across the deck. They were both terrified, while Adrien maintained some semblance of calm, hefting his hatchet while cradling his knee.

"Carnage, leave them!"

Carnage halted, his smile fading as he looked to the helm. "Why?"

"Because I ordered it. Do you need another reason?"

Trigger knew it was a risky response. Yet he was meant to be the Admiral. That authority needed to be cemented, or else the title was an empty chair.

"Heh. Fair enough." Carnage shrugged, folding his arms. Each of the men looked to Trigger in awe, the order weaving its desired effect.

"Yes, I command the Thrallkin." Trigger declared, adjusting his coat and smoothing his hair. "Which is why you should listen to the offer I make."

The perplexed trio studied his face, attempting to see if it was some kind of joke. By the set of their features, they'd clearly decided this was not the case.

"What's the offer?"

"Your ships have fallen back and will not attempt another assault, not until we've left the Void. When they come for us, you will inform them that we mean no harm, and that we wish for them to join our fleet."

"Doubt they'll be inclined to join, considering how bad the current one's going."

"It goes poorly because it is led by fools. You have seen what Carnage and I can do. What do you think we'd be capable of, with an entire fleet willing to follow my command?"

"A fucking lot, I have to say." Adrien grimaced, rubbing his misshapen knee.

"The correct answer, though please, no swearing."

The trio studied him again, attempting to judge if this were a joke. Once again, the answer was negative.

"So, that's it?" Adrien asked. "Our ships come to save us, we make them your offer?"

"No. I'll make the offer. You make sure that they're willing to hear it."

The trio appeared doubtful, mostly due to the Thrallkin, who were considering their captives with hungry eyes.

"You will not be harmed further, you have my word." Trigger assured them, expecting the usual dismissive response.

"Well then, I guess we'll take you on that." Adrien replied, giving him a slightly pained grin.

"Oy, Admiral!"

The rest of the crew had emerged from below, embracing their brothers in tight crimson hugs. Bodi alone was refraining, his yellow gaze fixed on the passage above. It would soon intersect with their own, offering the risk of a skyward assault.

"Yes, Mr. Bodi?"

"You might want to look with your scope. Your old ship's in view, and they're doing something…well, weird."

Trigger snapped out his lens, aiming the glass towards the high sea. Surely enough, the *Blackbird* appeared, having somehow sped past the rest of the fleet. At first, Trigger was surprised, yet soon the reason became all too clear.

"Are they blowing up their own ship?" Carnage asked, his Thrallkin eyes not needing a scope.

"They are."

"…Right. Why?"

"I have no idea."

Carnage nodded, tugging at his too-small hat.

"Don't suppose you know why they're pushing out the cannons?"

"I do not. Though, judging by the ropes, they may be trying to slow their ship down."

"Hmm. Shouldn't they use their anchor for that?"

"One would think so, yes."

"Ah." Carnage nodded, scratching at his scalp.

"Admiral?"

"Yes?"

"What the fuck's wrong with your old crew?"

****

"Another bend, Captain!"

"Fire when ready, Mr. Frank!"

"Aye, Captain!"

BOOM!

The swirl of sawdust grew as the latest cannon erupted, blowing away the hull with an almost deafening crack. Smoke and splinters flew as the timber dropped away, the crewmen grunting with exertion as they seized the cannon's length.

"Get that rope fastened!" Barnaby ordered, unable to repress a broad grin. This was actually kind of fun.

"Aye, Captain!"

The men fixed the rope with record speed, though their tired bodies struggled to see the cannon moved. Eventually even Sheridan was forced to add her strength, her gloved hands propelling the weapon across the soot-stained deck. A moment later it had left their ship entirely, striking the sea with an astonishing splash.

"Dammit." Sheridan cursed, as the spray soaked her wig and dress.

"I'd say it's an improvement." Bradley ventured, admiring the way the fabric now clung.

The rope went taut, slowing the ship to a more manageable pace. Barnaby could hear those above them attempting to take advantage, adjusting the stern and sails as best as they were able. With bated breath, they waited, each man praying for the ship to turn. It did, summoning a cheer from their aching throats.

"Sunniday!" Sheridan yelled, peering outside a newly formed hole.

"Aye!?"

"How many turns do we have left!?"

"One more! It's a prick of a thing, though! Sharper than the rest combined!"

Barnaby nodded, counting their remaining cannons. They were down to five.

"We could try and use two." He remarked, folding his arms against the cold. The shattered hull was nurturing a rather wicked cross-breeze, the clearing of the smoke not quite worth the rapidly increasing chill.

"Might be our best option." Sheridan conceded, studying the pass below. They were about to intersect with the lower level, and it seemed that Trigger's ship would be sailing directly below their own.

"I wouldn't risk it." Frank declared, reading the look in her eyes. "We're moving awfully fast, and I doubt we've got the rope for you to reach their mast."

"He's so close." Sheridan sighed, leaning against the hull.

"We'll catch him on the final stretch. Right now, we're the lightest ship to ever set sail."

"True enough, I suppose."

"Captain! Final bends coming in less than a mile!"

"Thank you, Mr. Sunniday! Magwa, are you ready at the helm!?"

"Magwa born ready!"

"Thank you, Mr. Magwa! Men, prepare the port side cannons!"

"Aye, Captain!"

Barnaby watched as the weapons were loaded, their dark steel aimed at the vessel which housed them.

He was really starting to enjoy this part.

"Fire!"

The guns blazed with a thunderous boom, smashing the hull with irresistible force. Barnaby closed his eyes for the initial burst of impact, yet when he opened them he could see the men were smiling, their childish delight matching his own. After all, it was always fun to blow things up.

"Get the ropes ready!" He ordered, though he needn't have bothered. The men were already at work, fastening knots of intricate skill.

"Mr. Frank, when should we push?"

"Not yet." The Quartermaster replied, leaning outside the shattered hull. "Though, I'd get into position."

"You heard the man! Grab hold and get ready!"

"Aye, Captain!"

The crew seized the cannons, the majority on one, while Sheridan alone took hold of the second. Barnaby should probably have offered to help, yet if he was being honest with himself, he'd just be slowing the First Mate down.

The *Blackbird* rumbled as they hit rapid waves, the bend creating chaos in the seas flowing tide. Barnaby could feel the vessel gaining pace, somehow increasing their ludicrous speed. If they did escape the Void, they'd hit the open water like a drunk hits the floor.

"Now!"

The crewmen all groaned as they took the cannon's weight, wiry arms tensing as they pushed against steel. The weapons rolled forward at a measured pace, yet surely enough they fell once their wheels had left the deck. The following splash was larger than all that came before, saturating Sheridan from head-to-toe. The greatest casualty was her makeup, which had gone from lady-of-war to hooker-in-rain.

Not that he'd ever say so. He quite enjoyed having his cock intact.

"I'd hold on." Frank suddenly informed them, pressing himself against the hull.

It was solid advice, one which caused Barnaby to drop to his knees, before lying flat against the deck.

Crunch!

The *Blackbird* spun as the cannons touched base, the ropes stretching tight against splintered wood. The corner was tighter than a virgin's backside, grinding their stern against the edge. It was a terrible sound, one which dragged for a hideous length. The crewmen above were shouting and screaming, watching in horror as their ship fell apart. At least they had the luxury of view. Down where they were, Barnaby was free to imagine, his tired mind filling with a thousand dread thoughts. They were at serious risk of losing their rudder, and if that happened, well, they were as good as dead.

"The ropes, cut the damn ropes!"

The cry came from above, galvanizing them all into furious action. The tightness of the turn had caused them to overshoot, forcing the *Blackbird* into a perilous circle.

"Throw me a sword!" Sheridan screamed, as three men hacked at the very same rope. It was Bradley who responded, tossing his weapon to her waiting hand. The blade was caught with her usual grace, and a moment later the tether was sliced, freeing their ship from the cannons great weight. A sudden shift followed, sending them tumbling towards the port side.

"Magwa, what are you doing!?"

"Steering!"

"Not fucking well!"

"That Frank's opinion! Magwa hold another!"

"Maybe you should hold the wheel instead!"

"Does Frank want to steer? He welcome to try!"

The *Blackbird* shuddered on the pounding waves, its speed increasing with every foot gained. The Void was now passing as a midnight blur, the rest of their fleet lagging far behind.

"We're about to exit the pass!" Sunniday screamed. "Hold on for your bloody lives!"

Barnaby obeyed the order, as did everyone else. Frankly, he was half-expecting their ship to collapse.

KOOM!

Their prow struck the ocean, blasting a flood of salty water straight into their hull. The liquid wall threatened to tear Brnaby from the deck, clawing at his limbs with stinging waves. It subsided rather quickly, however, draining away through the ships smashed ribs.

"Did everyone make it!?" Frank coughed, his cheeks and chin covered with watery drool. A chorus of ayes was swift to follow, each man croaking through a parched and aching throat.

"Would you look at that." Bradley rasped, nodding towards the open sea. "Most beautiful thing I ever did see."

The man had a point. The clear blue soared for what seemed an eternity, an endless font of adventure and life. Compared to the void they had so recently faced; such total existence was brilliant indeed.

"Aye, she can be a right bitch, yet there's never a day when she doesn't astound."

Bradley glanced at Barnaby, following his line of sight.

"I don't mean the sea, you silly twats. Sheridan's dress slipped. Most glorious view the world can hold."

The crewmen burst out laughing, even Sheridan, who had covered herself at record speed. She almost appeared flattered.

"We should head above." Frank declared, grimacing as he stretched. "We need to plan our next move."

"We're the first out." Sheridan mused, adjusting her dripping wig. Her makeup had devolved even further, somehow regaining a measure of terror. It had smeared into war paint, etching runes of black across her cheeks. "That gives us options we'd be fools not to use."

"Such as?" Barnaby ventured, limping towards the stairs.

"We could barricade the port side exit. Hold the *Dragon* until our allies are free."

"How?" Frank frowned, indicating their near-cannonless deck.

"We could ram them." Barnaby shrugged, feeling oddly cavalier.

"And risk damaging the ship?" Frank exclaimed, appearing outraged at the thought.

Barnaby didn't speak. He merely gestured at their hull, or rather, their lack of one.

"Huh." Frank conceded, scratching at his head.

"Fair enough."

Chapter Twenty-Seven

"I don't know if I'm impressed or horrified."

"Horrified. Definitely horrified."

"They do seem to despise that ship."

"Why, though? It's been nothing but good to them!"

"I can't say, yet that's the second time they've blown out its sides, and there was also that time they set it on fire."

Trigger ran a hand through his hair, astonished by his former crew. He adored the *Blackbird*, and believed their sentiment to somewhat be the same. Yet all evidence suggested the contrary, the crew appearing to delight in burning and breaking the noble ship.

"Oh, hey. It looks like they're going to ram us."

"You're enjoying this." Trigger frowned, giving Carnage a reproachful glare.

"I enjoy a bit of chaos." The Thrallkin shrugged. "And your old crew is fucking insane."

"Half-rations."

"Worth it."

Trigger sighed, considering the options at hand.

"We can't dodge them." He declared. "They were swifter to begin with. Factoring in the weight they've lost, they'll be even faster, even without their main sail."

"We could fire on them. The rest have fallen back, so we have room to use our guns."

"That's my old crew." Trigger scowled. "We're not firing on them, not unless we have no other choice."

"Well, we aren't exactly brimming with options. They're going to pin us near the Void, and that means we're cornered. That's not a fight we can win."

"We don't need to fight. We have them." Trigger replied, nodding at their captives. "They'll delay the fleets fire, and give me the chance to speak with Sheridan. She'll join us, once she hears our plan."

"You're certain?"

"There's never been a more loyal First Mate. On top of that, she's brilliant, and fully understands the Empires taint. She'll leap at the chance to tear it down. Provided we keep the fashion, of course."

Carnage blinked at the final addendum, yet carried on without remark.

"Be that as it may, I don't believe our captives will speak. Particularly the one with the swollen nose. He seems the vengeful type, and this is the perfect opportunity to see us undone."

"He also seems the cowardly type. His sense of self-preservation will outweigh his need for revenge."

"Mine wouldn't."

"You aren't human."

"Heh. Can't argue with that."

Trigger nodded, accepting the Thrallkin's submission. He signaled for the sails to be lowered and furled, while also requesting that the white flag be raised. The crew were quick to obey, despite the dubious expressions flittering across their faces. They had not yet exited the pass, yet the current provided all the propulsion required, driving them out at an easy pace. They hit the open sea with barely a tremble, slowing to a halt as they left the Void entirely. Their restraint proved wise, as the *Blackbird* was on them in a matter of moments, the battered vessel barely avoiding a collision with their stationary hull. It appeared that they'd managed to completely lose their anchor.

Trigger took a deep breath, adjusting his coat as he moved towards the prow. Carnage was at his side, seemingly unconcerned by the ships potential threat. He probably should have been, as a shot rang out the moment he was in view, piercing the Thrallkin's shoulder in an explosive spray of blood.

"Cease your fire!" Trigger ordered, putting himself between Carnage and his crew. The shot had come from Sheridan, who was clutching a pistol with a sturdy hand.

"So, you are protecting him." The First Mate sneered, tossing the weapon aside. Her makeup had run during their traversal of the Void, the black smears enhancing her ferocious appeal. She resembled some savage Goddess, a statue worshipped in the caverns of the world.

"You look fantastic." Trigger grinned, his worries overwhelmed by his sense of relief. He'd missed her more than she could know.

"She's about to be a smear!" Carnage roared, shoving Trigger aside. He hadn't gone a step before the next shots were fired, taking him through the forearm and thigh.

"That's enough!" Trigger bellowed, placing himself before the smoking guns. Glancing over his shoulder, he could see the anger growing on the other Thrallkin's faces, and knew that if this continued, his former crew would wind up dead, or at the very least crippled beyond repair.

"Step aside, Captain." Frank declared, his own weapon raised.

"Admiral."

All eyes turned to Carnage, who was rising to his feet, apparently unfazed by the holes in his flesh.

"Pardon?" Sheridan snapped, reaching over her shoulder. As if by sorcery, a freshly loaded pistol was tossed to her palm.

"He's an Admiral now." The Thrallkin continued, digging his fingers into a wound. He extracted them a moment later, a bullet clenched between index and thumb.

"Don't you need a fleet to be an Admiral?" Gary asked, scratching at his sopping beard.

"You brought us one." Carnage grinned, dropping the bullet to the deck. As if in answer to his words, the remaining vessels emerged from the Void, directing their prows at the *Dragon's* great hull. They'd be surrounded in minutes.

"Care to explain?" Sheridan asked, returning her gaze to Trigger.

"That may take a while."

"Trust me, you aren't going anywhere."

He could understand his First Mate's tone. They'd come this far to rescue him, and found him in bed with the enemy. He'd be a bit put-out as well.

"Very well." He shrugged. "Shall I wait for the others?"

"No. If you have to explain it twice, you will."

Trigger nodded, running his fingers through his hair.

"It started at the duel, when I attempted to save Beaufort. He took advantage of the confusion and used it to betray me. He'd made a deal with Carnage, who was waiting for the chance to take me aboard."

"We know. Beaufort's in the brig, and Falcon saw it all unfold. He was the one who arranged this rescue."

"Didn't seem like much of a rescue." Carnage snorted, gesturing at the corpses draped across their ship. "You came here for slaughter."

"We came for him!" Sheridan snapped, pointing at Trigger. "Unfortunately, you have a habit of pissing people off, and Falcon couldn't resist trying to get you killed!"

"Ah." Carnage murmured, tugging at his hat. "Well, I guess that makes sense."

"It's the only thing here that does!" Sheridan growled, fixing her glare on Trigger. "We thought you were dead, and that was awful enough. Then, we discover you're alive, yet in the clutches of this vile thing- "

"I don't have 'clutches'." Carnage muttered, removing a bullet from his bleeding arm.

"-a fate we assumed was worse than death! We thought we'd find you a broken wretch, tortured and beaten like some mangy dog! Instead, we find you in good health, with a brand new vessel, and a brand new crew!"

The last of the fleet arrived as the First Mate finished, their cannons trained on the *Dragon's* deck. They were well and truly captured, their only chance remaining in Trigger's choice of words.

"You're completely correct." Trigger replied, rubbing his finger against his thumb. "I have to admit, when I woke aboard the *Bloodbath*, I braced myself for pain. I offered prayers to the Gods, and whispered goodbye to my wonderful crew, wherever they might be. Every moment I expected the blows to start falling, for the cuts and whippings to commence. Strangely, they never did."

He glanced at the collected vessels, making sure he had their eyes and ears. Thus far, he was holding them firm.

"Instead, I was greeted with wine, food, and an insightful conversation. An offer was made; one I could never refuse."

"What offer?" Sheridan demanded, her features still fierce, yet somewhat calmed by a questioning hue.

"An opportunity. One to set the world right, to use my skills to their fullest, in a cause of genuine worth."

"I'd appreciate specifics."

Trigger nodded, feeling the weight of the moment. Thus far, the cause had been a fleeting dream, an intangible fancy for a few select minds. To announce it here would make it real, giving it form in the world. Form meant agency, influence and history. To petition these crews was their only chance of success, yet it was also the moment when their failure could be born.

Trigger sighed, adjusting his coat. Nothing ventured, nothing gained.

"We're going to kill the Empress." He declared. "And bring the whole Empire tumbling down."

****

"What?"

The question came from Sheridan, her fearsome scowl fashioned from confusion and doubt. Barnaby couldn't blame her. He hardly believed it himself.

"We're going to kill the Empress." Trigger repeated. "And not just her. The royal family, the nobles, her entire system of oppression and control. Carnage and I will see it undone. We were hoping that you'd help."

Every vessel present was filled with murmured thoughts, the crewmen asking questions to any comrade they could reach. Barnaby stayed silent, however, pushing himself to the front of the pack. It wasn't easy, yet the base of his cane was a welcome aid, crushing the toes of his more stubborn blockades. Trigger gazed at him as he stepped to the fore, those blue eyes narrowing as they searched for recognition. They found it, growing wide as the shock settled in.

"Barnaby?" Trigger asked, studying the scars deforming his face.

"Aye." Barnaby nodded, leaning against his cane.

"You've…matured."

"That's one way to see it. Don't mind me though. Tell us more about this grand idea."

A slight frown creased the Admiral's brow, his keen gaze flicking across the crew.

"I will, though I do have a question I'd like to hear answered."

"Fire away." Barnaby shrugged.

"The *Blackbird*. Who serves as her Captain?"

"That would be me." Barnaby beamed, tapping his cane against the deck. To Trigger's credit, he hid any horror the words might have caused.

"Well then, I thank you for tending to my vessel and crew. You've done a marvelous job."

The Admiral's words were followed by a loud and hollow splash, as several broken timbers tumbled from their hull.

"You're welcome."

"Oh, enough, for God's sake! Are we going to talk, or battle? There's money on the table, and a race to be won. If we aren't going to see them dead, then I'd rather head-off and earn a pardon!"

The declaration came from a nearby ship, and was met with approval by the rest of the fleet, who roared and sneered at the *Dragon's* hull.

"To what end?"

The question was spoken softly, yet quelled the growing shout and jeers.

"What do ya mean?" Asked the Captain, whose name he'd never bothered to learn. Truth be told, Barnaby had avoided the bulk of their fleet, finding them distasteful in both manners and speech. By comparison, Trigger had refined his crew, spoiling other pirates in Barnaby's eyes.

"Say you win the pardon." Trigger continued, running his fingers through his hair. "What then?"

"We get the Empire off our backs." The Captain sneered, looking to his men as though Trigger were an idiot.

"So, you intend to retire?"

"What?"

"From piracy. That must be your intention, as the pardon is only retroactive. Any new crimes you commit will incur the Empire's wrath."

"Well, yeah." The Captain replied, unfolding his arms. "But we wouldn't be punished for our greater misdeeds."

"No, I suppose you wouldn't. What do those entail, exactly? Murder, surely. I'd also assume some rape and assault, and your standard charge of piracy. Do you intend to abandon these practices? Will you never reoffend?"

"Ah, yeah, sure!" The Captain nodded. "We'll just do a bit of stealing, nothing too severe, you know?"

"A wise plan." Trigger smiled. "Out of interest, however, would you tell me the punishment for theft?"

"Uh..." The Captain uttered, knitting his brows together.

"Hanging!" Cheered a crewman, clearly glad to be involved.

"Indeed." Trigger replied, giving the man an affirming nod. "Now, what's the punishment for assault?"

"Hanging?"

"Right again. Now, tell me, what offences are there that *don't* result in hanging?"

Silence reigned as the fleet considered. Barnaby couldn't help but grin. The lunatic bastard might actually win.

"Buggery!" Announced a crewman, earning a round of approval from his Captain and mates.

"...True." Trigger conceded, rubbing his finger against his thumb. Sheridan was gazing at him intently, searching his face for some emotion or thought. "Though, remind me, what *is* the punishment for buggery?"

"Exile or stoning, depending on how rich you are!"

"That it is." Trigger replied, his tone now laced with a simmering rage. "Neither is desirable. Would all of you agree?"

"Aye!"

"Excellent. Then I repeat my earlier question. What end is there in winning the Tides? Yes, it frees you to retire, yet to do so would return you to the very nation you fled. A miserable existence, bowing to the whims of a merciless regime. Even worse, it does nothing to protect you if you continue your lives. Your next offence could be your last, and will incur just as harsh a penalty as any made before. The Tides is a lie, a balm to soothe an irritant itch. It is just another way for the Empire to hold us, to bleed us dry for its profit and goals. Every pirate here is currently slaving for the Empress. You're just too blind to see it."

Once again, a wave of murmurs engulfed the ships, though this time the tone was of a darker sort. The pirates spoke in anger, both at Trigger, and the idea he had thrust in their heads. It was a tenuous situation, one that could swing in one of two ways. They would either acquiesce to the Admiral's will, falling into line without further complaint, or their anger would get the best of them, causing them to lash out at the man who had opened their eyes.

Barnaby had gained an understanding of pirates. He could already see where their preference lay. If Trigger was to succeed, he'd need someone to tether their rage.

"He's fucking right." Barnaby declared, stamping his cane against the deck. The murmurs ceased, every crew turning to consider his words.

"Look at me." He began, gesturing at his face and cane. "These are the price of freedom. A price we've all paid, in one way or another. Should a man have to suffer, just so he can be his own? Is it fair, is it just, that a single person can control our lives?"

"No!" Yelled the crowd, gleefully drinking his false rage.

"Then I say we have no choice!" He declared, hoisting his cane above his head. "This man offers us liberty, true freedom! A life we can call our own! A world remade in the image of the free! What sort of pirates are we, what sort of *men*, if we choose to deny such a glorious chance!?"

The fleet trembled as the crewmen roared, stained timbers rattling in a hurricane of cheers.

Barnaby fought to suppress his grin. They had them. Despite it all, they fucking had them.

"I wear no sword!" He continued, limping towards the edge of his ship. "Yet I do carry this, and I prize it above all else in this world. I pledge it's use to the cause, from now until my dying breath!"

He lay his cane across the banister, struggling to stand without its aid.

"Well, I do carry a sword!" Announced the unknown Captain, stepping towards his bobbing prow. "And I'm more than happy to throw it in!"

The Captain's crew cheered, each of them holding their weapons aloft. The cry swept the fleet like a plague born on wind, every crew joining the deafening din. His own crew seemed the only exception, their weapons sheathed as they studied the fleet.

"Well?" Barnaby asked, looking towards his silent men.

A hatchet appeared, quivering slightly as it struck near his hand. It settled neatly in the banister, its obsidian bright in the smoke-tainted sun.

"Magwa will fight." The Kalyute declared, giving them all a pointed grin. Barnaby nodded in reply, watching the others to gauge their response.

"Fuck it." Gary announced, shrugging his shoulders and drawing his sword. "I'm in."

"Fuck yeah!" Bradley boomed, hefting his pistol over his head. The rest of the crew was swift to follow, lending their shouts to the fleets mighty cry. Sunniday, Frank and even Sheridan, every voice pledging their arms to the cause. The Thrallkin themselves were howling with glee, their crimson limbs raised as they basked in the cheers. It was a maelstrom of ecstasy, a momentous reunion of scattered minds. Trigger alone stood calm at the center, considering it all with pristine restraint.

Barnaby picked up his cane, using the shaft to bolster his frame. As he did, Trigger's gaze flicked back to him, those blue eyes brilliant from even this length.

The Admiral gave a tiny nod.

He returned it, before testing himself once more on his cane. He might have imagined it, yet for just a moment, he'd felt a great weight descend on his limbs. That would have bothered him, once. Now, however?

Well.

He knew he could take it.

Chapter Twenty-Eight

It felt good. It felt familiar.

It didn't feel like home.

Trigger walked the *Blackbird*, running his hand along its length. At one point, he'd known it all, every scratch and scar.

No longer.

She was different now, aged and weathered by another's hand. She'd seen things he wouldn't believe, and he'd done the very same.

"You've treated her well." He declared, removing his palm from the sea-slathered wood.

"We really haven't." Sheridan laughed, tossing her hair to one side. She'd prepared herself for his visit, donning her most elaborate dress, and cleaning her most dazzling wig. It practically shone, the blonde hair flowing like a river of silk.

"I was the first to blow out her sides."

"True. Though, we set her on fire, tore out her anchor, and *then* blew out her sides. We threw away her cannons, as well."

"All for a good cause." Trigger grinned.

"Not really, considering it came to naught."

"You're still bitter?"

"More annoyed, than bitter. It's hardly an epic rescue when your target saved themselves."

"You'd rather Carnage *had* tortured me?"

"No, no. It just would have made a damn good story."

"This hasn't?"

"Well, if we'd been rescuing you, the story would be done. As it currently stands, we'll be at this for months."

"That's a tad optimistic."

"Oh. Excellent." Sheridan sighed, giving him a sarcastic smile. He would have replied, yet they were interrupted by the tap of a cane, signaling the Captain's return.

"Barnaby." Trigger nodded, turning to face his altered friend. He still found it hard to decipher the boy, his former face lost behind a lifetime's worth of pain.

"Admiral." The Captain nodded. "They're ready for you."

"Thank you. How do they seem?"

"Exactly as I expected. Pompous and outraged. This is a poor idea."

"It is necessary." Trigger shrugged.

"It really isn't."

Trigger didn't argue, he simply marched towards the brig. The boy had grown an attitude.

It suited him.

"Admiral. Captain."

"Admiral. Captain."

"Admiral. Captain."

Every crewman saluted as they ventured through the ship, their voices filled with the utmost respect. He had gained a kingly status among the crews of their fleet, who considered his 'taming' of the Thrallkin a legendary feat. Strangely, however, they afforded Barnaby the same deference, his reputation bolstered by Beaufort's earlier lies. His later actions had served to validate them, giving the young man considerable influence. Trigger was glad that they were allies. He had no wish to grapple with such an adulated man.

"You've kept them in line." Trigger remarked, as they descended the well-swept stairs.

"Nah. They're behaving because you're aboard. Many are hoping you'll make us the flag ship."

"I see."

"I'm one of them."

"You don't enjoy being Captain?"

"Gods, no."

"Unfortunate." Trigger grinned. "You have a talent for it."

"I have good help." Barnaby shrugged. Sheridan snorted her agreement, ducking beneath a low beam.

"That you do. I regret that I have to diminish it." Trigger declared.

"I don't." Sheridan chimed.

"You've yet to serve with the Thrallkin."

"They can't be worse than this crew."

"She's not wrong." Barnaby conceded. "We are a motley sort."

Trigger restrained a smile. The Captain's tone was full of affection, an unspoken love for his unorthodox crew. It was a necessary sentiment, especially for the hardships that were sure to come.

"Ah, is zat a cane I hear? Rise, Mr. Falcon. We have visitors!"

They exited the stairs, coming face-to-face with the stinking brig. At first the smell proved quite overpowering, yet Trigger was swift to adjust, particularly when he discerned the adorable source.

His cat sat arched before the bars, a yellow stream blasting from its snow-white thighs. It looked to them as they entered the room, its golden eyes glowing as they set on his face.

It ceased its assault with a pleasure-filled meow, fluffy paws silent as it raced towards his feet. It brushed against his boots with a marvelous purr, burying its face in his ankles and shin. Trigger didn't bother with propriety. He swept it up with a childish grin, holding it tight against his chest. The purring grew louder as the cat raised its head, pressing its nose against his own.

"I missed you too, buddy." He beamed. He caught his companions staring from the corner of his eye, yet their smiles proved a match for his, all present glad for this heartfelt reunion.

Well, those not trapped behind bars.

"Captain Trigger." Beaufort greeted, leaning his weight against the door. "You survived!"

"I did. Though it's 'Admiral' now."

"Captain Admiral? How bizarre."

Trigger didn't laugh. Nobody did.

"Fair enough." Beaufort chuckled. "Hostility is reasonable, considering ze circumstances."

"Most would have you keel-hauled." Trigger replied, placing the cat beside his foot.

"For making zem an Admiral? Zat would be an ungrateful response."

"You didn't make me anything." Trigger declared, doing his best to keep his temper in check.

"I set you on ze path. Is zat not enough?"

Trigger opened his mouth to reply, yet his words were cut short by the brigs more recent acquisition.

"Gods, be silent, you jabbering oaf!"

Falcon shouldered Beaufort, attempting to push the big man aside. He failed, captivity having only somewhat reduced the swordsman's vast frame.

"Would you like me to move?" Beaufort asked, giving the Captain a mocking grin.

"You should have him keel-hauled." Falcon spat, stepping away from Beaufort's side. "Not only is he a traitor, he is utterly insufferable."

"If we keel-haul him, you'll be getting the same." Sheridan snarled. "Though, That's fine by me."

"Keel-hauled? For what? Attempting to kill Carnage? The greatest fiend our world has seen?"

"He's really not." Trigger replied, rubbing his finger against his thumb. The words brought Falcon's gaze to him, the Captain's eyes swelling with confusion and rage.

"We came to free you." He declared, his fingers wrapping about the bars. "To repay you for sparing my brother. Instead, we find you've turned against us. That you've joined the Thrallkin we sought to destroy. That alone is reprehensible, yet you then joined the bastards in killing our men. Men who sought to save your life!"

"They sought gold." Trigger shrugged. "At least, I believe that to be the case. If they were trying to save me, well, they certainly had an unusual style."

"You forfeited safety when you sided with Carnage."

"At the time, maybe. Things change, however, sometimes rather swiftly. Safety lies with the Thrallkin now, as does your salvation."

"Speak plainly."

"Very well." Trigger conceded, adjusting his coat. "Carnage is a member of our fleet, a very valuable one, in fact. I cannot allow you to kill him, though I understand your earlier attempts. He has made many mistakes, and the animosity you bear is a justifiable response. This makes it easy to forgive you, and to offer a second chance. Renounce your vendetta on Carnage, and lend your aid to our cause. You will suffer no punishment, and will be granted your own Captaincy, once we acquire a vessel of use."

"You're kidding." Falcon spat, gazing at Trigger with open contempt.

"I zink it's a good deal." Beaufort shrugged. "You should take it."

"You would." Falcon sneered. "I, however, am done with compromise. I have bandied too much with the lesser and the foul."

He looked to Sheridan as he spoke, his features creased by hate.

"There is nothing lesser in unity." Trigger frowned. "To discount a being for the way they are born…that demeans you, not them."

"So, all are equal, in your eyes?" Falcon scoffed. "Bloodthirsty beasts, bred solely for war? A swollen wench, playing at Captain? That Godless savage, spreading his filth? You really think you can succeed, with a fleet composed of such degenerate souls?"

"I beat you." Trigger replied, narrowing his eyes.

"Yes, but you're like me." Falcon shrugged. "You used your servants well, true, but that only speaks to your breeding and wits. Traits shared by the bulk of your foes."

"We have little in common." Trigger replied. "None of which has substance."

"You're closer to me than you are to them." Falcon sneered. "You're a man of status, however far you've fallen. Your family might curse your name, yet that doesn't change the blood in your veins."

He stopped speaking as Trigger chuckled, running his fingers through his hair.

"Do you know *why* my family curses my name?"

"You lost a battle, and a prince. Yet more proof that your cause is doomed."

"No." Trigger replied, brushing away the dust from his sleeve. "In that area, they were quite supportive. They knew it wasn't my fault. Unfortunately, their kindness alone couldn't dismiss my stress. I had to resort to my usual method."

"Which is?"

"Buggering the stable-hand." Trigger shrugged, relishing the disgust that claimed Falcon's face. "Manuel, a delicious man from across the east sea. We'd been at it for years, though unfortunately, this was the time that our antics were seen. He was quietly executed, while I was dismissed by family and friend. In the end, I believe they were actually glad for the military disgrace. They seemed to feel it was less embarrassing, and used it to justify their removal of ties."

"You're grotesque." Falcon spat, aiming the wad at Trigger's feet.

"No, I'm not." Trigger frowned. "Neither are my crew. I understand that. It's one of the reasons I accepted this fight."

"You're comfortable with this?" Falcon sneered, turning his gaze to Barnaby. "All your hopes, your lives, pinned on the plans of an exiled faggot?"

It was an interesting question, for many reasons. All eyes fixed on the youthful Captain, his scarred face devoid of expression or thought.

"Yeah, I'm good." He shrugged, tapping his cane against the deck. "After all, as was pointed out, he's already kicked your arse."

Falcon's cheeks purpled with outrage, while Trigger shared a grin with his gorgeous First Mate. Even Beaufort was chuckling, his maimed hands resting against his thighs.

"Well, Falcon, I'd say zat ze matter is closed."

"Hardly!" Falcon snarled, slamming his heel against the bars. "So what if this savage-loving cock-sucker agrees with his filthy lord? Do you think the rest of the fleet will? Do you honestly believe that they will follow you, once I tell them what you are?"

"You're assuming you'll get the chance to tell." Sheridan replied, drawing a dagger from the length of her glove.

Falcon backed away, a degree of panic replacing his hate.

"You can't just kill me here."

"Can't we?"

"No, he's right." Trigger declared, placing his hand on Sheridan's wrist. "Killing him would send a terrible message. It would be anointing our cause in the blood of our own. Worse, it would imply that I'm afraid, no, ashamed, of being who I am. That is not the case, and I'll not have the thought entertained, even if it's restricted to our three minds."

Sheridan considered him a moment, before returning her dagger to its silken sleeve.

"As you wish."

"Count your blessings, Falcon." Beaufort grinned, slapping the Captain across his back. "You've spoken your way to freedom. Zough, I believe my position is still quite precarious. Am I correct, Admiral?"

Trigger ignored the mockery. Did he despise the man? Yes. Would he enjoy seeing him dead?

No. Such petty hatred was beneath him. Well, he liked to think so, at least. Besides, part of him knew that while he was the one that Beaufort betrayed, the man's actions had proven far more harmful to another in the room.

"I'll not judge you." Trigger shrugged. "You betrayed the *Blackbird*, and her crew, neither of which belong to me. The decision is Captain Barnaby's. Whatever he deems appropriate, I will follow and support."

He'd expected some measure of surprise from the Captain's scarred from, yet the boy remained still, completely unmoved by the decision's great weight.

Trigger resisted a sigh. That was the problem with pain. Feel enough, and eventually, your only choice was to simply go numb.

"How wise." Beaufort declared, propping himself against the bars. "Tell me zen, Captain, what is my fate to be?"

They waited in silence for the Captain's reply, the only sound coming from the tap of his cane.

"Eh, let him go." Barnaby shrugged. "He's lost his ship, his crew, and any respect he might have had."

"Merciful." Sheridan frowned, as they watched the grin spread across Beaufort's lips. "Too merciful."

"It is his decision." Trigger declared. "And we will sup- "

"I wasn't done." Barnaby continued. They all studied his impassive face, his eyes made dark by the shadows of the brig.

"We'll cut a hand off, first. His right one, I think."

****

Barnaby watched with satisfaction as the dinghy hit the water, Beaufort cradling his bloody stump as the waves rocked him from side-to-side. For a moment their eyes met, loathing engulfing the swordsman's glare.

Barnaby chuckled, turning away to study their fleet. It was a bizarre sight, one that spoke of an unknown future, where either glory or failure awaited.

Each vessel sailed in unison; their wet hulls connected by thick lengths of rope. No prow claimed the rank of first place, their pace kept in check by Trigger's command. The Oracle-birds had massed overhead, their numbers dwarfing even those of the duel. No Tides had ever been finished like this.

They'd waited at the end of the Void, collecting all vessels that survived the great flow. One-by-one their fleet had grown, until every ship left belonged to their fleet. It had taken days of negotiation, threats, and the occasional bout of violence, yet Trigger had won them all to his cause. He had given them a plan of action, revealing the first of their coming assaults. Barnaby had to admit, he was starting big.

"Keep her steady, Magwa!" He ordered, as the *Blackbird* veered slightly off-course. The Kalyute corrected, keeping their broadside fixed on the shore. The White harbor was once more in view, its stunning sights marred by all he had seen. The marble was stained in decadence, the gilded edges wrought from the blood of the weak. The poor, unfortunate souls, who even now clamored on the shit-tainted docks, a writhing mass pinned beneath the wealthy's cold gaze.

He hoped they would have the sense to run, once Trigger made his opening shot.

"Sunniday, do you see her?"

"I do, Captain. She's on her balcony, and she's a Gods-damned sight, I have to say!"

Barnaby peered through his scope, a parting gift from Trigger's First Mate. He'd been somewhat sad to see Sheridan go, yet both of them knew it was for the best. Besides, Frank's expression had been worth the sorrow. The moment he'd learned of his coming promotion, well, he'd almost burst into tears.

"Damn." He whispered, as the Empress filled his glass-enhanced gaze. She was *right there*, no more than a quarter mile beyond his reach.

Barnaby lowered the scope, wishing he'd been able to see her face. The mask was on, however, the white features blank to all they beheld.

"We're in range." He whispered, playing a tune with the base of his cane. Three thumps sounded in reply, letting him know that Trigger had heard.

The Admiral had clambered aboard last night, accompanied by Carnage and a few of his crew. They'd hidden away in the *Blackbird's* hull, holding a clandestine meeting with the crew of the *Seal*. Popular rumor held that the ship held a rifle, one unmatched in all the seas. Rumor had proved reality, the polished barrel speaking of perfect design. It could turn a novice into a marksman, and in the hands of a man like Trigger, well...

"We're about to cross the finish, Captain!"

Barnaby craned his neck, seeing that the words were true. The line sat before them, begging for a vessel to break ranks, to surge on forward and claim the prize. Beyond it sat the royal fleet, suspicious as to their unnatural restraint. It was not uncommon for a victor to cross the line with their cannons blazing, attempting to sink their rivals. Such peace was unheard of, an alien sentiment to the pirate creed.

Hopefully, Trigger had changed that. If not, their whole plan could fall into ruin.

Barnaby took a breath, watching as the finish grew close. Their ranks held.

The cannon ports opened on the royal fleet's ships.

Their ranks held.

The crowd cheered, demanding a winner to emerge from the pack.

Their ranks held. They held all the way, straight across the fucking line.

Barnaby joined the cheers of his crew. It was better than the silence of those on the shore. It was the last bit of joy he might feel for a while.

He limped below deck, making his way to the shattered gun deck. He found Trigger waiting, the long rifle clutched in his steady hands.

"We're through." He nodded, as Carnage and Trigger turned to him. "We held."

"I knew we would." The Thrallkin beamed, clapping his hands.

"The royal fleet?" Trigger asked, showing no joy at the plan's success.

"They're here. The Empress is on her balcony, no doubt preparing an impromptu address."

"That means you're up." Carnage declared, giving Trigger's shoulder an encouraging pat.

"I know." The Admiral sighed, moving towards the crack in their hull. He stopped at its edge, dropping to one knee as he readied the gun. The barrel was aimed at that porcelain face.

"She dressed for the occasion." Trigger remarked, closing one eye.

"I'm sure she looks fantastic." Carnage replied. "Don't miss."

Trigger took a calming breath, his hands as steady as a blacksmith's tongs.

"I never do."

The End

James Parfitt is an Australian author, Voice Actor and Animator, born and raised in the wilds of Emu Plains. He enjoys reading, writing, fighting, and the occasional pint. You can find more of his work on his Youtube channel, Hero House.

Printed in Great Britain
by Amazon